The Phoenix needs a hero ...

"OK, you better sit down for this," the vase said. Since Phillips was already sitting, it continued. "I'm called the Soulkeeper of Kiribati because I'm carrying the essence of a mighty warrior who the phoenix protected over the years. His name was Mychus of Kiribati, and he was honest, and brave, and strong, and sharp of eye and mind. He was the first in line. Every so often, when the big bird decides humanity needs a hero, he makes sure the right person ends up with the essence. And, according to the phoenix, it's time for a hero, and the right person is you."

Paul Phillips snorted. "I'm no hero. I'm just a radio reporter."

"Look, I don't make the choices. Maybe you're not a hero right this minute, but the bird thinks you got it in you."

Other Books by Warren Bluhm

The Imaginary Bomb

Refuse to be Afraid

A Scream of Consciousness

The Imaginary Revolution

A Bridge at Crossroads

How to Play A Blue Guitar

Edited by Warren Bluhm

Resistance to Civil Government – Henry David Thoreau
Letters to the Citizens of the United States – T. Paine
A Volume Of Secrets

The Roger Mifflin Collection
The Haunted Bookshop – Christopher Morley
Men in War – Andreas Latzko
Trivia – Logan Piersall Smith
The Man Who Was Thursday – G.K. Chesterson
The Demi-Gods – James Stephens

MYKE PHOENIX

THE COMPLETE NOVELETTES

WARREN BLUHM

MYKE PHOENIX: The Complete Novelettes

Cover image "Man in light" © Styleuneed
Dreamstime.com

ISBN: 978-0-9910107-6-9

▼

To Carol Jean

Introduction

PERHAPS my most cherished Christmas gift of all time came in 1965, when I was 12 years old and my parents presented me with a copy of *The Great Comic Book Heroes* by Jules Feiffer, a celebration of the superheroes of the 1940s with a compilation of stories featuring Superman, Captain America, Batman, the Human Torch, Plastic Man and more more more.

"To Warren – The comic book fiend of 1965, Dad and Mother," it is dearly inscribed. And I was. We had moved across New Jersey two years earlier, and for the first year in that wilderness where comic books were scarce, I had lost track of Spider-Man, the Fantastic Four, and the other friends I had discovered in the summer of 1963 and enthusiastically absorbed their adventures. Fifteen months later in the spring of 1965, I had blundered into a rack of comic books in Bernardsville and found Fantastic Four #39. I would be in college before I missed another issue.

And so, when I heard about Feiffer's book, it leaped to the top of my Christmas wish list, and I spent that day marveling over the early exploits of Green Lantern, Wonder Woman, Sub-Mariner and the rest. It was the first time I heard about Captain Marvel, the greatest hero of the Golden Age who was felled and driven into obscurity by a lawsuit from DC Comics, who thought the World's Mightiest Mortal was too similar to their Superman to pass copyright muster. Feiffer needed special permission to reprint Captain Marvel, and even then he was allowed only a single page.

Perhaps most intriguing to me was Will Eisner's legendary Spirit, a weekly (!) comic book that appeared in Sunday newspapers (!!) before my time. I was intrigued by the idea of only a week, not a whole month, between adventures. And the way he drew girls raised odd feelings in my 12-year-old gut.

The book was my constant companion for the rest of my kid-hood, and not only for the wonderful stories and Feiffer's reminisces. The thing was 9 x 12 inches, the perfect writing surface, and so it plays a key role in my own origin story. I spent many an hour writing my own comics – Greatman, Brink the Atomic Man, the Fabulous Five – and writing songs and later poems, while sitting cross-legged on my bed with a piece of paper propped on the inside cover of Feiffer.

It was there that I created Captain Zap, a silly superhero whose adventures ran for 23 issues in my high school years and I circulated among my friends.

If I had my choice, I would have continued along those veins and my heroes and stories and songs would be known to you. But life led me to believe it would be more practical to apply my writing abilities in the service of journalism, and so I spent the decades after emerging from college plying that trade, first in radio and then in newspapers and eventually online.

From time to time I would tinker with my old passions, scratching out the beginnings of stories and novels and even recording cassette and later CD albums of my songs to share with family and a very small handful of friends. In the mid to late 1980s I started to think hard about making something of this creative bent, and I wrote a couple of novels – one of which I published as *The Imaginary Bomb* 20 years later – and the drafts of the first four stories in this collection.

I always wanted to be Will Eisner, or Stan Lee – who wrote more than a dozen comic book stories a month – or Lester Dent, who as Kenneth Robeson wrote a Doc Savage novel every month from 1933 to 1949, or Ray Bradbury, who wrote a short story a week for most of his life. I envisioned reviving the monthly dime novel or, more precisely, I envisioned a new format: A monthly magazine featuring a superhero, but not a comic book because my artistic skills were not terribly skillful. I believed I didn't have the time to write a 50,000-word story like the old masters, but maybe I could write a monthly story that would take the reader about as long as a comic book or hourlong TV drama. Call it a dime novelette.

And so was born Myke Phoenix. He owed much to Captain Marvel – he was a mighty warrior who appeared when needed, exchanging his superpowerful body with that of Paul Phillips, a radio news reporter who bore some resemblance to the fellow I saw in the mirror every morning. Paul/Myke was guided by a mysterious spirit who lived in an ugly green vase, which called to him from a shelf in a cluttered antique store not unlike Ralph's in my adopted hometown of Green Bay. The echoes of Billy Batson and Shazam and Captain Marvel and Warren Bluhm are deliberate, my homage to the hero and the wizard and "write what you know."

I completed four installments, started several more, and mapped out a year-and-a-half worth of further adventures. But I did not have the wherewithal or connections needed to publish a monthly magazine, so the stories and ambition went into a box, to be revisited from time to time with a sigh, until print-on-demand made self-publishing practical.

The Adventures of Myke Phoenix – the original four novelettes and the short story "Ghosts" – appeared in its first primitive form in April 2008, to indifferent response. I spent the next few years writing and publishing other books but always came back to my original dream of writing monthly adventures. The problem was I couldn't advance the story after all those years, not even to write "The Puzzle of the Talking Dinosaur," the climactic battle with Myke's arch-nemesis Deinonychus.

Then I got the idea of sending Paul Phillips into the future. After all, I was 25 years older; maybe I'd be more comfortable telling an older Paul's story. Next thing I knew, I was sending *The Song of the Serial Kisser* to the world via the new magic of Kindle Direct Publishing. A friend's joking comment on Facebook gave me the idea for a follow-up adventure, *Firespiders*, and lo and behold, I'd released two Myke Phoenix novelettes in two months.

That set my course for 2014: I plotted a 12-issue story arc and determined I would write and release them a month at a time, in time to prepare a collection in time for Christmas giving. It worked! "Talons of Justice" came out in October 2014, and *Year of the Dinosaur* a couple of months later. Myke Phoenix was on his way!

But he wasn't. Myke and my expanded cast of characters went back into hibernation, other non-Myke stories and books sprang to mind, and here we are five years later collecting the existing adventures into this volume with the final-sounding subtitle of "The Complete Novelettes."

Is this, in fact, the end of the Myke Phoenix story? Perhaps not; I did deliberately plant the seeds of further adventures into both the epilogue of "Talons of Justice" and the final moments of "A Myke Phoenix Christmas." But my interest as a creator has evolved toward the novel – or at least the novella – and so I believe it's safe to say these will be all of the Myke Phoenix novelettes. We shall see what happens next.

Thank you for reading these stories. Thank you for the encouragement over the years. Thank you for visiting Astor City and its peculiar inhabitants for a while. Your support means more than you can imagine.

Warren Bluhm
May 2019

Table of Contents

The Ancient Warrior

Prologue

AFTER all these years, it just seems like someone ought to tell the story the way it should have been told all along.

When Paul Phillips walked into that antique store, Astor City was a typical small Midwestern city, kind of like Green Bay without the Packers, if you know what I mean. There was nothing, really, to distinguish it from any other medium-sized city – the same crime, the same nice people, the same morons, the same saints, the same sinners.

Why this man in this city was chosen for what had to be done, only the chooser completely understands. Don't worry, we'll get to that.

But: Astor City. A little town that sprang up a couple hundred years ago at the junction of two pretty impressive (if not mighty) rivers: The Shikaakwa River and the East Shikaakwa River. Nobody said the settlers were particularly creative, but they did have a knack for locating a place to live.

Within a couple of decades, they had a pretty impressive (if not mighty) middling-sized city, and within a couple of centuries they had a good-sized city with, again, the same crime, the same nice people, the same morons, the same saints, the same sinners, as any number of middling-sized cities you could name.

Obviously, something changed, or else you wouldn't be reading this story because there'd be no story to tell.

What happened was:

The universe shifted, and something dark burst from a yawning crack in the nature of being.

It raced through the void with an attitude of purpose as fleet and as certain as death, as if it were running from its own demise. It was a black lightning bolt against blackness.

The dark something from the crack in existence did not turn from its perfectly straight path, not even when it passed too close to stars and black holes, where reason said it should have been sucked into nothingness.

The unreasonable something-dark sped between asteroids, past comets and through planets – ever silent, ever relentless, ignoring even the curves in the cosmos as it pressed straight on.

When the dark reached the planet you and I call home, it did not speed through, or between, or past. Kind of like ointment melting into an eye, it oozed over the entire outer atmosphere and began to sink slowly down, spreading itself more thinly as it worked its way into the sky, settled into the soil, and dissipated in the water.

Something dark and beyond reason was now part of the very fabric of Earth.

That's the bad news.

The good news is that every action generates an equal reaction, and so something noble and worthy and true blasted into existence at around the same time.

It's a little harder to describe in just a few words, so let's just begin by saying there was this bird. And through the ages, the bird sought out men who were noble and worthy and true, to fight the dark.

So: There was this bird. There was this man.

And there was this pottery.

And it was 1995.

Act 1: The storm gathers

PAUL Phillips took one last slug of coffee as he waited in the cubicle next to the newsroom. He turned up the monitor. What the heck was Hi talking about now?

"What part of 'limited government' are you having trouble with, my young friend?" the voice on the radio was saying. "Either you are free to do as you please with your private property, or you're not."

"Well, it's your property, but –"

"There's always a but, isn't there? There's always somebody who has a better idea what you oughtta be doing with your property, so 'It's your property, BUT.' And now it's not your property anymore: The government has first title, the bank has second title, and you're going to take care of THEIR property the way they want, not you."

Paul watched through the glass as Astor City's Midday Voice worked the phone line. Hi Dawson was not a pretty man. Bushy red eyebrows, beady eyes, receding hairline, bulbous nose, and a rubbery jaw that always seemed to jut out angrily. He saw Paul watching him and smiled, winking.

"Pally, I have news for ya," Dawson said. "You're delusional. You started talking to us about how the government sticks its nose where it doesn't belong time and time again, but here you are again with your big buts. 'The government is USUALLY the problem, BUT this time it's the solution.' OK, Councilor, I got newshound Paul Phillips getting ready for the 12:30 news, but I'll give you the last word."

"Look, Hi, the people elected me to watch their wallets and take care of the city. The Quackenbos Labs expansion is good for the city, it'll create jobs, and the adjacent land has been an eyesore for years. This is a perfect case for eminent domain."

Dawson took a deep drag from his ever-present cigarette and exhaled into the microphone.

"Councilor, your eyes have turned a deep shade of brown, and there is so much I want to say, but I promised you the last word. Thanks for calling." And before the councilor could respond, "You got the Hi Dawson Show on WACR, The Voice of The Community."

There's the sounder — a synthesized trumpet fanfare followed by synthesized strings plunked authoritatively.

"From your news voice, WACR, I'm Paul Phillips," he intoned. "District Attorney Kenneth Ronnegan still refuses to confirm that Astor City businessman Alan Pinkstaff is the subject of an ongoing grand jury investigation. As WACR News told you last week, the grand jury is considering whether to hand down indictments charging the 38-year-old president of Pinkstaff Investments with commercial gambling, racketeering, drug trafficking and fraud — "

Five minutes and 13 stories later: "Paul Phillips, WACR News."

"Let me ask you something, Newshound." The chatter after the newscast between Hi Dawson and Paul Phillips had evolved into one of the show's most popular regular features. Dawson never told Paul what he was going to talk about, which kept him on his toes. "How does Alan Pinkstaff get away with it?"

"Well - I'm not sure he does. There is this grand jury."

"So they say. It's all secret, right?"

"Right, but –"

"So how does he get away with it? He doesn't just run a few slots at his gas stations. He's also into drugs and everything else that turns decent people into lowlifes. He's the scum of the earth. Period."

"Allegedly," Paul said nervously. "That's what the grand jury is about."

"And somehow all the garbage slides off him." When Hi Dawson was on a roll, he was on a roll. "He's Teflon. The guy caters to every lowlife instinct in people, and they can't touch him."

"Well, it's one thing to think you know what's going on, and another thing to prove it," Paul said. "Remember that whole innocent until proven guilty thing? And the line between the street trade and Alan Pinkstaff's office isn't as clear as you make it sound. In fact, I think that might be Alan Pinkstaff's lawyer on line one for you, Hi."

The beady eyes twinkled. "Good one. They know the truth is the best defense against libel, so they got no case against me," Dawson said. He glanced up at the clock over Bill the engineer's head. "OK, we'll be back in three to take more of your calls on the Hi Dawson show."

As the commercials played, Paul Phillips stepped through the door separating the news cubicle from the main studio. Hi Dawson was letting loose the bone-rattling cough that he had been suppressing since the microphone went live.

"Those things are going to kill you one of these days," Paul said, nodding at the ever-present pack of cigarettes next to Dawson's hand.

"Yeah, yeah, yeah," Dawson hacked. "You and my mom. I keep telling you to ask her out."

"Hey, Hi, I think you're being a little too rough on Pinkstaff," Paul said. "He gets his day in court like anyone else."

"He doesn't though, does he?" As we established, Hi Dawson was not a pretty man. When he was angry or on the defensive, he was even less pretty. "Jeez, Paul, I think I know my job. Let me do it, huh? You're the one who's writing all the stories."

"Yeah, the stories that say 'allegedly' everywhere. He isn't convicted yet, and you have to say 'allegedly' until he is."

"Well, isn't he? The worst crime boss this city has ever seen?"

Paul knew he was turning a slight shade of pale. "Well, you think so. It's not my job to have an opinion."

"Oh, yeah, the 'objective reporter' thing," Dawson said, putting the words in air quotations. "Come on, buddy, you have an opinion, you just don't have the cajones to say it out loud."

"I *don't* have an opinion," the news hound objected.

"OK, whatever you say."

I'm just looking out for you, Hi. He's got some big-time lawyers."

"Don't get me started on lawyers," Dawson snarled, then suddenly laughed. "Better yet, great idea for the next segment. C'mon, Paulie, lighten up, it's just a show. Even this jerk face Pinkstaff can figure that out."

"You really don't realize how much power you have, do you?"

"Power! All I do is get people riled up and help 'em get the mad out of their systems. When they wake up tomorrow morning, nothing's going to be different, the bad guys'll still be running the world, so they'll need me again tomorrow afternoon to help them blow off some more steam. How's Dana?"

"Good, thanks. We're going antiquing tonight."

"You hang onto that one. She's a babe."

"She is, isn't she?" Paul said. "I'm still surprised that someone like her would give me the time of day."

"You and me both!" Hi roared. "Come on, you're a good guy, Paul. She's smart enough to figure out a good thing when she sees one. And you should, too – seal the deal."

"Do you know how much a radio guy makes? I can't take care of her."

"You don't need to. Remember what it says on her office door? 'Dana Dunsmore Advertising Agency.'

She doesn't need anyone to take care of her, but she likes you anyway. Go for it, buddy."

"Coming back, Hi," said Bill the engineer as the Hi Dawson theme came up in the background. Hi waved at Paul Phillips as the "on-the-air" light blinked on.

"The Hi Dawson Show. You know the numbers. Dial 'em and let's yell at each other. We were just talking in studio about lawyers — let's talk about those parasites for a while. Call me up with your horror stories; here's the number."

Paul Phillips sighed as he walked through the revolving door entrance to WACR a few hours later. The ten-story building had been erected in the 1930s, so art deco streamlining shot up its sides between the windows, and the stylish old-time lettering was carefully preserved over the marquee: W A C R. It had been the first radio station in Astor City, and unlike many operations, it was still proud of its heritage. It was the most beloved radio station in Astor City because it was still true to its original mission: "Voice of the Community." Bo Ranfort, the station's owner and manager, steadfastly refused to replace local announcers and news reporters with syndicated programs, even though he could be a much wealthier man if he did. The Voice of the Community had a harder edge than it had back in the '30s when Ralph the Clown was a local radio show, but the city had a harder edge now, too.

Between waiting around outside the grand jury room and then covering a late-afternoon fire downtown, it had been a long day for Paul Phillips. Ten years or so of long days had taken their toll: He had streaks of gray running through his light brown hair, and laugh/worry lines creased the edges of his eyes. This year, the square jaw was clean-shaven; Phillips had experimented with a variety of mustaches and beards through the years.

He'd have been happy to trudge home, crack open a beer and read this month's issue of *Fantasy and Science Fiction* magazine, but he'd promised Dana a dinner and an excursion to an antique shop.

When he walked into his apartment, Frick and Frack were rolling on the floor, tails clamped in each other's mouths. At his approach, Frack leaped into the air, her limbs flailing in four directions, and raced into the bedroom. Frick was after her in a second. Phillips chuckled; it's too bad his cats were so standoffish with each other.

When he opened the cabinet and pulled out the bag of kitty food, the sounds of play ceased, there came a small thunder of stampeding paws, and suddenly there were two little animals perched expectantly on the counter, purring loudly. Frick — black with white paws — sat quietly in the spot where his dish was always placed, while Frack — white with black paws — tried to reach into the bag while Paul was scooping out her portion.

"Patience, my dear, patience," he grinned.

It was 6:10. He'd told Dana 6:30, so he changed only his shoes and zipped out the door.

Dana Dunsmore loved his punctuality most of all. She once said she'd never be able to date a "normal" man after spending time with a radio man, who had to meet deadlines twice an hour in the course of his everyday business. Despite getting behind a slow-moving car with an "XYZ Driving School" sign on its roof, Paul Phillips was buzzing the front door at Dana's apartment complex at 6:29:30.

"Yes?" the electronic sound on the intercom was barely recognizable as Dana's voice.

"It's Paul."

"I knew that." The door emitted a harsh vibrating buzz, and he opened it. Up the stairs, third door to the left. She was waiting at the door with her purse and a kiss. Dana Dunsmore always had a smile for him, blue eyes shining, full auburn hair surrounding a face that glowed with life. She wasn't a classic beauty — not Garbo or Monroe — but in the presence of that smile, Paul Phillips' heart always melted.

"How are ya, Scoop?" He had hated it when she first started calling him that; now it was somehow endearing.

"Tired. A lot of hurry-up-and-wait stuff today, and then a fire right at the end."

"I can smell it!" she said, leaning in toward his hair. "Anybody hurt?"

"Nah, it was barely worth writing up for the 5 o'clock news, just a lot of smoke."

"You want to skip going out and stay in?"

"Are you kidding? I've been looking forward to this all day." Dana looked at him skeptically. "Really," he insisted. "I need a taco salad desperately, and I want to check out that antique shop. Honest!"

"All right, all right," she laughed. "Off we go!"

The desk went on forever, massive, beautifully polished mahogany that seemed nearly as big as the room. A banker's lamp rose out of the middle. Otherwise, the huge desk was dark-shining bright and empty. Oh, yes — there was also the length of granite with a silver nameplate attached: ALAN PINKSTAFF.

The owner of the desk was working late, scanning a small pile of papers. He fit the larger-than-life desk: Beneath the gray three-piece suit that had been stretched over a 6-foot-7 frame, it was clear this man had taken care to make his body strong and taut. His face fit the granite nameplate: tough, expressionless.

A second man appeared at the door. He was big and sturdy, but he felt puny in the same room as Alan Pinkstaff. He always drew himself up and walked into the giant man's presence almost at attention to stave off the feeling he didn't belong in the same room, but the tactic never worked.

"May I help you, Mr. Pinkstaff?" he said, more meekly than he intended.

The owner of the desk did not look up. He waited until the second man opened his mouth to repeat the question, then said, "I'm annoyed."

"Yes, sir?"

Resting both palms flat on the desk, still looking down at his papers: "Hi Dawson."

"Oh."

Alan Pinkstaff pushed back from the desk and turned his chair around, so that he was looking out the window. He still had not looked at the other man.

"And this man Phillips, the reporter. They annoy me, Stephen. Both of them. Something must be done about them."

"Right away, sir."

"Even sooner would be better. Dawson, the noisy lout, first, please, but the reporter, too. Thorns in the side are so — unpleasant." This last with a sigh.

The other man left so quietly, it was as if he were never there. The owner of the desk watched a dark cloud drift over the east edge of the city. The streaky lines below the cloud indicated rain moving in.

There was a flash of lightning, but Alan Pinkstaff's office was too insulated to hear the thunder that followed. He turned his chair slowly back to his desk and resumed his reading.

Act 2: The Soulkeeper of Kiribati

PAUL and Dana had their heads bent against the storm, so they walked right past the store and didn't realize their mistake until they reached the next corner. When they doubled back, they found the place just where they expected it.

"I suppose we should have noticed the big sign sticking out of the side of the building that says 'ANTIQUES' big as life," Paul said.

"Who's looking up?" Dana laughed.

A temporary sign with movable letters stood in a clutter of old things in the display window:

CARLSON'S PRETTY NEAT ANTIQ ES

NOW OPEN

GOOD DEALS CLASSIC ITEMS

Despite the downpour the couple eased themselves cautiously through the front door; even before they entered, they could see through the window that everything inside was stacked haphazardly and precariously.

"Doesn't look 'pretty neat' to me at all. What a mess," Paul said, stepping around an old metal pedal-powered fire engine.

"Oh, hush," Dana replied. "Look at all this great stuff. We'll be here for hours!"

"I have to cover a committee meeting at 9:30 in the morning. As long as we're out by then, we're fine." She gave him a playful shove, and they started looking.

There were the usual glass and ceramic things that someone must have found attractive at one time, then abandoned to an eternity of being sneered at on shelves like these.

"Ugh, look at these," Dana said, picking up an especially hideous pair of orange-yellow salt-and-pepper shakers. "They're the color of throw-up."

Paul's eyes glazed over in amusement. "My grandmother had a pair just like those."

"Oh, please."

"Seriously. How could I forget something like that? Maybe I should buy them for old times' sake."

"You do and I'll never speak to you again."

"Find what you're looking for?" came a cheerfully crotchety voice from nowhere. They had to peer through the junk in the voice's general direction to see the old man, so well did he blend in with his surroundings.

"Oh, this is wonderful! You have such great old stuff," Dana said. "We're just looking for now, thank you."

"Well, when you find it, just call out. I'm George."

"We will, George. Thank you."

"You like old records?" George asked Paul, who had stopped in front of a bin of Bakelite 78s. Mixed in with names that rang no bells were people like Bing Crosby and Artie Shaw.

"Oh, I love the music," Paul admitted, "but I don't have a machine to play them with."

"I got a roomful of Victrolas down that aisle, to the left, and then all the way back."

"No, no, I'm sure I couldn't afford it."

"Come on, son," George said, touching his arm lightly. "It can't hurt to look. Got some good ones cheap."

"I don't have the room!" Paul insisted, following George anyway. A row of 1940s children's books caught his eye: Bambi, Peter Pan, Radio Rangers, Captain Midnight; but he followed the old gray head as Dana looked after them with a grin.

They were almost to the Victrola room when he heard someone behind him say, "Buy *me*, Paul."

Phillips looked back as he walked. "What did you say?"

"I said watch your head," Dana called. "There's something hanging from the —"

Too late. Paul Phillips banged his head against a huge cardboard box of Wrigley's Spearmint Gum, which careened against a bookshelf and whizzed back toward his head. He caught it and steadied it on its wires.

"Marvelous," he muttered.

"Oh, you like that, eh?" George said with a glow in his eyes." It's an old store display item. Yours for 20 bucks. Worth three times that already."

"No. Thanks, anyway."

"Paul — buy *me!*"

The voice had a feminine alto tone, but it had an oddly male quality to it. Phillips peeked around a green jeweled vase into the next aisle, but there was no one there. He glanced in every direction, in fact, but there was no one in the store except himself, Dana and George.

"Come on, now, mate. Tuck me under your arm, buy me and take me home."

Paul suddenly realized the voice was coming from the green vase.

It was pale green, with glass jewels — crystal, red and blue — arranged in rows around its top and bottom and studded randomly about. There was a crude painting of a red bird, sort of like an eagle, on one side. Paul picked it up and turned it in his hands. It was crudely made and oddly misshapen: The more he examined it, the more surprised he was that it could rest on the shelf without toppling over onto its side.

"Oh my gosh, that's the ugliest thing I've ever seen," Dana giggled, eyes widening in delight.

"Did you hear that?" Paul asked.

"No. Hear what?"

"Somebody said, 'Buy *me*.'"

"I don't think so, unless it was this poor ugly vase calling out to you."

"Ugly, eh? Hey, babe, if you weren't so cute, I'd take offense at that," the vase said, and Paul jumped. "Careful, guy! Don't drop me. Just march me over to the counter and make a deal with George."

"What the bejeebers *is* this?" Paul muttered.

"What *is* it?" Dana asked.

"You didn't hear any of that?"

"Come on, Paul. If you want that silly thing, just buy it and stop acting goofy. It'll fit right in next to your science fiction bookcase."

"Actually, the perfect place would be next to your comic books," the vase said.

"I don't *have* any —" Paul began, but thought better of it.

"Well, buy it or don't buy it, it's your decision. Let me see that," Dana said, taking the vase gingerly. "It's wonderfully atrocious. If you don't want it, I'll buy it. People won't believe it exists unless we show them."

"Your girlfriend's a real comedian," the vase said as she turned it over in her hands. "If it wasn't the truth, I wouldn't like that at all." By this time Paul was trying very hard to ignore what he was hearing.

Thankfully, the vase didn't say another word after Phillips handed it to George for safekeeping until they were finished browsing. Besides the vase, Paul brought home four old vinyl record albums — one rock, two big band and the soundtrack to "Exodus" — and a nifty old pair of bookends. Dana bought a small truckload of costume jewelry and old books.

Paul Phillips was weird all the way home. Of course, he denied it every time Dana asked, "Why are you being weird?" However, he wasn't so weird that he didn't appreciate the long, loving kiss she gave him when he dropped her off.

"Sleep well tonight, Scoop, you deserve it. Are you sure you're OK?"

"Yes. I'm just a little tired," he lied.

"OK. Thanks for the nice time. I love you!"

"You've got one great lady there," came a voice from the back seat. At the sudden sound of the vase's voice, Paul Phillips nearly swerved in front of a truck. "Watch it, lad! Take care of yourself, will you? You're our best hope."

"Now what? Whose best hope?"

"Relax, relax, I'll tell you all about it when we get home."

And the vase refused to respond the rest of the way home, even when Paul threatened to heave it out the window to rid himself of the hallucination.

A very odd thing happened when Paul Phillips entered his apartment, even more odd than that which had already occurred. Frick and Frack were sprawled on the couch and easy chair, respectively, and only opened their eyes halfway to acknowledge the return of the master of the house.

However, when he withdrew the peculiar green vase out of the bag and set it on the coffee table, Frack's eyes widened and so did her tail. She leapt up, arched her back and hissed angrily at the poor ugly thing. For his part, Frick took one look and scampered out of the room to a safe place under the bed, making a bizarre whimpering sound all the way.

"What the heck is going on here?" Paul murmured. "What is this thing, anyway?"

"I'm the Soulkeeper of Kiribati," said the vase, "and it's about time you asked, too. I was starting to think you had no powers of inquiry whatsoever. And you're supposed to be a reporter."

"Kiribati? What is that, some kind of cult?"

"It's a country, you ninny. No one knows geography anymore! Kiribati! Ever hear of the Phoenix

Islands — in the Pacific?" If the vase had arms to wave in exasperation, they surely would be waving now.

"The Phoenix Islands, yes. Kiribati, no," Phillips admitted, picking up the vase, "and now that you say it, this dumb red bird looks like it's supposed to be a phoenix."

"Oh my gems and garters, the man *does* have something between his ears," the vase said. "That's right, it's a phoenix, the fabulous bird that lives for half a millennium, there's only ever one phoenix in existence, and when he's ready to die, he builds a little altar and sets himself on fire. The new phoenix is born in the flames. Kiribati is a nice place for the whole deal because it's out in the middle of the ocean, where there's lots of privacy. By the way, if you look, you'll see he's red and GOLD, not just a dumb red bird."

"Well, pardon me." Even through his dazed confusion, Phillips now noticed the gold embellishments. "Wait a minute," he said. "I thought the phoenix was an ancient Egyptian myth. What does this have to do with a bunch of Pacific islands?"

If it had lungs, the vase would have sighed. "Whoever picked you as our best hope was out of his or her mind. The connection between the Phoenix Islands and Egypt is if you live for 500 years, there's plenty of time to fly from one to the other a few times. They were called the Phoenix Islands because some hotshot explorer stumbled on a phoenix being born there."

"What explorer?"

"The one who found the Phoenix Islands!" the vase snapped. "Don't you want to know why I said you are our best hope?"

"Well, yeah, I guess I do."

"OK, you better sit down for this," the vase said. Since Phillips was already sitting, it continued. "I'm called the Soulkeeper of Kiribati because I'm carrying the essence of a mighty warrior who the phoenix protected over the years. His name was Mychus of Kiribati, and he was honest, and brave, and strong, and sharp of eye and mind. He was the first in line. Every so often, when the big bird decides humanity needs a hero, he makes sure the right person ends up with the essence. And, according to the phoenix, it's time for a hero, and the right person is you."

Paul Phillips snorted. "I'm no hero. I'm just a radio reporter."

"Look, I don't make the choices. Maybe you're not a hero right this minute, but the bird thinks you got it in you."

"Let me guess now," Phillips said, and a smirk started to play around the edges of his mouth. "All I have to do is shout 'Whiz-Bang' or something, and a magic lightning bolt will miraculously turn me into a big guy in a superhero suit named 'Myke Phoenix.'"

"I told you I'd fit next to your comic books, didn't I?' said the vase, and Paul Phillips laughed out loud. "But don't worry, the transformation just happens, you don't have to say anything goofy. You just have to think about it or be in danger, and ZAP! there you go."

"You're not kidding, you're serious," Phillips giggled. "What if I don't want some other soul running around inside my body?"

"Don't worry, it won't be your body."

That stopped the reporter in mid-giggle.

"Wait a minute. What exactly do you mean by that?"

"That means his body is exchanged with yours. When you become Mychus, you have your own mind and soul, but it's his body."

"What happens to *his* mind and soul while I'm borrowing his body? No, wait — what happens to *my* body while his is here?"

"First question first," the vase said. "Mychus' spirit passed to the next world a long time ago, so it's OK to use his body. It's in tiptop shape and ready at your beck and call. And *your* body will be kept in safekeeping while you're using his."

"Safekeeping. What the heck does *that* mean?"

"Will you stop sweating the small stuff? You've got a lot more to worry about than where we'll protect your body while you're battling the Forces of Evil in the World."

"Me – against the forces of evil in – one guy and I'm supposed to –"

"Well, yeah, you're one guy, but you have Mychus' body and skills –"

"His skills?! How, through osmosis?"

"Well, yeah, sort of. And the body has been made pretty much indestructible, so you don't have to worry about that. And you've got me around to answer any questions and help out –"

"Terrific! I have a talking pot as a sidekick."

"Lose the attitude, pal. You need me more than I need you. And worst case scenario, you have the phoenix."

"Do I get to see this mythical bird?"

"Listen, if you ever see the phoenix, it's probably because things are so bad you need a miracle."

Paul Phillips shivered. "What do you call a being with my soul and some old guy's body?"

"Hey, you called yourself Myke Phoenix. That sounds like a good name to me."

If the ugly green vase had eyes, it would have winked. As it was the crystal-and-blue-and-red jewels seemed to sparkle a little, and then Phillips sensed that he was alone again.

"Hello?" he asked the vase, but he knew somehow there'd be no reply. "Oh, come on! You haven't told me anything yet." He stood up, grabbed the vase and shook it. "This is STUPID! Tell me what this is all about!!"

He stopped and realized he was standing alone in the middle of his living room shrieking at an ugly green vase. Phillips set the vase down, walked into the kitchen, pulled out a glass and a bottle of wine, and poured himself a sedative.

What now? As a reporter he felt a compulsion to tell someone what had just happened. Being someone who valued his freedom, he felt a compulsion not to say or do anything that would cause others to lock him away as a madman. The two needs balanced nicely; he chose to do nothing and go to bed.

Strangely — given the fact that he'd encountered a misshapen talking green vase that told him he was humanity's best hope and thus was about to become a comic book superhero — Phillips fell asleep quickly and did an amazing imitation of a rock until dawn.

Act 3: The storm breaks

PAUL Phillips dreamed of a small dinosaur. The monster had captured him in a strange castle by the sea. He could smell something like processed tuna, and through the open portal he could see a coastline.

"You think you know ssomething about pain, do you?" the little dinosaur hissed. "You have only begun to ssuffer at my handss."

And then the dinosaur laughed, an evil reptilian sound that would begin like a chuckle and finally erupt into a belly laugh – if reptiles laughed.

The little creature reached up a clawed hand and began to torture him with a tiny piece of wet sandpaper along his cheek. A low rumbling reached his ears. He endured the strange sensations for several minutes before he realized he was asleep and there was a tiny, rough tongue licking his face.

Paul opened his eyes to a white, furry face with pointed ears and the sound of contented purring.

"Frack, get the heck out of my space," he mumbled as he returned to the land of the living and eased back the covers. He sat on the side of the bed for a minute, stretching and collecting his brain while two felines mewed plaintively, hungrily.

"All right, all right," he sighed at last, forcing his body onto its feet to feed the cats.

The first thing he saw when he entered the living room was the ugly, pale-green vase, and it brought a sinking feeling to his stomach.

"I was hoping you were part of the dream," he told the pottery, turning into the kitchen for the coffee and cat food.

"I exist. I'm real. I think, therefore I am," came the feminine, somewhat male voice seemingly out of nowhere but from the general direction of the vase. "I trust you slept well, oh chosen one?"

"Don't be sarcastic. No, I didn't sleep well, oh sentient urn. I was dreaming about a talking dinosaur."

"Deinonychus!" the vase exclaimed. He stopped in his tracks.

"I beg your pardon?"

"Deinonychus. You were dreaming about her. The phoenix will tell you about danger in your dreams."

"The phoenix is in my head?"

"Well, yeah. It's part of the deal."

"I don't want a mythical bird in my head."

"Just the dream state. If it's any consolation, it's not a myth. The phoenix is real, and so is Deinonychus."

"And who is Deinonychus? No, let me guess. She's an evil super-villain."

"Nobody really thinks of himself as a villain," said the vase, "but Deinonychus probably qualifies. Of all the reasons we called you, she may be the biggest — even though she's not very big in a literal sense."

"Spare me, at least until I get a cup of coffee," Paul Phillips said. "I think I'm taking an early flight to Nervous Breakdown City."

The vase kept talking without heed to Phillips' need for caffeine or even the howling kitties' Friskies fix.

"This is a time of emerging evil in the world," it intoned. "You'll find that Deinonychus is one of many strange villains. Prince Cormorant. Dr. Skull. Even Alan Pinkstaff is a manifestation of the darkness at work in the world."

"Right. I can see Alan Pinkstaff in a skintight uniform," Phillips called from the kitchen. He dropped a measure of Breakfast Blend into the coffeemaker and popped open a can of cat food.

"Hey, the comic book analogy ain't perfect," the vase replied. "Most heroes and villains don't really wear spandex."

"That's a relief."

A few minutes later the cats were happily eating and Paul Phillips settled into the armchair across from the vase with a cup of coffee in his hand.

"So, tell me, Soulkeeper," he said after his first sip, "what kind of a name is Mychus anyway? It sounds Greek."

"Something like that," the vase said evasively. "Let's say his origins are lost to history."

"So what hot superpowers does Myke Phoenix have, anyway?"

"It's about time you asked, I started to tell you last night but I got tired of your flapdoodle," the vase said. "Your skin will be impervious to harm, your wits will be sharper than a hound's tooth, and you'll be stronger than any mortal ever imagined."

"Oh, and let me guess. I'll have x-ray vision and the power to communicate with animals."

"Get a grip," the vase said. "I read you the whole list. Don't be greedy. Don't you think that's power enough to be bestowed on one man?"

"Since I don't believe any of this, I'll be happy with whatever you've bestowed."

"Oh, you'll believe soon enough, Paul Proxmire Phillips. Alan Pinkstaff makes his first hostile move today."

A chill passed up and down Phillips' spine, and not because of Mr. Pinkstaff.

"How did you know my middle name?" He had not used his middle name since he was 6 years old. No one even knew he had a middle name. No one.

The vase was silent again.

"The problem in Washington these days is there are too many people who think *1984* had a happy ending. You know, the Orwell book — where Winston Smith dares to defy Big Brother, and the Powers That Be have him arrested, tortured and brainwashed. The last line of the book is that Winston was happy at last because he loved Big Brother, even though Big Brother was killing him at the time. Well, the problem in Washington these days is that the people in charge think it's a happy ending when people love Big Brother and want the Government to take care of them and make life easy for them, and even think for them!"

Paul Phillips grinned as the monitor barked on the wall. Hi Dawson was on a roll today. This was going to be one of those days where everyone he got on the phone hung up in disgust before he could even "click" them off the air. It wasn't anything he said; it was the pompous tone that his voice assumed when he was sure only he had the answer.

Paul set down his notes and tape recorder at the editing station and walked into the studio during a commercial break.

"You're definitely on a roll today, Hi."

"I am the greatest thing that ever happened to this town," said the red-haired man. "Someday, you watch, I'll be national with this show. It's only a matter of time."

"Right."

"Say, do me a favor, huh, Paul?" Dawson shifted gears suddenly, digging into his pocket. "I left a carton of cigarettes on the front seat of my car. Here's the keys."

"Are you kidding me? I have a story to write."

"PLEASE, Paul. My breaks aren't long enough. I hardly have enough time at the top of the hour to get to the back door for a smoke, let alone run out to my car."

"That's probably a good thing. Those things are going to kill you."

"Yeah, you said that yesterday, Mom," Dawson said, and coughed loud and hard.

"See what I mean?"

This time Hi Dawson just stared at Paul Phillips sadly and desperately.

"All right," the reporter said grudgingly. "I know a nicotine fit when I see one. You want the whole carton or just a pack for now?"

"Leave the sarcastic humor to me, Paul. I'm better at it. A couple packs will do, thanks."

"On my way."

He trotted down two flights of stairs to the parking lot at the rear of the WACR building. Hi's car was a bright red sports car of the type built for men in midlife crisis, with the license plate "IT'S ME."

Phillips opened the driver's side door, sat down behind the wheel, and leaned over to grab the carton. He fished out two packs, then thought again and grabbed a third. Hi Dawson had a serious problem with these things, but Paul knew he was an enabler despite the warnings he inflicted on his friend. He set the carton back down and eased himself out of the car.

Checking to make sure it was locked, Paul Phillips slammed the door, and his life changed.

The sports car erupted in flames. The explosion sent a small, black mushroom cloud billowing four stories into the air. Pieces of expensive sports car were blasted in every direction, and Phillips was aware of the sound of glass breaking as the shrapnel and shock waves shattered windows on buildings and cars all around the parking lot. Twenty feet away a second car blew apart as its gasoline tank exploded, and he realized with dread that the other car was his own.

Then Paul Phillips began to wonder why he wasn't dead.

He did feel very warm from the conflagration around him, but he saw that his skin was not blistering or burning, and he had no cuts or broken bones, even though he had felt huge chunks of metal burst against him.

Then he noticed his clothes had changed. He was wearing a white uniform, with gold trim and red buttons up the left side of the torso and securing the pants. The uniform was tailored to his body but loose-fitting. There was a red symbol of some kind on his chest.

He would have examined the symbol more closely if he had not realized just then that it wasn't his chest. It was muscular and shaped like a barrel.

Through the flames and smoke, Paul Phillips stared at the palms of his hands. They were huge and meaty, not like his hands at all. More like a weightlifter's hands. More like —

Warrior's hands.

"Hokey smokes," he said. "The vase was telling the truth! I wasn't hallucinating!" Either that, of course, or he was now.

The thick smoke made him cough, and he ran from the burning cars. Looking down, he saw that the symbol on his chest was similar to the one on the vase — a more stylized phoenix, but definitely intended to depict the ancient bird.

He was Myke Phoenix.

Looking up, Myke saw faces at the windows. Faces aghast at the war scene they were witnessing. Faces refusing to comprehend the destruction. Faces afraid for anyone caught in the middle of it all.

And then, fingers pointing and voices shouting at the large man dressed in white walking unscathed and seemingly unaffected by the smoking disaster all around him.

"I better get out of here," Myke/Paul muttered. He made a quick dash for the back entrance to WACR.

Once inside, he heard the clatter of panicky footsteps on the stairs and fearful voices calling "Paul!" "Paul's down there!"

"Oh, boy. How do I turn back into myself?" he said out loud.

Suddenly, he was Paul Phillips again.

"That was too easy," he muttered.

He stared at the backs of his small, soft hands and clutched at his chest. The muscle felt reassuringly flabby. At that moment, the first of his would-be rescuers appeared, breathless, at the top of the stairs.

"Paul! Are you OK? What happened?"

"I'm not sure. Hi's car blew up after I shut the door — or I guess it must have been a few seconds later as I was walking away or something."

"Did you see that guy?"

"What guy?" he asked, hoping he looked more sincere than he felt.

"The guy in the white suit."

"No, no, I dove through the door as soon as I realized what was happening," Phillips said, lying more easily as the shock wore off a bit.

"There's blood on your shirt!" someone shouted.

He became aware that his right hand stung, and he was surprised to discover that his palm was sliced open and burned around the edges of the cut. The gash had not been on the warrior's hand, and nothing had happened to cause a cut since he had reverted.

"Let's get that taken care of," someone said, and Paul suddenly became aware there were eight men and women around him. "You must have caught a little shrapnel. You're lucky that's the only thing that happened to you."

"Yeah, I guess so," he said dazedly. Apparently the change was not instantaneous: The exploding door had slashed his hand before the invulnerable Myke Phoenix could make an appearance. At that moment the pain caught up with his consciousness, and Paul Phillips grabbed his right hand and squeezed, yelping as he did.

"That's a good sign," said a voice he recognized as that of station owner/manager Bo Ranfort. "I was afraid you were in shock, the way you were ignoring that gash across your hand. Let's get up to the lounge, we've got some bandages there until we can get you stitched up at the hospital."

There was a shuffling disruption above them. "Stand aside — hey! Out of my face," and the curiously rubbery face of Hi Dawson appeared at the landing. "Paulie! Are you all right?"

"I think so," Paul replied, a little more confident about it now, "and no, I don't know what happened."

"I was looking out the window and my car went up just as you slammed the door," Dawson said. "Why are you still alive, buddy?"

The question made Paul Phillips' heart beat just a little harder. How could he put off someone who'd seen it happen?

"No, I was already walking away when I felt the explosion," he attempted. "I was blown clear, but I cut my hand somehow."

"No, it was just as you closed the door," Dawson insisted. "I'd swear it."

"We're all shaken up, maybe the sight of the explosion made your mind play a trick on you," Ranfort said, adding with a smile: "Say, Hi, who's on the air?"

The next couple of hours would always be a blur in Paul's memory. Dana arrived at the hospital just as he and Bo Ranfort drove up; he never was sure whether someone had called her, whether he called her, whether she just responded to the fact that Hi Dawson had been late coming back on the air and was hysterical when he reappeared, or whether she simply heard the explosion near WACR like everyone else in town.

In any case, she was there, and she refused to leave his side as a receptionist slowly checked him in ("But this man's bleeding to death." "Fine. Show me his insurance card and we'll get him to a doctor just as soon as one's available."), as a physician dug into his wound to make sure there was no other shrapnel ("Oh. Did that hurt?"), and as the doctor carefully stitched his palm closed. She even endured it all with a grim smile and an occasional squeeze of his good hand.

"Gosh, I feel like the luckiest person on Earth," she said as she drove him home. "Wellll — the second luckiest, at least, behind you after what happened. I don't know what I would've done if you'd been seriously hurt or, or —" and then her eyes welled up and the day finally caught up with her.

Paul reached over and patted her arm with his unbandaged hand.

"Dana, I'm not sure how I'm going to tell you this," he said, "but I have to show you something when we get to my place."

Act 4: Mychus the Warrior

DANA Dunsmore was trying not to cry, trying not to laugh, trying not to let the sheer terror in her heart travel the short distance necessary to be reflected on her face. Mostly she was trying to process the last few minutes without running, screaming, from Paul Phillips' apartment and calling for mental health professionals to haul him away.

"Let's sit down," Paul had said when they got to his place after he made that mysterious comment in the car on the way over. She'd sat on the couch where they always watched TV and snuggled, but instead of taking his usual place by her side, he went over to the easy chair facing her.

"The vase," he said, nodding in the direction of the bookcase where he'd set the ugly green thing from the antique shop. "It –" and now he stopped, shaking his head. "This sounds just crazy."

And then he sighed, deeply, and stared at the floor.

"What is it, Paul? For heaven's sake, what's going on? What about the vase?"

His head jerked up and he looked at the pale-green, misshapen, jeweled bit of pottery.

"I'm trying to!" he said, still looking at the bookcase.

"Trying to what?"

He looked back at Dana as if he'd forgotten she was there. "That's right. You can't hear it. It said, 'Just tell her, dummy.'"

"What?! Who said that?"

"The vase! The vase talks to me."

"OK –"

"I know it sounds nuts, but it gets worse," he said with a scoff, and then the words spilled out like a waterfall. "The vase belongs to the phoenix – you know, the big mythical bird? The phoenix watches over us, and the vase is called the Soulkeeper of Kiribati, and it contains the soul of a powerful old warrior, and the vase says I've been chosen to take the warrior's body and fight evil like a, like a superhero, and the phoenix says I'm humanity's best hope, and I thought it was crazy until the bomb went off and I turned into the guy and I lived through the explosion, and this is impossible, it's just impossible. Oh, shut up!"

"I didn't say anything, Paul –"

"Not you, the stupid vase! It said 'If this is impossible, why aren't you dead?'"

Trying not to believe her beloved Paul had become deranged, Dana Dunsmore forced her facial muscles into a look of calm acceptance, forced her voice not to quiver.

"That's a pretty amazing story, Paul." She didn't recognize the assuring, understanding tone that flowed from her mouth and throat when her instinct was to shriek in panic.

"You think I was hit in the head during the explosion after all, don't you, sweets?" said the man she thought she knew. "Dana, I *should* be dead."

"Oh, don't say that," she replied, barely listening now. Her beloved was seriously injured, some kind of head injury, he was out of touch with reality, and she didn't know how to bring him back, didn't know if he would turn violent or something if she challenged his silly story about vases and superpowers and evil. "But I do think we should go back to the hospital and have them check you over some more."

"You don't believe it. I don't blame you; I didn't believe it until it happened," he said. "All right. There's only one thing to do."

He looked her straight in the eye and his eyes changed color.

No, not just his eyes.

She knew she hadn't blinked, but in a blink he was not Paul Phillips anymore. In Paul's place was a blond-haired, blue-eyed Adonis dressed in white. There was a red-and-gold bird emblazoned on his chest – his big, solid barrel of a chest. The bandage on his hand was gone – not Paul's hand, but large and meaty hands like a warrior.

"Oh my stars," she whispered.

"I know, right?" he said gently, with an easy smile like Paul's but with a square jaw and sky-blue eyes that looked nothing like Paul. "Howdy ma'am, I'm Myke Phoenix."

"Where's Paul? What have you done with Paul?" she said shrilly, knowing at once the answer, knowing at once she didn't want to know the answer.

"Easy, easy, Dana," he said, taking her hand in his, exactly the way Paul Phillips did but with hands twice the size. "I *am* Paul, and I am Myke Phoenix. I don't know why or how, but this is what I've become."

It always amazed Paul how quickly Dana processed information and rolled with the punches. He knew that resiliency was what made her a great business owner. He could see her adjusting to this bizarre new reality before his eyes.

"You do know why this has happened," she said just above a whisper, incredulous. "You're our best hope. What the vase said."

"Oh no, not you, too, kid," said the blond-haired man who spoke in Paul's manner but without Paul's voice. "I'm a reporter, for gosh sakes. I'm trained to be skeptical. I can't take at face value that I've been chosen to be some kind of crime-fighting savior. What's really going on?"

"Why not take this at face value?" She rolled her eyes. "No, I get it, that's an idiotic thing to say. But what else should you do with this kind of power, Paul? You survived a bomb blast in this – this body. Whatever's in charge here has given you incredible powers to battle evil."

"I don't *want* to battle evil! I want to report it!" Paul/Myke said. "I don't even take sides. I'm a reporter — a good reporter!"

"Yes, you are. Don't you see?" Now Dana's mind was starting to gather speed. "The things that make you a good reporter — your desire for truth, your integrity — that's why you were chosen! They needed an honest person to do the job."

"Dana," he said quietly, "WHO needed an honest person? Who's behind the Soulkeeper of Kiribati? It's obvious there's some kind of crazy magic going on here, but who's in charge?"

She touched the symbol on his chest and stared at it thoughtfully.

"The phoenix is in charge," she said simply. "The phoenix chose you. The phoenix wants you."

"My goodness," said the vase on the table. "Why the heck didn't the stupid bird pick this lady instead of you? She's got it! It's so simple, you dolt! She's got it figured out, and she didn't have all night to think about it!"

Myke Phoenix looked at the dreadful-looking green vase with a crooked grin.

"I suppose you didn't hear that," he said to Dana, and the confused look on her face was his answer. "OK, OK, I'm our best hope. Now what?"

The next 23 seconds answered that question in rather dramatic fashion.

Two huge, ugly thugs kicked in the door to Paul's apartment, wielding equally huge, ugly pistols.

"Dana, get down!" Myke cried instinctively. He jumped up, grabbed Dana and pushed her behind him and into the kitchen. The guns barked twice. Dana screamed. Myke felt the bullets thunk against his chest, then heard two "plunks" in the carpet in front of him.

He stared down in disbelief. So did the thugs.

There were two flattened pieces of metal on the floor. There were no holes in his body.

The bullets had ricocheted off his chest.

That gave him a great deal of confidence.

He took a step forward, and the thugs began to fire in earnest. He waded into the volley of bullets as the thugs' eyes grew larger and they squeezed the triggers with more frequency, more intensity, more panic.

When he got close enough, one of the bullets bounced off his chest and into the left thigh of one thug. The man howled with surprised terror and collapsed in a heap.

Myke Phoenix yanked the other man's gun away with one hand and punched him – punched him with all his might. Big mistake.

He felt the man's jaw shatter and watched in awe as the thug flew back hard against the wall, cracking the plaster and causing three pictures, a shelf and the television to crash to the floor. Frick the cat, who had dived into the little space under the TV when the shooting started, now fled for the bedroom.

In all, 23 seconds had passed since the door was caved in.

After a few more moments, broken only by the groans of the injured thugs, Dana stepped out of the kitchen, holding Frack in her arms. The huge man in the odd white uniform was standing over the two assailants, breathing hard, staring at his large, meaty hands. He looked astonished.

"P— Myke, are you all right?" she said softly. He jerked his face in her direction, as if he'd forgotten she was there until she spoke. When the eyes-that-were-not-Paul's-but-reflected-Paul's-soul met hers, his expression melted.

"I'm fine," he said and then more certain but surprised, "I'm fine. Are YOU all right?"

She nodded, and Myke Phoenix reached down, picked up the two guns and bent one barrel, then the other, making them useless.

He stepped into the kitchen where only Dana could see him, and then he was Paul Phillips again.

"Oh, *Paul*," she cried, and eased firmly into his arms, sobbing.

"It's OK, we're OK," he said softly. "We'd better call an ambulance for those guys."

With his bandaged right hand gingerly holding Dana against his shoulder, he dialed 911 with his left and wondered how they would explain the strange blond-haired man who had come to their rescue.

"He told us his name is Myke Phoenix and he was chosen to help the forces of good in a time of special evil," Paul told the detective named Sgt. Fredricks, who lifted his eyebrows.

"That the way you remember it, ma'am?" Fredricks asked. Dana nodded. "Guy sounds like a nutcase to me. We'll put out a warrant for him. Handle it, Danny." Another detective flurried out of the room.

"Wait a minute. What do you want to arrest *him* for?" Paul asked, not without a tinge of personal concern. "The guy stopped bullets for us, saved our lives! He told us he's here to *fight* evil. You can't arrest him!"

Fredricks' look said, "Oh yeah? Just watch me," but all he said out loud was, "I got two guys here for attempted homicide, and there's some vigilante out on the street who committed aggravated battery and criminal damage to property."

"Give me a break, Sergeant. I won't press charges against a man who saved my life, who, who saved Dana's life."

"You may as well ask him to press charges against himself," Dana added, earning a sharp glower from Paul for her creativity.

Fredricks put on his most sympathetic look, which didn't look very sympathetic. "I know you kids have had a tough day, but look. The guy might mean well, but you don't go breaking into people's homes and beating people up, even if they deserve it."

"He saved our lives!" Dana cried. "They were shooting at us!"

"I get that, I do," Fredricks said. "I still got to talk to him. Just relax and let us do our job."

"Tell you what," Paul said more quietly. "If you promise not to arrest him, I'll have him come down to the station and give a statement."

"You know how to get hold of him?"

"I think I might – but come on, it was all self-defense, for crying out loud."

"I make no promises," Fredricks growled. "If he gets in touch with you again, have him call me at the station. But I'm not putting up with some goofhead vigilante poking his head where it can get blown off. He's gonna learn real quick there's such a thing as armor-piercing bullets, for one thing."

"It's not armor."

"WHAT?"

Paul knew he'd misspoken as soon as the words were out of his mouth.

"Eh, I said, he did no harm."

"No, not this time. That's my point," said Sgt. Fredricks. "This guy tried to help you out, and since he pulled it off once, he thinks he's a superhero. If he tries it too many times, some night we're going to find a corpse in a funny white suit. It's a different world out there."

Paul noticed Dana turning white and said, "OK, Sarge, I got the point. You talk it over with him when he comes to visit you. Right now, we're pretty beat."

"You got a place to stay tonight, Phillips?" Fredricks said.

Paul looked at Dana.

"He can bunk on my couch," she told the detective.

"OK, and we'll step up drive-by patrols in your neighborhood tonight," Fredricks said. "Whoever sent those two goons may be the same guy who planted the bomb in Dawson's car, and that means he may try again."

"Talk to Alan Pinkstaff. Hi and I have been pretty hard on him lately."

"You worry about your job, and I'll handle mine," the sergeant replied. "Take it easy, kids."

As the officers walked away, Dana Dunsmore threw her arms around her man.

"I'm so proud of you, Myke Phillips," she said with a big hug. "You just be careful when you go out fighting bad guys, OK?"

"OK, but you be careful, too," he said. "If you keep calling me 'Myke Phillips' like you just did, people are going to figure me out."

She blushed. "I'm sorry. Did I call you that? I didn't even realize it!"

"If I didn't know better, I'd start getting jealous of Myke Phoenix," he teased.

"Hey, the guy's hot. I don't blame her," said the ugly green vase on the shelf. It probably would have said more, but Paul Phillips looked at the vase in a way that reminded it that it was breakable.

Alan Pinkstaff towered over the man with the thin mustache.

"Stephen, men do not survive properly placed bombs," he said testily.

"They told me they're sure he was right next to the car."

"Bullets do not bounce off a man's chest like popcorn."

"I'm telling you, that's what Ernie and Burt said."

"So you think there's a super hero in a white suit roaming the streets."

"I can only tell you what our people tell me."

"And I can only tell you that I will not tolerate failure in the future, Stephen," said Alan Pinkstaff ominously. "You're dismissed for now."

As Stephen backed out of the room, he said, "You can count on me, sir. This won't happen again."

The phone on the massive desk rang. It was Pinkstaff's private line.

"Pinkstaff," he said calmly. His eyes bulged slightly when he heard the voice at the other end. "Oh. Hello. How are you?"

Alan Pinkstaff fidgeted in his comfortable chair. "They told me they're sure he was right next to the car."

Sweat appeared on his forehead.

"No, I agree, but that's what Ernie and Burt told my people."

He drummed his fingers on the desk nervously.

"I can only tell you what our people tell me."

Pinkstaff winced at the reptilian hiss in his ear. He rolled his eyes in panic.

"You can count on me, gracious one," he said, backing into his massive chair. "This won't happen again."

Alan Pinkstaff hung up and turned his chair to look out over the city. Flashes on the horizon suggested another thunderstorm coming. It wouldn't be long before the streets were drenched again.

Epilogue

PAUL Phillips adjusted the shoulder strap on his cassette tape recorder as he mounted the steps of the courthouse. He whipped open the big door and almost ran straight into Alan Pinkstaff.

"Watch your step, friend," said the man next to Pinkstaff, who was carrying a lawyer-like attache case.

The reporter and alleged crime boss regarded each other for a moment.

"Sorry," Phillips said, and started to walk around the two men. Pinkstaff touched him on the shoulder.

"Mr. Phillips," the large man said coolly. "I understand you had a couple of close calls the other day."

"Yes, I did, Mr. Pinkstaff," Paul said. "What can you tell me about that?"

"Now, hold on, Scoop –" the lawyer said, but Pinkstaff put up a hand to quiet him.

"I don't know anything about the attacks. I just wanted to tell you I'm glad you survived. What a wonderful thing you had a protector, because someone's not happy with you. But it's not me. I'm not the man your friend Dawson thinks I am."

"That's for the grand jury to decide, isn't it? I'm just a reporter."

"Yes, you're just a reporter," Pinkstaff said, his voice gaining an edge. "You just tell your stories, and if someone's reputation is dragged through the dirt, well, that's not your fault, you're just the reporter."

"That's right, sir," Paul said. "I didn't call the grand jury, D.A. Ronegan did. Don't shoot the messenger – literally."

"You tell the city I'm a crime lord, but it's not your fault that people are afraid to do business with me, it's the DA's fault," the big man snarled. "How convenient for you."

"That's the way it works. See you in court," Paul said, and poked the lawyer in the chest. "Don't call me Scoop."

He walked toward the clerk of courts office to check the day's calendar, and he couldn't resist looking back. Alan Pinkstaff stood talking quietly with his attorney and looked across the lobby.

The crime boss and the Voice of the Community locked eyes for a long moment, and then Pinkstaff turned with his attorney toward the door.

"Mr. Pinkstaff, I do think I'm forming an opinion about you," Paul Phillips said quietly.

And this completes the story of how Myke Phoenix first arrived in Astor City. His next adventure tested the limits of his new-found power, led Dana into jeopardy, and brought him face to face with an ingenious duck man.

The Strange Ultimatum
Of Quincy Quackenbos

Prologue

"QUINCY! My God — Quincy!! I can't find the boy." Mother was beside herself.

"Now, now, Mother, where did you see him last?" Father called across the beach.

"He was right here on the sand, playing with his infernal duck, and now I can't find him. We have to get out of here. *Quinnnnccccyyyyy!*"

"There, there, we'll just search the atoll until we find him. We have more time than you think before the bomb goes off." Father hoped his casual tone of voice would calm Mother and mask his own fear. "It won't take long; he can't have gotten far."

The little boy wished the big ships hadn't moved so far offshore. It was fun watching them, big and gray shining in the sun. Hiding from Mother and Father was fun, too, but the big ships had the giant numbers on the bow and those big guns and the little tiny people on the decks. Mother and Father were just Mother and Father; there wasn't as much to see.

"Hush, Quacky," he whispered as Father strode into view on the beach. His pet duck muttered in ducky tones under his breath, but the waves of the Pacific drowned out the sound.

THE STRANGE ULTIMATUM OF QUINCY
QUACKENBOS

He watched Mother and Father walking and crossing the beach and crossing the beach and walking, all the while calling his name over and over.

"Quincy! Quinnnnnccccccyyyyy ... ! Come out here right now!"

It was fun. As long as Quacky didn't let loose with a full-fledged honk, this hiding place could be good for hours.

But then a million million light bulbs went off, and a billion billion crashes crashed, and a zillion zillion campfires burned his hair, and Quincy held Quacky tight.

If Quincy knew what it felt like to melt, he would probably say he felt like he was melting. It felt like Quacky was melting in his arms, too.

And then Quincy knew what Quacky was thinking.

In fact, Quincy was Quacky. And Quacky was Quincy.

And then everything went quiet and dark for a very long time. He could tell it was night, and then the sun came up again. Instead of all the animal and insect buzzy sounds from the day before, though, it was really really quiet.

The first soldier who found Quincy screamed and ran away.

The nice soldier who came next talked to him like Dad did when he was tucking him into bed. "How are you feeling, son?" he asked, soothing, comforting, gentle; but he had a funny look in his eyes, too, as if he was scared or something.

"You're a pretty remarkable kid to be still alive, you know," said the nice soldier.

"Wak," said Quincy.

Act 1

Our guest today is a terrorist

THIS was it. It was all over. She was going to die.

And then she wasn't.

Daisy Englebert heard the horn, looked up from her magazine as she was crossing Fenster Avenue and saw the Astor City 7th Avenue bus, bearing down on her. She had no time to dive out of the way, so she flinched. Oh yes, she also screamed.

She was still in mid-scream when she felt the impact, but it came from the side, not from the oncoming bus. She was expecting to be struck and brutally hurled to the pavement and under the bus. Instead, strong arms lifted her up and out of the way, across the street to the opposite sidewalk, where the landing was rough but not final.

A large man with longish blond hair looked at her with concern. He was dressed in a white tunic or uniform emblazoned with the outline of a bird across his barrel of a chest.

"Are you all right, ma'am? Did I hurt you?"

"I don't think so," Daisy said disconnectedly, looking down at her not-shattered body and then staring at her hand. "I dropped my magazine! Where did my magazine go?"

"I think that's what got you in trouble in the first place," the big man said, but he turned, looked both ways, dashed back into the street and came back with the tattered periodical.

"Thank you," the woman said and blurted, "You're Myke Phoenix!"

"I sure am," the blond-maned man said. "If you'll excuse me, I need to go."

The big man glanced back just before he turned the corner and saw that Daisy Englebert was still standing where he left her, staring at him, holding her phone. When they made eye contact, it was like she came back to life. She tucked the magazine in her purse and started walking swiftly in his direction.

"Wait! I have to thank you!" she called.

"Not necessary," he called back, and ducked around the corner. He looked up and down the side street.

When Daisy turned the corner, no large man in a white uniform was in sight. In fact, all she saw was a solitary man with salt-and-pepper hair in a suit, walking away about a half-block away.

"Myke Phoenix was just here," she said breathlessly. "Did you see him? Where did he go?"

"The guy in white?" the man said. "Yeah, he was running that way and then jumped over the building. I still can't get used to that."

"I hear you," Daisy said. "Who knew superheroes were real? I guess I'll have to thank him some other time. He saved my life."

"Really? Say, I'm Paul Phillips from WACR Radio. Can I do an interview with you about that?" He pulled a small cassette recorder out of his pocket. "This isn't my work tape deck, but it would do the trick."

She stared at the handheld device as if it was radioactive. "No, no, no," she said. "It was really nothing special compared to what he's been doing around the city."

The reporter shrugged. "OK, I don't want to force you. Thanks anyway."

Paul Phillips went his way, and Daisy Englebert went hers, and she never suspected that she had been talking to Myke Phoenix all along.

Paul continued on his way to the WACR Building a few blocks away, where he was due to deliver the 2:00 news in less than an hour. As he entered the front lobby, he saw a man with bushy red eyebrows, beady eyes, a receding hairline, bulbous nose and rubbery jaw walking his way.

"Didn't you used to be Hi Dawson?" Paul smiled at WACR's midday mouth.

"Hello, Newshound," the not-very-pretty man said. "How's it going?"

"It's one of those days; can't complain."

"Who'd listen anyway?"

"Where are you going already, Hi? You're usually here all afternoon."

The beady eyes narrowed and Dawson looked unusually sheepish.

"I have a doctor's appointment," he admitted. "Don't say it!"

"What was I going to say?" Paul asked innocently.

"'It's about time,'" Hi said. "Right? Right? I know you were going to say it."

"Maybe I was. That cough of yours gets pretty scary lately."

"I smoke. I cough. Big hairy deal," but then his bravado softened. "Actually, this is a follow-up. They did some tests the other day, and they want me to come in and talk about the results."

"Sounds serious."

"Nah, they just want me to come so they can bill me for another office visit," Hi said. "Don't worry about me."

"Well, I'm glad you're having it checked out," Paul said. "Hey, I care, what can I say?"

"Yeah, yeah," the red-haired man said, waving him off as he walked away. "See ya later."

Paul heard a quacking sound over the on-air monitors that always had the radio station playing in the background.

"That's right, our industrial leader is on with Annette this afternoon," he said to himself.

"So if I hear what you're saying, Mr. Quackenbos, the people of Bikini Atoll had every right to sue the United States government?" said the voice on the radio.

"Oh, my, yes, Annette. The government literally blew up their home and rendered it unsafe for human life forever. Wouldn't you say they had a right?"

It was hard for Annette McPhearson to look at the person sitting across the table without staring and, perhaps, giggling. There was the constant temptation to reach over and tug at his face to see if it was a Halloween mask. That would mean, however, confirming that it wasn't a mask, and that scary thought was what kept people from tugging at the bill of Quincy Quackenbos.

Smooth white feathers, not hair, lay on top of the man's head, framing his perfectly human ears. A long duckbill emerged where his nose and mouth should have been, and webbing linked his fingers. Anyone who'd read about the duck boy of Bikini Atoll knew that this now-grown man, under the designer suit, had spindly legs that looked human but for the webbed feet, and that feathers covered his body to his tail.

Everyone knew the story of Quincy Quackenbos, the half-man, half-duck, and no one could look into the eyes of the man-duck without sympathy. Some have speculated that it was the constant exposure to well-meaning people's pity that drove Quincy to the mad sort of behavior we're here to tell.

"Oh, no, I agree they had a right to sue, which of course they did in 1975," Annette McPhearson said with her deep, earnest voice exuding empathy. "What I've never been able to figure out, frankly, is why you never took the government to court yourself."

"Wak, wak, wak!" Quincy Quackenbos laughed heartily, a quacky wheeze of a laugh. "Ms. McPhearson, I am a millionaire many times over because of my books, my patents, my biotechnology firm, my lectures, and my radio and TV appearances. Plus, the taxpayers have already paid the cost of raising me in a government facility from age 5 to

18. It would be extraneous to sue the government and take any more money from the good citizens of our fine nation."

"The military set off a hydrogen bomb knowing full well you and your parents were still on Bikini Atoll. The bomb killed your parents and should have killed you."

"No, I killed my parents," Quackenbos said sadly, resignedly, "They were given plenty of time to get off the atoll, but little me and my pet duck were hiding from them, and no parents would leave their son behind under those circumstances. I only wish I had been old enough to understand what was about to happen. I was just being a typical, self-centered, playful, stupid 5-year-old boy with a pet duck, and we ended up killing my parents."

"You're much too harsh on yourself," Annette McPhearson said mechanically, having seen the producer wave his hand for the commercial break. "This is Your Afternoon Delight on WACR, the Voice of Astor City. A reminder that our resident Neanderthal, Hi Dawson, will be back at 9 a.m. tomorrow to make fun of our president and otherwise insult your intelligence. Just kidding. We'll take your calls for entrepreneur Quincy Quackenbos right after the news with Paul Phillips."

"Myke Phoenix collars two hit men — good afternoon, I'm Paul Phillips," the news guy intoned from the other studio, and Quackenbos tilted his ear toward the on-air monitor. He listened intently to the story of the mysterious man in white who apprehended the murderers.

"I'm very intrigued by this Phoenix fellow," he said. "He's supposed to be bulletproof and very strong, isn't he?"

"That's what I've heard," Annette McPhearson said absently. "Sam, how many calls? Good."

"He's also solved a couple of odd cases that the police set aside months ago as unsolved. There's a mind inside that remarkable body."

"I guess. I'm sorry, I had some quick paperwork and wasn't paying attention. Do you want to comment on Myke Phoenix when we get back from the break?"

"Wak! I was just going to ask if I could."

"You're the guest," Annette said. "We'll be back on in a minute." 65 seconds later as the music returned, she chirped sweetly, "Welcome back to Your Afternoon Delight. I'm Annette McPhearson and our guest today is the multimillionaire man-duck — I hope you don't mind that description —"

"Not at all."

"— Quincy Quackenbos, who told me off the air that he's fascinated by Astor City's mysterious new vigilante, Myke Phoenix."

"Yes, I heard that news story that said he was back in action earlier today. I'd love to meet him. No, that's not strong enough. Actually, I'd love to study him."

"He has a lot of people wondering about his background," she agreed.

"No, you don't understand," Quakenbos said slyly. "I mean, I'd like to study him."

"Study him?" Annette McPhearson made a curious face. "You mean, like a lab animal?"

"To tell the truth — I hope this doesn't sound too insensitive — that's exactly what I mean. Why can't bullets hurt him? What makes him so incredibly strong? How does he solve unsolvable crimes? He's a fabulous specimen, and

I'd like to see what makes him tick — short of dissecting him, of course."

"Mr. Quackenbos, frankly, that sounds terrible! Talking about him as a 'specimen' sounds, I don't know, inhumane."

"Oh so?" Quincy Quackenbos replied, and his voice became a little higher and yes, a little duckier. "And my 13 years of living in a science lab *was* humane, I suppose?" After an awkward pause, the duck man's expression softened. "Forgive me, Ms. McPhearson, for twisting your words. I wasn't speaking literally. Wak, no, I'm talking about a series of simple medical tests, not unlike a physical if you will, just to understand why Myke Phoenix is, well, Myke Phoenix! In fact, I demand that Mr. Phoenix appear to submit to these tests. Wak, yes, I want him to meet me here in this studio before the end of this broadcast!"

"What if he doesn't want to be studied," she asked warily, feeling control of her program slipping away slowly but inexorably. "After all, perhaps he has some secrets he doesn't wish to share."

"Let me put it another way," Quincy Quackenbos smiled. "If Myke Phoenix won't surrender to me by 4 o'clock, I will blow up Astor City with the hydrogen bomb I've planted at a secret location downtown."

"Wha — Who —" For a moment it was Annette McPhearson who sputtered like a duck. "Oh, I'm sorry, Mr. Quackenbos, you had me going for a moment. I thought you were serious."

"I assure you, I'm utterly serious." Suddenly the human eyes above the impossible duck bill were cold steel. "If Myke Phoenix refuses to come to my lab for a simple examination, I'll detonate the bomb that I've planted here in the city somewhere. I promise no one will be hurt unless he refuses — or, of course, if I'm taken into custody for making this little proposal. I've planned for its detonation under either of those circumstances."

"Let me get this straight," Annette McPhearson said. "You promise not to hurt Myke Phoenix, but you're going to set off a nuclear bomb if you don't get your way."

"That's a *very* good way to sum it up, Annette," Quincy Quackenbos said patronizingly.

"You made these arrangements not even knowing if we'd talk about Myke Phoenix on the show?"

"Oh, come now, it's a three-hour show and, as you said before, I'm the guest. Of course I was going to steer the conversation around to Mr. Phoenix sooner or later. Now, then, why don't we take some of those phone calls?"

Act 2

Existential panic

IN the WACR news studio, Paul Phillips was pretending to type a news story at his computer terminal, but listening to the conversation about Myke Phoenix, when Quincy Quackenbos delivered his strange ultimatum.

"Oh, for crying out loud," he said to no one in particular. This day was never going to end, it seemed. He'd tracked down a couple of killers for the police, then rescued a lady who didn't look both ways before stepping into the street, and now it seemed he was going to have to save the city from nuclear annihilation.

Station owner-manager Bo Ranfort burst into the newsroom seconds later.

"Paul! You know this Phoenix fellow. Get him on the phone! Get him over here now!"

"He probably was listening to the broadcast," Phillips responded with some assurance. "I'll bet he gets here in no time at all."

"My God," Ranfort said, his usual concrete calm cracked just slightly, "some nut blackmailing a city with a leftover nuclear bomb. On our radio station!"

"Quincy Quackenbos is a pretty intelligent cookie. I bet he made the bomb himself, he didn't need to find leftovers in some terrorist network," Paul Phillips said way too calmly for his boss.

"What difference does that make! We have to get Myke Phoenix," the station manager said.

"Relax, Bo. Myke will probably get here in a hurry, and there has to be some reasonable explanation for the way Quackenbos is behaving. I'll go get hold of Myke."

The boss walked swiftly back toward his office while Paul walked the other way. He turned the corner and ducked into the men's room, where he checked to make sure he was alone. The on-air radio feed also could be heard in this room.

"How dare you scare us with that stupid comment about nuclear bombs," a voice was shrieking over the phone line. "Why can't you just ask Mr. Phoenix for his help politely, like a normal human being?"

"Alas, I'm not a normal human being," a ducky voice replied. "I'm a freak of nature — well, no, that's not quite correct, either. Humanity, meddling into the forces of nature, created me; science gone mad created me. Now, I've decided to go a little mad myself. Do you know how silly it is to be half-man, half-duck, and not insane? No, no, the time has come for me to lose my mind, and therefore I'm going to blow up the city if Myke Phoenix doesn't surrender to me. You might say I'm quacking up," he said with a chuckle that was a little too forced to be sane. "It all makes common sense, don't you think?"

No, it didn't, but Annette McPhearson was doing a good job of sounding calm despite what must be growing panic. "Let's take another call, shall we? Good afternoon, you're on from the east side."

"I'd like to know if Mr. Quackenbos considers his threat an existential scream for light in the otherwise absolutely black darkness of life in our contemporary society," a man's voice said.

"Oh, please," said Paul Phillips, except that he wasn't Paul Phillips anymore. His voice was a bit deeper and fuller, and when he took a breath, his chest was much larger and broader than it had been a moment ago. He looked into the mirror and saw the chiseled body of Mychus the Warrior, better known in Astor City as Myke Phoenix.

"I don't think I'm ever going to get used to that," said Myke Phoenix, staring into sky-blue eyes under a mane of blond hair. Paul had hazel-colored eyes and brown hair, but behind the unfamiliar eyes he still felt the same. He couldn't even feel the change, except physically. One instant he was Paul Phillips, and the next he was Myke Phoenix. That's just how it went.

He stared a second longer, then said, "I better get to the studio."

The D.S. Dunsmore Advertising Agency was abuzz with activity, as always, for there were clients to call, commercials to write and design, and files to file. Dana Dunsmore was holding the phone away from her ear but could still hear the shouting on the other end.

"I can't call every radio station in town and tell them to change your ads as of 6 o'clock this morning," she said firmly. "For one thing, it's already 2 in the afternoon and more than half your ads for the day have already run by now." Someone was giving birth to a cow on the other end of the line. "No, I can't get them to run make-good ads for a change you made this late in the campaign ... All right, all right, I'll see what I can do, but don't expect a miracle — no, I don't think you want to do that. Another agency wouldn't be this patient with you." Until the phone landed on the hook, the birthing was still audible.

So her heart was already pounding when the intercom beeped.

"Dana? Have you been listening to the radio?"

"I know, I know, the Gaffney ads are all wrong; she just called."

"No, it's about Paul's station."

The last time Dana Dunsmore heard something had happened at her boyfriend's radio station, her boyfriend had been caught in a bomb blast and turned into a superhero.

She didn't have fond memories of that day. Dana's heart began to pound.

"What about Paul's station?" she managed to say.

"Somebody's talking about setting off an H-bomb unless Myke Phoenix surrenders to him."

The last time Dana Dunsmore had heard what was going on at Paul's radio station, she'd run out of the building in a panic to make sure Paul was all right. A lot of business needing her approval didn't get approved that day, and she had promised her employees she'd never leave them in the lurch like that again.

So much for promises.

Dana canceled her appointments for the rest of the afternoon and ran out of the building. She nearly literally jumped into her car, turned the ignition key and closed the door in one smooth motion. WACR was already tuned in on the radio.

"– so I disagree with your premise, at the end of the day. Things are never as dark as they seem. Thanks for calling. Wak! Wak! Wak!" The ducky laugh reminded Dana that Paul had said Quincy Quackenbos was going to be on with Annette McPhearson this afternoon. HE wouldn't threaten to set off an H-bomb, would he?

"Mr. Quackenbos, can we stop this horrible charade now?"

"Annette, Annette, Annette, this isn't a charade. I'm perfectly serious," the duck man's voice said. "This is certainly an explosive situation, isn't it? Wak! Wak!"

At that moment there came another voice from off-mike.

"Hi, everyone," the voice said cheerfully. "I'm Myke Phoenix." There was a long, lingering pause, and then he added, "Well? I understand you want me to take some tests."

"Mr. Myke Phoenix," Quincy Quackenbos' voice was positively gleeful. "This is truly a pleasure."

The relief in Annette McPhearson's voice was unmistakable. At least for now, the idea of nuclear annihilation could be set aside.

"Won't you have a seat, Mr. Phoenix?" she said, indicating a place in front of a microphone.

"OK, but it's Myke. Mr. Phoenix was my father." There was an awkward pause, and then he laughed. "That, um, was a joke."

The other two laughed along, Annette nervously, Quakenbos boisterously and a little wildly.

"Please tell me you're not playing along with this," Dana said to the radio.

"So, erm, Myke," Annette said lamely, "Welcome to the show. We have so many questions about you – who you are, where you came from –"

"Probably not the best time to talk about that," Myke said apologetically.

"Not a good time at all for that," said the ducky voice. "Really, we must be going. Come, come, young man, we have much work to do."

"Where are we going?"

"You've agreed to let me study you, and so we're going to a place where I can do that," Quackenbos said cheerfully.

"Forgive me for leaving early, Ms. McPhearson, but I have assistants making my labs ready for us. Thank you so much for having me on your program today."

"PAUL!" Dana Dunsmore screamed as she drove along Astor Boulevard. "What are you *doing*, you crazy LOON!?" She screeched around the next corner and pointed the car toward Quackenbos Laboratories.

Act 3
Peril at Quackenbos Laboratories

THE building was low to the ground and sprawling; it occupied 20 acres of the Astor City Industrial Park along the East Shikaakwa River. It was a granite building with big, smoky-black windows covering the upper half of each wall. On the facade next to the entrance was a huge silver "Q" with a huge silver "L" next to and slightly below it. From the outside, Quackenbos Labs seemed like any other business.

It appeared to be a plain old square building from the street, but once inside with his host, Myke Phoenix saw that it was a weird labyrinth of corridors, none of them especially long. Some hallways were straight and narrow; some curved around glass-walled labs that afforded no privacy to the researchers at work; some jagged along walls made of concrete with vault-like doors that towered over everyone. Myke knew he'd be hard-pressed to find his way back to the entrance on his own, should it be necessary.

"It was nice of you to surrender so promptly and peacefully," said Quincy Quackenbos. "You'll find that I'm a man of my word — this won't hurt you."

"You've said that a couple of times already," said the man in the white suit. "Since you're a man of your word, I assume you really intended to set off that nuclear bomb, and that would've hurt a lot."

Quackenbos waved a webbed hand. "Oh, that," he said with a wak. "There was no nuclear bomb. Mere dramatic license. It would be too much bother for me to actually build one."

Myke Phoenix eyed his odd little host carefully. "So I'm free to go anytime?"

"Wak, wak, wak. I didn't say that."

"If there's no nuclear bomb, what's keeping me here?"

"The *conventional* bomb in WACR's basement, of course," Quackenbos replied with a ruffle of his head feathers, "the one I'll detonate and blow your friends to rubble, if you leave prematurely."

"If your first bomb threat was a fraud," Myke Phoenix said as Quincy Quackenbos disappeared momentarily around a sudden corner, "why should I believe this one?"

"Good question," the manlike, duck-like voice said as thick glass slabs suddenly dropped from the ceiling, surrounding Myke Phoenix, "and here is your answer."

Something dropped from the ceiling into our hero's hands. He had only enough time to see that it was an electronic device wired to a putty-like substance before it exploded, hurling him against the glass and leaving acrid smoke hanging in the small enclosure.

As the smoke was cleared by a fan in the ceiling, Quackenbos stepped back into view, and his eyes widened in obvious pleasure. "Why, your body doesn't seem to be damaged in the least. Amazing! Can you get out of there?"

Phoenix coughed twice. "This glass appears to be bombproof, and you want me to try punching my way out?"

"Well, that's one thought. Perhaps I've left you an alternative." Quackenbos raised his eyes.

Myke looked up at the ceiling, where a small red button was visible just inside the glass. He knew he could reach it with a standing jump; no ordinary man could. Instead he punched the side of the enclosure with all his might, shattering it into a thousand pieces. Quincy Quackenbos jumped.

"Well! That was impressive," he said. "Why didn't you try the button?"

"Maybe I couldn't reach it," was the reply, "or maybe I could reach it but don't want you to know the full extent of my ability; or maybe I figured there was no proof that pushing the button would release the glass walls."

"Aha. A good answer, although not an especially cooperative one."

"I said I'd take your tests," Myke said with a trace of annoyance, "I don't recall saying I'd cooperate."

"I see: If I tell you to jump off a cliff, for example, you won't, necessarily. Yes, yes, a wise course."

"All right, Quackenbos. What's next?"

"Well, when you coughed a moment ago, you determined what's next," the man duck said, reaching into his pockets to take a small plastic mask in one hand and a grenade-like object in the other. Myke Phoenix took a deep breath as his host held the mask over his bill and dropped the grenade. A sickly green gas flooded the corridor.

Still holding his breath, the man in the white suit stalked toward the duck man. The tingle in his nostrils told him it would be unpleasant to inhale.

His intention was: He would pick up his host and rip off the gas mask, with a comment to the effect of "I'm tired of these games, Mr. Quackenbos."

What actually happened was: He walked toward his host and fell through a trap door, plummeting about 50 feet in darkness. His actual comment was to the effect of "Yikes!"

Myke Phoenix landed on his feet on a dirt floor, but the momentum of the fall forced him into a tumble. The good news was he was inside the body of Mychus, an invulnerable ancient warrior, and so no bones were broken or separated from their rightful place. The bad news was he looked pretty ridiculous, because it was not at all a graceful tumble.

There was what at first appeared to be further bad news, as dim lights along the wall revealed the presence of two timber wolves in the corner, pawing at the soil. The walls seemed to be made of poured concrete.

"Hi guys," said Myke as the wild canines inched toward him tentatively. "Now wait a minute, fellas, everybody knows that wolves don't attack people unless they're provoked."

At that, the big silver beasts leaped.

Myke Phoenix resisted the temptation to throw his hands up defensively or strike at them. This was a good decision, because the wolves stood on their back legs with their front paws against his massive chest, licking his face.

"Hey, cut that out!" he giggled. "We still have to find a way out of here."

As if to accentuate that point, a vague "ka-CHUNK" sounded somewhere in the distance, and Myke Phoenix heard a low hum and an odd scraping sound. Like a preposterous trap in some preposterous old movie, the walls to the small dungeon began to move toward him.

"Hokey smokes!" he muttered. He had a pretty good feeling the walls would break against his indestructible body; his two furry companions, however, were in danger of being squashed.

"Hey! Quackenbos! Don't you know timber wolves are an endangered species?" he shouted.

"Well, then, you'd better find a way to get them out of danger," a ducky voice quacked over a speaker somewhere.

Myke squinted in the semidarkness, searching for a seam that would reveal a possible opening. The walls eased closer.

"This won't hurt you," Quackenbos had said. He hadn't said anything about whether it would hurt anyone else, like two poor wolves.

One of the animals began to howl, and it was only a moment before they began to harmonize. Myke turned and turned, seeking, seeking a way out. The walls were closer still.

He hauled back and punched the side of one wall with the force of five sledgehammers, but the walls kept moving, untouched. The concrete might yield to repeated blows, but there was no time. Then the proverbial light bulb flashed in his mind.

"We're on a dirt floor," he whispered excitedly, fell to his knees, and began to dig. The wolves joined in the game, although their big paws were not able to move as much soil as their companion's huge hands.

He had only enough time to dig a shallow pit, but there was room enough for him to wrap his expansive arms around the two wolves and pull them down to safety. The converging walls met above them with an authoritative THUNK. All was still.

"We're OK for now, kids," Myke Phoenix told his companions gently, "but I have to tell you — stop squirming! — we're trapped 50 feet underground with two big concrete walls overhead. I think I could lean up and get them to break, but chunks would fall on top of us. I'd be OK; you wouldn't. Any suggestions?"

The only response was quick canine breathing from both sides of his face in the dark. At the rate the wolves were panting, the oxygen wouldn't last very long. Myke Phoenix considered telling the animals to calm down, but he was beginning to feel a bit claustrophobic himself.

After a minute there came another distant "ka-CHUNK" and Myke felt the concrete sea above him begin to part.

As the walls returned slowly to their original positions, he heard a now-familiar wakking sound above. "Magnificent! Wak, wak, wak," said Quincy Quackenbos, "simply magnificent! You're all I heard you would be."

"I'm glad you liked it," said Myke Phoenix as he clambered to his feet with the wolves next to him. He brushed soil off the front of his uniform and looked straight up. Quackenbos was leaning over the edge of the precipice, 50 feet up. "What was the point of all this?"

"The bomb, to test your indestructibility," said the man-duck. "The gas, to see if you were bright enough not to breathe and, if you were, to test your lung capacity. The pit, again to test whether your body can be broken. The wolves, to try your compassion. You are really too good to be true, my friend. You passed every test with flying colors."

"Frankly, I'm not sure we qualify as friends, Mr. Quackenbos," said Myke Phoenix, gathering the two wolves under his arms, dipping into a deep knee bend and leaping the 50 feet up to the corridor.

Quincy Quackenbos blinked in amazement. "My word," he said, flabbergasted. "Nobody can jump like that!"

"Just call me nobody, then," came the reply as the wolves scampered away, "but I prefer Myke. Now, I think I'm finished here. Let me go, before I —"

It was really a bad time for Dana to burst into the room, followed by a secretary saying frantically, "I'm sorry, Mr. Quackenbos, she just burst in and I couldn't stop her."

"Dana, what are you DOING, you crazy LOON?" Myke said.

"You have no business calling anyone a loon," Dana shot back. "How can you just waltz into danger after this maniac threatened to blow up the city?"

"At least *I* can't be hurt — but this maniac could threaten to do things to you and force me to —" Myke Phoenix stopped in mid-sentence and glanced at Quincy Quackenbos with an expression that could only be summed up with the word, "Oops."

THE STRANGE ULTIMATUM OF QUINCY
QUACKENBOS

A little leer played at the corner of Quackenbos' bill. "Soooo — this lady means something to you, does she, Phoenix?"

"Err — well, she's in the advertising business," Myke ad-libbed. "She's helping me develop my public persona."

"A superhero with a marketing specialist, eh?" Quackenbos said. "Very interesting, but not terribly convincing. I'd say she has a personal stake in your well-being, the way she burst in. Ms. Hughes, show this woman — Dana, was it? — into Conference Room B and lock her in. Gently, please."

"Go with her, Dana. I'll be OK." Myke Phoenix watched helplessly as Ms. Hughes escorted Dana out of the room.

The superhero and the duck man looked at each other.

"Let her go," Myke said in a low voice.

"When we're done," Quincy leered.

"I'm telling you, if you harm one hair on her head, Quackenbos, I swear I'll —"

"Blood tests. Stress tests. A lock of your hair. A little aerobic exercise. That's all we have left," the duck man said, holding his hands in front of his chest, palms facing out, to calm his reluctant guest. "Then I'll have the bomb deactivated and release your Dana."

Watching Quincy Quackenbos approach him gingerly, expectantly, Myke couldn't help but think of a vulture circling its prey.

Act 4
Do Ducks Have Souls?

"THIS is the most astonishing thing I've ever seen," said the man in the white coat as he struggled over Myke Phoenix's arm. "It won't go in."

"What do you mean, it won't go in? Why won't it go in?"

"Well now, that's the question," the doctor said, pulling the syringe back. "See here? I can find the vein in the crook of the arm, but look here, when I try to take the blood sample —" he pushed and poked and prodded with the needle, but Myke Phoenix's skin would not yield.

"Gimme that," Quackenbos said loudly. He grabbed the syringe and pushed it against the meaty arm with all his might.

There was a popping sound and Myke Phoenix said, "Ouch!"

Quincy Quackenbos stared at the now needle-less tube. The needle itself rolled on the floor briefly after ricocheting off the ceiling and wall. Myke Phoenix rubbed the spot where his host had been pushing; it was red, but there was no puncture wound.

"If it makes you feel better, that hurt," Myke said with almost a whine in his voice.

"Incredible," Quackenbos breathed. "Wak! This is incredible. The man is bulletproof and can't be cut. Dr. Simpson, do we have a bazooka?"

THE STRANGE ULTIMATUM OF QUINCY QUACKENBOS

"Now hold on just a New York minute," Myke protested as the doctor nodded and began to back out the door. "I will not stand in front of the business end of a bazooka!"

"Ah ha! So you do have limits," Quackenbos exclaimed. The doctor paused by the door.

The truth was that Myke didn't know whether his marvelous body could withstand a bazooka shell, but he wasn't about to find out by letting his odd host try it. "Let's just say I don't care to be shot at today, OK?"

"No. Not OK." The expression on the peculiar duck face darkened. "You're not leaving until I get into your bloodstream."

"Why? What do you need my blood for?"

"Nothing," Quincy Quackenbos blurted, as if something private had slipped out. "That is to say, there's no one on the planet with abilities like yours, and I want my people to determine if something in your blood gives you this power."

"He means to kill you."

"SIMPSON!?"

The doctor stepped forward. "I couldn't say anything because I was afraid, but I think I'm safe while you're here, Mr. Phoenix." Quackenbos lunged at Dr. Simpson; Myke Phoenix grabbed his arm. "Quincy, I'm sorry, but you can't go through with this."

"Go through with what?" Myke asked.

"He wants to kill you and then use whatever he finds in your blood to produce a serum to make more of you — a

personal army of super-powered beings, if you will. He —
Urk!"

The odd gurgle at the end of the sentence was caused by
Quincy Quackenbos' springing out of Myke's light grip and
getting his hands around Dr. Simpson's throat. "You fool!
You've ruined everything!" he quacked. "I'll kill you! I'll
kill you! I'll kill you!"

Myke Phoenix clawed at the duck man's hands, but
there were several seconds of extreme discomfort for the
doctor before Myke succeeded in freeing him.

"You're stronger than you look," Myke said. "I'd hate
to get into a fist fight with OOLGH!"

The fowl blow to Myke Phoenix's solar plexus was
entirely unexpected and caught him off guard, so he was
staggered ever so slightly but just long enough for Quincy
Quackenbos to run away.

Ms. Hughes had dutifully locked the door to
Conference Room B, but every room in the building had an
interface that responded to Quincy Quackenbos'
biometrics. He slapped a webbed hand against a panel next
to the door and yanked it open.

Dana Dunsmore was standing at the far corner of the
conference table, her arms folded somewhat defensively but
with a glare in her eyes.

"Let me out of here right now," she growled, "and my –
client – too."

"As a matter of fact, I was inclined to do just that,"
Quackenbos said, circling the table, "until your –
boyfriend? husband? – stopped cooperating. Now I have no
other choice."

Dana circled, too, keeping the table between her and the duck man.

"What's that supposed to mean?"

"Well, I'm guessing he didn't have time to tell you there's a bomb in the basement of the WACR building," he said. "I'm just going to have to set it off."

"You were lying about the atomic bomb," she said. "You're probably lying about this one."

"Funny, that's what Myke Phoenix said, too. You may be right," Quackenbos said, and his eyes narrowed. "But do you really want to test that theory? Sit down."

"I don't think so."

"Oh, I hate when people say no to me."

Quincy Quackenbos jumped – flew? – over the table and grabbed Dana's arms, forcing her into a chair.

"Now," he said, breathing heavily, "I want you to sit right there just for a minute. I'm going to walk into the next room and set off the bomb, and then we'll tend to you and the superhero."

Dana lunged at the duck man, who stepped aside and pushed her to the floor.

"Stay!" he said, lifting an index finger as she struggled to get back up.

Quincy Quackenbos ran to the door on the other side of the conference table and slammed it shut. A moment later the other door burst open and Myke Phoenix strode into the room.

Seeing Dana on the floor, he rushed over to her.

"Are you all right?"

"Yes, I'm fine," she said, brushing hair away from her eyes and pointing at the door. "He went that way – said he was going to set off a bomb."

"I don't think there is a bomb, but we can't take that chance," he said, and went out the door.

From his office window Quincy Quackenbos could see the red and blue flashing lights of the Astor City emergency response unit's squad cars.

If he had been clever enough to install a secret exit to the labs when he built them, now would have been a good time to use it. He hadn't been that clever.

If he were evil enough, he could have used that woman, Dana, as a hostage to break to freedom. Right now, he didn't feel that evil.

"This is the end," he said out loud, and he was surprised at the despair in his voice. Deep inside the duck man's breast, Quacky wanted nothing more than to fly away to the nearest wetlands, find a hen and swim around with her for the rest of their lives. Quincy wanted to hide in the bushes, but that was how their mutual troubles had begun.

He pulled open the top drawer of his desk. There, settled next to his appointment book and an unopened tin of sardines, was an automatic pistol.

He picked it up and examined it, holding it in one webbed hand. Strange how such a small metal device held the power to perform the huge task of evicting the very soul from his body — or both souls, as the case might be.

"Do ducks have souls?" a TV interviewer had asked him once when he described how he and Quacky occupied the same body. Of course ducks have souls; he felt

Quacky's presence always; he *was* Quacky, and also Quincy. The bomb at the atoll had somehow made them one being that was the sum of its parts.

Enough reflection. Quincy Quackenbos held the gun's barrel against the side of his head, winced, and pulled the trigger.

Nothing happened.

"The safety," he muttered in frustration. He was about to push the little button to release the gun's lethal power when the phone beeped.

It was Quincy Quackenbos' private line. There was only one being who could be on the other end of that line. He looked at the gun and considered which alternative would be better: the bullet or answering the phone.

However, the beep of the telephone had distracted him long enough to remember that as long as he was alive, there was hope. He picked up the receiver.

"Quackenbos."

"From what I hear on the police sscanner, you're to be arressted shortly," said a reptilian voice at the other end.

"Yes," he said solemnly.

"Come, come, come. Cheer up, Quincy. And for goodness ssake, put that gun away."

Quincy Quackenbos looked around the room, looked at the gun. "What gun?" he lied.

"Dear fellow, I didn't come this far by not knowing the people who work for me," the voice said with a trace of bemusement. "You're feeling extremely depressed right now, or my name issn't — well, anyway, I need you,

Quincy. You won't be in prison for ssuch a very long time — after all, there were no bombss really, were there?"

"No."

"There! It's just a tiny little extortion charge, perhaps ssimple assault. And when you come out, we'll have much to do together, Quincy, you and I."

"Yes," Quincy Quackenbos said sadly.

"Thanks to you, we've learned many things about this Phoenix persson," the voice reassured him, "and by the time you get out, we'll have all the information we need to exterminate him and get on with business. Now, put down that gun."

Myke Phoenix slammed open the door and stamped across the room.

"It's over now, Quackenbos," said the barrel-chested man. "Put down that gun!"

"Wak," Quincy Quackenbos chuckled, and suddenly found hilarious the fact that his mysterious ally and the superhero had demanded the exact same thing. "Wak! Wak! Wak! Wak! WAK! Wak!"

The strange little man-duck placed the receiver gently back in its cradle, eased the pistol onto the desk, and settled his head in his hands. It was impossible to say whether he was giggling or sobbing; perhaps both.

Ducks have souls that are designed for flying, you see, and this one was about to be caged.

Epilogue

"DON'T do that again!" Dana Dunsmore told Paul Phillips as she hugged him for all her life. "How could you just waltz in and surrender to that man?"

"What choice did I have? He said he was going to blow up the city. I couldn't take the chance he was bluffing. And what do you mean, don't do that again? What were *you* doing there?"

"I just wanted to help, honey," Dana said. "I know, I know, I just made it worse."

"Oh, I really don't think Quackenbos would have hurt you, and Myke didn't get hurt, either. Of course, I made a point of refusing to let them try the bazooka."

"The bazooka?!" She searched his face to see if he was kidding and decided he wasn't. "I don't think I want to hear anything more about it."

"Deal," he said. "So — what do you want to do tonight?"

"Tonight? Hadn't thought about it. What do you want to do?"

He drew her close and nibbled lightly on her neck.

"Oh! That tickles!" Dana Dunsmore told Paul Phillips with a giggle. "You may do *that* again, anytime!"

She hugged him for all her life, and he hugged back. But then he gently released the squeeze.

"I hate to do this, but I left some stuff at work," Paul said. "See you tonight - my place or yours?"

"Mine is a mess," she said. "I'll freshen up, stop and rent a tape, and be at your place around 7. I can't wait to see Frick and Frack again."

When Paul got back to WACR, he spotted Hi Dawson's red mane in a recording studio, saw that the "On Air" light wasn't lighted, and pushed the door open.

"Hey, it's God's gift to radio," he chirped. "How'd it go with the doctor?"

When Dawson turned around, Paul saw that his face was ashen and the bulbous nose was wet with – tears?

"Shut the door, Newshound," Hi said.

Paul let go of the door and it whispered shut.

"What's wrong?"

The red-haired man heaved a wheezing sigh. "It's the Big C."

"Cancer?!"

"No, chickenpox," Hi said sardonically. "Yes, cancer. Lungs. Stage 4, whatever that means. I think it means sayonara."

"Don't think like that, buddy. They cure this stuff a lot of times these days. They're sure about this?"

"Sure enough that they scheduled me for chemotherapy starting day after tomorrow. They'll do a few of those and then see what's happening."

"I'm so sorry, Hi."

"Yeah, thanks," Dawson said. "Not as sorry as I am. You told me so, right?"

"Shut up," Paul Phillips said. "You need someone to go to the hospital with you or anything?"

"Nah, my brother's coming up from Greenville, he's going to stay a few days."

If Hi Dawson's brother was coming to visit, this was pretty darn serious, Paul thought to himself, but let it go.

"OK, well, anything you need, just let me know. You're going to beat this, Hi."

"I have to. I need these lungs. I am the greatest thing that ever happened to this town," said WACR's midday host. "I'm going to take my show national before I'm done, you watch."

"That sounds more like it," Paul said. "Hang in there."

When Paul Phillips entered his apartment and turned on the lights, he saw two cats sitting on his kitchen counter and looking indignant. The black cat with white paws was Frick. The white cat with black paws was Frack.

"What? I'm only an hour late," he said to the irritated felines. "You're just lucky you're here for me to feed you and not radioactive dust, thanks to me."

"You ain't so great," said a voice from a bookcase in the living room, a voice that sounded neither male nor female. "He didn't really have a nuke and you know it."

Paul jumped. "Yikes! I wish you wouldn't do that."

"Do what, point out the obvious?"

No other human was in the room. It was laid out with the usual furniture you might find in a living room: a couch, an easy chair,a reading lamp, a coffee table, a TV set, and a bookcase with a bunch of books and, on the top shelf, an ancient-looking ugly vase studded with random red and blue jewels and adorned with a red bird of some kind.

"I'm still not used to having talking pottery in my apartment."

"Pottery, smottery. I'm the Soulkeeper of Kiribati, and don't you forget it."

"Right. So, today I caught a couple of crooks, saved a bookworm from getting flattened by a bus, and defeated a crazy duck, all while getting my usual seven newscasts done," Paul said. "Is that a good enough day to justify being a little late to feed the cats?"

"Don't ask me about it, ask the cats."

"They're not talking."

"They're not eating, either."

"Oh, yeah," Paul said. After filling the cat bowls with dinner, he sat down next to the bookcase and looked up at the vase. "What else you got for me besides nasty duck men?"

"Quincy Quackenbos isn't so nasty," the vase said. "He just has some anger issues to work through. In another universe you might even be pals. But he is part of the Forces of Evil in the World."

"I figured that out."

"You haven't figured much out. Did you figure out he's working for her?"

"Who's her?"

"She is Deinonychus."

"The talking dinosaur you talked about? Where does she come in?"

"If I told you once, I've told you a bunch of times. Of all of the reasons we called you, she's the biggest, and baddest."

"I can't wait to meet her."

"Oh yes you can," said the vase. "Don't get cocky, kid."

"No problem there, with you on the shelf," Paul said. "Do I ever get a 'hey, good for you, arresting crooks and saving damsels in distress and stopping duck men' out of you?"

"Ain't my job to buck up your self-esteem. But for what it's worth, you didn't do too badly today."

"Well, thank you, O Soulkeeper of Kiribati," said the reporter who also was Mychus the Warrior a k a Myke Phoenix.

There was a knock at the door. When Paul Phillips opened it, he saw a beautiful woman with auburn hair waving a VHS tape and grinning a big grin.

And all was right with the world, at least for a few hours.

The World's
Nicest Bad Guy

Prologue

"STOP that! Stop it at once!" Sandy MacKenzie hurried across the room toward the two tiny combatants. "Jenny! Joshua! What's this all about?"

"Josh was laughing at me 'cause I can't come here anymore," the little girl sniffed.

Sandy MacKenzie's heart ached for the girl. Jenny's mother couldn't afford the center after today, and the scholarship fund was dry.

"Oh, Jenny," she said, drawing the girl into a hug, "We'll miss you so much. I wish you didn't have to go away, either."

"Perhaps that won't be necessary," came a voice from behind her.

The voice belonged to a small, bald man with thick glasses; his eyes were huge behind round lenses too large for his face.

"May I help you?" she asked him.

"No, but I hope I can help you," he replied, handing her a small piece of paper. "I've come to make a small donation."

The visitor had a huge grin that was too sinister to be completely friendly, but Sandy didn't notice that. She was staring at the cashier's check for $25,000 that he was extending to her.

"Perhaps this will help replenish your scholarship fund," said the stranger.

"Oh my," said Sandy MacKenzie, "it really will. Jenny, you don't have to leave. Thank you so much, sir!"

"It's my pleasure," said the man with the big glasses. "This is the kind of thing I like to do with my earnings. There's always more to go around."

Sandy was so thrilled about the stranger's contribution, she didn't make the connection when she heard the radio news story about a quarter-million-dollar jewelry heist.

"Well, now that's something that doesn't happen every day," said a voice from somewhere in the room.

If you were looking at the room from the outside — oh, that's right, you are — you might be hard pressed to understand who was talking. It was a small but comfortable apartment, and a man was cooking himself a hamburger and bean casserole, but he was alone, and he wasn't talking. The only other living creatures were a black cat with white paws and a white cat with black paws — and they weren't talking, either.

But, apparently not surprised by the mysterious voice out of nowhere, the man broke what should have been the silence.

"What doesn't happen every day, Soulkeeper?" He looked up from stirring the pot, and his eyes fell on a frankly ugly green vase randomly adorned with jewels on top of his bookcase.

"Someone evil has just done a kindness," and now it was clear the vase was speaking.

"I suppose no one is totally bad," the solo cook said.

"True," said the voice, which was neither a male nor female voice. You might say it was masculine with a touch of feminine, but you might just as easily say it was a feminine voice that was somewhat masculine. "But it doesn't happen every day."

"Is it something Myke Phoenix needs to get involved with?" asked the man, a pleasant looking man in his mid to late 20s.

"Not right this minute," said the vase. "But you'll probably bump into him one of these days soon."

"How do you know stuff, anyway?" asked Paul Phillips.

"Know stuff?" The vase sounded coy.

"Some bad guy did something nice," Paul said. "And you think I'll meet up with him someday soon."

"I'm in tune with the flows of good and evil in the world. That's what I do," said the Soulkeeper. "And since Mychus is a force for good, it's inevitable that you might clash at some point. That's just common sense."

"Well, let me know when it's time to meet the generous bad guy," Paul said. "Just not tonight. Dana's coming over to watch 'X-Files' and 'Homicide.'"

"You know, a few hundred years ago, Friday nights were a lot more interesting," the Soulkeeper said.

Act 1:
The odd metamorphosis
of Bartholomew Skull

THE psychiatrist caught herself glancing at her email while the patient droned on. Mustn't do that, she said to herself, and made the screen go blank.

"My mother always told me I could do anything I wanted to do, if I set my mind to it," the patient said. "I always thought of her anytime things didn't go the way I wanted."

"Tell me about one of those times, Mr. Skull."

"It's *Doctor* Skull, actually, but please, in this setting, you should probably call me Bartholomew."

"All right, Bartholomew," she said. "You're proud of your degree."

"Aren't you?" the patient said. He was a funny-looking man, eyeglasses so thick they could have been made from the bottoms of bottles, close-cropped hair so short he might as well be bald. "Your shingle out front has 'Dr.' in front of your name, after all."

"Good point," the psychiatrist said. "We put in a bit of time and work to earn the right to use the title."

"Exactly. We might as well ask people to recognize that."

"All right, Dr. Bartholomew Skull," she said, "tell me about a time when things didn't go as well as you wished."

"Well, the story I tell people most often is when I was a high school boy and other kids would taunt me because my glasses have always been so thick."

"Kids can be cruel."

"Oh, yes! They can," the patient said, shaking his head. "But, it turns out, so can I."

"Tell me."

"Well, there was this one lad, Barney, who would pass me in the hall and slap me on the back of the head. Sometimes he slapped so hard that it knocked my glasses loose."

"That must have made you angry."

"Well, I didn't look forward to it every day, that I can tell you."

"Go on."

"One day as I went by, he slapped me on the back of my head, same as always, but something snapped. I was carrying a rather large textbook in my hands, and I ran back to him and took that book in both hands and swing as hard as I could. The book caught him square in the back of the head." He giggled. "I didn't know my own strength. He lurched forward, tumbled into a locker, and fell flat on his face."

"How did that make you feel?"

"Oh, glorious, at first, but then I was scared that he would hit me back, harder. I ran up to him to apologize, but he shook me off when I tried to help him back to his feet. He just walked away and never bothered me again."

"Perhaps being cruel back to a bully is the only thing he will understand."

"Oh, that wasn't when I was cruel to him. That was just retaliation, a tit for a tat."

"Keep going, then."

"When I realized he wasn't going to strike back at me, I lost all my fear," Dr. Skull said. "I rigged his locker so that when it opened a line of firecrackers went off in his face. He was in the hospital for a week, and he still has the scars."

"That *was* cruel," the psychiatrist said.

"He always suspected, but no one could prove I did it. I organized a fundraising campaign to help his family pay for the medical expenses."

"To help atone for your sin?"

"Oh, nothing so noble. It just seemed like the right thing to do."

"I see."

"You see, it's like I have a devil on one shoulder and an angel on the other, always trying to talk me into doing a bad thing or a good thing."

"You hear their voices?"

"Oh, no, of course not," he laughed. "I'm just being metaphorical. I said it's 'like' that, but not literally."

"Excuse me."

"But doing something nice gave me a good feeling. And so, when I committed to a life of wrongdoing, I decided that I would always use my evil abilities for good whenever I could."

"How do you mean?"

"You know what I mean. People are always looking for something good to come out of an unpleasant situation. Well, I try to practice that. Whenever I do something that people might consider bad, I try to balance it by doing something good. You need to help people look on the bright side of things, after all."

"That might make you the world's nicest bad guy."

"Do you really think so? I'd like to think I am."

The psychiatrist looked at the clock on the wall. "This has been very productive, but I hate to say this, the hour is almost up."

"Really?" Dr. Skull looked at the clock. "That went so fast! No need to apologize, I have a very important appointment this noon."

"You're not going to do something bad, I hope," she said.

Bartholomew Skull just smiled.

Doris Jensen was having a bad day. It's OK for most people to have bad days, but when you are a customer service manager at Harold's Department Store, it's not OK to show it. Therefore, not only was Doris Jensen having a bad day, but she had to be so courteous, so friendly, and so helpful that no one would ever suspect how very much she would like to be anywhere else in the world than behind the customer service desk. It wasn't anything she could put her finger on exactly; she was just having a bad day.

The odd request from the little man with the thick round glasses didn't help. She had now searched through three catalogs trying to answer his question. Finally, as yet another child began to scream at his or her mother over some imagined need, she slammed the catalog shut with a sigh and decided to give up.

"I'm sorry, sir, we seem to have that item in every size except – ulp!!!" Doris Jensen had been having a bad day, and the gun now pointed at her chest certainly didn't help.

The little man with the thick round glasses smiled pleasantly as he brandished the pistol. "It would grieve me to have to use this, and I hate to be a bother, but would you mind filling this sack with the day's proceeds, please?" He handed her a cloth bag over the counter.

Doris took the sack and glanced around the room. There were three seedy-looking characters behind the robber; each had their hands in their jacket pockets, looking for all the world like they would do great bodily harm to anyone who interrupted the nice little man's work. This was clearly not a good situation.

"I wish I could help you," Doris lied, "but the armored car just picked up the receipts. All I have here is a few dollars."

"Come now, Ms. Jensen –" how did he know her name – Oh! the name tag on her blazer – "I've shopped here every afternoon for the past month, and the daily receipts have been picked up here, every day, approximately 15 minutes from now. Let's have the money."

Doris tried to discreetly move her hand to the alarm button under the counter. "Tut, tut," said the leader of the thugs, and there came a flurry of movement and a clicking of guns and suddenly four barrels were aimed at her head, as if she were a TV detective who had just reached into her blazer.

"Now, I like to think of myself as a very sweet, patient man," said the little gentleman behind the glasses, "but I really would prefer to get this over with and leave, and I think you'll be much more relaxed after I'm gone. Isn't that correct?"

"Uh-huh," Doris Jensen admitted.

"Well, then!" he exclaimed, still smiling broadly. "Put today's receipts in the sack, and we'll stop troubling you!" The cordially menacing way he spoke made her quite nervous. She put the day's receipts in the sack. "There, that's much better. Now," taking a 50-dollar bill from the bag and a small card from his wallet, "here's a little something for your trouble, and my business card."

"Dr. Skull, Philanthropist and Thief," she read. "Specialist in Good Deeds, Compliments and Robbery."

"At your service," said Dr. Skull with a flourish and a grin, "and may I say you've been a great deal of help, young lady. You're quite professional, and I thank you kindly. I'm terribly sorry to have interrupted your day."

"Dr. Skull – is there a first name?" she asked, still looking at the card as the entourage moved swiftly and carefully out of the store.

He stopped in the aisle and looked back at her, started to speak, then changed his mind. "You couldn't pronounce it," he said with a wave, and then he was gone.

Doris Jensen watched the door for a long time after the strange little man disappeared, as bedlam reigned around her. This really was turning out to be an extraordinarily bad day.

"Alan Pinkstaff is still a punk, and a crooked one at that." Hi Dawson's voice spewed venom through the monitor. "And I'm not just saying that because he blew up my car."

Paul Phillips smiled as he walked the corridor toward the WACR newsroom. He knew Hi had no proof that the city's resident crime boss had bombed his car, but it made for dramatic radio, and every day that Pinkstaff ignored Hi's tirade made the charge more convincing.

"Oh, Paul," came a voice behind him. Phillips turned to meet Bo Ranfort, the station manager, and he stopped in his tracks.

Ranfort was accompanied by a small, thin woman, probably in her early 30s, who was wearing a long, baggy, orange dress with intricate black-and-white embroidery. It took his eyes a second to focus before he saw the dragon lurking in the design of her dress amidst the paisley. She had jet black hair, pale skin, and far too much makeup. She had painted her eyes, painted her eyelashes, painted her lips, painted the creases on either side of her mouth, brushed an unnatural blue on her eyelids, and dabbed her cheeks with something that made her pale skin even whiter. The effect was not unlike embalming.

Bo Ranfort touched her shoulder and said, "This is our new late-night announcer, Glinda Northington."

"So charmed to meet you," said the face that should be dead with a smile that revealed a row of straight, gleaming too-white teeth. "I've listened to you on the news for years."

Paul Phillips choked back the need to stare and extended his hand. "It's a pleasure," he said with some caution. "Welcome."

"OH, MY!!!" She jumped back as their hands touched and put a hand to her chest. He looked at his right hand, confused.

"What happened? What did I do?" he asked. "Are you all right?"

"Oh, yes, yes I am," Glinda Northington said, out of breath. "It's your aura. You're so GOOD! I've never sensed such an embodiment of goodness in all my years."

Paul Phillips looked to Bo Ranfort for some assurance he was not dealing with a loon.

"Glinda is a psychic," the manager explained. "We thought it might be fun to have a New Age presence to start the night shift."

"Now there's an interesting idea," Paul said with all his powers of diplomacy. "Well, I've got to get the next newscast ready. Good to meet you, Glinda."

"Thank you," she replied, still breathless. "I'm looking forward to working together."

"Me, too," he called over his shoulder as he escaped toward the newsroom.

"Why should it be the government's business when you decide to open a store? Do you know how much paperwork these phony bureaucrats make people fill out just for the 'right' to enter the so-called free market? No wonder the economy's a mess!"

The Hi Dawson Show was in "hi" gear. He seemed like his old self despite everything that was happening to him,

Paul Phillips thought as he turned down the monitor to concentrate on preparing his next newscast.

"10-33 in progress at Harold's – caller states there are men with 10-32's at the customer service desk," a woman's voice piped out of the police scanner. The first code, 10-33, announced an emergency; the second 10-code, 10-32, warned there were guns involved. He looked at the clock. The department store was a four-minute drive from WACR; the newscast was in 11 minutes. Plenty of time to grab some news copy, jump in the truck, get down there and do the 'cast from outside Harold's. He threw a tape recorder over his shoulder.

"I'll be on the remote transmitter for the half-hour news," he called to Hi Dawson's engineer as he passed the main studio. Paul Phillips said a grateful prayer for radio's flexibility as he walked briskly toward the station garage. He would have the story on the air before any of the TV crews could get out of their shops.

Harold's was a small chain in terms of the quantity of its stores, but people who could afford it would drive for miles for the quality of its merchandise. There were already three squad cars and an unmarked detective's squad outside the front entrance when Paul drove up in the four-wheel-drive truck marked "WACR – Voice of the Community."

They were letting shoppers in and out; whatever had happened must be over. "Hello, WACR," said the officer at the door. "Say, do Hi Dawson and Annette McPhearson really hate each other or is that all put on?"

"Hi likes Annette," Paul said, starting to move past the cop, "but she has no sense of humor."

"Hey, wait a minute, I don't think I can let media in there."

"Store's still open, isn't it?"

"Well, yeah, but not that section –"

"I need a bracelet for my girlfriend," Paul said, plunging inside.

Sergeant Fredricks always seemed to be the detective on duty when a story broke, and every time Paul arrived at a crime scene he would say "Oh, cripes. Reporters already." Sure enough, those were his exact words as Phillips approached the customer service desk.

"Good to see you, too, Sarge. What you got?"

"I got heartburn, trying to solve a robbery with reporters looking over my shoulder. Get outta here, I'll give you a statement in maybe a half-hour."

"Great. See you in 30." Paul already had enough to lead the newscast with word there'd been a robbery at Harold's and the culprits had gotten away.

He saw a small group of shoppers watching from outside the cordon.

"Was anybody hurt?" he asked them. "Did you hear any shooting?"

"Oh, no," said an elderly woman, "they were as nice as could be."

"Nice? Nice robbers?"

"Well, at least the man in charge was," she replied. "He said 'please' and 'thank you,' and I heard him apologize to the clerk for being a bother."

Paul glanced at his watch and saw he had to dash back to the truck to deliver the news. It seemed the kind bad guy the vase mentioned had made a public appearance.

As he hurried to the exit, the story wrote itself in his mind: "A nice man has just held up Harold's Department Store," he would begin.

"Major Dawkins, I have to run to the grocery store, and the petty cash fund is empty."

Major Dean Dawkins of The Salvation Army sighed. How were they supposed to feed the hungry and homeless when the people who used to donate generously were starting to feel the pangs themselves? These were troubled times. "I'll write you a check," he told the kitchen worker. "Come up to my office when you're ready."

There was a well-dressed man waiting outside his office when he got upstairs. He was wearing a fine suit, the kind you don't usually see in this town, except perhaps at Harold's. "Just the man I'm waiting for," said the man through thick glasses that magnified the twinkle in his eyes. "I've come to make a small donation."

Long after the man left, Major Dawkins still could not take his eyes off the bag filled with enough cash to feed Astor City's hungry for the next five months.

Act 2
The nature of badness

FOR a few moments there was no sound in the room except the ticking of the clock on the wall.

"Dr. Skull, you do realize you've just confessed to a felony," the psychiatrist said uneasily. "A rather serious felony, at that."

"Why, yes, yes I have," said the odd little man with the thick glasses, "and in some states you would be required by law to report this information to the authorities. Thankfully, this is not one of those states. We're bound by doctor-patient confidentiality."

"Why are you telling me this? Why did you seek psychiatric care in the first place?"

"Why, for the very reasons you've been so helpful already," he said, blinking. "I wish to understand the motivations for what I do."

"Um, go on."

"Even I can see what a fascinating case I am. I'm compelled to do evil, I'm very good at it if I say so myself, and yet I'm also compelled to share the fruits of my labor with those less fortunate. Why do you suppose that is?"

"What do you think?"

"Ah, very good. These sessions are about what I think, not you," Dr. Skull said. "I've already told you about the figurative voices that I feel in my mind, the angel and the devil. Why does the devil win most of the time, do you think?"

"Why does the angel even have a say?"

"That's a very interesting question."

"No one thinks of himself as totally evil," the psychiatrist said. "In fact, you're one of the few people I've met who seems to embrace his own evil. I think you're simply trying to compensate, or balance the evil with some token of good."

"It's not just a token, I'm sincerely happy to be able to do some good in this world. That's part of why I keep doing evil: It's what I'm best at. If I used my doctorate for plain old everyday good purposes, I might be making a comfortable living as a university professor or the like, but I couldn't possibly afford to have the impact I'm having on lives."

"You're bad for the purpose of doing good."

"Correct. Why is that so bad?"

By a curious coincidence, a very similar conversation was taking place at that very moment in a small but comfortable apartment across town from the psychiatrist's office.

"I'm telling you, just because he's a nice guy doesn't mean he's not part of the embodiment of evil," the strange vase on Paul Phillips' shelf was saying. "Hitler did some OK paintings, he loved his dog, and Eva thought he was a real sweetie –"

"Oh, back off," Phillips said. "I know that as much as you do, but it doesn't excuse holding up a department store." He looked apologetically at Dana Dunsmore, the auburn-haired beauty who shared the secret that the

Soulkeeper of Kiribati had intruded into his formerly normal life to give him the powers of Mychus.

"What did it say?" asked Dana Dunsmore.

"He says Hitler was a nice guy, too."

"Now, wait a minute, said the ugly bejeweled vase, "you're quoting me out of context and giving your girlfriend the wrong impression."

"Well, then fix it so she can hear you and I don't have to keep repeating everything you say!"

"Oh. OK. How's this, babe?"

"Hey, I heard that!" Dana said in astonishment. "But don't call me babe!"

"Oh, sorry, doll," the vase replied. "Anyway, I was telling your boyfriend here that this Skull character is part of the evil influx that brought me and him together. It's guys like this that convinced the phoenix to call Mychus back into action."

"And he says just because he's polite to his victims doesn't mean he's not part of the influx," Paul continued. "After all, in some ways Hitler was a nice guy."

"Good grief, that's not what I said!" the vase huffed. "I used him as an example of how the evil isn't manifested in every little thing the guy does. Look, I warned you. If you don't wanna take my advice, that's just fine. Just be careful around Dr. Skull, all right?"

"I think you hurt the Soulkeeper's feelings," Dana said with an amused smile. "Is Dr. Skull the talking dinosaur that Paul had a dream about?"

"I wouldn't kid about Deinonychus, lady," the vase cautioned. "No, you'll know HER when you see her."

"What makes Skull worse than your run of the mill impolite stickup guy?" asked Paul. "I mean, besides the fact that he hits places with a lot more money than a convenience store."

"You'll find out." The red and gold gems on the vase seemed to twinkle as it spoke its last words for now.

Major Dean Dawkins waited awkwardly at the glass window in the lobby of the Astor City Police Department. After a couple of minutes, the woman behind the glass looked up.

"I'm sorry, I didn't see you there," she said with a smile. "How can I help you?"

"I need to see the person in charge of these Dr. Skull robberies," replied the major.

"That would be Sgt. Fredricks. I'll see if he can talk to you. Take a seat."

The major sat next to a woman in jeans and a red flannel shirt. She had her arms folded and her legs thrown forward, ankles crossed, as she slumped in the chair. She was frowning hard, her jaw set.

"Are you in trouble?" he asked sincerely.

"I will be after I get my hands on that kid," she snarled. "They caught her shoplifting earrings, and I'm gonna kill her."

"Sometimes being hard on your kids is the best way to let them know you love them," said Major Dawkins, still gently.

The woman's eyes softened just a little, but she said, "I had to take off from work to come down here and bail her out. I'm gonna kill her."

"You don't mean that."

"Yeah? Just watch me," said the mother, but now her eyes were welling over. Major Dawkins offered her a tissue and his business card.

"If you and your daughter need someone to talk to about this, or anything, I'm at The Salvation Army office. Good luck and God bless."

The door to the interior of the police department opened with a clunk to reveal a man in a wrinkled vest. He had a 5:00 shadow and an unlit cigar between his teeth. "I'm Fredricks. What can I do for you?"

"Hello, I'm Major Dean Dawkins," he said, extending his hand. Fredricks took it cautiously. "I think I can help with these Dr. Skull robberies."

"Oh, yeah? What do you got?"

The major sighed. "A man who sounded very much like the description I heard on the radio came to my office yesterday and gave me a bag filled with thousands of dollars. I thought it was too good to be true."

Fredricks took the unlit stogie out of his mouth. "Let me get this straight. You think this guy robbed Harold's and then turned around and gave a big chunk of the money to you? Let me clue you in, friend, the people I usually deal with ain't that generous."

"I know it sounds incredible, but he looked just like the description. A small man with thick round glasses, very polite. He was even wearing a fine suit that could have come from Harold's."

"Oh, cripes," Fredricks said. "They did steal a suit on the way out. We didn't tell that to the media. Come on in, Major, I'll have you fill out a statement."

"I'm happy to help," the major said. "I have to tell you, though, this hurts. We could use the money."

"I get that," Fredricks said. "Maybe that's his angle. The guy's stealing from the rich and giving to the poor. Wait until those idiots in the media get a load of this."

Sandy MacKenzie's heart filled with joy watching Jenny giggle and run across the playground. The sweet little girl wouldn't be there today without the generosity of that nice odd man. She sighed. If only everyone would give a little bit of their good fortune to families in need, the center wouldn't have to deal with crises like Jenny's mom had.

Sandy walked into the playroom, abandoned when Noontime Recess had come. Someone had left the television on, and a young bleach-blonde reporter was standing in front of The Salvation Army office.

"Is he a hoodlum or Robin Hood?" the young woman asked as she walked along the sidewalk. "Sources have told TV-19 Upfront and Personal News that the mysterious robber who calls himself Dr. Skull stopped at a bank as he was getting away from Harold's and then drive straight here" – pointing awkwardly behind her at The Salvation Army – "to make the biggest donation this group has received in a year! I have with me the head of the Astor City Salvation Army chapter."

From regular get-togethers of local nonprofit organization leaders, Sandy recognized the face of Major

Dean Dawkins, although the caption at the bottom on the TV screen identified him as "Dean Dinkins."

"It's just tragic," the major told the reporter. "The man gave us enough money to sustain our entire operation for weeks, and now I'm afraid we'll have to turn it all back."

Sandy MacKenzie had a sudden sinking sensation. The scenario sounded all too familiar.

"Police have now released a composite sketch of Dr. Skull, based on descriptions from Major Dinkins and people from the bank robbery," the blonde said, and then the sketch appeared on the screen.

It looked just like the kindly man who had come to the child-care center. Sandy's sinking sensation struck bottom.

Act 3

Hoodlum or Robin Hood?

"I see you haven't made your identity a secret," the psychiatrist said. "Business cards that say 'Dr. Skull, Philanthropist and Thief'? Don't you think that will lead the authorities straight to you?"

"If only they knew where I live," the odd little man said. "I'm not in the phone book."

"The Salvation Army gave the money back," she said. "How does that make you feel?"

Was that anger that washed over his face just briefly, replaced by a sad expression?

"It makes me feel like I should have laundered the money somehow, to disguise my intentions," said Dr. Skull. "But that feels dishonest."

She snorted; she couldn't help it. "Dishonest? You're a thief. You're inherently dishonest."

"I suppose that's true."

"Why don't you use your genius to accomplish some good in the world?"

"That sounds so judgmental," Dr. Skull said. "I *am* accomplishing good; I thought you understood that."

"You're only giving people false hope if they have to give the money back to its rightful owners."

She wondered if challenging his view of reality was a good idea, but it seemed worth the risk. He seemed to smolder for a moment before responding slowly and evenly.

The flashes of anger were something new, and there was a quality to them that made her more than uneasy. They were more than a little scary, they were – oh, let's face it. She was suddenly terrified."

"I've given a lot of money away. Only the Salvation Army has given it back," he said, earnestly more than angrily now. "I couldn't do as much as I have if I had to earn it honestly."

"You don't know that."

"I do know that! Do you think I haven't tried?" he snapped. "The quickest way to make money in this world is to take it — grab it from the foolish and give it to those who need it."

He caught his breath and smiled, at ease again. The teeter-tottering between rage and calm was starting to make the psychiatrist dizzy.

"A pirate's life for me," Dr. Skull said. "I am the Robin Hood Bandit. Haven't you watched the evening news lately?"

"Robin Hood in a pig's eye." The voice of an elderly woman barked through the phone into the airwaves. "The man stole my silver tea service."

"Beg pardon?" asked Annette McPhearson. The afternoon open line was well under way on WACR radio, the Voice of the Community.

"That service belonged to my grandmother. I took it in to Jenkins Jewelry to have it appraised, and that hoodlum took it with the rest of his loot. I'm not a wealthy woman, and he stole from me just like everyone else."

"Well, these titles, the Robin Hood Bandit or the World's Nicest Bad Guy, those are just titles for news stories. It doesn't condone what he does."

"Of course it does! You people don't know how much power the media has. You're making this man a hero."

Paul Phillips cringed. He never gave Dr. Skull any of those flattering titles, but local TV had, and all of the electronic media were painted with the same brush in people's minds.

"Don't you love getting lumped in with the worst of them?"

Paul looked up and saw Hi Dawson, the red-haired gadfly who torched the airwaves before Annette's show every day.

"What do you mean, Hi?"

"I saw that look on your face just now. The old lady honked you off talking about how all the media is making Dr. Skull a hero."

"Yeah, you got that right," Paul admitted. "Sometimes the way other journalists act is enough to make me quit the profession."

"Nah, don't do that, you're pretty good at it," Hi said, and then started coughing. Then he coughed some more, and coughed again, until it was clear that if he wanted to stop coughing he would have a hard time doing so.

But after a few moments the coughing fit did subside, and Hi Dawson half-sat, half fell into a chair.

"I suppose I shouldn't ask how your treatment is going."

"I'm OK," Hi said in a tone that suggested he wasn't. "I have my second chemo treatment on Friday morning. They're telling me I shouldn't work my shift, but I can't afford to miss work."

"We get sick days."

"They say I'm going to need them later."

"How are you really, Hi?"

The not-pleasant face with the bulbous nose looked much more serious than usual.

"I'm scared, Paul. This is damn serious. I —"

Just then a lanky fellow with a cheerful expression walked into the room. He started to say something, then noticed the somber looks on his co-workers' faces.

"Oh, hey, sorry, I can come back."

"No, that's OK, Sam, I'm just heading out anyway," Hi said, rising a little unsteadily.

"Are you OK, Hi?"

"I got lung cancer, Sam," Hi said with a grim smile, clapping a hand on Sam Wainwright's shoulder. "No, I'm not OK, but I'll see you tomorrow, I promise."

Sam Wainwright's real name was something else, but he adopted a radio name from one of his favorite movies. He was the morning news guy who often handled the police beat.

"I'm really sorry if I interrupted, Paul," he said.

"Don't worry," Paul replied. "I don't think Hi wants to talk about it anyway. Hey, what's new downtown?"

"I was going to tell you, one of the guys at the cop shop said they think they have a general idea where Dr. Skull and his gang are operating.

"Fredricks tell you this?"

"Ha! Good one," Sam said. Sgt. Fredricks did not cooperate with reporters, period. "It was Henderson. He wouldn't give me an address but he said we should watch out for activity on the south side."

"Try calling Lt. Tomlinson," Paul said. "He's usually pretty helpful. I'll keep an ear on the scanner."

As if in response, the police scanner squawked into action.

"All units, report of suspicious characters approaching the Fourth State Bank," the dispatcher intoned. "Might be Dr. Skull and his gang."

"Well, that's not the south side but it's the right criminals," Sam said. "Are you heading over there, Paul? Oh!"

Paul Phillips was already gone.

The distinctive roaring clatter of a helicopter passed overhead, and the Fourth State Bank security guard craned his neck to see where the flying machine was going. When he brought his attention back to earth, the muzzle of a pistol was aimed between his eyes.

"I'll use this," warned the man at the other end of the gun, "so behave."

One of the customers saw the gunman back the guard into the bank, and she yelled, "He's got a gun!" Someone else screamed. Dr. Skull entered the lobby behind a total of three gunmen.

"Ladies and gentlemen, please, please," he said loudly but calmly. "There's nothing to be worried about. This will be over in just a few minutes."

A huge man with an ugly scar across his nose walked up to a teller station and tossed a large duffel bag on the counter, brandishing a large gun near the teller's face.

"Fill it with cash and make it snappy," the thug growled.

"Pookie! Where are your manners?" the cheerful man with the thick glasses chirped.

The big man rolled his eyes. "Fill it with cash and make it snappy, *please*," he said, folding his arms across his chest with his hand still holding the gun, but more gently.

The other two men — not as imposing as Pookie but also pointing guns — mimicked the lead henchman's behavior with other tellers.

"This is not acceptable behavior, gentlemen," said a deep, booming voice from the staircase to the second floor. Eyes turned to see a blond-haired man with a huge, barrel-like chest standing between floors. He was wearing a white uniform with a red-and-gold symbol on the chest, a symbol that seemed to depict some kind of bird.

"It's Myke Phoenix!" someone cried.

"Oh, fiddlesticks," said Dr. Skull. "We did such a good job of planning this operation, too. Pookie, remind me to prepare a surprise for Mr. Phoenix next time. We'll be going now, folks. Ta-ta!"

"You're not going anywhere, Skull," the superhero in the white suit called across the lobby. One of the henchmen fired his gun at Myke Phoenix, who walked into the hail of bullets unharmed, grabbed the gun and knocked the man out with a light punch.

"I don't mean to be contradictory, but yes, I am leaving now," Dr. Skull replied, motioning to the nearest accomplice. "That one, Pookie."

The huge man with the ugly scar across his nose grabbed an elderly woman and held his gun to her head.

"All we ask is a 10-second head start, Mr. Phoenix," the little ringleader said pleasantly. "If you leave the bank at any time during those 10 seconds, we'll deprive this poor woman of her life. I would hate it very much if that happened, wouldn't you?" Pookie, the remaining gunmen and Dr. Skull ran out the door with their hostage.

Myke Phoenix gave them 15 seconds just to be sure. He could hear police sirens converging on the bank now. Myke dashed out the door, looked both ways, and saw the woman lying on the sidewalk four doors away.

She was groggy when he reached her, a welt swiftly swelling on the back of her head.

"Are you all right, ma'am?" he asked.

"I think so," she replied. "They pulled me down the street and then hit me on the head."

"Did you see which way they went?"

"No. No, I'm sorry, young man, I didn't see."

The sirens were just around the corner. Myke Phoenix looked in every direction but saw no sign of the bad guys; he also knew he had a newscast to deliver shortly. The superhero dashed into a convenient alley; Paul Phillips walked out of the alley as the first squad car reached the woman.

He'd have to find Skull another time. Darn it all anyway.

"I'll get you yet, Dr. Skull," he muttered.

"A man asked me to deliver this to the person in charge. Is that you?" asked the little boy.

"That's me," said the man behind the desk of the Place to Stay homeless shelter. He took the envelope.

There was a note inside with $250 cash. "I wanted to give more but my fundraising effort was less than successful. I sincerely hope to do better next time," it read.

"Thank you, son," said the man behind the desk. "Who was it who gave this to you?"

"Some guy," said the little boy. "He smiled a lot, but he made sure I walked in the door with the envelope."

"Maybe he's still outside." They rushed to the front door and looked both ways, but of course the street was empty.

"I guess he wants to be anonymous," the desk man said. "What a nice fellow. He didn't say his name?"

"Nope, he just smiled."

Sam Wainwright whipped out his notebook and showed it to Paul. "The lieutenant was as helpful as you predicted," he said in the deep, melodic tone that made him popular with the listeners. "He gave me the address where they figure Dr. Skull is staying."

"2562 Industrial Lane," Phillips read.

"It's one of those new office buildings they haven't finished yet," Sam said. "They think he's set up shop in one of the suites, and guess what? The lessee is something called DS Enterprises Ltd."

"Sounds a little obvious," Paul replied, "at least in hindsight. Are they going after him?"

"They're staking the place out, waiting until they're sure Skull is inside before they raid the place. I don't think they'd head there after the bank heist, do you?"

"They might if they don't know the police are onto them. Thanks, Sam, good job. I'll head on over there, uhh, with the remote equipment, just in case."

"Want me to write up a little story, 'police are close to nabbing Dr. Skull'?"

"NO!" Phillips made Sam Wainwright jump. "Sorry, Sam. If we run a story like that, it might be enough to tip off Skull and his gang, and it'd be the last tip we ever got from the P.D. Just sit tight and listen for that address on the scanner."

Paul's reservations about using the information on his day job, however, did not preclude him from acting on it for his other occupation.

Act 4
Showdown at Trail's End

MYKE Phoenix wished his uniform wasn't such a shining white. He couldn't approach the office building on Industrial Lane without being spotted in the moonlight. He'd tried putting Paul's trench coat on, but Mychus the Warrior's body was somewhat more massive than Phillips the reporter's was.

A helicopter rumbled in the distance, and one of the nearby factories hummed with activity, as he skulked as invisibly as possible toward DS Enterprises Ltd. Crossing the street furtively, he realized he could have come here as Phillips, in Phillips' coat, and then changed into Myke Phoenix when he needed to. Hindsight is 20/20.

He really began to use hindsight when the helicopter thundered into view overhead, dropped a net over him and snatched him off the ground.

"Hokey smokes," he cried. He really was going to have to work on being sneaky. Whoever was inside that building must have seen him coming a long time ago, if they had time to call out the helicopter.

Paul Phillips loved to fly; he wouldn't take a book when he was taking an airplane trip, because he knew he would spend the entire time looking out the window at the fields and cities below anyway. Now, however, dangling from a helicopter in a net, he was not having the time of his life.

The net was made of steel cable; Myke Phoenix could easily tear it open, but that would mean dropping a few hundred feet onto downtown Astor City, and he wasn't sure if Mychus' remarkable body could survive such a plummet. He looked up – yes, he probably could climb up to the 'copter, tear the top of the net and haul himself inside, given enough time –

The bad news was that as soon as the helicopter reached the middle of the river, it dropped the net.

"Yikes!" said Myke Phoenix. The river rose up terrifyingly to greet him.

"OK, he's in," the voice on the radio shouted over the aircraft's whirling roar.

Dr. Skull picked up the microphone with his ever-present grin. "Excellent, excellent," he said. "Now come back here as quickly as you can. We're moving."

"Are you sure we oughtta move now, boss?" asked Pookie warily. "We got some stuff in the back that won't fit on the helicopter."

"We'll have to leave it behind, dear boy," Skull replied. "If Myke Phoenix can find us, the police can, too. Remind me to be more subtle when I name our future hideouts, Pookie; using 'DS' was pure hubris."

"Huh?"

"Hubris, lad, hubris – fatal pride! Didn't they teach you anything at school?"

"I dint graduate."

"Why am I not surprised?" Dr. Skull sighed. "Well, you can always go back for your G.E.D. It will make you a more clever accomplice. Now, let's go. I hear the helicopter."

Myke Phoenix took a deep breath, and it took all his powers of concentration not to exhale it all from the shock of plunging into the cold, dark water. He knew his adopted body had a chest like a barrel; now he was going to learn the hard way how much air a barrel can hold.

The steel net helped him sink to the bottom of the river swiftly. To his dismay the speed of his descent was such that he plunged into the river sediment to his knees. He was trapped in a net made from steel cables, underwater, and stuck at the bottom.

Don't panic. Don't exhale.

First things first – he got a good grip on the netting and gave it a sharp yank. He almost gasped in surprise (but thought better of it) when the steel cable tore like tissue paper.

I still don't know my own strength, he thought, but he couldn't pull his legs up out of the muck so easily. He watched a small bubble come out of his nose, then another, as he began slowly to let the air out of his lungs.

He peeled himself out of the cable, reached down and dug at the mud around his knees, kicking and digging and holding his breath and trying not to be alarmed. Just as he felt panic beginning to form a seed in his heart, he broke free of the river bottom. Now it was simply a race to the surface.

How deep is the river? Paul Phillips had lived here for a decade and never asked, never known. Now, as the lungs of Mychus began to burn with wanting to do their job, he prayed that it was not a long journey to the surface. There was no oxygen left in his lungs, it was all carbon dioxide now, and it was screaming to come out so that he could breathe in more oxygen. Doing what comes naturally would fill his lungs with murky water just now.

Was that the light of the city just ahead or was he seeing stars as he started to lose consciousness? He didn't know. He only knew he had to keep moving his arms methodically, pulling himself through the water and heading up as directly as he could.

And, then, there was air.

Glorious, sweet air. The rank stuff from his lungs exploded away, and he breathed hard, noisily, roughly again and again, treading water.

It took several minutes to compose himself, and then Myke Phoenix started to swim to shore, a grim purpose to his stroke. Dr. Skull was still at large and had to be found.

Major Dean Dawkins opened the file cabinet and stuck the form he'd just completed into the appropriate folder. He sighed as he pushed the drawer shut. Would anyone, ever, see that piece of paper again? Were all of these forms necessary? Did they feed one hungry child or give one homeless family a night of shelter?

He had joined the war on poverty out of compassion and caring, and he still cared. What bothered him were the many tasks he was required to do that had little to do with fixing what ails humanity. At the end of the day, after his energy had been spent on doing the Lord's work, he still had to stay late to document it all like this.

The phone on his desk rang, and for a moment he considered letting it ring.

"Can't I be done for the day just once?"

It might be someone in desperate need. He picked up the phone.

"Salvation Army, Major Dawkins, how may I help you?"

There was a gasp on the other end. "I didn't expect you to answer."

"Well, I'm here. What can I do for you?"

"This is probably silly and unnecessary," the woman said, "but if something happened I wouldn't be able to forgive myself, so I had to call."

"All right, that got my attention," the major said.

"You see, I'm Dr. Skull's personal psychiatrist."

"I see," he said skeptically.

"I assure you, this isn't a crank call."

"You'll forgive me if I don't believe you."

"Just don't hang up the phone!" the woman said as he reached to hang up the phone. The urgency in her voice convinced him to stay on the line.

"What is it you want, doctor? I assume you're a doctor.

"Yes. I just want you to know that Dr. Skull was displeased that you gave back the money he donated."

"I couldn't very well keep it, knowing it had been stolen in a bank robbery," Dawkins said.

"Be that as it may, he was very unhappy," she said. "He's never committed a violent act, but I always suspect there's a rage under his smiling demeanor, and he doesn't like to be contradicted."

"You think he'll hurt me because I didn't take his ill-gotten money?"

A loud swarming sound roared overhead, temporarily so loud that it drowned out any attempt at conversation.

"What was that, major?"

"It was only a low-flying helicopter," he said. "Everything's fine here."

"A helicopter? Everything's not fine. You've got to hide. I think that's him."

"He's coming for me in a helicopter?"

"Major, do me a favor and just hide."

"All right, I'm hanging up and I'm hiding."

Major Dean Dawkins hung up the phone, turned, and met the eyes of a large man with an ugly scar across his nose.

"What's the rush, padre?" the man said cruelly.

"Manners, Pookie," said the odd little man who had delivered the cash a few days earlier, as he stepped off the stairs from the roof. "Hello, Major, so nice to see you again."

Dr. Skull took the gun from Pookie's hand and aimed it between Major Dean Dawkins' eyes.

"What do you mean denying the poor people of Astor City the benefits of my contribution?"

Dawkins stared down the barrel of the gun.

"You stole that money," he said softly.

"And I gave it to you, for your ministry," Dr. Skull hissed. "How dare you judge me?"

"Um, boss, manners," Pookie said somewhat timidly.

His eyes widened and his nostrils flared, but the villain relaxed into his more familiar smile.

"Quite right, Pookie. Quite right. I have a proposition for you, major, and I want you to listen carefully. Someday soon, perhaps after you hear of a crime in some other city, you will receive a money order in the mail for a tidy sum."

"You're going to steal more money —"

"Tut, tut, I said no such thing," Dr. Skull grinned. "You will receive a generous donation, and this time you will gladly accept it, put it in the bank and start using it on behalf of your flock."

"I can't throw bad money after good."

"Very clever. Not only can you throw bad money after good, but I insist." The eyes flickered behind the thick lenses, and the barrel of the gun reappeared in front of the major's face. "Shouldn't we all share our good fortune with others, son? Their lives depend on us, and your life depends on doing good with my contribution to the cause."

Major Dawkins nodded at the gun barrel. "When you phrase it that way, how can I say no?" he said grimly. "Of course, and thank you."

"You're welcome," Dr. Skull said. "Was that so hard? Now, our helicopter is going to come back and land on the street to pick us up, so I'd appreciate your staying right there until we depart. And please don't pick up the phone again."

"We can just prevent that possibility," Pookie said, and ripped the phone cord out of the wall.

"That was rude, my friend, but perhaps necessary," the villain said. "Sorry about the damage, major."

They walked out the front door of the Salvation Army chapter into the glare of a spotlight. It was not the light from the 'copter.

"Police. You are surrounded. Set down those packages and put your hands up. You're under arrest."

"Oh, my goodness, I certainly am not," Dr. Skull called cheerfully back.

Just then a large man clad in white appeared at Pookie's side, wrested the gun out of his hands and tapped him roughly on the chin. The henchman collapsed in a proverbial heap. Myke Phoenix gripped the odd little man by the arm.

The helicopter returned, soaring over the surrounding buildings and shining its own spotlight over the scene. The armed officers were sitting ducks for the helicopter's armaments – but Dr. Skull exhaled resignedly and gave his henchman in the 'copter a prearranged wave that meant, "Go away and save yourself."

"Surrendering to avoid bloodshed?" Myke said. "Good move. Maybe you are the world's nicest bad guy after all."

"Tut, tut. The maximum for armed robbery is 20 years, my friend," Skull said with a smile. "We'll be out in no time. Under the circumstances, killing several police officers would not be a practical thing to do."

As the emergency response unit walked Dr. Skull and Pookie in handcuffs toward a squad car, radio reporter Sam Wainwright strode up and poked his microphone in their direction.

"Why did you share your loot with charity, Dr. Skull?"

The man in the thick glasses grinned broadly as he was placed rather abruptly into the back seat.

"We should all do our bit to make life a little easier for our fellow travelers on this mortal coil," he called to the reporter.

The exchange would sound terrific on the morning news, Sam exulted as the squad car drove away; he was especially pleased because the TV vans came up now, after Dr. Skull was gone.

Paul will be happy with this audio, Sam said, and then he stopped in mid-stride, looking around. Why wasn't Paul here yet?

Just as Sam was starting to worry – and a moment before he could start thinking that he never saw Paul Phillips and Myke Phoenix together – Paul walked around the corner.

"Hey, Sam," he said in greeting. "Wild night, huh?"

"You said it. I just got a great sound bite from Dr. Skull," Sam gushed.

"That means you saved my life, buddy," Paul said. "I was tied up and didn't get a thing."

"I thought you got here first."

"That was the plan, but it didn't work out."

"What happened?!"

"It's a long story, and maybe I'll tell you about it someday. For now, I'll meet you back at the station. We'd better get this story out there."

"I thought you were bringing the remote stuff."

"I was going to do that, but – well, I told you it's a long story," Paul Phillips said.

Epilogue

THERE was one small problem remaining. Sandy MacKenzie didn't want to give the money back.

"That $25,000 allowed several children to have the child care their parents otherwise couldn't afford," Sandy said to anyone who would ask. "If we have to return it, we may end up having to close our doors altogether."

The daycare center became a cause célèbre at WACR Radio, as talk show hosts and the community in general debated.

"The city should let her keep the money," Annette McPhearson argued every afternoon for a week and a half. "It's not her fault that it was stolen, the insurance company has covered the jewelry store's losses, and the center could certainly use the cash.

"It ain't the government's responsibility to give away other people's money, no matter how much they do it every day, folks," Hi Dawson argued every midday before Annette's show. "The money was stolen, we know where the money is, the money should be returned. Tell you what, though – if everyone in this city sent two or three bucks, we'd be able to give the center that much money and then some."

And so, the fundraising was on. Some people gave more than two or three dollars. A week and a half later, Sandy MacKenzie was presented a check for $192,261, courtesy of WACR, Voice of the Community.

Sandy was thrilled, the children were happy, and all was well in Astor City – at least until a few weeks later, when a prince who wished to rule the world saw an opportunity to begin his quest for dictatorship in a middling-sized community called Astor City.

In the Lair
of the Cormorant

Prologue

PIERCE Shelley could be called a number of things, but fool was not one of them. Those who knew him well said he was cold, arrogant, aloof, and extremely intelligent. Most people felt Shelley was the smartest man they'd ever met — it was his lack of warmth that lost him the election back in '88, when he could have risen to the U.S. Congress but was beaten by the very bright *and* very charming woman who still represented the district that includes Astor City.

Shelley's party did not forget the work he had done over the years, and for his loyalty he was rewarded with an ambassadorship after he lost the election. Many wondered why he would accept the posting to a tiny little nation barely larger than Astor City itself. That was because they did not know as much about Cormornia, and Prince Cormorant, as Pierce Shelley did.

Shelley loved to ski, and Cormornia was nestled among the beautiful ski resorts of the Swiss Alps. Shelley loved to talk about deep and philosophical things, and in many circles Prince Cormorant was considered one of the great thinkers of the age. Pierce Shelley loved to be alone, and Cormornia did not receive many visitors. Only the wealthiest people in the world could afford the trip to Prince Cormorant's little country, and only those who loved winter and snow and skiing would care to make the trip.

When the president offered Pierce Shelley a choice between the embassies in Sweden or Cormornia, it was a remarkably easy choice. Both countries had almost everything Shelley desired, but Cormornia promised solitude.

But now, after nearly six years as ambassador, Pierce Shelley had just learned something extraordinary about his host, and he was terrified.

The cool emotionlessness that bothered his acquaintances served him well now, for he was able to banish any sign of discomfort or fear from his face and body language.

"Your Majesty, I've known you for a long time," he said evenly. "If it wasn't for that, I'd be inclined to say you were joking, but you are very serious about this, aren't you?"

"And why not, my old friend?" smiled Prince Cormorant with a grin that was entirely too wide, too calculated. "The world belongs to those who are willing and able to take it. It is only right and proper that I rule it."

"The entire world in the hands of one man?"

"The world belongs to those who are willing and able to take it," Prince Cormorant repeated. "For all of my life, I have been willing but not able. Now, at last, I soon will be able. You do see how this makes sense, don't you, my friend?"

"Why, yes," Shelley agreed. He could follow the prince's twisted reasoning because he was as bright as the prince. That was why he was so terrified. "But what you propose is just not — well, may I be blunt?"

"Are we not friends?" Prince Cormorant replied.

Pierce Shelley failed to notice that the prince had not directly answered his question. "What you propose is inhuman, Your Majesty. I don't believe the world would stand for it."

"The world will have no choice. It must bow to the promise of a new day. It is my will, the will of the world's rightful ruler." Underneath his huge, beaked nose, Prince Cormorant's mouth drew into a pursed and even line. Beneath large, out-of-control, crested eyebrows smoldered an emotion beyond Pierce Shelley's understanding, and Shelley suddenly knew one thing with a chilling certainty:

Cormorant, Prince of Cormornia, was quite insane.

Act 1

Cormorant Landing

STREAMING beams of light seeped into the room. It was time to wake up, and Pierce Shelley felt like he had barely slept.

He rose from the sumptuous bed and stepped to the window, which faced the east. Sure enough, he noted, pulling back the drapes, it was another beautiful morning in the Alps. Sunlight was bursting over Cormornia from between the mountains, filling the little principality with the promise of a new day.

A promise of a new day. Cormorant's evil promise. It had taken only that long for the terrible secrets conveyed to him by the prince to find their way back into Pierce Shelley's consciousness.

He crossed to the computer terminal that would link him to the headquarters of the diplomatic corps in Washington. The screen blinked at him softly, not at all as brightly as the sun over his shoulder.

"Urgent that I return to Washington for consultation. Prince Cormorant is —" he typed, then looked at his words with an ironic laugh. Prince Cormorant is what? What could he write that wouldn't be greeted with hoots and ridicule? The leader of this postage-stamp country wants to declare war on the human race? From a military perspective, the rest of the world had the power to crush Cormornia before breakfast. He wouldn't be taken seriously.

"The problem is, it's not a question of force," Pierce Shelley said aloud, and caught himself. Was Cormorant mad enough to plant monitoring devices in the U.S. Embassy? Lord knows Washington was not concerned enough to make security a major priority for its diplomats in Cormornia.

But what message could he send that would allow him to get back to the States to issue the warning?

"A personal emergency has come up. Request permission to return home," Shelley finally wrote, lamely. "While in town would like to brief HQ regarding —" here we go again; what could he say? "regarding protocol with respect to security." There, that was vague enough not to attract too much attention, but it had that important word "security" in it. Washington always loved to talk about security. He dispatched the brief message.

Moments later the phone rang and Pierce Shelley nearly jumped through the ceiling.

"Shelley here."

"My dear friend," came the oddly clipped tones of the prince of Cormornia, "I've just decided to visit your homeland next week. Would you care to join me?"

"Why, I'd love that, Prince," said Pierce Shelley cautiously, trying not to sound alarmed. Had Cormorant been monitoring his heavily encrypted dispatch, or was this sudden trip a coincidence?

"I want to visit this Astor City that you speak so highly of, the land where you were born. May we include this town in our itinerary?"

"Of course, of course," and a thought occurred to him that gave him authentic enthusiasm for the idea of the trip. "By all means, I'd love to show you Astor City. It's not as magnificent as your own country, of course."

"Nonsense, my friend, nonsense. I will be honored and pleased to see the sights of your hometown. Will you ask if your president can meet me when we reach Washington?"

A churning began deep in Shelley's bowels. So that was it. Cormorant was almost prepared to act. He wanted to scream, no, you madman, I won't let you near my president! but all he said was, "It's certainly a possibility. I'll do all I can to try to arrange it."

After he replaced the receiver in its cradle, the U.S. ambassador to Cormornia went back to the window blazing with morning sunshine. The talk of Astor City had reminded him of the bizarre rumors he'd heard, about a crime fighter with amazing powers who had recently emerged there. What was his name? Something birdlike.

Myke Phoenix. That was it.

The man apparently was bulletproof and had already foiled a small number of criminal enterprises. It wasn't clear where Phoenix had come from, but he was quickly turning into something of a legend.

The shadow that had settled across Pierce Shelley's face began to lift into an ever-so-slight smile. This Myke Phoenix character would know what to do about Prince Cormorant.

Paul Phillips turned up his collar as a cool breeze chased brown leaves across the runway at Astor Field. As the plane approached, he realized he had time to call into the radio station, so he ducked back into the terminal, where an array of pay phones was positioned not far from the gates.

His colleague Sam Wainwright answered the phone in the WACR newsroom.

"The prince's plane is just arriving, so I probably won't have anything for the top of the hour," Paul said. "The welcome ceremony will probably be happening when the newscast comes up."

"OK, Paul. Did you hear about Hi?"

Hi Dawson was the station's acerbic midday host and Paul's best friend among his co-workers. "What about him?"

"He got real sick right after his shift ended, and they took him to the hospital. Sorry to be the one to tell you."

"How bad?"

"Like he told me last week, it's lung cancer, right? It sounded pretty bad."

"OK, thanks for letting me know," Paul said. This was not good. Hi had only recently learned about his illness, but it seemed to be progressing a lot faster than even the pessimistic doctors were predicting.

The Astor City North High School Band had struggled for weeks to perfect the nuances of the Cormornia national anthem, and the result was more than serviceable. The musicians seemed much more at ease, however, when they were able to turn their attention to "The Star-Spangled Banner."

The reporter for WACR Radio waited patiently for the anthems to be completed so the brief ceremony could get underway.

"Half of this job involves standing and waiting," he muttered with a half-smile. "No wonder the pay is so miserable."

Ambassador Pierce Shelley stepped to the podium. He looked older than Phillips remembered, but it had been a few years since he'd seen him last. Shelley looked over to the press table and saw Phillips there, gave a nod in his direction and a small smile that almost seemed urgent. The message Paul Phillips received from that smile was that Shelley wanted to talk to him – odd, from a man whom he recalled as being so uncomfortable with reporters.

"I have spent the last few years in a wonderful country almost as pretty as this, my hometown," Shelley told the audience, "and I can think of nothing more appropriate than to use this soil to greet Prince Cormorant to America. I give you Cormorant." The fact that Pierce Shelley's speech was remarkably shorter than usual did not occur to Phillips until later.

The man who stepped to the podium was as peculiar a physical specimen as anyone present could remember. He was tall and lanky, with slick, jet-black hair that came to a long, sharp widow's peak in the middle of his forehead. The predominant feature of his face was his nose, a thin, hooked proboscis that gave him a distinctly birdlike appearance. Wild and feathery eyebrows accentuated his avian features. Anyone who had ever seen cormorants diving for fish along the coast couldn't help but marvel at the resemblance.

He waited — and waited — until the bustling crowd settled into an embarrassed silence. Then he cast his wide, staring eyes around the group, turning his head in small, sudden jerks. The resemblance to a predatory bird was complete.

"Dear friends," he chirped in the Cormornian accent that defied comparison to any other nation, "it is indeed my pleasure to be in America and in my dear, dear friend Pierce Shelley's town of home. It is as lovely as Pierce has said." The words, calculated to draw applause, succeeded.

The prince droned on for some minutes about the usual things that political leaders drone on about: what good friends our nations are, how we can help each other, etc. etc. Paul Phillips stifled a yawn. He was getting some acceptable sound bites to run on the news, but nothing terribly earthshaking.

When the speech ended, the crowd clapped politely and Phillips walked up to the podium to retrieve his microphone. The Prince of Cormornia and Pierce Shelley were talking just behind the dais.

"Paul Phillips, isn't it?" Shelley said, extending a hand. "My goodness, I think you were with WACR back when I was running for Congress."

"Yes, I got here a couple of years before that election," Phillips replied, taking the hand. Shelley was sweating. "You were on the County Board."

"Of course, of course," Shelley said, and stepped closer. Prince Cormorant had struck up a conversation with the mayor. "Phillips, do you know how to get hold of Myke Phoenix?"

The question was so sudden and unexpected that Phillips blushed. "What made you think to ask me?" he stammered.

"You're in the media, you've covered him. You have a few contacts, I guess."

"Sure, I know how to contact him, you just took me by surprise. Does the Prince want to meet Myke Phoenix?"

"No." Pierce Shelley's face turned extremely somber. "It's for me. I must talk to him personally. It's a very serious matter, and I'm not sure anyone else can help."

Paul Phillips' recollection was that it was hard for Pierce Shelley to admit he needed help of any kind, so the comment got his attention. "OK. Do you want him to come to your hotel?"

"That would be great," the ambassador said. "Late tonight, if possible."

Prince Cormorant stepped over to the two men with a broad smile. "Well, Pierce," he said, clapping Shelley on the back of the shoulder so hard that Shelley winced, almost as if in pain. "Introduce me to your reporter friend."

"Hi, Paul Phillips," the reporter stuck out his hand, but the Prince did not take it. Phillips suddenly felt extremely uneasy, but he pressed ahead. "Welcome to our little city."

"It is as magnificent as I have been told."

"What brings you here to America, your highness?" Phillips said, taking advantage of the opportunity and aiming his microphone at the beak-nosed royal.

Immediately a huge, dark hand clamped onto Paul Phillips' wrist. He dropped the mike and cried out in pain. The owner of the dark hand towered over the reporter. He wore a turban and looked as if he had spent his entire lifetime in the sun of a Middle Eastern desert. He said nothing, but his eyes burned with a protective rage.

"It's all right, Dabu, it is merely an interview," Prince Cormorant replied. The large bodyguard released Phillips' hand, which throbbed but did not appear seriously damaged, and resumed his silent watch by the prince's side. "Please forgive Dabu, he is well-meaning but overly enthusiastic."

"Don't mention it," Paul said, stooping to pick up his microphone. "I didn't mean to startle him. Now, I think the question was 'What brings you to America?'"

"I wish to make allies with your president in a variety of mutually beneficial — what is the word? — not adventures. Ah yes, endeavors. There are a number of mutually beneficial endeavors our two nations can conduct together, and I wish to enlist the support of your leaders."

"What kind of endeavors do you have in mind? A tourism or business exchange of some kind?"

"No, no, something far more sweeping than that," said Prince Cormorant. "I have a vision of a new day for

Cormornia, for America, perhaps for the world to live in peace, and the time has come to share this vision with your president."

"Tell me more."

"I'm sorry, Mr. Phillips. Your president hears my proposal first."

"Fair enough, sir," Phillips said with a grin. "It was a pleasure to meet you, your highness, thanks for your time. Good to see you again, Mr. Shelley."

"Please remember my request," Shelley asked pointedly.

"Sure, no problem," replied Paul Phillips. The prince and the U.S. ambassador to Cormornia walked away toward a waiting limousine, and Pierce Shelley cast a glance back in Phillips' direction.

Something sank deep in the radio news reporter's stomach, and he knew from the look on Shelley's face that Myke Phoenix should accept the ambassador's invitation as soon as possible.

For there on cool, emotionless Pierce Shelley's face, just for an instant but etched indelibly for anyone who knew to look, was an expression of abject terror.

Act 2:
Another Interview

PAUL Phillips brushed back a lush thicket of auburn hair, found an earlobe, and nibbled gently.

"Oh! you devil," said the owner of the ear, an attractive young woman dressed in a floppy sweatsuit. "I'll give you five hours to cut that out."

"Sounds like a deal," replied Paul Phillips, "but it turns out I don't have five hours – Myke has to work later on."

"What! Now you tell me? Why didn't you say something if you have to go back to work tonight?"

"No, no, Dana, not until after 10," he said, and then he told her about Pierce Shelley's mysterious request.

"It sounds like the man's in some kind of trouble, all right," she said. "Does the United States get along with Cormornia?

"Near as I can tell, Cormornia's not big enough to worry about. It's just a little tourist trap in the Alps."

The apartment was empty except for the couple and a couple of cats, but suddenly a third voice entered the conversation. Perhaps what was most odd was that neither of them was surprised to hear the voice.

"You folks have lots of expressions to cover situations like this," said the voice, which sounded neither male nor female but an amalgam of both. "I think the best one is 'Don't judge a book by its cover.'"

"Cormornia *is* a threat?"

"Bingo!"

The new voice was coming from the top shelf of the bookcase along the wall. Specifically, it appeared to be coming from a misshapen vase of a peculiar green hue, which had red and yellow gems of some kind encrusted in it.

This was the Soulkeeper of Kiribati, the mysterious vessel that somehow facilitated the process that switched Paul Phillips' body with that of Mychus, a powerful ancient warrior, and transferred Paul's consciousness into Mychus' body.

Paul sat up on the love seat and leaned toward the goofy-looking piece of pottery.

"Is Prince Cormorant dangerous?" he asked.

"Do dogs bark at strangers?" replied the vase. "The guy oozes evil. Didn't you notice when you met him?"

"He does have a way of making you uncomfortable."

"Not 'you' in general, just people like you who have the ability to sense these things," said the vase. "You felt Cormorant's evil out on the tarmac. It was an unpleasant feeling, wasn't it?"

"The guy made everyone around him uneasy."

"Suit yourself. I'm just tellin' ya, he's a bad guy."

"What else do you know about him?" asked Dana.

"That's pretty much all I do know," the ugly vase replied. "I don't get around much. Shelley will probably fill Myke in."

"You heard Paul tell me about the airport?" Dana said. "What else did you hear?"

"Don't worry, doll, I'm very discrete about who I tell what I know."

"Great, it's a ceramic voyeur," she said, "and don't call me 'doll'!"

"Well, the bottom line is, Myke Phoenix better meet Pierce Shelley tonight," said Paul Phillips. "There's something scaring him badly."

"Be careful," the vase said.

"That's the first time you've ever told me to be careful, Soulkeeper."

"It's the first time you've needed it."

The fifth floor of the Astor Heights Hotel was reserved for most of the delegation from Cormornia. It was a sumptuous floor of the hotel, but not the very best — Prince Cormorant himself had taken the very best, the penthouse five floors above.

Pierce Shelley had been reading a book, but he had long since set it down and begun to pace the floor of his suite. Where was this Phoenix? He picked up another book, set it down, adjusted the painting on the wall, sat down, stood up, and sat down again. His knee bounced up and down.

After several seconds, the ambassador got up and walked to the balcony overlooking the small city he called his hometown. He opened the drapes to stepped out and yelped in surprise.

There was a giant man outside the sliding glass door.

He was dressed all in white, a white tunic over white trousers — close-fitting trousers, almost tights. There was a red symbol on his chest that appeared to be a bird rising from fire. He was a blond-haired man with a strong, square face.

"You must be Myke Phoenix," said Pierce Shelley, relaxing noticeably. "How did you get out there?"

"I thought I'd cause a scene if I walked through the lobby," the large man smiled. "Sorry to scare you. I''m told you're looking for me."

"Yes, yes, come in," Shelley replied, motioning him into the suite. "I don't know if you can help me or not, to be honest, but I don't think Washington will believe me."

"What makes you think I will?"

It was Shelley's turn to smile. "From what I've heard, you specialize in the unbelievable."

"Touché. What's the problem?"

"I think Prince Cormorant intends to assassinate the president."

Myke Phoenix distinctly heard the sound of his heart beating a half-dozen times before he could speak again.

"Come again?"

"I know it sounds preposterous, but I believe that's his goal, and I think he has the cunning to pull it off."

"Why would the leader of a little country like Cormornia want to kill the president of the United States?"

"He wants to rule the world."

Once again, there was a long pause before Myke Phoenix said, "Get out of town. If I didn't know who you are, I'd swear you were kidding, Mr. Shelley."

"Prince Cormorant is a computer genius. He has found a way to tap into every source of information in the world. The man seems to be almost omniscient as a result," Shelley said. "In fact, I cabled Washington asking to talk about security questions, and he asked me on the plane over here what my questions were."

"Big deal. So he can intercept communications —"

"It's not that simple. I put the highest priority security scrambling codes on that cable."

"And why do you think he wants to rule the world?"

"He told me. He says the world needs a benevolent dictator to eliminate all the pain and violence and sadness. Believe me — I sat at his breakfast table and heard him say he wants to make the whole world as peaceful as Cormornia."

"— by assassinating the president."

"He believes if the world can be thrust into chaos, the people will be more receptive to his kindly hand."

"Have you told your people in Washington about this?"

"I intend to," Pierce Shelley said, and the fearful look reappeared on his face, "but I'm not sure I'm going to make it to Washington. That's why I had to tell someone. That's why I had to tell you. You seem to make your living fighting evil."

"Actually, it's more of an avocation than a living," said Myke Phoenix, "but that's not the point. What can I do? Is there any proof I can bring to the police?"

"No. I tried making a tape recording of my conversations with the prince, but when I played it back, there was only a bad hum. He must have some way to jam electronic devices."

"Well, then I'm stuck. What do you want me to do?"

"Why, stop Prince Cormorant, of course."

Myke Phoenix stared thoughtfully into the air for a few moments. "I'm not sure how much I *can* do at this point other than keep my eyes and ears open," he said, "but I will see if there's any record of this scheme that I can shake loose, and in the meantime, I'd appreciate it if you can find some evidence, too. Right now it would be his word against yours."

"I know," Shelley fretted. "At least I've told you so that, if anything happens to me, you can protect the president."

"I hope it doesn't have to reach that point," the big man in white replied, and he stepped back onto the balcony. "Be careful, Mr. Shelley. I'll stay in touch."

Pierce Shelley followed Myke Phoenix onto the balcony, but the little perch overlooking the city was empty again.

The U.S. ambassador to Cormornia sighed heavily. He felt a heavy burden was lifted. At least he had told someone. He rubbed his hands together and was surprised at how sweaty his palms were.

"Warm in here," he said under his breath, unbuttoning his shirt.

He pulled off his T-shirt and saw a red welt on the back of his shoulder, then realized it was in the approximate place where Prince Cormorant had clapped down when he met the reporter.

"What the devil is that?" he said, his chest glistening with sweat.

Every morning at 9:45, the Astor City Police Department sent one of its detectives into the conference room to brief reporters on any news from the past 24 hours, and to answer any questions. This morning Sgt. Fredricks had the duty.

"OK, vultures," he said with only a trace of humor on his face, "I got a good one for you today."

"This have to do with the ambulance call at the Astor Heights this morning?" asked the beat reporter from the Tribune.

"You got it, lady," Fredricks replied, pulling a report from his sheaf of papers. "At approximately 7:19 —"

"Could I have a white balance?" one of the TV photogs asked. A reporter held a white pad of paper in front of Fredricks' face while the photographer turned some knobs.

He scowled big-time at the reporter before resuming. "Ambassador Pierce Shelley was found dead in his hotel room at approximately 7:19 this morning."

"Wasn't he on the city council or something a few years ago?" asked a TV guy as Paul Phillips' eyes bugged out.

"Wow, you guys are sharp," replied the surly detective. "Preliminary reports indicate cause of death was a massive coronary."

Paul wanted to shout a hundred different expletives of surprise. All he could muster was a murmured, "Hokey smokes!"

Act 3

Prescription for sudden death

THE sky over Astor City was a bright blue, and wispy clouds trailed peacefully high above, in sharp contrast to the churning in Paul Phillips' stomach. Shelley's death was much too timely for it to be merely a heart attack, but you just don't go marching into police headquarters and accuse an international diplomat of murder.

"I suppose he'd have diplomatic immunity anyway," he said out loud as he drove toward the Astor Heights Hotel. "Holy cow, what a mess."

A mess that next could include an attempt on the life of the president. It was more than Paul Phillips cared to think about, but he had no choice. It was up to Myke Phoenix to unravel the situation.

He knew better than to inquire at the front desk about a trip to the penthouse. As a reporter he wasn't going to be welcomed with open arms. Paul Phillips strolled through the lobby and found the stairs.

It was 11 floors to the top, and he was tempted to switch to Myke Phoenix to take advantage of the powerful body's better conditioning. "Nah, gotta take care of this body, too, it's the one I started with," he said to himself and started the upward trek.

The climb was remarkably uneventful, and Phillips was beginning to wonder about Shelley's remark that Prince Cormorant was thorough to the point of appearing omniscient. It seemed clear that he hadn't even bothered to guard the stairwell. "Seemed" being the key word here.

He pulled open the door to the 11th floor and found himself face to face with silent rage in a turban.

"Why, hello again, Dabu," gulped the reporter. "Remember me? Paul Phillips from WACR radio." He held out a hand. Dabu took him by the shoulders and lifted him bodily off the ground.

Paul Phillips had two choices. He could switch to Myke Phoenix and blow his big secret, or he could hope and pray that Dabu did not intend to kill him right away. He prayed.

"Helllp!" he added.

The big, silent man threw Phillips over his shoulder like a rag doll and walked down the hallway toward the elevator. As he bounced on Dabu's shoulder, Paul breathed a sigh of relief. It appeared he was merely going to be shown the way back down.

As they stood waiting for the elevator car to climb to the penthouse, the clipped accent of Prince Cormorant sounded from the end of the corridor. "Who do you have there, Dabu?"

Dabu placed Phillips back on his feet and bowed toward the prince. The reporter opened his arms sheepishly as if to say, well, here I am.

"Ah, Mr. Phillips from the radio," said Prince Cormorant. "You are here to ask me about poor Pierce. I am shocked, just shocked. He was much too young."

"Well, yes sir, that is why I'm here, and I wonder if I could ask you about something he told — a friend of mine." It wouldn't do to say that Shelley told "me," because the prince might have a good idea that the conversation was really with Myke Phoenix.

"You may ask anything you like. We are in your wonderful free country, after all, are we not?"

"It's really fairly awkward. I'm not sure how these questions will be taken," Phillips said with an eye on Dabu.

"He will not harm you unless I ask him to," Prince Cormorant smiled much too broadly, "and I do not treat the mere asking of questions discourteously."

"I understand. Well, then. Pierce Shelley seemed to believe you intended to do harm to our president."

Either Cormorant was a fine actor or Shelley had been mistaken, for the prince assumed an expression of utter surprise and shock. "Harm the president! Pierce thought that I — I scarcely can believe it. And he told you this?"

"He told a friend," Phillips replied, maintaining the tiny subterfuge. "He said you want to rule the world and he was afraid you planned to throw our country into chaos by killing the president."

The quiet bodyguard took a step forward. The prince waved Dabu back.

"Oh, my poor Shelley, I see where he got this," Cormorant said. He stepped toward the window and looked over Astor City, then turned back to Phillips. "I told him not long ago that I wished I could rule the world, so that I could spread peace and justice everywhere such as we know in proud Cormornia. I was simply fantasizing and he — how do you say this? — he took me liberally."

"Literally?"

"Yes. He took me literally. No, no, no, I was merely making a thought, a conjecture. Oh my, I hope it was not his agitation over this misunderstanding that broke his heart."

"I couldn't say," Phillips said, trying to weigh the prince's words. He usually could tell when a politician was lying, but he wasn't as familiar with royalty. This could be an act, but it was a very good act. Prince Cormorant appeared for all intents and purposes to be legitimately hurt by the idea he would want to hurt the president. After a moment, he put his reporter face on. "Would you care to comment on any of this for the record?" He pulled his mini-recorder out of a pocket.

Prince Cormorant's peaked face darkened ominously, and for a few seconds Paul Phillips thought he would be placed in Dabu's custody after all, but finally the prince softened his expression and said quietly, "No. Pierce Shelley was a dear friend and I wish to remember him so. I will have a statement later today when I am more composed."

Phillips tucked the recorder away. "I understand. Well, thank you for your time. I'm sorry to bother you at a time like this. Just doing my job, you know."

"And you seem to do it well," Cormorant said, extending his hand. "I appreciate your asking me about what the ambassador told your friend," he said as they shook hands. "I fear some reporters in your country would not do me such a courtesy before they spread such terrible rumors."

"That's not how we operate in Astor City, at least," Phillips replied, rubbing his hand. Something sharp had pricked his palm. He looked; there was a small drop of blood just under his forefinger.

"Are you all right?" the prince asked earnestly.

"Yes, of course. I just seem to have cut myself somewhere."

"I see. Well. Until we meet again, Mr. Phillips."

As if on cue, the elevator door opened. Paul Phillips' last view of the penthouse was the face of Dabu, glowering.

Paul Phillips was exhausted when he dragged himself up to his apartment a few hours later; it had been a long day. Two black and white cats reminded him immediately the day was not over yet: There were two insistent mouths to feed before he could rest.

As he tipped a cup of kitty food into each bowl, the mysterious voice emanated from the lower shelf. "That couldn't have gone too badly, you didn't need to change into Mychus' body."

Phillips looked up from pouring the cat food, and Frack pawed at the cup. "How do you know I didn't change? Can you monitor everything that happens?" he asked the vase.

"Do I look all-knowing and all-seeing?" the vase dripped sarcasm.

"Well, no, but sometimes you know stuff that most pottery wouldn't know."

"Touche," said the vase. "I do sense when you make Mychus come and go, and I'm privy every now and then to an emanation of good or evil, but no, I don't know everything. Sweet of you to think so, though."

"The man murdered Shelley in cold blood, I'm sure of it," he said, wiping his palms on his shirt, "but I don't know how I'm going to prove it. I don't know if local police can do anything when visiting royalty kills somebody." He raked his sweaty palms through his hair.

"Are you OK?" the vase asked suddenly.

"What? Oh, sure, I'm just tired. This has been a long, mind-boggling weekend." As the cats ate ravenously, Paul flopped into a chair.

"You're sweating."

"This is the third floor. I walked up."

"You're not usually this tired."

"I haven't usually confronted the prince of some little country about a murder I think he committed."

"What's that cut?"

"What cut?"

"On your hand!"

Paul Phillips stared at his hand. The puncture wound was still there, and the skin had reddened around it. "Oh, this," he said with a wave of dismissal.

"This what?"

"Knock it off! It's just a little cut, I'm just tired, now quit it already."

The vase persisted. "Where did you cut your hand?"

He thought a moment. "I noticed it at the hotel. Right after I —" Paul Phillips sat up straight. "Right after I shook Prince Cormorant's hand."

"Let me remind you of something else. You saw the prince clap Pierce Shelley on the shoulder and the ambassador winced."

"What? When?"

"Right after he told you he needed to see Myke Phoenix."

"Hokey smokes, you're right. How did you know that?"

"Maybe I know everything after all," replied the vase. "The important thing is, that wound was probably caused by a small needle, which means you've probably been poisoned by whatever killed Shelley. It must be some kind of substance that looks like a heart attack if the person doing the autopsy doesn't suspect poisoning. You have to turn into Myke Phoenix."

"Now wait a minute," Paul Phillips said, beads of sweat forming on his forehead. "Maybe I should call an ambulance. What's turning into Myke going to do?"

"It will heal this body. When you're there, stuff like this can be taken care of."

"Where?"

"Where your body goes when you're using Mychus's!"

"What about when that bomb went off and my hand was slashed? The cut was still there when I changed back!"

"Not the same. Fixing cuts is more complicated. If you transform now, it'll cleanse the poison — the sooner the better, if you catch my drift, big guy."

"The big stuff gets patched up but not the little things?"

"You'd prefer the other way around, maybe? Just be glad it works on the big bad things," the vase twinkled. "I keep telling you, don't sweat the small stuff. Now change into Myke Phoenix, doggonit!"

In a blink of an eye, Paul Phillips became Myke Phoenix.

The phone rang.

"Oh, great," said the blond giant. His voice did not sound like Paul Phillips' voice — both resonated, but Myke Phoenix had a deeper tone to match the broader chest. He thought about letting the answering machine take the call, changed his mind and picked up the receiver. "Paul Phillips' phone."

"*WHO* is *this?*"

"Oh, hi, Dana. It's Myke."

"Why aren't you Paul?"

"Paul's not here now." He kept trying to remind her that they needed to treat Paul and Myke as two separate identities, even over the phone — anyway, he didn't want to tell her just yet that Paul had been poisoned by the would-be ruler of the world. "There was just some stuff that I was more suited to doing than Paul."

"Does that lazy reporter have you moving furniture again?" she asked coyly.

Myke laughed. "No, it's just a project we're working on together. He can tell you about it later."

"Well, when he has the time, have him call me, *Myke!*" She said the name with ironic emphasis.

"Sure thing, Dana. He'd probably want me to tell you he loves you."

"Uh-huh. Good luck on the project!"

He replaced the receiver and looked at the vase. "How long does my real body have to stay in limbo to be cleansed?"

"This is probably just a semantics thing," the vase said, somewhat evasively, "but the body you're in is real, too."

Myke Phoenix threw up his arms in frustration in a manner very similar to the way Paul Phillips did it. "You know what I mean, Soulkeeper. Just answer the question."

"Your original body is fine now."

"That's it? I pop it in the oven and it comes out fine a couple of minutes later?"

"It depends on what the problem is – cleaning out poison just takes a few seconds," the Soulkeeper said. "Repairing a severe injury can take a lot longer."

The steel features of Mychus the Warrior softened. "Is there any way this could be made available to anyone? Think of all the people who could be saved."

The vase was silent for longer than usual before it responded. "Sorry, kid. The phoenix can only offer these powers to one man at a time," the misshapen pottery said, "but the fact that you'd think to ask that question means the big bird made a pretty good choice."

Myke lapsed into thought, a little bit awed at the size of his still-new responsibilities as a doer of good deeds. "Well, what do I do next?"

"It's just a suggestion, of course," said the vase, "but next I'd probably change back into Paul Phillips, call Dana back, and fix myself some dinner. You may recall only the cats have been fed."

Myke Phoenix began to laugh, and he was Paul Phillips when he finished chuckling. "That sounds like a great idea," he said.

Act 4
The Blood Test

SHEILA Farrell always came to work early. The Astor County Medical Examiner's Office was understaffed and over budget, so she always had an hour or two of paperwork to catch up on before the office opened.

Therefore, she was accustomed to being the only person in the county office building when she arrived, usually around 6:00 in the morning.

It was a bit surprising, and somewhat alarming, when she turned the corner and found a man in a trench coat waiting in the corridor outside her door.

"Dr. Farrell? I'm sorry to startle you," the man said. "I need to talk to you."

As she got a better look at the man, she relaxed a bit. He was a very handsome man, with a strong, square face and blond hair. He was also huge, at least six and a half feet tall, but there was something gentle in his voice that scattered her alarm to the wind. She didn't know why, but she had no fear he would harm her. For lack of a better word, there was just something nice about him.

"OK, come on in," she said, "but you have an advantage over me. You know who I am."

"Sorry," the big man replied. He'd forgotten that the woman he interviewed as a reporter all the time had never met his alter ego. He parted the trench coat slightly, to reveal the red and gold emblem on his chest. "I'm Myke Phoenix."

"Well," said the medical examiner. "Why aren't you out bashing criminals' heads together?"

"That's not all I do for a living," he laughed. "I have some information regarding Pierce Shelley's death, but only you have the power to confirm it."

Dr. Sheila Farrell caught on quickly. "Let me guess. You don't think he died of a heart attack."

"That's correct. In fact, I'm sure of it."

"Look, fella," she said, "I saw the man's heart. He was a candidate for a quadruple bypass if he'd ever bothered to see a doctor. The case is closed. Heart attack."

"Aren't there substances that would look like a heart attack unless you knew it was poison?"

"Sure, but you've been watching too much TV. Stuff like that doesn't happen in real life."

"Pierce Shelley was afraid for his life the night he died."

That got her attention.

"Why? How do you know?"

Myke Phoenix told her about the meeting at the Astor Heights Hotel, Prince Cormorant's slap on Shelley's shoulder, the plot to rule the world.

"Come to think of it, there was a welt on the back of his shoulder," Farrell said. "I chalked it up to an insect bite, but I suppose it could have been a needle."

"He also poisoned me."

"Wait a minute. You're still standing."

It was time to stretch the truth. "He shook my hand and I felt a needle," he said. "When I'm in this body, nothing can puncture my skin." He hadn't lied. Both statements were true, after all, even if they didn't quite match.

"So he tried to poison you, and it didn't work," she said. "Look, Mr. Phoenix, even if I buy this story, I don't have the budget for that kind of test. The chemicals I'd be searching for would be in such minute quantities that it would be a one-in-a-million shot to find 'em. Hello? You still with me?"

Myke Phoenix was staring out the window at the rising sun. Inside the ancient warrior's body, the mind and soul of Paul Phillips were torn with doubt. Off on the horizon, a bird flew across the searingly bright mass of light in the sky. It was impossible to identify what kind of bird it was against the glare of the morning sun. but it reminded him of something.

"This will sound a little crazy," he admitted, "but I'm here because the supernatural bird known as the Phoenix brought me to this town. Maybe if you attempt the test, the Phoenix will see to it that you find the chemical."

"You're absolutely right," said Dr. Sheila Farrell, "it sounds crazy. What's even nuttier, I'll try it for you. Come back around 5 this afternoon."

"This afternoon? I'm not sure if Prince Cormorant will stay until then."

"Then you'll have to chase him to his next stop if he leaves," she replied. "This test takes 10 hours."

Paul Phillips had seen the prince's itinerary. The group was only going to stay in Astor City for a day — that evening it would be flying to Washington. And in 24 hours,

Prince Cormorant would be preparing to meet, and kill, the president of the United States.

"You go ahead with the test, and thank you," Myke Phoenix said earnestly. "I'll find a way to keep Prince Cormorant in sight."

The man in white glided out of the room. Sheila Farrell picked up the syringe and test tubes necessary to draw blood and set them next to Pierce Shelley's body.

As she slipped on her plastic gloves, the medical examiner muttered, "I'm nuts to be doing this." At the same time, something in her heart reassured her. There really did seem to be something inherently good about this Myke Phoenix character.

Was the mood at WACR eerily somber, or was Paul Phillips feeling eerily somber as he walked into WACR? Sam Wainwright's voice sounded shaky as he delivered the hourly newscast.

Sam was the morning and noon news voice, and Paul took the afternoon shift. The two of them took pride in the number of times they had scooped the Astor City Tribune, the local newspaper that had 10 times as many reporters to cover the city.

"What's wrong?" Paul asked his colleague when he emerged from the news studio. "I can tell you're upset just by your voice."

"Hi is gone – no, that sounds worse than it is. Hi called in sick – no, that's not right either," Sam said. "They let him go home yesterday afternoon, but he got taken to the hospital early this morning, and –"

"What, Sam? How bad is it?"

"They're saying we should visit him today or tomorrow, because it's not going to be long now," Sam choked.

"No," Paul said. "I can't believe that."

For a moment the only sound was the tinny on-air monitor spewing an electronics store ad. Paul turned toward the bulletin board on the wall and pretended to read something there, but he couldn't see through blurred eyes.

It was too much too fast: The crazy man who wanted to kill the president, the ambassador's murder, the attempt on his own life, and now his friend's death sentence. Hi Dawson was going to die young because of those stupid cigarettes he chain-smoked all his life.

They say there are five stages of grief: Denial, anger, bargaining, depression and acceptance. Paul Phillips moved quickly from denial into anger and stayed there.

In the penthouse of the Astor Heights Hotel, Prince Cormorant was having a private supper. Staring across the city at the horizon, he thought he saw a bird flit across the sinking sun. "It is an omen," he said. Clearly he had caught a glimpse of a cormorant or some other bird of prey, and he felt empowered by the sight. The entourage would proceed to Washington in about an hour, and the unpleasantness of the past 24 hours would be behind them.

The prince felt a twinge of loneliness. He would miss Pierce Shelley; his death was an unfortunate consequence of his grand plan to save the world from itself under his beneficent goodness. No more borders, and therefore no more border wars, just one great big world with everyone free to live their lives in peace under Prince Cormorant's terms.

He absently flicked his ring open and closed, exposing and then hiding the drug-tipped needle. Amazing that such a tiny device would be the instrument to escort an entire planet into a new reality.

A knock came at the penthouse door, and Dabu glided into view. Ah, beloved Dabu, always near and yet invisible, such an imposing presence and yet able to fold himself into the background.

After he opened the door, from the sudden tension in his back, Dabu signaled the prince to be alert. His massive body hid the identity of their visitor for a moment.

But the coming Prince of the World feared no man. He stepped into the foyer to greet the newcomer. His bodyguard stepped aside, and Myke Phoenix emerged from the shadow with a grim smile.

Before Prince Cormorant could utter a word, the white-clad warrior raised a fist and strode towards him. Moving faster than one of his bulk should be able, Dabu intercepted Myke and seized the raised right arm in an unbreakable grip.

Well, for most people it would be an unbreakable grip. Myke Phoenix bent his knees and pushed Dabu with his left arm with such force, the giant needed both hands to keep his balance. While Dabu was still staggering, Myke quickly followed with a right cross that lifted Cormorant's bodyguard off his feet and sent him crashing into a glass table near an easy chair. A few seconds passed before it was clear Dabu would not be awake for whatever came next.

"How about that," Mychus the Warrior said, standing over the unconscious hulk. "He can dish it out, but he can't take it."

The white-clad hero raised his fist towards Prince Cormorant, who flinched ever so slightly but drew himself up into a huff.

"You would dare strike the crown prince of Cormornia?"

Myke Phoenix held his fist back a moment, looked at it, looked at the crown prince of Cormornia, and shrugged.

"Well, yes. Yes, I would," he said as gently as he could. Then he slammed his fist into the great beaked nose — but not hard enough to make the prince unconscious. He had had no interest in a conversation with Dabu, but he had a few words for Prince Cormorant.

"Pierce Shelley was a friend of mine," the white-clad warrior hissed, standing over the cowering prince. "In a few minutes you're going to get a call from the White House. They won't be mentioning the results of certain tests I had the medical examiner run, but needless to say the president has had a change of plans and won't have time to meet with you. You probably have diplomatic immunity, so even if I had proof that you killed Pierce, you wouldn't be prosecuted — but you're not going to have the president's death on your hands. The crown prince of Cormornia is going to have to find another way to become prince of the world."

Cormorant picked himself off the ground and dusted himself off.

"I have no idea whatsoever what you are talking about, young man, but because I am a magnanimous prince, I will forgive your confused and misguided attack," he said unctuously. "I know you Americans are a reckless and foolhardy sort. Please, accept my hand in friendship."

They shared a firm handshake, and suddenly Prince Cormorant yelped in unexpected pain. He looked at his palm — the needle had snapped against Myke Phoenix's skin and pierced the hand of the prince of Cormornia.

"You'll probably want to have that taken care of," Mychus the Warrior said as he closed the door behind him.

Epilogue

HI Dawson finished coughing and lay back on his pillow, exhausted. Paul Phillips tried to hide how alarmed he had been by the ferocious way Hi had to gasp for air as his lungs resisted the effort.

"I'm so sorry, Hi," Paul said quietly.

"What about?" said the man on the hospital bed. "Hey, I'm gonna die famous. 'Biggest radio star in Astor City dead of lung cancer at age 37.' It's a great tragic story."

"Come on, Hi, you'll beat this, you're not going to –"

"I'm going to die in this bed, Paul," Hi Dawson wheezed. "Get real."

Dawson was the top-rated talk show host in town, Astor City's version of the national shows that were changing the landscape of commercial radio. Although the syndicated shows were not good for local radio announcers – why hire a kid disc jockey when you could hook your signal up to a satellite for a fraction of the cost? – the trend toward sharp-tongued commentators opened the one available local door for Hi Dawson. Someday he may have been one of those national stars, had his chain-smoking habit not wrecked his body.

"Look – Myke – I want to thank you for being my friend," Hi said. "And I want to thank you for all you've done for this city, going after Pinkstaff and all those crazy villains."

"I'm just a reporter," Paul said modestly, ignoring that Dawson hadn't called him Paul. The illness played with his memory, after all –

"I said 'Get real,' didn't I? Not much time left," Dawson croaked. "I saw you change that very first day, Paul. Don't BS me. You got the cigarettes outta my car, slammed the door, car blew up, Myke Phoenix walks away."

There was no way to deny it. As Paul had long suspected, Hi Dawson had witnessed the moment Paul Phillips first exchanged bodies with the ancient mighty warrior named Mychus. As he had learned then, the exchange often happened automatically, as a defense mechanism, when deadly danger menaced.

"I don't know what to say," Paul said truthfully. "Why didn't you tell me you know?"

"Obviously" – he coughed twice, suppressed a more serious round of hacking – "you needed to keep it a secret. Better to say nothing."

"Well, I guess I owe you big time."

"You're a good guy, Paul, and I mean that in every sense of the word," Hi Dawson said. "Keep fighting – the bad guys." And he fell into what looked like an uncomfortable sleep.

Paul Phillips would never see his colleague and good friend alive again. But now he had a better idea just how good a friend he had been.

Ghosts

A short story

"ASTOR City was founded in 1877 by the famous industrialist Jefferson Davis Astor," said Jessica Daniels as she led the small group down the corridor. "These are photographs taken in that era. You can see many of the original buildings that Mr. Astor built are still serving our downtown. Of course, he built this wonderful mansion for his wife, Emily Wellington Astor, who turned it over to the Astor Historical Society when she died in 1943, and ever since it has served as the city museum."

"Look, there's Harold's," a young man told his date, whose eyes glazed over. "Only the sign says it was VandenHouven's General Store then!"

"Isn't that nice," the young woman said without a great deal of conviction.

"And look at all the logs piled next to Jefferson's Dock," he went on. You know, most of the wood that was used to develop this part of the country passed through the Astor City port."

"Wow," his companion said flatly. Jessica had seen this before: someone who loved local history dragged a friend to the museum instead of to dancing or a movie. Sometimes it was the boyfriend who was bored; this time it was the girlfriend.

"We owe who we are and what this community is today to the people in these photographs," Jessica said, partly to send a message to the bored young woman. "The Astor City Museum exists to make sure we always remember these brave pioneers and the debt we owe them."

The boyfriend nodded as he peered into the old pictures, hoping to spot other details that would still exist a century later. The girlfriend yawned; Jessica Daniels sighed.

"Well, that sure was a dandy little speech, Miss, uh, Daniels," said an elderly man in the group who paused to read her name tag. "And may I say it's a privilege and an extraordinary treat to see what you fine folks have done with my little town."

"Thank you," Jessica Daniels said, blushing. "Are you originally from around here?"

"You might say that. I was born in Richmond, Virginia, but I always thought of this as home," the old man said, extending a hand. "My name's J.D. Astor, and this is my wife Emily."

As she took the man's hand, a chill ran from Jessica's shoulders down her back. Somewhere in the old mansion, the wind began to howl.

"I don't mean to be rude, Mr. Astor, but you can't possibly be Jefferson Davis Astor," said the museum curator, a pleasant but somewhat officious man named Timmerman. "He died 75 years ago."

"I see," said the cordial old man, "and next you'll be telling me this vision of beauty isn't Emily."

"Oh, I'm sure you are Emily Astor, if that's what you say," Timmerman told her, "but of course you can't be THE Emily Astor."

"Well, I never," said the woman. "Let me tell you something, Mr. Timmerman —"

"Now, Emily, you must agree we did drop in a bit unexpectedly," the man said.

"I must admit, however, that the resemblance is striking. I would almost believe you *are* J.D. and Emily Astor if it wasn't that you're both, uh —"

"Dead. Yes, we did die, didn't we, Em?"

"I'll never forgive you, either, Jeff. Nearly 30 years alone in this drafty old house."

"Don't make such a fuss, Emily, you'll give this nice man the wrong impression."

"What's that supposed to mean?" she insisted.

"Merely that you are the most charming woman who ever walked this earth, and you're being rather cantankerous at this particular moment," he smiled like a Virginia gentleman.

Timmerman glanced at the portrait of the old couple on the wall, then at the apparition before him — back and forth, back and forth. "What is the meaning of this? Why are you here?" he said at last, beginning to become a trifle angry.

"Frankly, young man, I'm not sure what we're doing here," J.D. Astor said soberly, then broke into a grin, "but as long as we're here, we may as well have a look around, eh? No offense intended," the old man said, extending a hand.

"None taken," said Timmerman — and his hand passed right through Jefferson Davis Astor's.

"Oops," the old man said with a smile. He took his wife by the crook of her arm, and the couple walked through the doors of their mansion and into the street.

Timmerman stared at his hand, then at the door, then at his hand, then at the door, and then he fainted.

"Why, it's just as that young man said," said J.D. Astor. "George VandenHouven sold his store."

"I don't wish to complain, Mr. Astor," Emily replied, "but you may recall I told you about that these 50 years ago."

"I'm sorry, my sweet. There are so many things to remember. Well, they certainly have perfected the automobile since I was here last."

"Yes, and such pretty colors," said Mrs. Astor. "But, Jeff, there's so much more noise than there was before. Such a clatter!"

"Progress, my dear, progress. Remember how the neighbors were up in arms when they built the sawmill by the river? That noise was a tenth of this."

"Jeff," she took him by the arm. "Why are we here? It was so lovely where we were. I'd just as soon be back there."

"So would I, my dear. Let's just visit a few minutes. Look! You told me they'd added sound to the motion picture. Perhaps we can go inside here."

"What if we can't leave? What if whatever power brought us back to Astor City wants us to stay?"

His face was locked in a grin, but his eyes betrayed him. She could see he was just as worried as she was, but he maintained a joviality in his voice for her sake. "All right, dear, let's try to leave." He put his arm tenderly around Emily. "Now, close your eyes, darling, and concentrate. Let's go home."

They held to each other, eyes closed, and simply faded away. A passerby overheard J.D. Astor say to his wife, "There, see? We're heading home now. And how lovely the city looked!"

Timmerman, recovered and dashing up the street to talk to the Astors, watched them vanish and fainted again.

Glinda Northington The Nighttime Psychic smiled at Annette McPhearson Your Voice of Reason over her cup. Glinda was sipping herbal tea; Annette liked her coffee strong and black.

"Can I tell you a secret?" Glinda winked. Annette suppressed a laugh; she was surprised by the wink because she had thought Glinda's eyelid was too caked with makeup to move.

"I've been dabbling a bit in the spirit world," said the unearthly face. "You know, witchcraft."

Oh, spare me, thought Annette McPhearson, but she said, "Oh! Really?"

"Yes, indeed, and I was sure I'd made contact this morning, just before I left for work."

"What do you mean by 'contact'?"

"Well, I was experimenting with an ancient chant to call back the spirits of the dead. I read the chant from the book just the way it said, and I suddenly was filled with the strangest tingling. I literally had goosebumps all over my body!"

"Did you meet any dead people?" Annette McPhearson asked, wondering why she was pursuing this bizarre train of thought.

"No," said Glinda Northington, sincerely grieving. "I wanted to so much, though. The feeling was so strong, I was sure they were there! There were two of them — I know I felt two presences."

"Well," Annette replied, not knowing what else to say, "maybe next time."

Over her shoulder Annette heard a hearty laugh, like a Southern gentleman enjoying a mint julep at sunset. When she looked around, of course, no one was there.

The Puzzle of the
Talking Dinosaur

Prologue

THE vase had warned Paul Phillips about Deinonychus from the very beginning.

"No one really thinks of himself as a villain," the Soulkeeper told him, "but Deinonychus probably qualifies. Of all the reasons we called you, she may be the biggest – even though she's not very big in a literal sense."

It was hard to take seriously the idea that a four-foot-tall talking dinosaur could be the most evil of evils, although by the time the events of this book had passed, Paul Phillips was convinced.

Since the events we spoke of in the previous four stories from *The Ancient Warrior* to *In the Lair of the Cormorant*, some three years had passed. During that time Myke Phoenix fought many of the Forces of Evil in the World, beginning with those I've shared with you: Alan Pinkstaff, the crime lord; Quincy Quackenbos, the genius half-man, half-duck; Dr. Skull, the world's nicest bad guy perhaps but still bad as can be; and Prince Cormorant, the madman who would rule the world.

With the emergence of a force for good came an insurgence of evil. There was Professor Insidious, a scholar who shared Cormorant's view that people needed a dictator to live educated and fruitful lives, with the purpose of course of serving the professor's every whim. There was another skirmish with Dr. Skull and his gang after he manufactured their escape from prison, and he remained at large. There was the riddle of Jay Looney, a military engineer who saved his most amazing and lethal weapons designs for his own purposes. And as predicted, Quincy Quackenbos served a fairly short prison term, returned to his business long enough to hatch another scheme, but disappeared before he could be apprehended.

And through it all, Myke Phoenix remained a thorn in the side of all things evil, especially Pinkstaff, the crime boss who reigned over the Astor City underworld – or was it really his reign? As we revisit the city about three years after the coming of Myke Phoenix, District Attorney Kenneth Ronnegan has finally caught up with the criminal mastermind, with the help of the city's superhero protector, and put him on trial for his crimes. Still, there is an undercurrent of whispers that Alan Pinkstaff answered to someone even more evil and corrupt than himself – someone who was preparing to strike at those who would dare to arrest the kingpin.

Before we begin to describe those events, however, let's visit a well-known restaurant on the outskirts of Astor City, where a moment we have long expected was finally about to happen.

The little fuzzy box in Paul Phillips' pocket was a lot heavier metaphorically than in actual life. He had been working on the presentation for a long time, and he knew pretty much what he wanted to say.

The restaurant was Dana Dunsmore's favorite. So was the wine he ordered for her and the flowers he asked be displayed on the table. He was wearing the shirt and tie that he knew she liked best. Everything appeared to be perfect. She even declared it so.

"Oh, this is perfect, Paul," Dana said, smiling that disarming smile that filled him with so many feelings it was almost hard to talk. But he started talking anyway, just the way he imagined it.

"You know, Dana, we've been dating a few years now and it's been pretty terrific –"

"Don't spoil the moment, Paul."

He stopped in mid-sentence. "What do you mean?"

"This wonderful night, how great you look tonight – hey, you always look great, but tonight, well, there you are – What you're working up to say, you don't need the preamble. The last five years have been preamble enough. Just get on with it."

"You know –?!?"

"Just ask me, Scoop." She couldn't stop grinning that grin, those eyes couldn't stop sparkling in that way that melted him.

The best radio reporter in Astor City, who always knew what to say and even had prepared his speech tonight, couldn't speak, so he drew the box out of his pocket.

"Oh! A little fuzzy box! I knew it," Dana said, and although her grin was as wide as could be, it grew wider. "Let's see the ring!"

"Hey! Let me do this," he said in a sullen voice, his big speech shot to pieces, although he was starting to grin, too.

"You did get a ring, right? That's what's in the little fuzzy box?"

"First things first," he insisted, trying to regain control of the situation. "Dana Dunsmore, will you marry me?"

"Of course I'll marry you, silly. You think I would hang around for five years if I wouldn't? What took you so long?" He was dumbstruck. She grabbed his hand. "Paul, you're the most caring, thoughtful, sweet, dedicated guy I've ever known" – and, leaning in to lower her voice – "and for the last three years, you've been a superhero, too! Oh my stars, I'm the luckiest girl in the world."

He produced the ring, and she oohed and aahed and shed tears for its shiny brilliance, and she slipped it on her finger, where it resides to this day.

After many years of hugs and kisses, and three years of working a romance around superhero adventures and the fight of good against evil, Dana Dunsmore was officially betrothed to Paul Phillips. There was a wedding in their future! But first – as always seems to be the case in stories like this one – there was an unspeakably evil menace to dispatch.

Act 1

The breathless man

AT first no one noticed the man leaning against the corner of the building in the 1800 block of Hansen Street, gasping for air as if he had been running longer than he should. He held his long trench coat closed tightly, but it was a cooler autumn morning than had been predicted, so he was not the only one on the street who looked cold.

The tall man's given name was Morton Montgomery Davis, but only his mother ever called him Morton. He had come to insist that his friends and business associates call him by his last name, Davis, but many condensed that to Dave, which was all right, too. That the district attorney called him Morty was, well, mortifying to him, but at the moment he didn't care what anyone called him.

Dave now was pressed against the side of the building as if it would crumble to the ground if he were to move. His breath came in quick, short intakes that rattled as if he had a bad cold or worse. It was worse.

After resting against the building only made the gasps come faster, he gathered his energy and pushed himself to the first door he found, which happened to be that of a car seat re-upholstery shop.

The rich smell of leather greeted his nose when he pulled open the door, but he didn't draw deeply as one who appreciated the fragrance.

Instead, Dave spoke in a wheezing gasp. "You gotta help me," he panted to no one in particular. "Call an ambulance."

"What in the name of wide, wide world of sports happened to you, buddy?" said the man behind the counter.

"I've been stabbed," Morton Montgomery Davis said as emphatically as he could, which was not very emphatically, given that his ability to take in oxygen was heavily compromised. "Just make that call."

When Dave heard the sound of three buttons being pushed – 911 – he knew help was on its way. As if knowing their job was completed for now, his legs buckled under his weight, and Dave crashed to the floor.

The counter clerk heard the man in the trench coat breathe once, deeply, as if finally permitting himself to enjoy the leathery perfume of the shop. Then he noticed a spreading pool of red staining the floor where the man lay. As if the blood released him from some strange paralysis, the man who had been standing without moving behind the counter dashed over to help.

"Holy Schmitt, I've seen this guy's face in the newspaper," the clerk said. "He's one of the Pinkstaff boys."

Before the clerk could figure out how to help – which is fine because there was nothing he could have done – the bleeding man gave a mournful cry, exhaled raspingly and lay absolutely still. A siren whooped a few blocks away.

"White male, about 6-3, 220 pounds, dead of a stab wound to the chest," came the voice over the phone. From the description Sgt. Fredricks of the Astor City Police Department, Detective Division, had a pretty good idea what the answer to his next question would be.

"Got an ID?" he asked anyway.

The pause at the other end confirmed his fear. He was not surprised when the voice said, "It's Davis, Sarge."

Two nights ago Morton Montgomery Davis had talked to Fredricks at a fast-food place 35 miles away, to avoid being seen by someone who might see the two of them together and do the math. The detective had been prepping Davis one last time to testify against his former employer.

"You OK, Sarge?" The detective sergeant realized he was still on the phone.

"Oh. Sorry, Will, I was just sitting here getting real damn mad, that's all."

"I don't blame you. I'll go back to the upholstery shop and see if I can scare up any witnesses."

"Great, thanks. I'll probably be over there with you soon." Fredricks set the receiver down more carefully than necessary, fighting the urge to slam it down in a rage.

"Pinkstaff," Fredricks hissed. "This time he's gone too far."

The large claw, positioned where the index finger would be on a human hand, tapped on the table as its owner stared out the window deep in thought. A casual onlooker might mistake the pose for a typical reverie, except for the fact that there was nothing typical about this thinker. For one thing, there were the claws.

Each digit of the four-fingered hand ended in a dagger-like claw, the one larger than the others, and the thumb not quite opposable like a human hand. What might pass for a thumb looked more like the end of an old-time can opener. Even more imposing "can openers" protruded from the front of the beast's feet, which supported its weight on two toes.

Each of the claws looked razor sharp, as if a swipe of that inhuman hand would rend flesh like a knife slicing through warm butter.

A reptilian, or perhaps birdlike, eye stared into the night. Now, it's said that the average human blinks anywhere from four to 30 times per minute. This particular eye just stared into the night – stared – stared – stared – and about, oh, 48 seconds after we started paying attention, the eye slowly closed and then opened again. You might call it a blink, but it seemed more deliberate than that.

This went on for quite some time, the tap-tap-tapping of the claw on the table, and the reptilian, perhaps avian, eye staring into the night and blinking slowly every four-fifths of a minute.

Then came a hiss. It might be described as a guttural hiss, if hisses can come from the gut. It was not quite the kind of hiss a human might make, and it was not quite the kind of hiss a snake might make. So, after all, to call it a guttural hiss would probably be as accurate as one could be.

Up until this moment, except (one might say) for the tap-tapping of the index finger on the table, the strange reptilian beast seemed to be merely an animal, perhaps an astonishing throwback to the Cretaceous Era of dinosaurs. But then the beast did something no dinosaur was ever suspected of doing: It spoke.

"Pinksssstaffffff," said a hissing, guttural but oddly female voice. But then the feral rage collected itself into cool determination. "Thiss time he has gone too far."

Astor County District Attorney Kenneth Ronnegan was not easily rattled. Few people ever saw him lose his calm, collected demeanor; fewer still ever saw him lose his temper. That's why the explosive expletive caught most people in the room by surprise.

"How does this happen?" Ronnegan shouted. "How does Pinkstaff get to Morty Davis the night before his damn testimony?"

Just as suddenly, the contorted face of the D.A. relaxed into a more neutral expression, the feral rage collecting itself into cool determination.

"I'm sorry," Ronnegan said quietly. "We've worked too hard, and we've built too solid a case, for this to be a complete disaster, but it's still a disaster."

"You got that right," barked Sgt. Fredricks of the Astor City Police Department, who was not as practiced at containing his anger as was the district attorney. "I got people running double-time now to find the link between the hit and Pinkstaff. I just can't promise you we'll get it done by morning."

"Pinkstaff has to know we have a strong enough case to send him away for a very long time with or without Dave's testimony," Ronnegan replied. "This is a message to the other witnesses."

"Probably is," Fredricks agreed. "'He's tellin' them nobody's safe. 'If I can get to Dave, I can get to you.'"

The trial of Alan Pinkstaff had been a topic of headlines for months, ever since the fighting D.A. first filed charges of commercial gambling, racketeering, drug trafficking and fraud against the investment broker. The evidence was insurmountable that Pinkstaff Investments was the front for one of the largest criminal enterprises Astor City had ever seen. And now that he had all of his ducks in a row and spent four days selecting a jury, one of Ronnegan's key witnesses bleeds out on a sidewalk. This was not a particularly encouraging development.

"Tell you what," Ronnegan said. "You do what you need to do at your end, and I'll rework the witness list for morning. By the time we're done with him, there'll be barely enough scraps for the vultures."

Which, ironically, was exactly what the owner of the horrific claw was planning herself – although the fighting district attorney had meant to evoke a figurative image.

Interlude

IN the moments before it happened, when he believed to his shock and surprise that he was going to die, he became aware of something in the sky.

What that something was, he couldn't yet fathom. He was too busy not dying, fighting with all his consciousness not to close his eyes, not to fade into somewhere else, knowing that if he went to sleep now he would awaken in the next life.

And he remembered a day when the sun was shining and the grass was greener than it ever would be again, and running across a field laughing with the joy and abandon a child has because there is no other place to be than right here, right now.

He remembered the first time he kissed a girl and she kissed back and suddenly he wasn't all alone in the world anymore, and joy and abandon rose in his soul like everything sunny and amazing.

He remembered a canyon so big and wide that all he could do was stare and say, "Wow," and the awe was so deep that he felt joy, and the abandon was so deep he had no other words.

And then he knew he could not fight anymore, he knew that his body was spent and he could not help but let go, and the *sunshine consumed everything, and everything went white, except for something in the sky – something – in the sky –*

Act 2
The first assassination

THERE was something of a smirk in Alan Pinkstaff's face as he watched District Attorney Kenneth Ronnegan walk up the aisle to the prosecutor's desk in Astor County Courtroom No. 7.

"You look tired, Kenny," the crime lord called across the room. "Come on, buddy, it's Friday. Don't let the jury see you looking like you started the weekend early."

Ronnegan's head snapped up and he looked like he was about to say something, but he just pulled himself up short and sat down. He took some papers out of his briefcase and made a show of organizing them on the table.

"Not gonna get to me, you little weasel," he muttered. Then he pulled himself up short. This was the first time Pinkstaff had ever called him "Kenny" with a taunting laugh instead of "Ronnegan" with a contemptuous sneer. Usually the crime boss was the picture of complete calm, eerily so. He rarely spoke above a menacing, low growl. Today he seemed positively giddy.

The fact that he was acting so out of character meant only one thing: Alan Pinkstaff was relieved, more relieved than he had been for a long time. But that fact had a corollary: Alan Pinkstaff had been frightened, and he still was frightened.

Now it was the fighting district attorney's turn to smirk. He sauntered across the room and stood in front of the defendant's table holding a manila folder full of documents. He waggled it playfully next to his ear.

"Al, if you thought having Dave whacked was going to hurt my case, your attorney has not been keeping you informed about just how much trouble you're in," Ronnegan said, returning giddy for giddy. "I don't need Morty Davis' testimony to put you down like the sick dog you are."

Alan Pinkstaff's face returned to its normal stone, eyes like slits and shooting daggers at the fighting D.A. The daggers followed Ronnegan's back all the way back to the prosecutor's table.

"All rise," intoned the bailiff. The judge swept through the door behind his bench and settled himself between the U.S. flag and the state flag, which hung limply on poles to either side of the big chair.

"All right, let's get started. Ready to call your witness, Mr. Ronnegan?"

"Yes, I am, your honor," Ronnegan replied, with an easy smile to the defense table.

"Bring the jury in," the judge commanded.

Paul Phillips slipped a new cassette into the recorder, set the counter to 0000, and made sure the machine was plugged into the courtroom's media sound system properly. With him in the little soundproof room with the glass window in the back of the courtroom were a couple of TV camera operators and the courts-and-cops reporter for the local newspaper, the Astor City Gazette.

"So who's the first witness today now that Dave Davis has been kacked?" asked Ben Furillo, cameraman for Channel 9.

"Hard to say," offered Connie Gates of the Tribune. "I'm guessing Fredricks to talk about the bombing in the WACR parking lot. Are those doughnuts?"

"Yeah, I bought a box on my way over to the courthouse," Phillips said. "Want one?"

"Mmmm, yeah, thanks," she said, lifting a long john out of the carton.

This was happening as the judge was instructing the bailiff to bring in the jury. Paul looked at his watch and saw that it was 9:01 a.m.

"Figures. I have to call in a live report for the 9:06 news," he muttered to the other reporters. "Don't let anything important happen while I'm gone."

"Mmph-mmph," Ben Furillo said. "And thanks for the doughnuts."

There was a phone booth in the courthouse rotunda that was a bit of a throwback even in those days. WACR manager Bo Ranfort had asked whether it would be useful for the news staff to carry cellphones, but Paul had assured him that as long as there were public telephones, the small portable phones would rarely be needed. He encouraged his boss to spend the cash on more practical equipment or even raises for the team.

He called the direct line to the studio.

"WACR Studio, Greg Waters, may I help you?"

"Hi, Greg, it's me, ready for the report from the courthouse."

"OK, Paul, stand by, we're about a minute out. Cutting it a little close today, aren't we?"

"Yeah. Sorry."

Paul still wasn't used to Hi Dawson not being there. The self-proclaimed greatest thing that ever happened to Astor City radio, Hi was a flamboyant and popular talk show host whose death a few months earlier had shaken the station to its core. Dawson's tirades against the Pinkstaff organization had helped shame the district attorney's office into taking the criminal enterprise seriously and starting the investigation that led to the ongoing trial.

But Hi Dawson was a chain smoker, and the inevitable cancer ended his life prematurely.

Paul was still reeling from what Hi told him the last time he visited his friend and colleague at the hospital – that he knew about Paul's secret life as the super-powered Myke Phoenix, and protected the secret for the rest of his life. He was still thinking about his old friend when he heard Greg say, *"The trial of Alan Pinkstaff took a dramatic turn overnight with the apparent murder of a man who was scheduled to testify this morning. Our Paul Phillips is live at the Astor County Courthouse with the latest. Paul?"*

He probably could have recorded the 45-second report a few minutes ahead of time, but Paul wanted to keep the segments as up-to-the-minute as he could. The courthouse bustled with activity. In another courtroom a judge was holding conferences on ongoing cases, miscellaneous felonies and misdemeanors. The sessions took just a few minutes each, so two dozen cases were scheduled at 9 a.m. The judge handled them by pulling files off a big pile and calling the defendant's name. Outside the courtroom attorneys conferred with their clients about what would be happening when they entered.

For seven more seconds, as Paul Phillips walked from the outer door up the hallway toward the Pinkstaff courtroom, it looked like any other day covering a trial in the Astor County Courthouse.

And then, without warning, Paul Phillips wasn't walking up the hallway anymore. He didn't even notice he had made the change until a woman carrying a sheaf of papers close to her chest gasped in surprise and stopped in her tracks.

"Myke Phoenix!" she said breathlessly.

The blond man with the barrel chest and white uniform stopped in his tracks himself. He glanced at the shirt with its buttons down the side and the phoenix emblem, then looked around, all senses alert.

Only one thing could make him change into Myke Phoenix in an instant: imminent danger. Usually he controlled the change, but if Paul Phillips didn't realize he might be about to die, it happened automatically. Myke braced for whatever was about to happen.

And, of course, that's when the screams began.

"The trial," Myke said sharply, and dashed toward Courtroom No. 7.

In all the years ahead that he spent fighting bizarre supervillains and other menaces, Myke Phoenix/Paul Phillips never forgot the scene that greeted him as he pushed past fleeing spectators and burst into the courtroom.

THE PUZZLE OF THE TALKING DINOSAUR

At one table District Attorney Kenneth Ronnegan was standing, backing away with his eyes fixed in the direction of the defendant's table.

On the table stood a crouched-over creature. It was some sort of lizard, standing on two legs, leaning over the dying body of Alan Pinkstaff. Its face resembled recreations of the tyrannosaurus rex, but it was not nearly as large an animal as that. Perhaps it was four or five feet tall, with a tail as long as the rest of its body, and those awful, sharp talons on all four limbs.

Here your faithful narrator must inject a personal preference. The creature had just used its terrible claws on the person of the crime lord Alan Pinkstaff, in a manner intended to end his life. She was gruesomely successful, although when Myke Phoenix arrived Pinkstaff's body was still desperately trying to operate normally with so many of its vital organs compromised. I have described every scene that Paul Phillips and his alter ego encountered through the years to the best of my ability, but I do not wish to belabor in graphic detail precisely what this strange creature did to Alan Pinkstaff.

Suffice it to say that if you imagine what those razor-sharp claws could do to a large, doughy man in a terrible combination of ruthless killing efficiency and uncontrollable rage, the reality was 10 times worse than your imagination.

Claws dripping with gore, the creature turned and viewed the newcomer in the aisle with curious intent.

"Myke Phoenix," said a reptilian voice, drawing out the "s" sound at the end so the witnesses heard "Phoenickssssss." And these were the first words the grim assassin had spoken.

"Deinonychus," Myke Phoenix whispered in shock. "It has to be."

For years the Soulkeeper had warned him that the real mastermind behind the crime syndicate – indeed, behind the uptick in evil in the world – was a ruthless, talking dinosaur. Intellectually, ever since he first began his sideline occupation as a superpowered crimefighter, he knew anything was possible. Not until he saw Deinonychus standing over her prey did he fully believe.

What happened next was more of a blur in everyone's mind, it happened so quickly. The small dinosaur leaped off the defense table and over the wooden gate and fence separating the attorneys' tables from the audience. It scooted up the aisle straight at Myke Phoenix and, before the superhero could react, raked its terrible claw across his chest, shredding the front of his uniform. Bursting through the doors and out of the courtroom, it disappeared, leaving the echoes of screams and shouts through the corridors as it left the building.

Normally Myke Phoenix would have raced after the horrible creature immediately.

Instead, he stood in paralyzed shock in the middle of the courtroom aisle. Witnesses who had been screaming in panic a moment before looked on in stunned silence.

Myke Phoenix was invulnerable, you see. Men and women with bad intentions had tried for years to hurt him, to no avail. Nothing known to humanity could even puncture his skin.

But now, in front of all those people, a red stain was spreading across Myke Phoenix's chest.

Interlude

HE was a boy, standing in the middle of a meadow with bumblebees hovering around the goldenrods. The sun was shining so bright that the sky around it looked white, not blue.

Just like that, he broke into a run. He wasn't running to or from anywhere, he just felt like running, like the day was so shiny bright and the aromas were so strong and he had so much to feel he just had to run.

"I'm alive! Life is good! Life is great!" he would shout if he could put anything into words, but he couldn't. So he just ran.

He didn't know why, but the feeling felt a little bit like defiance, as if shouting "I'm alive" was standing up to the truth of it all, as if the energy that sped him across the field was nothing but a distant memory.

The field shimmered in the heat, and in the back of his mind he thought he heard the sound of a predator snarling – and a beating of wings.

Act 3
The puzzle

AFTER a few moments of stunned silence, it was if everyone exhaled. Medical personnel burst into the courtroom to tend to what remained of Alan Pinkstaff, although his spirit had probably already passed to the great beyond. One or two people stepped up to Myke Phoenix; one reached up with a gentle hand on the mighty warrior's shoulder.

"Myke? Are you all right?"

He parted the tear in his uniform to examine his chest and discovered a slash – deeper than a mere scratch, but not deep enough to cause serious damage. The wound was oozing rather badly, though.

The woman who laid the comforting hand on Myke's shoulder pulled a large handkerchief out of her pocket and pressed it against the superhero's chest, where it quickly became saturated with bright red blood. She looked around for another cloth, but Myke Phoenix shook his head and gently pushed aside the apparent offer of help.

"I have to stop her," he said, and dashed out of the courtroom.

We'll follow Myke Phoenix in a moment. First we must notice that, while people dashed here and there around the courtroom in horror and panic and grim determination to restore the peace, the person who comforted Myke Phoenix and sacrificed a handkerchief to stem the bleeding reached into a pocket and pulled out a plastic baggie, then dropped the blood-soaked cloth into the baggie and sealed it.

Myke Phoenix followed the screams down the corridor and out the door of the courthouse. Standing on the grand stone steps, he looked in every direction but saw no immediate sign of trouble.

"Where did she go?" he asked the first person he met on the stairs, a young woman.

"Who?"

"The talking dinosaur!"

The woman stepped back and took a look at the large man in the torn, white uniform stained with blood talking about a talking dinosaur.

"Get away from me, you maniac!" she shouted. "I'm going to go find a cop." With that she darted into the courthouse, yelling for help. (She was embarrassed later to find she had called the real Myke Phoenix a maniac and there really was a talking dinosaur, but that's not really important to the telling of this tale.)

There was a clear indication which way the dinosaur had gone – people screaming, waving their hands, holding their hands to their mouths and looking in that direction – and he followed the chaos. But oddly, the trail petered out after a few blocks of running, even though Myke Phoenix could run like the wind in his mighty warrior's body.

"How does a talking dinosaur disappear?" he muttered to himself as he walked back to Paul Phillips home. "What the bejeebers is going on here?"

The vase would know. That much was certain.

"I don't know," said the vase. "Why didn't you change back to Paul Phillips?"

"I'm bleeding!" Myke Phoenix cried, ignoring (or perhaps answering) the question. "Why am I bleeding?"

"I don't know!" said the vase, sounding a bit more flustered than usual. "Just change back to Paul."

"What good would that do?"

"Everything! Just do it!"

So, in a blink – actually less than a blink, it was always that instantaneous – the superhero with the stained white uniform was replaced by a normal looking man in his early 30s who looked like a radio reporter and, more important, did not have a jagged slash across his chest.

"All right," said Paul Phillips. "At least it doesn't hurt now. What just happened?"

"How many times do I have to say 'I don't know' before you understand that I don't know?" came the voice of the vase. Paul would never learn how the vase talked; after a while he had just accepted that the vase came with a voice out of nowhere. "Obviously, her claws are so sharp and powerful that they can cut skin that can't be cut."

"That's impossible," Paul muttered incredulously.

"Impossible? No fooling, Philip. But let me give you a clue," the vase said. "The species Deinonychus died out millions of years ago, and they didn't speak English. 'Impossible' is what she does."

"How can a dinosaur be alive after millions of years? And speaking English?"

"Does it really matter right this minute? The thing tried to kill you and proved that it has the means."

Paul Phillips had no answer for that. He was frustrated enough to pick up the vase and heave it against the wall but resisted the urge. It would be many years before he realized that it would have been OK to do that because the vase – which looked like, and claimed to be, fragile ancient porcelain – was unbreakable anyway.

"What do we do now?" Paul said. "We can't just let that thing run loose in the city."

"This isn't a monster movie, buddy. She's not going to be walking the streets if she can avoid it. I think you have to bide your time for a while."

"Why am I doing this at all?" Paul said suddenly. "What's the point? I mean, why me? What made you call out to me in that antique shop and say, 'Buy me?'"

"You're going to do *this* now? Look, I don't make the calls, my friend, the Phoenix does. But maybe it has something to do with the fact that it took you years before you asked that question."

"Huh?"

"The Phoenix picked you out as someone who would take the power to battle evil and run with it. You never needed more of a reason than that there are the bad guys, and you have the power to do good."

"The Phoenix. How does the Phoenix know me from a hole in the back yard?"

"I've never figured out the 'how' of it at all," the vase intoned. "How does the body of an ancient warrior show no signs of aging past its peak condition? How is it that I'm the only vase in the world with a consciousness? How did Mychus' body get bulletproof? How does the Phoenix know you from a hole in the back yard? How did it know you would use that mighty body only in honorable ways? I don't know how it all works. I only know why, and that's good enough for me."

"OK, then, why? Why has all this happened?"

"The 'why' is as simple as good and evil, mate," the vase said. "Something dark and unreasonable is trying to take charge of this world, and you stand against it in all its forms."

"Why?"

"Because you're the good guy."

"What does that even mean?" Paul said.

A black and white cat jumped onto the kitchen counter. Then a white and black cat jumped up. Without thinking, Paul Phillips opened a cabinet, retrieved a can of cat food, and filled two saucers that were standing on the counter. The cats began to purr and eat the food.

"Did you see that?" the vase said.

"See what?"

"You fed Frick and Frack. Why did you do that?"

"They're my cats. They were hungry. I fed them."

"Why? Why did you take two animals into your home and take care of them?"

"I wonder about that myself sometimes," Paul said with a slight chuckle.

"No, you don't. It's what you do. Because you believe in caring for others."

"I dare say some of the forces of evil in the world have cats they take care of."

"True, that," the vase replied. "But you're the one who saw a talking dinosaur shred a human being and then ran forward to try to stop her."

"Point taken. So what do we do next?"

"For starters, now you can change back now if you want to."

"What do you mean?"

"It's OK to change into Myke Phoenix if you want. It's fixed."

"What's fixed?"

"Mychus' body. The wound is repaired."

"Repaired!"

"Yeah, remember when Prince Cormorant poisoned you and turning into Myke Phoenix sent your body to the repair shop? It works both ways."

"How?"

"I don't know how it works. You're just ready to go if you need to."

Paul willed the change into Myke Phoenix. The uniform was spotless and white again, with no slash across the chest. He unbuttoned the buttons up the side of his tunic and looked at his chest. There was a long, thin, white scar from one side to the other as if he had been scratched years ago.

"That thing opened up my chest barely two hours ago," Myke Phoenix said. "How is this possible?"

"You may have forgotten this part, pal, so let me explain this to ya," the vase's voice floated in the room, neither a masculine voice nor a feminine voice, musical yet powerful. "Mychus the warrior died a couple, three thousand years ago, but the Phoenix has called people back to use his body a few times since then. You're the latest in the line, although you're the first to go all superhero-ey on us. Most of 'em just went about their business and saved the world on the sly. Must be the pulps and comic books of the last century that put the superman complex in your head."

"You're the ones who put me in the superhero uniform."

"That look like spandex to you, mate? You made that connection. The point is, the Phoenix has a way of keeping that body young and powerful and – well, until today – invulnerable. The repairs happen when the body goes wherever it goes when you don't need it."

"Some kind of magic mausoleum? A fantasy hospital with high-tech surgery? What?"

Short pause. "I don't know. I'm the conduit that knows a lot, sees a lot, senses just about everything. But I don't know all and see all. Toss me in a hot-air balloon and I'd be the wizard who says, 'I can't come back, I don't know how it works.'"

"Can I – can Mychus be killed?"

"I wish I knew, friend," the vase said. "I know you – Paul Phillips – will die someday like the rest of you mortal types. I know the Phoenix will die and rise from the flames in a couple hundred years. Until you came back bleeding like a stuck pig, I would have said Mychus will be around forever. Gotta say, I don't know that for sure anymore."

With the purported leader of Astor City's underworld slaughtered in broad daylight, the focus of law enforcement turned to finding the killer. Leads were tracked down, a paleontologist was consulted, and searches were searched, but it was as the vase had predicted: Deinonychus did not want to be found, and so she was not.

But after a few days the hoodlums and gang leaders and strange villains who had reported to Alan Pinkstaff were surreptitiously called to an undisclosed location and gathered around a table. A few minutes after the appointed time, the little dinosaur strolled into the room.

This caused no small amount of alarm. The news had been full of the strange reptile who had raced into the courtroom and sliced all life out of their leader. Even those who had not seen the video footage knew this must be that same strange reptile. Those who were not repelled at the sight were merely terrified.

"Gentlemen, and ladiess," the dinosaur said, with a nod to the small representation of female criminal bosses in the room, "My name is Deinonychus. Alan Pinkstaff was my employee, as are all of you."

She was able to get out a brief explanation of Pinkstaff's fatal misstep – having Dave Davis killed in a too-clumsy display of force, and how all of the arrangements were still in place among the various criminal enterprises he had led, except that now she was going to be more visibly in charge – before one among the shocked throng of hoodlums gained his voice back.

"Alan Pinkstaff was a friend of mine," said a man in a fine, tailored suit. "He was going to prison. I don't see the need to kill him."

Deinonychus regarded the man with narrowed eyes. Her tail flicked ominously.

"Jason Santelli, isn't it?" she said, and the crime boss nodded. "When you have someone killed, is it your underlings' practice to question your judgment?"

"I don't have people killed, I'm a businessman," Santelli said. "And I'm not going to take orders from a giant gecko."

"Oh, come now, we're all business associatess here," the dinosaur said reprovingly, hopping up on the table and leaning over Jason Santelli so that her snout was only a foot or two from his face. "You've never, ever had to make an example of someone who got out of line?"

"Well, I –" Santelli began.

Almost faster than the eye could see, Deinonychus' right arm slashed forward. The cheeky crime boss lifted his hands to his throat, but it was already clear he would not be able to stem the sudden and heavy flow of blood.

But to drive home her point, the dinosaur lifted her foot and used its terrible claw to dig into Jason Santelli's chest and pierce his heart.

For a few seconds, the only sound in the room was Jason Santelli dying miserably.

"Now, then, boyss and girlssss," the dinosaur hissed, the civilized tone of voice yielded to a guttural, reptilian hiss. "Are we clear here?"

Interlude

THIS is very interesting, he thought to himself. It's not at all as sudden as you'd think sudden death would be.

A kind of peace was overtaking his soul, even though a corner of his heart was telling him to fight the inevitable.

Sensations like floating on a clear summer lake or lying in a field of thick, waving grass on a sunny day conflicted with the gurgle of blood flooding like a babbling brook. And yet, he felt calm.

The celebratory roar of a dinosaur over its kill had not been heard for millions of years. Seconds from the end of his life, Myke

Phoenix felt strangely privileged to be present to hear that ancient sound.

That ancient sound – and another that he had never heard before –

Intermission

A one-room cabin in the woods on the side of a mountain.

Never mind which cabin. Never mind which woods. Never mind which mountain.

For our purposes, you need only know it was a cabin, with one room, in the woods, on the side of a mountain.

The woman got out of her car and walked up to the door. She knocked tentatively, and immediately came a rustling sound from inside the cabin. The door opened a crack, and the barrel of a shotgun eased slowly through the crack.

"Oh, please, you're not going to use that," the woman said, pushing the door open gently but firmly. "You're evil, but you're not a killer."

If we had not already met the present-day version of the creature inside, the sight of him might make our collective jaws drop. He was not exactly a man, although he was as tall as a man and walking on two legs. His head and face – and indeed, his entire body – were covered with feathery hair, and he had a bill. Not a wide, flat bill like a cartoon character, nor were his eyes large half-ovals that took up most of the top half of his face. Have you ever seen a duck? That kind of bill, and those kind of eyes.

The area around where his human chin would be – but not on the bill itself – showed a dark stubbly substance that was not quite feathers, not quite hair, and the tufts on the top of his head were disheveled. Those were the main clues that Quincy Quackenbos had been alone for some time.

"What are you doing here, Doc?" the duckman said, for she was a Ph.D.

"I've got something for you," the visitor replied, handing him a package. He opened it and pulled out an evidence bag with a blood-soaked handkerchief.

"What's this?"

"That's Myke Phoenix's blood."

Quincy quacked a scoffing quack. "Impossible. The man's skin can't be broken, not even with the sharpest blade known to man."

"This wasn't done by a man," said the visitor. His eyes widened.

"She came out in the open? Attacked him?"

"That's right, you don't get the news out here," she said. "Pinkstaff is dead. She walked into the courtroom and butchered him. Myke Phoenix got there a couple seconds later."

"She must have gotten tired of the big oaf running the syndicate like a bull in a china shop. Should have seen that coming. But she didn't kill Phoenix?"

"She was in a hurry, so she just wanted to get this sample."

"That makes sense," Quackenbos said, lifting the bag closer to his eyes against the light. "Huh. So he bleeds after all. This will be very useful in my experiments."

"Deinonychus wants something sooner rather than later. She had me sit in the courtroom to collect this on the chance he'd show up soon after the killing, and he did."

"Well, if I wasn't in hiding after that last debacle, this would be a lot easier. I could use the labs at my business."

"That'd be a little awkward now, wouldn't it?"

He looked at her with a mixture of annoyance and irritation. "Just 'a little awkward' that Quincy Quackenbos was removed as the head of Quackenbos Laboratories? The board put Brian Duckworth in charge. Not a bad choice, actually; he was a great vice president, and I hear he's doing fine without me. But as for this" – rattling the evidence bag – "I should be able to make some progress now. Thank you."

Duck man and the woman sat in silence for a few moments.

"OK, well," she said, rising. "That's what I came to give you. See you in the funny pages."

"You can't stay for a while? Catch me up on what else is happening in the big city?"

"Sorry, I can't stay away from the office for too long or I'll be missed."

"I understand," Quincy said with more than a trace of loneliness in his voice. "Thanks for this."

And with that Sheila Farrell, Astor County coroner and forensic officer, closed the cabin door gently behind her.

Act 4
The second assassination

TIME passed. Months went by, to be precise. And for the people of Astor City, the streets had grown more dangerous.

A gloomy night on the docks; a little fog in the air; a night watchman doing his rounds.

A nightstick applied to the side of the man's head. Down he went.

The thug holding the nightstick struck the man a second time, and a third.

"What are you doing, Jake? The guy's down, don't kill him." This was one of the thug's accomplices, in an earnest stage whisper.

"You heard what she said," Jake replied. "Excessive force at all times, to intimidate."

"You heard what *who* said?" This was not the voice of a thug, nor was it said quietly. It was a clear, distinct challenge that rang above the sound of the lapping water, the hum of the warehouse lights, and the distant sound of 2 a.m. downtown traffic.

"Oh, no," said the man who had scolded Jake.

"Oh, yes," said Myke Phoenix, who proceeded to apprehend the four thugs rather handily. A bruised chin here, a rude banging of two heads together there, and a short chase and tackle, and the four men were in custody.

As the superhero tightened the cords that would hold them for police, he asked Jake again.

"You said she wants 'excessive force at all times, to intimidate,'" Myke said as approaching sirens began to howl in the distance. "What's that all about, Jake? Who said that?"

"Who do you think?" the thug replied glumly.

"Well, if I had to guess, I'd say it was the talking dinosaur," and Jake's expression told him that was a correct guess. "The way you went after that guard, you crossed the line from misdemeanor battery to felonious assault. You'll be going away for a while, Jake. Why do you listen to her?"

"You're kidding, right?" Jake said, and turned his head so the right side of his face shone in the dim light.

That was when Myke Phoenix first noticed that Jake, and in fact all four of the men, had a jagged scars on the right cheek from a recent wound – a mark that would come to be known as the Sign of Deinonychus.

There had always been hoodlums on the streets willing to commit crimes, stick up convenience stores and other businesses, grab purses and the like. But now there was a meaner element.

A convenience store would be held up, and the clerk would be shot in the shoulder without provocation. A hardware store would be robbed, and shelves full of merchandise would be knocked over as the thug departed. A purse would be grabbed and the woman shoved to the ground or cut with a knife.

It was if some dark, sinister force was demanding that criminals get meaner, to instill a greater sense of fear among law-abiding citizens.

And the murders –

Astor City was a medium-sized city where homicides had been rare. But beginning with the deaths of Morty Davis and Alan Pinkstaff, the toll began to skyrocket. A year earlier, the time between homicides could be measured in months – barely a dozen people killed in a fit of passion. But now, it was measured in days, and more often than not it was a cold-blooded execution.

Police were overwhelmed by the increase in criminal activity. Rounding up all of the culprits was impossible. And when criminals were apprehended, they bore a scar on their cheeks, a kind of promise that if they failed to be sufficiently brutal, they would face a punishment more frightening than a scratch on their faces.

District Attorney Kenneth Ronnegan was angry and frustrated. He even asked the governor to send the National Guard in to patrol the streets.

But Deinonychus was angry and frustrated, too; there were too many people still fearless – or if they felt fear, they tucked it inside and converted the emotional energy into defiance. She wanted to conquer this city, to crush its spirits, to use Astor City as a base to spread the force of evil around the world.

And the most defiant of these defiant ones were Kenneth Ronnegan and the superhero, Myke Phoenix. Ronnegan with his police and his sheriff's deputies and his

National Guard resisting her minions' efforts to break the city's spirit. Phoenix with his ability to crush the plans that the law officers could not crush.

Both of them had to die.

A comfortable home on the outskirts of the city with a view of the woods out the back window. A young couple at the kitchen table. An ugly green vase displayed on a shelf in the middle of a collection of Depression glass.

Except for the fact that the vase was talking, the scene could be any middle-class home.

"You know that the Phoenix arranged for you and I to meet after a pretty enormous blotch of evil smacked this world and started to spread," the vase summarized the past several years. "And I've told you over and over again that Deinonychus is the earthly epicenter of the evil. What's happening now is that she's making her first big moves."

"*First* big moves? Backing Alan Pinkstaff and Quincy Quackenbos and half the other menaces I've been fighting all these years were small steps?"

"Paul," said the auburn-haired beauty across the table, "the vase is right. What's happening in the city is even worse than before."

This was, of course, Dana Dunsmore, whose role in the superhero business was largely that of sounding board and supporter. As president and owner of a growing advertising and marketing company, she did not have super powers and could not directly assist in the fight against the forces of evil in the world. But she did much to keep her fiancee focused.

"You may have to kill her," the vase said after a few moments.

The blithely stated words took a few more moments to sink in. When he spoke at last, Paul Phillips' voice had an incredulous tone.

"Kill her? How? I'm not a killer. I'm one of the good guys."

"You were there when she killed Pinkstaff. You saw what she's capable of," Dana said gently. "You may not have a choice in this."

"And I gotta admit, I'm not sure you *can* kill her," the vase said. "If she can cut you with those claws, she's tapped into some kind of force we haven't seen before. All I know is you may have to meet her deadly force with deadly force of your own."

"Understood, but that doesn't have to be my first choice," Paul said. "I'm not sure I have it in me."

"Mychus sure had it in him. He understood, like you do, that killing isn't the way of the Phoenix. I don't think the big bird has ever resorted to killing, but it's the most powerful creature on Earth. When it was kill or be killed, Mychus did what he had to do."

"Mychus isn't here!" Paul Phillips snapped. "Well, his body is here, but I'm not him."

Dana leaned across the table and took her husband's hand.

"I'm not sure I want you to take this on," she said. "I'm not sure I wanted you to take any of this on. But it's your destiny, isn't it? This is the time it's all been leading to. You were chosen to be Mychus for this reason, this moment, because for some reason you're the soul who can beat this evil power."

"I know," Paul said. "Someone has to stand up to Deinonychus and her minions. I just want to stop her short of killing, no matter how evil she is."

"That's a big reason why the Phoenix chose you, you know," the vase said. "I'm just tossing out the possibility that you may not be given a choice."

It was not long before that possibility presented itself.

The small auditorium at Astor City Hall was slowly filling with reporters and electronic equipment. A bailiff walked to the windows and lowered the blinds to screen the clear, bright morning sunshine from the room.

Paul Phillips set his WACR microphone on the podium with the mics for the other radio and TV stations in town, unwound his cable and plugged it into the portable cassette recorder he carried on a strap over his shoulder. He recorded for a few seconds and played it back to make sure the machine was working properly, then pulled a notebook out of his pocket and settled back in the front row.

District Attorney Kenneth Ronnegan was next to the podium setting up several large mugshots on easels with the help of his son, Assistant District Attorney Kenneth Ronnegan Jr.

"Looks like you caught some bad guys, Ken," Paul called up to the younger man, who turned and smiled back at the reporter.

"Just wait a little while, Paul," Ken Jr. replied. "Dad will tell you all about it."

As was the custom in those harder times, a couple of sheriff's deputies were stationed at the back door of the auditorium, and the county attorneys were joined on the stage by Sheriff Rod Skortje and Col. Mark Fielding of the National Guard.

The time came, and Paul pressed the "play" and "record" buttons, which were side by side on the cassette machine panel.

"Hi, folks, you all ready?" Kenneth Ronnegan Sr. said. Nods and murmurs of assent from around the room. "OK, we're hear to announce this morning the arrest of seven high lieutenants responsible for the crime spree that has plagued this city in recent months. This is the result of hard work by our police and sheriff's investigators with the help of the state. We have even harder work ahead, but we're not going to rest until we've apprehended and brought to justice the menace responsible for all of this, the talking dinosaur, Deinonychus."

"And how exactly do you propossse to do that, you pompousss windbag?" came a reptilian voice from the back of the room. Everyone turned to see the two sheriff's deputies drop to the ground, bleeding, and a four-foot-tall creature standing defiantly in the doorway.

With everyone's attention on the dinosaur in the room, no one noticed that Paul Phillips was gone and Myke Phoenix was standing in front of the podium.

The superhero's intention: To stand in the center of the aisle and declare, "I don't know what you're planning here, Deinonychus, but you're going to have to get past me first."

What actually happened: Myke Phoenix planted himself in the center of the aisle and started his little speech: "I don't know what –" At that point the dinosaur launched herself into the air toward the stage high over the heads of the crowd.

Myke jumped up to try to block her, but she slashed out with her claws and deflected his trajectory.

He landed with a thud on the floor in front of the stage, and Deinonychus landed deftly on the podium facing District Attorney Kenneth Ronnegan Sr., scattering the microphones and lifting her right arm high in the air.

"Nooo!" shouted Kenneth Ronnegan Jr., Rod Skortje and Mark Fielding in unison as they each stepped forward, but she was too fast. The district attorney's throat was slashed so savagely he was as good as dead before he hit the ground.

But she was not the only lightning-quick being in the room. A white barrel-chested streak of vengeance crashed into the dinosaur from behind before she could turn her attention to the three other law officers. The reporters scrambled for cover, but two or three of the cameramen stayed at their stations. They captured the image of Myke Phoenix and the dinosaur rolling on the floor until the strange creature struck out with the terrible claw on her foot and ripped a piece of flesh from the superhero's leg just above the knee.

Pushing him away, Deinonychus leaped up and raced back up the aisle and out the door. The reporters gave her plenty of room to pass.

The two deputies groaned on the floor by the door. Behind him, Myke Phoenix heard the sheriff and colonel shouting for medical help and reinforcements. He eased himself onto his feet, tested his wounded leg, and cast a steely glance beyond the door.

This was too much. This had to end. And it had to end today, one way or another.

Whatever he had to do to stop the menace of Deinonychus, he had to do it – even if it meant the end of Myke Phoenix at the hands of those terrible claws. Even if the soul of Paul Phillips might perish with him.

This had to end.

"No more," Myke Phoenix said quietly, and then he shouted it with a roaring ferocity no one had ever heard from the mysterious super being: "NO MORE!"

The protector of Astor City took a deep breath and sprinted after the dinosaur.

Interlude

THE smell of tobacco smoke is generally acrid, but there was something different about this aroma. It did not sting the eyes or the nose and throat; it was simply a smoky odor, somewhat pleasant actually.

He did not see a face or a hand lifting cigarette to lips – the body that held the soul had long since passed to dust – but he somehow knew it was Hi Dawson.

"Hey there, guy," Hi said.

"Am I where I think I am?"

"Almost. I expect I'll see you in a minute. Don't worry, it's kind of fun over here. And – cigarettes in heaven, and nobody hassles you or cares about it. I should have known!"

"I can't die, Hi."

"Sure you can. Everyone does when they're ready."

"I can't, not now. I have to stop her."

"I'm not sure anyone human can stop her, Myke. Don't sweat it. She'll be stopped."

"How?"

"Come on over and we'll watch together. You're gonna love this. That's it, let go, here you come – hey! Wait. What?"

Act 5
Volucris ex machina

AS he ran, Myke Phoenix realized he was limping. He looked down at the unfamiliar sight of a large gash in his thigh. This wasn't going to do.

He stopped and ripped the right sleeve off his tunic, quickly fashioning it into a tourniquet on his leg. Like the day Alan Pinkstaff was murdered, he could easily follow the path the talking dinosaur must have taken – although unlike that day, this time the path was strewn with the occasional wounded person, slashed at random as the horrible beast ran toward whatever sanctuary she was seeking.

Down the streets of Astor City he ran, until he saw her a block ahead and screamed "DEINONYCHUS!"

Two jeeps sped past with helmeted men in brown uniforms, followed by a couple of troop transport trucks. The National Guard was joining the fray. As he began to close the gap between himself and the prehistoric horror, Myke Phoenix saw other military vehicles approaching from the other direction.

The little dinosaur stopped on the sidewalk in front of the marquee for one of the city's handful of skyscrapers. Darting her head birdlike in every direction, she decided going up was the best alternative and hopped up on top of the marquee, then used her claws to start climbing the brick structure.

Myke Phoenix gave a running jump to the top of the marquee. He landed with a THUD and a bullet bounced off his shoulder, knocking him against the wall.

"Hey!" he said, turning toward the sniper on the street who had taken a shot at the scrambling Deinonychus and instead struck the equally lightning-fast superhero. The marksman shrugged his shoulders apologetically.

"What happened to 'Be sure of your shot?'!" Myke hollered.

"I *was* sure," the sniper called back. "I never had a target move that fast."

No time to dwell. Myke Phoenix looked up to see the dinosaur halfway to the roof, dodging here and there to what nooks and crannies she could find, now that she knew men with rifles were willing to take a shot.

"Why would she trap herself up on the roof?" he mused, then realized with deadly certainty that she was confident she would not be trapped up there. Deinonychus would hold the high ground until her prey was dead, then scurry away and disappear as only she could. "Not gonna happen," he said firmly if not confidently.

And with that, Myke Phoenix braced his mighty legs and took a running vertical leap up to the top of the 23-story building. A sharp twinge as he left the ground reminded him again that a piece of his thigh had been ripped out, and his trajectory took him just shy of the roof. He had to scramble up over the edge before he could stand under the bright blue sky.

She stood on top of the little structure where the stairs led out onto the roof, tail flicking like a whip. She drew her claws, stained with Kenneth Ronnegan's blood, up to her face and licked them. If a dinosaur could smile, she smiled now.

"Myke Phoenix, protector of Assstor City," she scoffed, drawing out the "s" sound so the last word came out "ssssittee." "You have no protection against the likes of me."

"You may be right," he replied, "but I'm going to stop you anyway."

"There is no ssstopping us," hissed the dinosaur. "We already rule this city and this world. You are merely a hindrance."

"Now, see, you seem to be a little confused there," Myke said, strolling almost casually toward the monster with the flicking tail. "You have a lot of people scared, but you don't rule anyone. They just avoid you and go about their business same as always."

"The effect is the same. We are free to do as we please, and they –"

"They have me," said Myke Phoenix, suddenly grabbing her by the tail and pulling her off her feet. The momentum of his grab pulled her off the structure. He swung the little dinosaur around three times and slammed her against the corner of the staircase entrance, crying out at the exertion.

Rather than stun her as he hoped, the impact had the effect of launching her into frenzied action. All four razor-equipped limbs thrashed wildly about, seeking flesh to rend. He jumped back warily, and Deinonychus scrambled to her feet.

She took a deep breath as if to launch into another speech about ruling the world, but instead she launched herself sideways and onto the top of a large air-conditioning unit. There she crouched, looming over the roof, claws extended and ready to slice.

Several TV towers had been erected on the roof to serve the local stations. Protruding from the sides of these towers were smaller antennae and dishes that caught microwave transmissions from the main studio or remote broadcast locations and relayed the signals to and from the stations.

Murmuring, "Sorry about this, folks," Myke snapped off one of the smaller steel structures and held it like a 9-foot-long baseball bat.

The dinosaur's brow lifted, but the expression on her face was one of contempt and defiance. When Myke Phoenix swung the tower at her head, she leaped – not away from the oncoming club, but onto it, so that as he followed through he gained the extra weight of a 4- or 5-foot-high dinosaur to swing. The tower and lizard crashed together, digging a small crater into the roof, but more important, the dinosaur clambered up the metal wreckage right at the white-uniformed man who had been wielding the metal weapon.

Rrrrip! Myke Phoenix jumped back, but not fast enough to avoid having his once-wounded chest slashed a second time, a little deeper than he had been a few weeks earlier. He shoved back mightily, and his attacker flew across the roof into the side of the air-conditioning unit.

The two combatants circled each other, and Myke Phoenix noticed with some sense of satisfaction that Deinonychus was limping slightly and shaking her head as if to clear cobwebs. At least he'd hurt her a little, too. He was aware of a sticky wetness on his chest, however, and his tourniqueted leg throbbed.

Time was a-wasting. He had been cut and bleeding only the once before, and these wounds were worse. This was unknown territory.

Better to strike sooner than later.

Mustering his energy, Myke Phoenix threw caution to the wind and launched himself directly at the deadly claws.

The brute force approach worked. He landed directly on top of the gruesome beast and was able to pin her lower legs to the ground with his knees. Better, he was able to grab her by the neck and start squeezing, with the aim of throttling the very life out of her.

She thrashed back with all of her might, squirming under his greater weight, whipping her tail against the side of his head, flailing at his arms with her shorter but deadly fore-claws. She was able to scratch him but not seriously enough to loosen the grip around her neck. Her eyes bulged with more than a hint of panic.

"Not – this – time – you little – lizard!" he gasped, ignoring the slicing pain and holding on for dear life. "It ends here!!"

Thrashing with the force that comes with desperation, she slowly maneuvered her left leg out from under his knee. Realizing too late what she was about to do, he leaned backward to secure the leg, relaxing his grip on her neck ever so slightly.

Ever so slightly was enough to make all the difference.

Deinonychus snarled and darted her head forward, biting Myke on the side of the face. She pulled her leg up against her chest, extended her terrible claw, and kicked him in the sternum with a raking blow.

A horrible gash in the middle of his abdomen sprayed crimson as Myke Phoenix fell backward.

The dinosaur pulled herself to her feet, gasping but triumphant, bright red ooze dripping from the large talon at the front of her foot.

"Myke – Phoenix," she said hoarsely. "Protector of Assstor Cccity. Who protectsss the protector, eh? Who protectsssss the protector?"

Myke Phoenix, bleeding and breathing quickly and shallowly, did not reply. His eyes did not seem to be focused on anything as he stared into the sky.

The celebratory roar of a dinosaur over its kill had not been heard for millions of years. That chilling cry rang across the roof of the skyscraper now, a roar that cut fear to the depths of any heart that heard it.

Deinonychus raised her head to the sky and roared, a raspy roar from a throat that had been on the verge of being crushed, but a full-body roar that declared her the victor and survivor of the death battle.

She closed her eyes to feel the thrill of victory in all of its power and glory.

Seconds from the end of his life, Myke Phoenix felt strangely privileged to be present to hear that ancient sound.

But then –

There came the sound of huge wings flapping, and a cry as unspeakably, hauntingly beautiful as the dinosaur's roar had been unspeakably terrifying.

Deinonychus opened her eyes in shock.

The bird descending from the sky toward the talking dinosaur was like no bird anyone there had ever seen, except perhaps for Deinonychus herself. Its wingspan was greater than that of a small airplane, and its feathers virtually glowed in the sun, especially the multicolored tail feathers of reds and golds and blues and greens. Its beak was the color of a rose, and the rainbow hues extended to its neck.

When it opened its mouth to give voice, the sound was not the threatening screech of a predator but a melodic song that seemed to breathe hope and peace into the very air.

It was not an eagle, but it was at least as big as an eagle.

It was not a hawk, but it moved with the speed and grace of a hawk.

It was not an owl, but it was stealthy as an owl.

It was like no bird Myke Phoenix had ever seen.

It was like every bird Myke Phoenix had ever seen.

It was an absolutely unique bird.

Unique: Because only one existed.

Myke Phoenix, balanced delicately on the precipice of death itself, stared at the great bird with what appeared to be indifference or unknowing, but after a few moments, he gasped, with awe dripping from each agonized syllable, "Oh my ever-loving stars. It's the Phoenix."

And for the first time, Deinonychus looked scared.

Before the little dinosaur could say a word, the Phoenix's great talons wrapped around Deinonychus and snatched her from the ground.

And then the Phoenix soared, climbing higher and higher above the city until it appeared to be a mere flash of color against the blue, and the monster it clutched was a speck of dust in the sky.

The resigned shriek of a dinosaur knowing it was about to die had not been heard on this Earth for millions of years. Deinonychus did not realize she would be spared – killing is not the way of the Phoenix, after all – and so she wailed and shrieked, helpless in the grasp of the great and gentle claw, for several minutes until her cries were nothing but a memory in the distance. And intermingled with the frightened screams of the dinosaur was the song of the Phoenix, a song that soothed the very soul of everyone who heard it over the city.

"Glad – I saw that," said Myke Phoenix, now alone on the roof watching helplessly as his life's blood flowed away. "I'm – glad." He closed his eyes and leaned back.

The heart of the mighty warrior Mychus slowed, skipped several beats, and stopped.

A squad of National Guardsmen found Paul Phillips unconscious on the roof, sprawled in a pool of blood. They turned him over gently, fully expecting to find a horrible wound, only to discover he was whole. They roused him to a groggy half-awareness.

"Whose blood is this?" a soldier asked. "We saw Myke Phoenix come up here; is he all right?"

"I don't know," said Paul Phillips. "I don't know, but I think he might be dead."

The wind on the skyscraper's rooftop was fierce but warm. It was a sunny day, and the city was safe for now.

Paul Phillips slipped into an exhausted sleep, dreaming of dragons.

Interlude

THE unexpectedly sweet aroma of Hi Dawson's heavenly tobacco began to fade from his consciousness, and he sensed himself being pulled away from the presence of his old friend.

"I'm glad I saw that, too," he heard Hi's spirit say. "OK, newshound, I guess this was a false alarm after all. Go off and fight the good fight some more. I'll talk to you again when your time really comes. And, Paul?"

The last words seemed to be an echo from far, far away.

"Mychus says to tell you, 'Good job, superhero.'"

Epilogue

PAUL Phillips and Dana Dunsmore looked at each other across the table. Outside, a storm had settled into a gentle, rhythmic rainfall.

She broke the silence.

"Is Myke dead?"

"I don't know," Paul said. "I swear I felt my heart stop. It was a pressure in my chest like my heart had skipped a beat except constant, as if it had stopped altogether. Next moment I was changed back and I was exhausted, but the pain was gone."

She grabbed his hand and tried somewhat unsuccessfully to smile. "I'm glad you're OK. Without the Phoenix, I think you would have died."

"That's what I'm trying to tell you, love," he said. "I think I did die."

"Well, that sure was a helluva mess," chimed the Soulkeeper of Kiribati's androgynous voice, breaking its silence. "But Mychus will be OK, eventually."

"What do you mean, 'eventually'?"

"I mean you should rest and take it easy for a while," the vase said. "And by 'a while' I mean about three months."

"Three months?!"

"Yeah, well, some repair jobs take a little longer than others."

"Has Mychus been dead before?"

"You're kidding, right? Remember the part where he lived 3,000 years ago?"

"I mean, has he been killed before, like this?"

"Not like this," the pottery said. "And not very often. But yeah."

"It takes about three months to fix?"

"More or less."

Several seconds passed in silence.

"It was beautiful," Dana said. "The Phoenix. I've never seen anything more beautiful."

"It was, wasn't it? I was barely aware it was there, but I could tell," Paul said. "I was drifting in and out, I thought I was dying. I *was* dying. At first I thought the bird was another vision of heaven."

"The big bird tends to stay out of the way," the vase said. "It likes to live on its own and let life unfold as it will. Every so often, it decides it needs to intervene, but it's always when life and death are at stake."

"Every so often? That's the only time the Phoenix has appeared in the three years I've been Myke Phoenix."

"When you're a mythical bird that lives 500, a thousand years, there's a long time between 'every so oftens.'"

The reporter with the crimefighter alter ego looked out the window as if he saw something in the dark.

"I've never quite understood why Deinonychus and her kind do what they do," he said. "Oh, the underlings, the thugs, they're motivated by fear – it's 'Do as you're told or be shredded.' But she just seems to force her power on others, to lord it over the underworld, to try to rule the world, just for the sheer pleasure of it."

"Evil is a disease," the vase said. "In the end, it can't be explained any other way."

"Where do you suppose the Phoenix took her?" Dana asked "Why wouldn't she just kill her?"

"That's not the way of the Phoenix," Paul Phillips and the Soulkeeper of Kiribati said in unison.

She chuckled. "Somebody owes someone a beer."

"I don't drink," the vase said.

The two humans laughed.

"So, Myke Phoenix is out of commission for about three months, more or less," Paul said. "What am I going to do with my spare time?"

"Oh, I don't know," Dana said with a big grin, and she waggled her ring finger so that it sparkled in his eyes. "I do believe we'll think of something."

Bo Ranfort, owner and president of WACR Radio, stood in as best man, and Dana's sister served as matron of honor, as Paul Phillips and Dana Dunsmore were joined in holy matrimony.

It was a low-key wedding ceremony before a relatively small group of friends and colleagues. The bride wore a pastel-blue gown, the groom a tuxedo, and everyone agreed they were the most beautiful couple anyone had seen since the last wedding they'd attended. (Neither radio nor the advertising business is particularly sentimental.)

On their wedding night, Dana Dunsmore Phillips settled her head into her new husband's chest and wrapped her arms around him.

"Is it OK for me to say I'm glad Myke Phoenix is out of commission for a while?" she said. "I've kind of enjoyed having just plain old Scoop around the last few weeks."

"Of course it's OK," Paul said. "I know how you feel. It's been nice living a normal life again."

"But you'll be OK getting back to the superhero business, too, right?"

"Of course, I've been chosen for this," he said sardonically. "Something is bound to turn up that needs Myke Phoenix to fix it."

More time passes

THEY moved into Dana's apartment, which was somewhat large than Paul's – because owning an advertising agency yields a greater income than working as a reporter – and after a few years they moved into a sumptuous middle-class home on the outskirts of Astor City.

The Forces of Evil in the world did not stop with the disappearance of Deinonychus. Myke Phoenix had plenty to keep him busy, and perhaps we will share some of those stories someday.

But now it's time to move the saga forward a few years – to the present day, to be exact. Some of those years have been filled with adventures, and some of those years were more quiet. When next we gather to speak of Myke Phoenix, it will be in the waning moments of one of those quiet years.

How quiet was it?

"It just seems like we don't need Myke Phoenix anymore," Paul Phillips said out loud one day.

He had no idea how soon he would find out how wrong he was.

Song of
The Serial Kisser

Prologue

THE great red-and-gold bird sailed high over the land, ever vigilant, ever wary. It's easy to grow lax over the course of a 500-year life span, but relaxation was not an option, not when a force of pure evil was afoot.

And knowing that force had not been vanquished, despite 18 years of intermittent struggle, was cause enough to stay vigilant. Someday a drooping of the head, a wandering of the mind, a distraction for a moment, would give the force an opening in the shield, and the resulting blow could be fatal for an entire planet.

The great bird's mission was to prevent that from opening. It could not permit itself a moment's diversion from the task at hand.

Its allies, after all, were mere flesh and blood.

And ceramic.

And so the great bird soared, and watched, and sang.

Act 1

A stolen kiss, a weary hero

THE Astor City Mall bustled with weekend shoppers. There was a craft sale in the aisles – homemade jewelry and clocks made from old LPs and birdhouses and artfully decorated mailboxes, you know the stuff – and that made the shoppers crowd together even more.

Randi Vermiere had been shopping all afternoon, and she was happier than she had been for a while. This was going to be her boyfriend's best birthday ever, no doubt about it. She had only three small- to medium-sized bags to show for the effort, but what was inside those bags was exactly what he had asked for.

Everyone seemed to be in a good mood even though it wasn't anywhere close to Christmas. Maybe it was the fact that winter would soon be over. She even heard someone whistling the pretty opening notes of "Spring" from Vivaldi's "The Four Seasons."

Time to buy something for herself. She saw a man wearing sunglasses set up between the bookstore and yet another women's fashion shop. Roses! She deserved a rose.

"I'll take one of those," Randi chirped to the vendor, pointing at a container full of fragrant red roses.

"Which one are you looking at?" the man in the sunglasses asked, and she realized he was blind.

"I'm sorry," she said. "I'd like a red rose."

"All right, here you are," the vendor said, reaching for the correct vase and plucking a nice one out for her. "Don't they smell lovely?"

"Yes, they do," she laughed, exchanging cash for the flower. "That's why I had to have one. This is a five-dollar bill."

"Thank you," he said, and counted out the change. "The aroma matches your lovely voice."

"You're too nice," Randi replied and walked away, the rose just in front of her lips, enjoying the sweet springtime odor.

She turned up a back corridor to the parking lot when she felt him come up behind her and whisper, "You look so good in purple," then start nibbling on her neck.

Randi blushed and smiled and closed her eyes. Where had he come from? She didn't expect him to be at the mall today. The smell of the rose combined with the sensation on her neck was divine.

He turned her around and planted a gentle, warm kiss full on the lips that gave her a familiar longing feeling in the general vicinity of her belly. Eyes still closed, she gave a little moan of appreciation. Oh my, she loved the way he made her feel.

That's funny, he shaved his mustache, Randi realized, opening her eyes just a slit – and then as wide as could be.

The man kissing her so lovingly was not – in any way, shape or form – the man she expected to be kissing.

"What the – WHO ARE YOU?" she screamed. And she kept screaming as he laughed and fled down the corridor and into the parking lot.

Detective Captain Fredricks tried to call up the notes-taking app on his smartphone, swore under his breath, tucked the device into his coat pocket and retrieved a paper pad and pen.

"This works better for me anyway," he said apologetically. "So you thought it was your boyfriend."

"Well, who else is going to come up behind me like that and start kissing my neck?" Randi Vermiere asked innocently.

"Oh, gee, I don't know – a rapist? What were you thinking, girl?"

"It wasn't like that! He was very gentle and sweet, like Tom – my boyfriend's name is Tom. I was sure it was him," she said. "Except that it wasn't."

"Right. Did you get a good look at him?"

"Well, yes. Well, not so much. I was so surprised. He didn't have a mustache like Tom. I saw that it wasn't Tom's mouth, and screamed, and he ran. The rest of his face, I don't know."

"Could you pick the guy out of a lineup if you had to?"

"Maybe," she said not so confidently. "His mouth, at least."

"Right. And you'd just bought a rose from the blind guy at the kiosk. Did you notice anyone hanging around, maybe watching you?"

"No, I was looking at the rose."

"I mean before, while you were shopping, did you see the same guy looking at you at different places?"

"Not really – I tune that out. Guys are always looking, you know what I mean?"

She was a good-looking girl. "Yeah, I know what you mean. OK, here's my card, if you think of anything –anything that might help us find the guy – give me a call. Especially if you think of something besides his mouth not looking like Tom's."

"He had a brown coat on."

"Cloth or leather?"

"Fabric."

"That's good. Blue jeans or business pants?"

"Pants. Brown pants. Kind of casual pants, not real business-like. And he had a nice laugh, it wasn't like a mean laugh. He was a good kisser. I hate to say that, but he kissed as good as Tom does. It was very nice, except for I didn't want to kiss him."

This was not going to be easy. A clean-shaven guy with brown casual pants and a brown coat. Could be anybody. The blind vendor remembers selling the rose to her. He obviously didn't see anybody nearby. Nobody saw the kiss, nobody saw the guy running away, they just heard the scream.

In this state kissing a lady who doesn't want to get kissed is not a felony. They call it fourth-degree sexual assault, which sounds serious but it's a misdemeanor with a $50 fine and maybe 15 days in jail max. A stolen kiss not generally an offense that brings out a captain of the detective squad to investigate.

The reason Fredricks was on the case was that it was the 27th stolen kiss in the last two weeks. The description in each incident was as vague as this one, but they all sounded like the same guy – sudden and unwelcome, but gentle and even nice.

"A serial kisser," Fredricks muttered. "What a freakin' waste of time this is."

The whole thing was perplexing. The guy had managed to find 27 public places where he could walk up to an unsuspecting woman and plant a big, wet one on them, or as big and as wet a kiss as they would allow. Even when he was caught on surveillance camera, he managed to keep the system from getting a good look at his face. The ladies were shaken up, some to the point of becoming anxious when their boyfriends or husbands approached them romantically, but there wasn't an overwhelming demand to track the guy down and press charges.

Fredricks was the only detective who thought it would be worthwhile to pursue the thing.

"What if he takes it farther than stealing a kiss?" he asked. "At some point maybe kissing her isn't going to be enough of a thrill."

"Well, that's why it would be nice to catch him, to make sure he doesn't," District Attorney Kenneth Ronnegan Jr. had said. "But in the meantime we have bigger fish to fry. Don't waste the resources."

The resources. The personnel. The damn budget. Once upon a time the cops just worried about catching the bad guys, protecting and serving. Now it was all about prioritization. Fredricks hadn't plucked a kitten out of a tree for a little kid for about 30 years, not while he was on the clock at least. What was the world coming to?

Maybe tracking down a serial kisser wasn't going to be his top priority. But he'd get the guy before he did any real harm. Or maybe an angry boyfriend would get to him first.

"Astor County Sheriff's Dispatch, Blanche speaking."

"Hey, it's Paul Phillips. How are ya, Blanche?"

"Nothing going on, Paul."

"What? No hot dates or anything?"

"Very funny. No, I ain't been seeing anyone lately."

"Don't worry, someone will come along. Say, anything worth writing for the news overnight?"

"I told you, nothing going on."

"You said that when I asked 'how are ya.' Now I'm asking if anything happened overnight."

"You're what, like a comedian? Have a nice day."

Someday he would get Blanche the dispatcher to lighten up. But today was not going to be that day.

Paul Phillips was the editor, reporter, typist, heck, he was the whole staff of the Astor City Beacon news blog. Once a hotshot radio news reporter, he was laid off when WACR decided that having a local news team was too expensive. He spent a few years with the Astor City Tribune until it decided that modern times required getting by with one-third of the news staff it had back in the day. Unwilling to give up his lifetime urge to tell people what was going on in their town, he eked out a living applying his journalistic skills online.

"It's hard to write up a news update when there's no news going on," he grumbled, apparently to himself.

"Don't look so disappointed, Paul. It's good news – the forces of evil in the world took the night off."

The new voice appeared to be coming from an ugly green vase on a bookshelf. The voice had a somewhat feminine but definitely male tone to it, and the vase was pale green with the painted figure of a red bird and crystal, red and blue glass jewels embedded around the top and bottom.

Perhaps the most amazing thing about this scene is that Paul Phillips did not seem to be especially surprised to hear a disembodied voice coming from the general vicinity of a butt-ugly green vase on his bookshelf.

Did I mention that in addition to being a hotshot reporter, for the last 18 years Paul Phillips had led a double life as Myke Phoenix, superhero and protector of Astor City? The vase was the Soulkeeper of Kiribati, and when bad guys threatened, Paul exchanged his everyday reporter's pudgy body for the invulnerable frame of a mighty warrior named Mychus.

"Yes, it's great that the forces of evil took the night off, but I got nothin' and people will start logging in for news in a little while," he told the vase.

"Are you talking to the furniture again?" came a third voice, this one definitely feminine. It belonged to a good-looking woman of a certain age with bright blue eyes, auburn hair with a hint of gray here and there – or were they highlights? – who walked into the room stretching and wearing a robe.

"The babe awakes. Hiya, doll." This was the odd voice in the vase, not Paul Phillips.

"Hello, ugly," she replied, this to the ugly vase, not Paul Phillips. At the beginning of their relationship, Paul was the only one who could hear the vase's voice. Early on the vase decided it was all right for the wife to listen in.

Dana Dunsmore Phillips had been Paul's partner for a little more than two decades and his wife for the last 15 of those years. Truth be told, she had evolved into the breadwinner of this little family as the owner of one of the biggest public relations/marketing companies in Astor City. Her company was a major sponsor of the Astor City Beacon, and she helped secure other sponsors when she wasn't putting out fires, managing people and otherwise running D.S. Dunsmore Advertising Agency.

"So did anybody get shot last night?" Dana asked Paul the way an average person might ask, "Who won the ballgame?"

"No," Paul replied ruefully. "It's one slow news day already."

"You got that United Way interview from the other day, you could write that up quick," she said. "Did you remember to make coffee today?"

"Yeah, have some," he said. "I forgot about that interview, thanks – I can make something out of that pretty quick."

"Whatever happened to the powerful forces of evil in the universe?" she asked the vase cheerfully. "This town has been pret-ty darn quiet lately."

"What, are you complaining? That used to be a good thing, evil taking the week off," the vase said. "Careful what you wish for."

"Evil can take the week off anytime," Dana said. "We haven't had a supervillain invade town for – at least a couple of years, isn't it?"

"I'd guess the Grasshopper Bandit was the last time we had a guy that nobody except Myke could handle, and that was two summer ago," Paul agreed. "It's kind of depressing."

"You're depressed because you chased off the Forces of Evil? I don't believe this," the vase said, and if it had lungs it would have exhaled in exasperation. "Don't worry, dummy, the Forces of Evil don't stay chased."

"Is something brewing?" Paul said almost expectantly.

"Just the coffee," the green thing said. "What are you depressed about?"

"I don't know," he said. "Deinonychus is out of the picture. Prince Cormorant was deposed, and he's in exile in Switzerland with none of the power and resources he used to have. It's the same with all of the really bad guys we've fought over the years. Lately it's just been everyday crooks and the occasional mobster. And even then, there's nobody like Alan Pinkstaff who almost ran the town with his crime syndicate. It just seems like we don't need Myke Phoenix anymore."

"You say that like it's a bad thing," Dana said, running her hands across his shoulders. "That's a victory, you big idiot. You're winning."

"I guess. Maybe that is a good thing, after 18 years even being a superhero gets a little old," Paul said, staring vacantly at his computer screen, and then starting. "I'd better write up that interview."

"If it's any consolation, the Forces of Evil never go away completely. They'll be back," the vase said. "And it'll happen just when you don't want them to."

"Can they come back soon? I need a story," Paul said, a slight twinkle returning to his eye.

"Don't push your luck." The vase went silent, Dana read the news on her smartphone, and the clickadee-clack of Paul's keyboard telling the United Way story was the only sound in the room for the next half-hour.

Act 2

The usual suspects

SONNY Boneau fidgeted at the table in the interview room. He heard the murmur of cops talking on the other side of the door, and he thought he heard the clunk of a coffee cup being set down on a counter behind the big glass that everybody knew was a one-way mirror so other cops could watch the proceeding. Sonny figured he'd been sitting by himself for at least 15 minutes.

"Come *on*," he hollered. "Let's get this over with. I ain't got all day."

He kind of jumped when his holler was met by the abrupt opening of the door. Detective Captain Fredricks walked in.

"Fredricks!" Sonny said with some surprise. "What'd I do? I thought you was riding a desk these days."

"Not so much," Fredricks replied. "How are you, Sonny? Do any break-ins lately?"

"No! I did my time and I'm clean now," the burglar replied. Both men knew it wasn't true, but Sonny hadn't been caught lately. "What are you trying to pin on me?"

"Well, I got a weird one I'm working on, and you strike me as weird," the detective captain deadpanned. "Do you know we have a serial kisser in town?"

Sonny Boneau sputtered. "A serial killer? I ain't no murderer. No way."

Fredricks smirked.

"Kisssser," he said, drawing out the "s" sound in the middle of the word. "We have a serial kisssser in town. Walks up to ladies and plants one on them."

"He just kisses them?" It was Sonny's time to smirk. "How 'bout that. Good for him!"

"No, not good. It's illegal to kiss a stranger without their permission."

"I still say good for him. Some girls need to be kissed."

"Not. Like. This," Fredricks said. "You like the idea so much, maybe it's you I'm lookin' for."

"What?" Flabbergasted. "No, that's not my style."

"Whose style is it?" Fredricks said. "Because you know, the way he cases places, picks where to do his thing without being picked up on security cameras, the M.O. sure reminds me of a talented burglar or robber. Yep, it does."

"What are you talking about?"

Fredricks was talking about having a conversation with anyone and everyone he'd ever busted for breaking and entering, shoplifting, or otherwise taking advantage of an innocent victim. After the kisser's victim list hit 20, Fredricks had spent the week shaking down the petty criminals of Astor City and asking them about the Serial Kisser.

And after a while, they began to get irritated. More about that later, because first I need to describe the 28th incident.

Rollie's Bar was one of those bars that, six weeks later, you and your friends are saying "What was the name of that bar we went to that night?" and darned if any of you can remember it. Pick a bar, any bar you've been in. Yeah, it was that kind of bar.

On the end of the bar sat a woman. Pick a woman you've seen at a bar and thought, hey, she's not bad. Not too pretty, but definitely not unpleasant to look at. Yeah, that was her.

Rhoda Tennyson was sitting at the end of the bar at Rollie's, pretty much minding her own business. She wanted to be alone. If someone came up and offered to buy her a drink, she might have said yes, but she was hoping nobody would offer. She wasn't horribly depressed or anything; sometimes you just want to be left alone and have a drink by yourself. Rollie's was one of those places where maybe a girl could do that. And sure enough, it wasn't a busy night, and she was most of the way through her metropolitan and feeling like it was a good night to be alone. A guy whistling some classical thing, Vivaldi maybe, walked past behind her and into the men's room.

"'Nother one?" asked the bartender.

"No, I'm good," Rhoda replied. He nodded and walked to the other end, where there were glasses to clean and dry.

The men's room door opened and closed. Rhoda picked up her glass and gazed blankly at the mirror, watching a guy walk most of the way past her, but then he leaned around and give her a kiss.

"Hey!" she said, wiping her mouth. "What was that all about?"

The man was already past the bartender, who looked around and saw the back of the guy's head, then turned back to Rhoda.

"What happened? You all right?"

"He kissed me! Just all of a sudden kissed me."

"What'd you say to him?"

"Nothing! He just up and kissed me."

"Doesn't sound so bad."

"It wasn't so bad, that's not the point!"

"I suppose not."

"Where did he go?" Rhoda asked, looking past the bartender. He followed her line of sight.

"Gone. I think he walked right out."

"Well, I'm calling 9-1-1."

"What, this is an emergency?"

"Rueben, the guy kissed me. Who knows what he's thinking of doing next?"

The 9-1-1 dispatcher transferred the call to Detective Captain Fredricks, who ended his conversation with Sonny Boneau and drove down to Rollie's Bar.

Rhoda Tennyson was not the most cooperative victim ever. She had just wanted to finish her metropolitan and go home to her cats. The more she talked about it, the less she wanted to talk about it.

"How about you?" Fredricks asked Rueben the bartender. "You get a look at the guy?"

"He was kind of in a hurry, walking past me already when the lady yelled," Reuben said. "All I saw was the back of his head."

You know that face people make when they want to swear but they decide to do it silently? Kind of a sudden downward jerk of the head and a grunt. That's what Fredricks did now.

That was fun. She looked so surprised. Seemed like a nice lady, all by herself. A woman needs to feel like she's not all by herself, like somebody noticed she's cute and kissable.

Why do I do that? They're always a little mad when I do that. I probably shouldn't do that.

But that was fun.

The man walked along Seventh Avenue, whistling the "Spring" theme from "The Four Seasons."

Paul and Dana Phillips didn't get out together much. He was always reporting the news or fighting evil, and she was waist-deep in running her business. They had to schedule a date to spend time together. The good news is they made a point to go on a date at least once a week, but it often involved popcorn and wine in front of the television set at home, watching an old movie.

Getting to Radicchio's was a special treat for both of them. The Italian restaurant was famous for its exotic salads and fabulous pasta creations, and the music was subdued enough that they could carry on an intelligent conversation.

They were in the middle of such a conversation when Paul spotted a familiar face over her shoulder. The face was passing by behind Dana, so rather than excuse himself and walk over, he simply called out.

"Bo! Bo Ranfort!"

The tall, well-dressed man looked in his direction, and his expression lit up.

"Paul! Dana! How the heck are you guys?"

Ranfort was the former owner/manager of WACR Radio, the Voice of the Community, which until just a few years ago had lived up to its slogan by providing 24 hours of locally produced programs including locally reported, locally announced news. After he sold the station and retired, well, remember I mentioned that Paul left WACR and became a newspaper reporter? That was after Bo Ranfort sold the station and retired.

After the usual pleasantries – Bo was with his wife, Candi – they got to talking about the old place.

"It's really gone to hell, hasn't it?" Ranfort admitted sheepishly. "I suppose I shouldn't have retired, but you just have to step away at some point."

"Not your fault, Bo, it's the business," Paul said. "They never found another talk show rabble rouser like Hi Dawson, so they hitched their star to a satellite dish like everyone else."

"I told that SOB to lay off the cigarettes, but he didn't listen to anybody," Bo said.

"Not his style," Paul agreed.

Bo and Candi had very nice things to say about the Astor City Beacon blog, and they agreed it was nice that the snow was melting and the days would be really warming up sometime soon, and then the Phillips' order arrived and the Ranforts went off to their own table.

"It's good to see Bo," Paul said wistfully. "He really was a throwback, and so was his radio station."

"You'd think he could have let people in the community know the station was for sale instead of selling out to that big chain," Dana said with a frown. "The advertising reps lost all of their ability to make a deal – if I've heard 'That's not the company's policy anymore' once, I've heard it 100 times."

"Isn't that the way of the world nowadays," Paul said, more of a comment than a question. "They make it easy to say, 'Sorry, it's out of my control, there's nothing I can do about it.'"

The food was great as always, and they each were with their favorite person, so the rest of the evening went comfortably. As Paul figured out the tip, Dana excused herself to go to the ladies' room.

She was relaxed and happy. Business was doing all right, Paul's venture and adventures were progressing, and the calendar's promise of coming spring takes the edge off the end of winter. Dana smiled; as she passed the men's room door she heard someone whistling Vivaldi.

The reader should not be surprised at this point to learn that when she was finished in the ladies room and stepped back into the corridor, Dana became the 29th woman in Astor City to be accosted by an overly affectionate stranger.

"Did he hurt you?" Paul asked earnestly.

"I'm fine, it wasn't a rough kiss, just – sudden," Dana said, and lowered her voice so only Paul could hear: "If I was in any danger, you would have turned into Myke automatically."

That much was true – Mychus the Warrior was known to switch bodies with Paul all of a sudden, seconds before an attack of some kind.

"What if he's some terrorist spreading germs?" Paul said. "I don't like this at all."

Dana shot him a look of extreme skepticism. "Terrorist? Really?"

Detective Captain Fredricks arrived at the restaurant just then. He and Paul eyed each other with surprise.

"How'd you find out about this?" the detective asked.

"Captain Fredricks, meet my wife, Dana. She's your complainant. Why did the police send a detective – a detective captain! – on this case?" the reporter asked.

"Pleased to meet you. I was in the neighborhood," Fredricks said. "That, and the fact that this guy has done this to a couple dozen other women in the last two-three weeks."

"What!" Paul said. "There's like a, serial kisser on the loose?"

"Don't be so freakin' dramatic," Fredricks said, a little irked that the reporter had come up with the same phrase as he. "It's a misdemeanor. Kind of weird that he's doing it so often, but nobody's –"

"That's not the point, Captain. Don't you think people might want to know that this is going on? Why didn't you tell us in the media about this?"

Because you'd blow it out of proportion and scare women more than they deserve to be scared, Fredricks thought.

"I don't feel like causing a panic over this," Fredricks said out loud. "You mind if I interview the victim here, old buddy? Did you get a good look at the guy, Mrs. Phillips?"

"Dana. Not really. I was just coming out of the ladies room, and he sort of swooped by, took me by the shoulders and gave me a big kiss."

"Did you see his eyes, his nose, what he was wearing?"

"Brown eyes, actually kind of friendly look to his face. His nose was sort of hooked, and he had a round chin. Clean shaven. Brown overcoat, casual brown pants."

Fredricks' eyes widened a bit. That was the most detailed description any of the 29 women had given so far. She was very observant. Maybe being a reporter's wife ...

"I thought you said you didn't get a good look at him."

"I notice details."

"Would you object to sitting down with a sketch artist?"

"I suppose not."

"I thought this wasn't a big deal," Paul Phillips said sarcastically.

"Compared to 29 murders, it isn't a big deal," Fredricks said. "But this is upsetting to the people involved."

"Darn right it is," Paul grumbled. "I can't believe you've been covering this up."

"Shush, Paul," Dana said. "He had his reasons. And now you know."

And the next morning, the readers of the Astor City Beacon news blog knew, too.

Act 3
The pact

A half-dozen shady-looking guys sat around a half-dozen bottles of beer and a basket of popcorn at one of those bars like Rollie's Bar. Only it wasn't Rollie's, it was – actually, no one remembers which bar exactly it was. The important thing was, Sonny Boneau and five other shady-looking guys were having a beer.

"This Serial Kisser SOB ain't good for our business," Sonny was saying.

"You got that right," one of the other guys, Ted Rademacher, said bitterly. "Jeez, Fredricks hauled me in the other day just because I did some time for robbery. Said this guy has the same M.O. I never kissed anybody I ripped off!"

"Ya dummy, it's the way he sneaks up on them like we sneak up on a mark," Jimmy Dehn said. "It's like he thinks one of us graduated from grabbing purses to kissin' the broads?"

"It's bad for business," Sonny repeated. "First off, the cops are walking the streets more. Second off, people are getting more cautious. It's like they don't mind if we steal their wallets, but oh hey, don't kiss me – that's a step too far, don't ya know."

As Fredricks had feared, the media was running with the "Serial Kisser" mania. It wasn't so much Phillips' blog, it was the TV stations. They were playing it cute, but they were also getting people riled up. It didn't help that he had now surprised more than 40 women with a sudden public display of unwanted affection.

"You know what we need to do?" Sonny Boneau said. "We gotta stop him ourselves."

"What?!" said Scarface Mahoney, who was a skinny 19-year-old pickpocket who got scratched by an overly affectionate yellow lab when he was a kid. "We're not the cops."

"Once the Serial Kisser is put out of business, people will calm down and they'll go back to carrying their purses loose and forgetting to lock their doors," Sonny said.

"You know, that actually makes sense," Jimmy said. "You think we should get the word out to watch for the guy?"

"Yeah, I do," Sonny said.

"Maybe we could recruit some of the boyfriends or husbands," Ted said. "They're pretty ticked off about it."

Sonny Boneau looked at Ted Rademacher with sincere admiration. "Teddy, that's the best idea you've had in 10 years. Yeah, of course those guys are gonna be motivated."

"But what are we going to do with the guy if we catch him?" Scarface asked.

The question hung in the air for a few seconds.

"We'll figure that out when we get him," Sonny said.

Paul Phillips emerged from the clerk of courts office and was heading down to a courtroom to watch a gentleman who was going to be sentenced for his 11th conviction of operating a motor vehicle while intoxicated.

"Mr. Phillips?" came a low voice nearby. He turned and saw a short man with a few days' worth of beard and a baseball cap pulled almost over his eyes.

"Can I help you?"

"Maybe, if you got a minute. I hear your lady got kissed by that nutcase last week."

That got Paul's attention. "Do you know something about it?"

"Just what I see on TV." That always irritated Paul more than it should; the TV reporters usually saw it on the Beacon first and then ran with the story as their own. "But a bunch of guys are working to catch the moron on our own."

"What guys? What's wrong with letting the police do their jobs?"

"It ain't a top priority for them, and you know that," the unshaven man said. "Anyway, it's some of us guys and we're thinking the boyfriends might want to help us look. And you with your connections inside the cop shop ..."

"Look, I wouldn't risk the trust I've built up with the police over the years by sharing stuff other than what's in the stories I write," Paul said.

"Yeah, yeah, I'm just asking if you hear anything or see anything that would help us catch him, tell us too."

Paul considered the suggestion. If he knew how to catch the serial kisser, he'd probably take care of the little creep himself in his Myke Phoenix uniform. But if there was some weird vigilante group forming, that might be an interesting story of its own.

"How would I find you?"

"Oh, I'm here a lot, I have a few cases pending, if you get my drift," the man said. "I'll watch out for you and we can talk here."

"Do you think your leaders would be willing to comment on the record for a story?" Paul asked, and he got a look as if he were a space alien. "I'll take that as a 'no.'"

Geoff Rogers was a little angrier than usual, but he refused to let it show. It didn't help business when he wasn't the sweet and cheerful blind man who sold flowers at the Astor City Mall.

It's not as if he didn't have a good reason for being angry. His friend Yancy took a look at Geoff's cashbox every couple of hours, and it was in disarray when he checked a few minutes ago. There were $5 bills mixed in with the twenties, and $10 bills with the ones. Obviously one or more customers had lied about what they were handing him, and at least one or more had lied when he inadvertently gave them more change than he should have.

Who would take advantage of a blind man? He wanted to fume and rant and rave, but he knew he had to project the cheerful front. Thank goodness Yancy was there to catch stuff like this.

"Calm down, relax, sell your flowers," Geoff said to himself. A shopper walked by whistling. "Be like that person, carefree, happy to serve."

"Can I buy one of these roses?" a soft feminine voice asked.

"You can buy as many as you like," Geoff smiled broadly. "Here, don't they smell lovely?"

"Oh, they surely do," she replied. A slight Southern accent. "But just the one will do."

"All right, that's two-fifty," he said.

"Here you are," the woman said, handing him a single bill.

"Is this a five?" Geoff asked.

"Oh, I'm sorry, it's a ten."

It *better* be a ten, he thought, handing her two quarters, two $1 bills and a $5 bill in change. He trusted his customers and folded each bill in a special way so he could tell them apart. But it all depended on them being honest.

"There you go," he said cheerfully. "The aroma goes perfectly with your lovely Tennessee voice."

"How did you know I'm from Tennessee?" she asked in delighted surprise.

"You sound like a southern belle," Geoff smiled.

Four minutes later, there was a commotion down the corridor not far from Geoff Rogers' kiosk. The southern belle had received an unexpected kiss in a side hallway.

"Just like a week or so ago," Geoff mused to himself, and then he made a connection.

Someone had been whistling just before the Tennessee woman walked up. Before that first incident, someone had walked past the flower stand whistling the same tune – some classical thing. You don't suppose – seems like a weird coincidence – but if it *was* a coincidence, he wouldn't want to get someone in trouble. But what are the odds? Two times he had heard someone whistling that tune, two stolen kisses a few minutes later.

He thought he'd mention it if the police came around asking about the southern belle. They didn't come around. But he did mention it to Yancy. It turns out that Yancy was a friend of Sonny Boneau.

"Sonny?" Yancy purred into his cellphone. "I think I might have a clue for you."

The blind vendor whistled the tune to Yancy, who recognized the melody.

"It's the 'spring' theme from 'The Four Seasons,'" he told Sonny. "You know, Vivaldi."

"Va-who?" Boneau asked.

"Oh come on, you know: Da-dum-dum-dum-dada-DOO, Dada-dum-dum-dum-dada-DOO, dada-dum-dada-dum-dum-dum," he sang.

"Huh. Yeah, I guess I've heard that riff before," Boneau said.

And the word went out.

The Astor City Mall was bustling with people that evening, and Geoff Rogers was doing good business. The roses always sold like gangbusters, but everything else was also moving. With spring just around the corner, people were snapping up the potted daffodils, too. He was so busy he almost didn't hear it.

Across the corridor. Someone whistling. Not just whistling, but whistling that little classical cadence, the one Yancy said was from Vivaldi.

"Are you still there, young man?" Geoff called out.

Scarface Mahoney had been hanging around near Geoff Rogers' flower kiosk for two or three hours and he was really, really bored. But he heard it, too, and his heart started pumping a little harder.

"Yeah. Was that him?" Scarface said, scanning the crowd.

"It sure sounded like the same guy," Geoff said, pointing. "Over that way."

"On it."

Scarface walked briskly in the direction of the whistling, and it wasn't too long before he matched the sound with the back of a head. Brown hair, not too light, not too dark. But the whistle made him.

A blond-haired woman turned down the back corridor toward the parking lot. A few steps behind her, the whistling man also turned down the back corridor.

"No way," Scarface Mahoney muttered, and picked up his pace.

She had a bag slung over a shoulder and was carrying shopping bags in both hands. The shoulder bag's straps looked easy to snap. If only Scarface was looking to grab a purse, it looked easy. But that wasn't the goal here. The man had stopped whistling and was only about five steps behind the blonde, but he glanced back and saw Scarface and slowed his pace.

The young thug slapped the man on the shoulder and saw that he was in his late twenties, beak nose, round chin.

"Hey buddy, are you wearing a watch? I wonder what time it is."

The guy, looking a little put out, pulled a cellphone from his coat pocket and lit the screen. "7:22." He patted his pants pocket as if to make sure his wallet was still there. Ahead, the door to the parking lot closed behind the blonde.

"Great. Thanks," Scarface said, spinning and heading back up the corridor. Just around the corner, he pulled out his own phone.

"Hey, Sonny, it's Scarface. I got him. Astor City Mall, right now he's in the east back corridor. Whoop! He's back in the mall," he said, turning his back on the whistling man.

"I'll make some calls. Keep an eye on him," Sonny said.

"Don't worry, I will," Scarface replied. "And I slapped the tag on him, too."

Damn kid, asking me what time it is. Why me? I was almost on her. It was going perfect. Probably a pickpocket; good thing I heard him and turned my wallet pocket away from him at the last second.

She was a pretty one, too. It would have been fun.

The challenge had increased in the week since that blog first revealed what he was doing. Funny that the police took so long to announce what he was doing. Being famous was part of the fun, he had to admit, but women were harder to find alone now, too.

That stuff about "we hope this doesn't escalate into something serious" was just rubbish, too. All he wanted was to kiss ladies. After all, women need to be kissed, and often, and by someone who knows how. It was fun, and most of them didn't seem to mind so much.

He whistled. The "spring" theme from "The Four Seasons." Spring was coming soon, and the ladies would start wearing their spring and summer clothes. It'd be easier to smell their scent then, and they'd be warmer to the touch.

It had been 20 minutes or so since that stupid kid broke up the opportunity. He walked past the flower kiosk. If he didn't know any better, he'd swear the blind guy was watching him go by. Whatever.

That little woman wearing the beret looks cute. Some people call that mousy hair, but I like it, especially with the beret as an accent. She turned down the back corridor. *Perfect.*

"Hey buddy, what's that on your back?"

Now what!?

"You talking to me?"

"Yeah, you've got some sort of sticker on your left shoulder."

He reached over his shoulder, and sure enough, there was a sticker there.

"What do you know. Thanks."

"No problem."

It was one of those name tag stickers that says "My name is." But it didn't have a name on it, just one letter.

"K."

He stared at the tag in dumb silence for a second. Where'd *this* come from? He looked around and saw the kid who had asked for the time about 50 feet away. He had two or three friends with him. Big, tough-looking friends.

He must have stuck the tag on when he slapped my shoulder. Why? What's this all about.

"K."

A TV commercial jingle incongruously spun through his head: "Every kiss begins with K."

He turned away from the kid and his thuggish buddies and saw three other thugs walking meaningfully in his direction.

"K." K for Kisser. Oh. My. God.

He ran. Two sets of brutes ran after him.

Act 4
The trial

"ASTOR County Dispatch, Blanche speaking."

"Hey Blanche, it's Paul Phillips."

"You just don't quit, do you?"

"I'm like clockwork, good lady. Every morning at 4:45, it's call the 911 dispatch center. And ask what's going on. You know that."

"Nothing going on, same as always."

"Nothing? Not even another kiss from the Serial Kisser?"

"Nope, he took the night off. The only thing we heard about the Kisser was a phony report that he'd been abducted."

"You're kidding."

"Yeah, somebody said there was a bunch of guys ganged up on someone and tossed him in a van, and another call said they were yelling about 'We caught the Kisser,' but when the squad got there, there was no sign of a van or the kids who called it in. Figure it was a prank."

"Probably. Where was this?"

"Down the street from the mall. That's the thing, the responding officers couldn't find anyone who actually saw this happen. Like I said, it was just kids in the mall playing games. No news for you, even if I wanted to give you some, which I don't."

"Thanks, Blanche, you're a peach."

The guy with the baseball cap was walking the hall at the courthouse. Paul caught his eye.

"Hey. Anything new to report out there?" Paul asked.

"I was looking for you," the cap said. "You want a piece of him?"

"A piece of who?"

"You know who."

"I think I know who, but what are you talking about?"

"They caught him. The guys caught him, the guys I told you about. You didn't hear this from me."

"I protect my sources with the best of them."

"Five o'clock this afternoon, the old Astor Brewery. You can have a piece of him, get him back for what he did to your girlfriend."

"What, you're going to beat him up or something?"

"Whatever you want. Just saying. We're going to have a little trial, gotta have due process, you know. Then everyone can take a piece of him."

"You're not worried the police will find out about this?"

"Who's going to tell? You protect your sources, right?"

The hood was finally removed, and then the duct tape, rudely.

The face underneath had brown eyes, a beak-like nose, and a round chin.

"That's him," a female voice said, emphatically, over in the corner.

"Yes. It is him," another feminine voice said, assuredly.

"What *is* this?" the man said. But the look on his face betrayed that he knew what it was, or at least that he knew why the two women said what they said.

His hands were tied behind his back, and he had been placed in a chair. There was a light over him, but he had been in darkness for something like 18 hours, so he couldn't see right away. Once his eyes adjusted, he saw there were about 30 men across the room, and four, no, five women off to the side. The women all were nodding. And he recognized them all.

"That's him," Randi Vermiere said, although he didn't know that was her name. "I didn't think I'd recognize him, but that's definitely him."

"Why am I here?" he said.

Sonny Boneau sat at a table in front of the men. (He didn't know Sonny, but you and I do, so I'm telling you to make it easier on us.) He snorted at the question.

"You know why you're here," Sonny said, and he whistled the first few notes of the "Spring" theme from Vivaldi's "The Four Seasons."

The Serial Kisser gasped as if hearing his own whistle for the first time.

"What – what are you going to do?"

"Make you stop," Sonny said.

"HOW?"

"Well, that's up to you, isn't it? You've upset these women, and some of these men, their boyfriends and husbands. You've upset the rest of us by bringing the law down on the streets harder than usual. We're upset, mister. We're very upset. And it's time for you to stop."

"Please! I haven't hurt anyone," the Kisser whimpered. "It's just a little fetish. I can't help myself!"

"You haven't hurt anyone?" This was one of the men behind Sonny. "I can't touch my girl without her jumping like I'm some kind of wild animal or a rapist or something. You did that to her, creep."

The crowd started to move in. He stood, awkwardly, because his hands were bound behind his back.

"Please!" he said, more of a shriek than a whimper now. "I want to stop – but I can't. I can't resist the impulse. You have no idea what it's like. I just have to kiss someone!"

"Well, maybe if we rearranged your kisser," the closest man said. And he slugged him, reeling him back a step.

"And maybe if we made sure it doesn't escalate into something worse," the next-closest man said. And he kicked him in the groin.

"Yeah!" the group roared.

More than a handful of the men stepped from the crowd then, surrounding the man, who fell to his knees holding his hands to his head in a feeble attempt to protect himself.

"OK, boys, that's enough," a strong baritone voice barked.

The voice belonged to a very tall, blond-haired man with a chest shaped like a barrel, who stepped in front of the frantic kisser. He was wearing a white uniform with buttons down the side of the tunic. The image of a red-and-gold bird was emblazoned on his chest.

"Hokey smokes," someone in the back of the room said. "That's Myke Phoenix."

"I don't care if it's the governor," the groin-kicker said. "This guy's going to pay." And he wound up his leg for another wallop.

Myke intercepted the flailing leg and flipped the man head over heels. He landed with a belly flop and a burst of dust on the floor of the abandoned brewery.

"Go home, folks, I'll bring this guy to the police station," Myke told the surly crowd.

"He's just gonna get off with probation or something," someone shouted.

"We'll let the judge sort that out," the big warrior said, "but I imagine he'll order some mental health treatment while he's at it."

The group started to file slowly out of the building. The wail of police sirens approaching the building sped up the process. Paul Phillips protected his sources of information, but he wasn't going to stand by and let 30 angry men take care of the Serial Kisser.

As the room emptied, Myke grabbed Sonny Boneau, Scarface Mahoney and the other folks who had met around some beers and said, "Hang on just a second, fellas."

"What did we do?" Sonny demanded.

"Let's see, kidnapping, false imprisonment, battery ... for starters," Myke replied. "And boys? It's still not safe for burglars and robbers on the streets of this town."

He turned to the Serial Kisser, who was looking at him with a grateful expression, and began to untie his bindings.

"I could just kiss you," the man said.

"Don't push your luck."

Epilogue

DANA pulled back after one of the most luscious kisses in the history of kisses, definitely somewhere in the Hot 100.

"What was that for?" Paul asked, holding her close so that their lips were in close proximity in case she wanted to dive in again and shoot for the Top Ten.

"Thank you for catching the bad guy and protecting my honor against that dastardly devil," she smiled with that look in her eyes that always melted him.

"Actually, I saved him from a fate far worse than he's going to get at the hands of the judge," he said, almost ruefully.

Dana reached up and wrapped her lips around his left earlobe. "That's because you're the good guy," she whispered.

"Yeah, I guess. The police would have caught up to all of that eventually, though. These were petty criminals, not exactly evil at the level that demands a response from Mychus the Warrior."

"Oh, cripes, I gave up a long time ago trying to get through your skull," said a familiar voice from the general vicinity of the knickknack shelf. The Soulkeeper of Kiribati was checking in again.

"What?" Paul said, accustomed to having his romantic moments interrupted by a wise-cracking piece of pottery. "You think Astor City needed Myke Phoenix to break that up?"

"Wendell Hanrahan sure needed Myke tonight."

"Who is Wendell Hanrahan?"

"The serial kisser, you idiot," the vase said. "You didn't hang around to find out his name? He was about to be killed by an angry mob of men, some who never did anything stupid in their lives before and never will again."

"Oh, come on, they weren't going to kill him."

"Never underestimate the power of a mob to commit stupidity once they're riled up, especially when they've been riled up by the Forces of Evil in the World."

"What are you talking about?"

"Think about it, if you have any synapses at all snapping tonight," the vase said. "Three dozen guys are prepared to commit aggravated battery against a serial kisser? Why do you think they got so agitated? It's the Evil."

"That's kind of a weird way to show itself."

"You wait. It's just warming up."

The house was well-built and energy tight, but a chilly breeze crossed the living room and through Paul Phillips' bones.

"Come on, Paul," Dana said, tugging gently on his arms and leading him to the next room with a wary eye on the ugly green vase. "I'm feeling the urge for some serial kissing of my own."

Spiders of Fire

Prologue

EVERY spring the Astor City Service Club held its Philanthropists' Ball on the luxury cruise ship *River Girl*, which operated on the Shikaakwa River during the warmer months of the year. This year's ball was the biggest yet.

All of the folks who could be counted on to donate to the important charities and foundations were there, having a good time, bidding up the auction items, tipping the celebrity waiters, dancing to the ballroom band, and generally doing their best to support the important charities and foundations while enjoying each other's company.

The furnishings were festive. The food was festive. The mood was festive. It was quite the festive night until the giant spider spit flame and set everything on fire.

There actually was some debate over whether it actually was a giant spider. Most everyone agreed that a stream of flame flashed through the night and set the decorations over the open deck on fire, which in turn set everything flammable on the deck on fire, which spread to the rest of the vessel. Not everyone believed that the stream of flame came from a giant spider in the water. Also, and this might not surprise you, some people who did see a giant spider in the water emphatically refused to say that's what they saw.

Everyone agreed that the ship leaned precariously to starboard (or to the right, if they didn't know their port from their starboard, or to the left, if they were facing the back of the ship when it leaned), pitching a couple dozen well-dressed people into the river and almost capsizing the boat (although some people objected to calling the ship a "boat"). Not everyone believed that the unexplained tilt was caused by a giant spider trying to climb on board. And some who saw spidery feet clinging to the rail refused to call them spidery feet.

Matt Metroleo, a staff member for the caterer, insisted that he wasn't drinking on the job and, more important, that he saw a giant spider start to climb onto the railing on the main deck and spit fire at the decorations on the upper deck, which caused the blaze that gutted the ship and nearly killed a bunch of people. A small handful of people, who *had* been drinking, vouched for Matt's veracity and accuracy, but a combination of factors strained credulity.

For example, no one before that night had ever seen a spider the size of an elephant. Everyone knows that spiders do not, as a rule, spit fire. And everyone assumed there was a more reasonable and logical explanation for the ship to tip dramatically on its side and catch fire.

The main problem was that no one could find a more reasonable and logical explanation. And so it became a matter for the city's resident superhero to investigate.

Act 1

Three Scientists

JOSIAH Petri stepped over the ruins of a table on the blackened, debris-filled deck of the *River Girl*.

"Wow, how did nobody get killed from this?" he mused to himself.

The devastation was as complete as could be without actually sinking the ship. What wasn't burned was severely charred, and with the stuff falling from the ceiling and all the furnishings ablaze, you'd think someone would have been hurt more seriously than anyone was.

Yes, here was probably the combustion point – the charring seemed to emanate from this point, low on the wall of the center-deck cabin where the ballroom was located.

The forensics investigator leaned in for a closer look, reaching his rubber-gloved hand to scrape a sample of the burned matter for further examination, when a hand clamped on his right shoulder and made him jump.

"What are you finding, Josie?" said a big man in a white uniform with the image of a red-and-gold bird emblazoned across the chest.

"Good grief, Myke, why can't you NOT sneak up on people?" Petri grumbled when his heartbeat returned to a semi-normal pace. "And please don't call me 'Josie.'"

"Have you looked at me lately? It's hard for me to sneak up on anyone."

Myke Phoenix was Astor City's resident superhero. Strong as an ox and possessed of an invulnerable body, he had been a thorn in the side of evil and plain-old-bad guys for nearly two decades. But, contrary to what he'd just said, he also had the ability to come up behind Josiah Petri without a sound despite his great bulk.

"Sorry about that, Josiah," the white-suited newcomer said, but with a slight smile that suggested he enjoyed surprising his friend. "I guess this is the wrong outfit to wear to a fire scene."

"That's why God invented dry cleaners, or whatever you use on that costume of yours," Petri said.

"Are you buying the giant spider theory yet?" Myke asked.

Now, it might seem odd to you or me that anyone would take something as outlandish as the giant spider theory seriously. But that's because you and I don't live in Astor City, which had been menaced by a talking duck, a taloned dinosaur whose capacity for evil bordered on genius, and numerous other fantastic threats in the years since Myke Phoenix had emerged as an equally fantastic force for good.

Still ...

"No, that seems too fantastic," Josiah Petri said. "The fire started here, but my first guess is a manmade source, a flame-thrower or something. I'll know more when I do a chemical analysis of the rubble."

Myke looked up and down the deck.

"How did nobody get killed from this?"

"You know, I said the exact same thing just before you scared next week out of me. Amazing destruction."

Somehow – probably due to Myke's super-sharp eyes – he saw something black against the black that didn't seem to belong. The big guy walked over to the railing and plucked the unusual thing from the floor.

"What do you suppose this is?"

The large something was a chunk about the size and consistency of a dinner platter, but with little bristles attached. Myke tapped on the chunk and it sounded sort of like plastic or fiberglass.

"It's sure not a piece of the boat or any of the furnishings," Petri said. "I'll bag that and take a look in the lab."

"Maybe it's giant spider dandruff," Myke said with a chuckle.

"Right," Petri laughed back, but both men sounded a little anxious.

Paul Phillips and his wife, Dana, had lucked out 16 years earlier when they bought a new house on the edges of the Astor City limits. The place was within their means, and it came with a wooded 2-acre lot so they had a little privacy and room to breathe. The way the neighborhood had grown up around them, if they built it today they'd have to come up with quite a few more pennies.

He sat in his easy chair looking out the back window at a cardinal flitting around the bird feeder. Paul was a 40-something man with traces of gray and white in his hair, but he was in fairly good physical shape – definitely not a couch potato but, to tell the truth, not as fit as his alter ego. But then, no one was as fit as Myke Phoenix.

Yes, the middle-aged man watching the bird feeder had the ability to switch bodies with an ancient warrior named Mychus, whose soul went to its reward a long time ago but whose mighty body was held in reserve for those moments when Astor City needed a defender against the forces of evil. How that process worked, where Mychus' body was stored when not needed, and where Paul's body was when he was inside Mychus – well, he tried not to overthink the situation. The Soulkeeper of Kiribati had always assured him he was safe, and in two decades the Soulkeeper had always been right.

"This is very weird," Paul said out loud. "I have a hinky feeling that the people who think they saw a giant spider weren't hallucinating."

It's not unusual for people to talk out loud when they're alone in their living room looking out the window. It's a little more unusual when they get an answer.

"You were the one who was complaining last week that you haven't battled any monsters or supervillains lately," a voice said from the general direction of a bookshelf.

There was an ancient, misshapen pale-green vase on that shelf, with a crudely drawn image of a red bird and clear, red and blue jewels arranged in rows across its top and bottom and studded randomly about. It held a prominent place among the other knick-knacks and books on the shelf, but it also looked out of place because it was so very old and, well, ugly.

This was the Soulkeeper of Kiribati, which held the essence of Mychus in safe-keeping somehow and also served as advisor – of sorts – to Paul Phillips. The same mysterious force that enabled it to carry a warrior's essence also kept it in touch with unseen powers in the world and universe.

"So you're saying there *is* a giant spider wandering around the city somewhere?" Paul said, turning his attention away from the cardinal and looking at the vase.

"Can't say for sure, but I wouldn't be surprised," the voice said. The sound never seemed to be coming directly from the vase but it definitely hovered in the general direction of the pottery. It was a masculine voice with feminine undertones, or else it was a feminine voice with masculine undertones. "As one of your favorite movie characters might say, there's a disturbance in the forces lately."

"'Force' – there's a disturbance in the Force," Paul said.

"I just said that, didn't I? It's an evil disturbance, too, not good, not good at all," it said.

"Like maybe a giant spider."

"Might be more than one. This is a major shaking."

Paul just stared at the vase for a few seconds, contemplating the idea of Myke Phoenix versus a squadron of giant spiders ...

"Hey, it could be worse. Could be zombies."

"Z – zombies?! There's no such thing as zombies!"

"How do you know?" The vase let the question hang in the air, and then added, "No. There's not. I was just spoofing you."

"Who would be behind a bunch of giant spiders that breathe fire? How do I find him? Or her," he added, recalling that his arch-nemesis, Deinonychus, was a female dinosaur of historic viciousness.

"I am a mere pot that sits on the shelf. I can only sense this stuff, I can't draw you a map," the vase said, modestly – for very few glass vases in the world have the power to detect evil in the atmosphere or carry the soul of a mighty warrior. "You're going to have to find the bad guys yourself, same as always. Or I suspect if you just wait long enough, they'll turn up again."

The forensics lab was in the corner of the Astor City Justice Center's basement, and they could use a little more space. Every year Josiah Petri asked the county board for more room, and every year they told him there wasn't enough money in the budget for expansion. He made do, but it wasn't ideal.

Petri had company when Myke Phoenix came by to visit, so the lab was even more cramped than usual. An older man – maybe 60 or so – was huddled over a microscope next to Josiah, and an extremely attractive younger woman – early 30s – was standing behind them.

"Astonishing," the older man was muttering. "Why, if this is what I think it is, everything we know is forever changed."

"That sounds ominous," Myke said, sounding as chipper as he could.

"Myke," Josiah said in greeting. "This is Dr. Travers from the University of Astor City, and this is –"

"Dr. Travers," the attractive woman said, extending a hand. "Dr. Terri Travers."

"Are you related by marriage or –?"

"She's my daughter, the best arachnologist in the country, and that's not just a proud papa talking," the bearded professor said with a grin. He almost had a Santa Claus quality about him. "Jacob Travers. A pleasure to meet you, sir."

"Arachnologist? As in somebody who studies spiders?"

"Yes, I taught her everything she knows, and she took it all to the next level," Travers said with a wink.

"Stop it, Dad, he's going to think I'm Wonder Woman or something," his daughter said. (If you think this could be not a throwaway line but a foreshadowing of a plot element that I'm tucking away for a future adventure, you may be right. But it works as a throwaway line, too.)

"So we're taking the giant spider invasion seriously now, Josie?"

"Just covering all the bases, Mikey," Petri said with a look that meant someday he was going to stop responding altogether – or worse – when Myke called him Josie.

"It's far too early in this investigation to draw any conclusions," she said. "But Dr. Petri did find some fascinating material in the charred debris." Was there more than professional admiration on her face when she turned to look at Josiah? Something to think about later.

"Yes," Petri said after an awkward pause – well, he appeared to have been distracted by her look, too. "DNA in the burned spots. As if the fire was organic."

"Spider DNA?" Myke gaped.

"As we said, it's too early to draw any conclusions," Jacob Travers said. "Right now it's all theory and speculation, and I'd hate to make any recommendations based on a theory. You'd think we were crazy if we told you what we were thinking."

"I'm guessing that you think this attack may have been carried off by one or more giant spiders that spit fire the way regular spiders spit webs," the big man in the white suit said.

They looked at him as if they'd been caught sending texts to each other in the back of the classroom.

But all Terri Travers said was, "Spiders don't spit webs. The silk comes from spinneret glands located at the tip of the abdomen."

Myke Phoenix waved his hands in exasperation.

"If there's a chance giant spiders are lurking around the city, don't you think the authorities would like to know sooner rather than later?"

The father and daughter exchanged a guilty but determined glance.

"It could not hurt to wait until we have some verification," she said. "If I can get these samples to the university lab and perform a microscopic examination, you'll have an answer by this afternoon."

"Well, maybe you should get these samples to your lab," Josiah Petri said gently, packing them up and shooing them out the door.

The forensic scientist and superhero looked at each other.

"I'll call the police," Petri said.

"I'll get in touch with my buddy in the military," Myke Phoenix added.

As Myke hurried away, Josiah Petri shouted, "And don't call me Josie!"

Act 2

Another party spoiled

DANA Dunsmore Phillips dressed up nice. One of the little pleasures in Paul Phillips' life was that his wife, Dana, dressed up most of the time. Today was no exception.

"Wow, Scoop, a lot of these people were at the Philanthropist Ball last night," she whispered to Paul. She was the only one who called him "Scoop," and the only one who could get away with it. "I guess a little fire doesn't get them down for long."

The lunch-hour reception was to announce plans for the major renovation of a well-known downtown Astor City office building. Once upon a time the first two floors had been a 5-and-10 variety store, the kind of quaint establishment made obsolete by the big-box stores on the edge of town, and the top nine floors housed the offices of a motley mixture of small to medium-sized businesses.

Now the structure was to gain new life as a complex of waterfront condominiums, with esoteric retail stores on the first floor and the second floor repurposed as a restaurant/ballroom/meeting place. With the area cleared and the old store's light fixtures and fine wooden trim exposed again, it wasn't hard to envision the possibilities.

The movers and shakers of the city were again gathered on that second floor, and the main players in this project were beginning to gather around a small tub of soil had been brought in to stage a ceremonial groundbreaking ceremony.

"So the spider scientists pulled the old 'neither confirm nor deny' maneuver on you, did they?" Dana said to Paul, who – when he wasn't trading bodies with a superpowered ancient warrior – spent much of his day tracking down news for the Astor City Beacon news blog.

"They made a lot of noise about wanting to test their hypothesis before coming out with a theory," Paul said, fishing in his pocket for a small camera. "But they made enough noise to show that they're taking the giant-spider reports seriously."

"Well, you were the one who was complaining last week that Myke Phoenix hasn't had any supervillains or monsters to fight lately," she teased.

"Oh please, now you sound like the darn vase," he chuckled. "There's Mark, I need to talk to him quick."

Mark Fielding was the mover and shaker whose dollars were being leveraged to give new life to the old building. For purposes of this narrative, he also was a colonel in the National Guard and as such had played a role years earlier in thwarting the plans of the evil talking dinosaur, Deinonychus, arch-nemesis of Myke Phoenix.

Between the two roles he had generated his share of news coverage, and so he knew Paul Phillips in all of his incarnations as he moved from radio anchorman to newspaper reporter to news blogger – although he didn't realize that he had also been working with Paul when he stood with the city's superheroic protector.

"Hello there, Paul," Fielding said, flashing his quiet but confident multimillionaire's smile. "Are you really doing the Beacon all by yourself? You have more news than the Tribune most days."

"Thanks, it's mostly smoke and mirrors and a little bit of hustle," the middle-aged journalist said, relatively modestly. "I need your National Guard hat for a minute – any thoughts about the cruise boat fire last night?"

"Wow, how did nobody get killed from that, you know what I mean?" Fielding said. "Did you hear anything about what caused it?"

"Some of the folks say they saw a giant spider that spat flame," Phillips said. "I thought maybe somebody had passed that along to the Guard, just in case."

"Oh, you heard that, did you," Fielding said, his smile waning just a hair. "Well, we really don't have any contingency plans for giant spiders, although we'd have to whip some up in a hurry if that proves to be true. But we need something more to go on than a few eyewitnesses who'd been drinking on a cruise ship at night."

It's amazing sometimes how things happen right on cue. While Fielding's response was hanging in the air and Paul reached into his mind for the next question, several ladies (and at least two or three men) screamed as a large window shattered and a stream of flame flashed over everyone's heads from the window halfway across the huge open floor.

You'd have to be looking directly at Paul Phillips to witness the transformation, and of course everyone was looking either at the stream of fire or toward the window where all the shouting was. One instant the reporter was whirling around to see what all the commotion was, and in less than a blink of an eye, his space was occupied by a huge, blond-haired man in a white suit emblazoned with the image of a red bird.

That's how fast Myke Phoenix could arrive on the scene when he was needed. Usually Paul had time to will the change, but in an emergency it just happened in less than a blink of an eye. This was an emergency.

The big spider was crawling through the 10-foot-tall opening created by the shattered window. It was black and hairy with eight legs and – well, you know what a spider looks like. Just imagine if it was the size of an elephant, and you can envision the scene. The ceiling was scorched, and little flames licked here and there, but the greater menace was the big, black hairy thing with eight legs crawling through the window.

Myke had just enough room to leap over the crowd and place himself between them and the monster. He wound up a fist and planted his mightiest punch in the middle of the thing's giant face.

Now, the mightiest punch of Myke Phoenix has stopped quite a few unearthly menaces in their tracks. This was no exception, although the punch did not have as much of an effect as he was accustomed. The big spider fell back against the wall, squealed an unearthly squeal, and jumped back out the window.

Apparently not especially staggered by the blow, the thing scurried away from the building and disappeared around a corner. It was a little unnerving to see something the size of an elephant scurrying, but "scurry" is the best word to describe how fast it traveled. Some people thought they heard a big splash from the direction of the nearby docks.

No one had been looking at Paul Phillips when the commotion broke out, but quite a few people were looking at Myke Phoenix now. So he jumped out the window and ran in the general direction the spider had gone, but as soon as he was out of sight he switched back to being Paul and made his way back to the reception as fast as he could. And since he had not seen what happened to Dana, he moved very fast indeed.

Several people had grabbed fire extinguishers and had the small ceiling fires under control. The room was buzzing – no one seemed to be seriously hurt, although there were minor burns here and there – and Dana came running up and threw her arms around Paul.

"Did you get it?" she whispered.

"It was too fast, and I wanted to make sure everyone was OK here," he replied.

"That punch didn't knock it out?" Dana's eyes widened.

"Slowed it down a little, but it ran away as soon as it hit the ground."

As the dust cleared, Paul's phone buzzed.

"Paul Phillips."

"Hey buddy, are you sitting down?" It was Josiah Petri's voice. "I just heard from the Travers family over at the university."

"Oh, yeah?"

"That chunk with the bristles that Myke found is definitely a piece of spider that got chipped off somehow during the ruckus last night. Only it's hundreds of times larger than any spider anyone has ever seen. What's all that commotion in the background?"

"Downtown just got hit by a spider hundreds of times larger than any spider anyone has ever seen."

"Hey," Petri said wryly. "What a coincidence."

Drs. Jacob and Terri Travers seemed contrite but defiant at the same time.

"It's unfortunate that we needed to delay a few hours, but if we had confirmed the existence of the great spider right away this morning without doing any tests, would it have made any difference when the spider appeared again?" Jacob Travers said.

"There might have been a National Guard squad nearby," Myke Phoenix said. "The military didn't want to get involved based on rumors and speculation."

"The military!?" Dr. Terri Travers pulled herself up into full umbrage. "That does it. I was afraid you'd want to kill this beast – that's why I delayed confirming its existence until I was absolutely sure."

"No offense, doc, but what do you do with a spider that's causing trouble except swat it?" Josiah asked cautiously.

"We should capture it for study!" she said. "Spiders are not horrid creatures; they're one of the most useful animals in existence. They keep pests under control in gardens and agriculture; they mean no harm."

"Except when they're burning down cruise boats and terrorizing crowds of people," Myke said. "Look, Dr. Travers, I'm sure most spiders are wonderful critters, but this particular spider is like nothing we've ever seen before. What evidence do you have that it's harmless? Because, I gotta tell you, it sure seems pretty dangerous to me."

"Don't you see? That's why we should study it," Terri Travers insisted. "Who knows why it's acting the way it is? You're right, it's like nothing we've ever seen before, and to our knowledge it's the only one of its kind. You can't just blindly destroy it."

"Oh yes we can, if it's threatening the people of this city," Myke said firmly. "Tell you what, I'll talk to Colonel Fielding and see if there's a way to capture this thing without getting a bunch of soldiers and civilians killed."

That seemed to calm the doctor's fury for a moment.

"There's one thing I still don't understand," Josiah Petri said. "I've never heard of a spider that shoots fire. How is that possible?"

"Well," Jacob Travers said, and father and daughter exchanged a troubled glance again.

"Well –?" Petri said, encouraging him to finish the sentence.

Terri Travers let out a sigh. "We discovered higher levels of radiation in areas where the stream of fire made a direct hit. Not dangerous levels, but it's definitely radioactive."

That little bit of information hung in the air for a good 10 seconds or so. If that doesn't seem like a long pause, consider that a good athlete can run 100 meters in 10 seconds. A lot can happen in that length of time, and so when nothing is happening it can seem like a very long pause indeed.

"A radioactive spider," Myke Phoenix said. "What is this, a comic book?"

"– says the guy wearing a superhero suit," Josiah Petri said.

Madison Macintosh was feeling more stressed than a 16-year-old girl normally feels – and if you've ever known or been a 16-year-old girl, you know that's a lot of stress. Everything looked beautiful, and yet it didn't.

"We're missing something," she insisted to groans all around. "I just don't know what it is."

"Oh, what-ever, Maddy," said Aileen Rabinowicz, rolling her eyes. "We've been here for hours, and everyone else thinks it looks fabulous. Let's go home."

Astor City Central High School was having its spring prom the next night, and a dozen girls – and three guys anxious to please them – had been decorating the gymnasium with streamers and balloons and all of the gaudy details that make prom the most romantic and precious time of the year, if not the entire high school experience. Madison, the prom committee chairperson, agreed that the gym looked special, but was it special enough?

She walked under the vast tangle of crepe paper and mylar thoughtfully, turning herself around to see it all from every angle. The others sighed and looked at the doors, hoping to escape after a good night's work.

Finally, Madison smiled and allowed herself to breathe.

"I guess it does look pretty wonderful after all," she said, lowering her eyes and beginning to turn toward the rest of the committee when – "What's that on the floor?"

Her attention had been captured by what appeared to be a puddle of water in the corner of the gym. Walking over, she discovered, well, a puddle of water in the corner.

As she approached, a drop of water – actually, to tell the truth, it was a big glob of water as opposed to a drop *per se* – fell from above and landed in the puddle.

Madison Macintosh looked up, took a second to inhale, and let out a blood-curdling scream.

Stretched across the corner of the gymnasium ceiling, about the size of the giant nets they use to catch field goals at football games, was a spider web.

Act 3
The web and the casualty

MYKE Phoenix, Josiah Petri, and Drs. Terri and Jacob Travers stood just inside the door of the Astor City Central High School gymnasium, looking up at the enormous spider web. Jacob Travers pointed at a big fuzzy glob on the wall behind the web.

"That looks like an egg cluster," he said. "Won't know until we get up there."

"Don't you need more than one spider to fertilize eggs?" Josiah said.

"Normally," Terri Travers agreed. "Although this is not a normal spider."

She started walking toward the corner of the gym.

"Hold on, professor," Myke Phoenix said, catching up and stopping her with a touch of the arm. "Now look, we don't know what we're going to find up there or what'll happen – but there's one thing for sure, it's no place for –"

"For what? For a woman?" Terri Travers snapped. "Are you that much of a complete neanderthal?"

"I was going to say, it's no place for someone who isn't bulletproof."

"Oh. Sorry," she said. "But still, there's no time to give you a fast course in arachnid pathology. So let's stop all the talk and get on with it."

"Sure, no problem," Myke said. "Just let me go first."

The web was more than 20 feet off the ground, and this was one of those times when Myke Phoenix wished he could fly instead of merely having invulnerable skin and super strength. It's astonishing how people always want a little bit more than they already possess.

They had procured a cherry-picker unit from the city, and Myke and Dr. Travers climbed into the bucket. With a city utility worker at the controls below, they were lifted up close to the web in the general direction of the big fuzzy glob on the wall.

"You don't see a giant spider around here anywhere, do you?" Myke asked.

"No, just the web," she said distractedly. "That definitely is an egg cluster. We should try to cut it away and get it back to the lab."

"What, so giant baby spiders can hatch and take over the university?" said the superhero. "I'm thinking it might be wise to just smush it at this stage."

"Spoken like the typical ignoramus who doesn't understand science," Dr. Travers replied, and then seemed to realize what had just come out of her mouth. "Sorry, no offense meant, it's just that our culture seems to smush first, ask questions later, to use your colorful word."

"Well, Mama Spider took out a cruise boat and caused a major panic at the Fielding Center this afternoon," he said. "I'm not real interested in seeing what her kiddies are capable of."

"You'll be happy to know that taking the eggs away from this environment will seriously deplete the new spiders' chances of survival," she said, somewhat sadly. I imagine we'll need something like a machete to cut that away from the wall as carefully as possible."

"If I can get up there, I may be able to pull it away from the wall."

"Don't be foolish, the proportionate adhesive power of an egg cluster that large would be impossible to remove by hand."

Myke wrapped his hand around a strand of the web and then tried to let go. It was sticky – sticky enough that he warned Dr. Travers not to follow but not so sticky that he was afraid he'd be stuck, being extremely powerful and all – so he climbed up and made his way slowly toward the egg mass. The thing was about seven feet long and three feet wide, protruding a foot and a half or so from the wall.

He tugged and pushed and got his arm under the mass, pulling and tugging to get it away from the wall. After a couple of minutes, it was almost detached.

"Careful!" Dr. Travers said, and she started to climb out of the bucket. She grabbed a strand of the web and, unlike Myke, was stuck fast. Pull as she might, strain as she might, she couldn't unclench the fist that was wrapped around the sticky strand.

The mighty warrior gave one last tug, and the egg mass fell to the floor with a sickening PLOP.

"Oops," said Myke Phoenix.

"SCREEEEEEEEEEEEEeeeeeeeeeeee," came a screech from behind the web near the ceiling.

"Hokey smokes," Myke Phoenix muttered. "Mama was up there all along."

Unfolding itself from its perch, the giant spider stretched itself out and took a menacing stance. Myke maneuvered himself into position on the web, standing between the big hairy beast and the cherry-picker bucket, and made a fist. He'd knocked the thing out a second-story window once; if he put everything he had into one massive punch, then maybe –

"No!!" the scientist cried in alarm. "You fool, can't you see? It's intelligent! It's sentient! She's angry that you destroyed her babies."

Myke looked over his shoulder.

"What does THAT have to do with anything? This thing is – OOLF!"

Technically, "oolf" is not a word, merely an approximation of the sound Myke Phoenix made when a spider leg caught him in the side of the head and sent him sprawling toward the gymnasium floor.

Fortunately, he recovered in time to land on his feet and spring back up to the cherry-picker with his powerful legs, because he was back in position blocking the spider from Dr. Travers when the eight-legged creature let loose with a stream of fire.

Terri Travers screamed in fear and pain as the flames raced over her hand, which was still stuck to the web. The good news is that the fire poked a hole in the web so she was able to pull her hand back; the bad news is that the fire first had to strike that portion of the web with her hand still attached.

Pulling his feet up off the web with an effort after each step, Myke advanced on the spider as fast as he could and delivered the haymaker he'd intended in the first place. He didn't have the solid footing of a ballroom floor to plant his feet, but the blow still shook the giant arachnid back on its heels. Once again the blow did not stop the big spider; it quickly lowered itself to the ground on a strand of web and scurried through the double doors to the outside of the gym. Josiah Petri, Jacob Travers, and the utility worker, needless to say, gave the thing a wide berth.

Explosions outside and further screeches assured Myke that the military had arrived on the scene, so he turned his attention to the wounded scientist. Her hand was not a pretty sight, and part of her right sleeve was burned away, exposing a bright red and blistered arm. The big warrior took her up in his arms and, not willing to wait for the cherry picker to ease them down, leaped to the floor, absorbing the impact with his mighty legs.

"Hopefully they've got a medic out there," Myke Phoenix barked. "That hand needs immediate attention."

The firing had stopped, so they ventured a peek out the door. The scene was strangely quiet, given that a giant flame-spitting spider had walked out the door and several explosions had followed. The National Guard and its tanks had arrived on the scene, and there was clear evidence the tanks had fired their guns – smoke, little fires, holes in the pavement, and the like – but there was no sign of the giant flame-spitting spider, and everyone was just sort of standing by in stunned silence.

Myke spotted an ambulance and raced Terri Travers over there. Colonel Mark Fielding, now in uniform, walked briskly toward them.

"Is this the professor who said we should study that thing, not shoot at it?" Fielding said earnestly. "Well, you'll be happy to know that after further study, shooting at it doesn't work anyway. Sloughed off bullets and tank shells like they were confetti."

Josiah Petri ran up to them, with Dr. Jacob Travers hustling up behind.

"Ouch!" Josiah said when he saw Terri Travers' hand. Red and blistered, the burn crept up her forearm and met the place where her lab coat sleeve ended with a ragged char. Her palm was blackened where it had been clutching the spider web.

"'Ouch' is not exactly the first word that crosses my mind," she said, gritting her teeth as a medic gave full attention to the injury.

"I'm sorry," the forensic scientist said, a look of something more than professional concern crossing his face. "I just wish there was something I can do."

"Your specialty is finding cause of death, so I'm happy that there's nothing you can do for me just now," she said with a grim smile. And perhaps she returned that look of something more than professional interest. "But you're wrong, Colonel Fielding, I believe you did injure the spider – and you, Mr. Phoenix, you clearly hurt her emotionally."

"I hurt its feelings?" the mighty warrior sputtered.

"Dropping the egg sac most certainly damaged the developing young, probably fatally," she said. "There was agony in that screech. I'm surprised she didn't attack you – but perhaps there's a clue in that action, or lack of action if you will."

"How do you mean?" Petri asked. She glanced back at him.

"She most certainly had cause to attack, but she fled. That tells me she doesn't really want to do harm."

"It tells *me* that Myke Phoenix's punches are the only thing that has stung her so far," Fielding barked back. "She did some serious harm to that cruise boat last night, and on purpose. What did you mean when you said we injured the thing?"

The arachnologist pointed with her left hand at several sticky puddles on the school parking lot.

"She's bleeding," Terri Travers said. "Or at least she bled. I don't know how fast she can heal."

"We should get you to a hospital, daughter," Jacob Travers spoke for the first time, ashen-faced.

"Not just yet, doctor," the colonel said, leaning in. "How do we kill this thing?"

Dr. Terri Travers' eyes welled with tears, and it wasn't because there was a third-degree burn covering her right hand.

"You swat it," she said softly, resigned. "Find a way to crush it. Or suck it into a vacuum cleaner."

Fielding gave a little snort.

"Where do you suggest we get a vacuum cleaner for a spider the size of an elephant?"

Terri Travers looked sadly in the direction of the man inhabiting Mychus the Warrior's powerful body.

"You don't need a vacuum if you have someone who can generate enough force to use the swatter," she said. "Now, if you'll excuse me, I think I'm going into shock now." And she closed her eyes.

"Get her to the hospital," Myke Phoenix said. "I'll take it from here."

In his time, Myke Phoenix had battled a talking dinosaur, a half-man-half-duck, and numerous other odd creatures that were not exactly human and not exactly like any animal ever seen before.

And now, a giant spider that spit fire. The part about a gigantic arachnid was quite enough without the extra added attraction of spitting fire.

"What is it about this town that attracts sentient freaks of nature?" Colonel Mark Fielding said to no one in particular.

"Some kind of evil presence settled over this area about 20 years ago," Myke Phoenix replied, not realizing it was more of a rhetorical question. "It's the main reason I was called into action in the first place."

Fielding stopped in mid-thought and stared at his superpowered friend.

"Really? All of these bizarre beings are connected?"

"Well, no, not connected exactly," Myke replied. "It's more like the evil attracts them to this general vicinity."

"You believe that," Fielding said quietly. "Well, I can't explain you, either, so it makes as much sense as anything."

They were working on a huge and unwieldy trap of sorts. Welders were welding a large, waffled steel plate onto a sturdy pole made of a more flexible steel alloy. It looked very much like a fly swatter if the insect were about the size of an elephant – although a spider technically is not an insect – this fly swatter was huge and unwieldy, with the exception that everyone was counting on the thought that at least one person could indeed wield it.

"It won't be ready for a little while, that seam has to cool off," Fielding said.

"Maybe we can slow it down in the meantime before anyone else gets hurt," Myke said. "I'll go out and look for the spider; ship the swatter to me when it's good to go."

Act 4
Swatting a spider

NIGHTTIME in Astor City was like nighttime in just about any medium-sized city in America. The lights shone brightly; the men and women smiled when they weren't frowning or shouting at each other; people were in too much of a hurry to really enjoy themselves or notice how grand the lives they were living really were; people were in too much of a hurry to really let it sink in how shallow the lives they were living really were.

In all of this, waiting here on the shore of the Shikaakwa River and on the high palisades overlooking the river at the edge of the city, a contingent of National Guard troops stood vigilant. The laughter and loud music downtown contrasted with the tense and even eerie silence of the expectant soldiers.

And then ...

"There it is!" A finger pointing at a stream of fire from the river shore.

"Yaaaaaaaaaaaaaaaaaaaaaaaaah!" Several men and women reacting to the flames licking over their heads.

"Yikes! Everybody out!" Men scrambling out of a tank engulfed in flames that raised the interior temperatures to intolerable levels.

Automatic weapons fire splintered the night as a monstrous figure with eight legs scrambled out of the river and over the tank, through an opening in the flames, and back into the dark.

"After it!" a staff sergeant yelled.

"Sarge, I thought they said the thing was the size of an elephant," a nearby private ventured. "That thing looked like a small building to me, like a house."

"I know. Maybe it's growing," the sergeant muttered, hopefully.

The radio crackled and came to life.

"It's up here! On the palisades!" the voice on the radio said. "They were right, it's as big as an elephant!"

The sergeant, being good at his trade, immediately ordered some of his unit to stay on the river shore and keep looking out at the water.

"If we just saw one as big as a house and there's one big as an elephant up on the palisades," he said firmly, "we have more than one of these things."

In a seventh-floor room at St. Valentine Hospital in downtown Astor City, Dr. Terri Travers' hand and arm were sufficiently wrapped in all that the medical doctors could do for them. Now it was a matter of waiting on the slow process of healing. She also was pumped with a sufficient quantity of the best pain-killing medication available.

"It's funny," she said to her companion, Josiah Petri, as a TV game show chattered away from the glowing box near the ceiling in front of the bed. "The drugs don't exactly take away the pain, but they make it so I don't mind it."

"That sounds uncomfortable," Josiah said.

"No, not really," she smiled serenely.

And then the television program was abruptly cut off and replaced by a stern-looking but attractive young woman wearing a stylish, low-cut blouse.

"Firespiders in downtown Astor City," the woman intoned dramatically. "Creatures like the one that destroyed the cruise boat *River Girl* last night have appeared on Presidential Avenue and near the palisades."

"More than one," Dr. Terri Travers whispered, and she sat up, making motions as if to leave.

"Oh, no, you don't," Petri said firmly, standing and grabbing her by the shoulders before she could fully swing herself to the side of the bed.

Her head sagged a little bit to the side. She smiled a slight, crooked smile and her eyes became slits.

"Oh! No, I don't," she purred, and allowed Josiah to ease her back down onto the pillow. "I am certainly in no condition to move from this bed tonight." She opened her eyes. "But they need my help! I have to tell them –" She closed her eyes.

"Tell them what, Dr. Travers?" Josiah asked. "Is it important?"

Her eyes fluttered open again.

"I forget," she admitted. "But call me Terri."

Years ago as a radio reporter, Paul Phillips had a small radio scanner on his desk that monitored the emergency chatter. Later he had a portable radio the size of a small walkie-talkie that he hooked to his belt and carried most places. These days he had a police scanner app on his smartphone, which he also used to listen to commercial radio, post breaking news on his blog, check for messages and occasionally make a phone call.

Inhabiting the body of Myke Phoenix, he had the smartphone securely Velcroed to his uniform and heard the two radio calls within seconds of each other, one from downtown and one from the park near the palisades. (In case you wonder about such things, the smartphone did not travel back and forth between this world and wherever the bodies of Mychus and Paul Phillips were stored when one was active and the other was wherever that other place is.

How the device knew to stay in this reality is a mystery beyond the purpose of the present narrative.)

Among Myke Phoenix's limits was an inability to be in two places at once. He had to choose which spider to chase. He was already heading toward downtown – where more people were likely to be – when the staff sergeant at the scene radioed that the beast at his location was significantly larger than an elephant.

"Good call, Mykie," he muttered to himself, and stepped up his pace.

He arrived at Colonel Mark Fielding's side in time to watch a spider the size of a two-story house rip the old art-deco "WACR" neon sign from the side of the building and toss it to the street below in a crash of glass and electric sparks.

"It's like something out of a Japanese monster movie," Fielding said.

"Except that's not a scale model of downtown Astor City and it's not a guy in a rubber suit," Myke said. "What now?"

Fielding took him by the arm, pulled him toward the spider and gave him a little shove.

"What else? Go get him."

Myke grinned and raced toward the spider.

He had to jump over crowds of screaming men and women running the other way. It took five or six bounds to carry him the couple of blocks and land at the great spider's feet, grabbing it by one of its eight ankles.

The thing turned its head, and Myke was looking into about eight eyes. It reared back and suddenly all he saw was flame.

"Whoa!" he said, losing his grip. Even an invulnerable superhero will flinch a little when he gets a faceful of fire.

The spider knocked a couple of cars over, almost as if for spite, and jumped onto the side of a building. Seeing that it was two stories tall to begin with, it attached itself level with the fourth floor and quickly scurried up to the seventh, then paused. After a moment the reason for the pause became more clear: It was looking, one by one, into the windows.

"Hokey smokes," Myke said. "That's St. Valentine's Hospital!"

The crash of the neon sign and overturned vehicles, and a bit of the screaming, could be heard up on the seventh floor. Josiah Petri walked over to the window and found himself face to face with an eight-eyed horror of a face. This, as you can imagine, was somewhat unsettling.

Before he had time to take in the sight completely and scream for his life, Josiah saw a large blond man in a white uniform land on the back of the giant spider's neck, raise his fists together, and punch down on the top of the spider's head. Man and spider slid down, but the great beast did not let go of its grip on the side of the building.

"She's looking for me," Terri Travers shouted from the bed. "She smells her child's scent from my burns."

"You mean it's looking for the smaller spider," Petri said.

"Yes, yes," she said. "The scent should be on Myke, too – he can lure her to the child."

But first Myke needed to be privy to this information. Currently he was on the other side of the window in a death struggle with a two-story-high spider.

Fortunately, the next thing that happened was the spider put its foot through that window, showering bits of safety glass across the room and allowing Josiah Petri the opportunity to finish letting out a somewhat manly shriek of terror.

When the foot withdrew, he leaned out and saw the white-costumed man hanging on to the spider's neck like a bronco buster.

"She's looking for the other spider – you have its scent on you – she's the mother – the scent will lead her away!" he said, summing up the situation as fast as he could.

"OK!" Myke said and allowed himself to be thrown clear. He struck the building across the street with a loud "Whoof!" and landed roughly but on his feet. Looking to make sure the giant spider was still interested in him, not the contents of the hospital room, he took off running.

"SCREEEEEeeeeeee," the big spider screamed.

"Come get me," the mighty warrior shouted as he ran up the hill as fast as he could – and, as you may have guessed by now, "as fast as he could" was very, very fast.

"Myke Phoenix is leading the big one up to the palisades," he heard over the scanner.

"Good, the swatter is ready and we have the little one cornered."

The swatter. Myke knew what he had to do, and now that he had a better grasp of what was happening, he had a sinking feeling in his heart. A mother protecting its child?

Fortunately, he was too busy trying to stay ahead of the scurrying giant spider to think too hard about it.

He made several great leaps up to the towering cliffs overlooking the river and asked the first soldier he saw, "Where's the swatter?"

"It's over there with the spider; we've injured it," the soldier said – and then he saw the monster crawling swiftly toward Myke Phoenix. "Holy Mother of –"

Myke took in the scene quickly. The spider the size of the elephant, dripping something ooze-like from a number of holes in its hide. Three tanks surrounding the wounded beast. A huge waffle with a massive handle attached. He wrapped his hands around the handle and, impossibly, lifted the waffle off the ground.

"Screeeeeeeeeeee!" both spiders screamed at once, as if understanding what was about to happen.

Moving faster than any human being could possibly be expected to move, Myke whipped the swatter over and the massive waffle flattened the smaller monster with the ugliest "SPLAT!!!!" in the long history of ugly splats.

For a moment there were no further sounds in the air except the random spattering of giant spider bits hitting the ground.

And then the remaining giant spider screamed.

This scream had a different tone than the screeches they had been hearing all night. Those screams had an angry tone. This scream was not angry; it was more heartbreaking than anything else. Myke lifted the giant swatter and tried to brandish it awkwardly, but the beast did not charge him as he expected.

"Fire! Fire! Fire!" Myke recognized the voice of Colonel Mark Fielding. Numerous automatic weapons and three tanks unloaded on the two-story-high monster, which seemed not to be terribly affected by the ordnance – until it staggered, just a little.

Eight gigantic eyes focused on Myke Phoenix. He did not know how to read the emotions on a spider's face; he only knew that eight eyes were boring into him.

And then the beast turned toward the edge of the cliff.

It braced to jump and launched itself into the night, tumbling end over end toward the jagged rocks below.

The latest unnatural menace to threaten Astor City was over. Myke Phoenix had come through again, but he didn't feel the thrill of triumph that often came at moments like this. He just felt unspeakably sad.

"It was like she didn't want to die up here at our hands," Fielding said, searching for a sign of spidery life among the rocks and waves in the darkness below them. "There's no way anything could have survived that plunge."

"There's never been a spider as big as a house," Myke said. "Who knows what kind of a jump it could survive?"

"Come on, Myke," the colonel sputtered. "Even if the fall didn't kill it, we pumped it full of bullets and tank shells. If it isn't dead now, it's well on its way to dying."

"I sure hope you're right," the tall blond man said. "I sincerely hope you're right."

THE END?

Epilogue

BEING ripped from its moorings and dropped to the ground had been catastrophic for the younglings in the spider egg sacs; none of them were viable. It appeared that only the mother and a single offspring had survived from the first batch.

It was over.

The bearded man sat staring across the lab.

"This was an unmitigated disaster, if I say so myself," he said out loud, a bit startled by the sound of his voice in the otherwise empty room.

Dousing it with radiation had indeed made the beast grow, as he had postulated, but it grew too much, and it was completely out of control. The experiment was a failure.

Worse, it had costs. His unsuspecting daughter may yet lose her hand to the severe burns. Dozens more people were injured, perhaps dead – the early news reports were spotty about that. This was a burden he would have to shoulder himself. If he had succeeded in creating a new breed of spider that would be even more efficient in eliminating garden pests, he would trumpet that triumph to the world. But this – this – better that the great spiders' origins remain a mystery.

"You old fool," he said. Too much radiation was easily solved. But how to make the beast more maleable, controllable – that would be the challenge next time.

Next time.

For there would indeed be a next time. The stakes were too high, the potential reward too great, to abandon the project now. If only he could enlist his daughter; her talent and knowledge of arachnids were far beyond his. But she had too much respect for spiders as they exist in nature; she would not approve this tinkering with the design. No, he would have to carry on the experiment as he had begun – by himself.

Dr. Jacob Travers sighed, took one last look around the lab for the night, and turned out the lights.

Invasion of the
Body Borrowers

Prologue

NO one really thinks of themselves as evil, not even beings from another planet who turn ordinary humans into zombies.

But please be assured, in the end these aliens were evil through and through.

That was really the disappointing part, because they generally seemed to be sincere enough. Trusting people is a good policy most of the time, although you need to be aware that not everyone deserves your trust but most folks do. In this case the aliens turned out to be "not everyone," which is a shame because contact with other worlds should be an exciting thing as opposed to a frightening thing.

In the case of *these* folks who came from outer space, it bordered closer to frightening.

It all started with a frantic call to ace reporter Paul Phillips, who was known to have connections with Astor City's resident superhero. The man's story was fantastic but rang just true enough to bring Myke Phoenix in on the case, and perhaps not a moment too soon.

Actually, that's not quite where it all started.

It all started when the night sky was interrupted by a huge meteor that flew overhead and crashed into a small hill a few miles away from the city.

At least at the time everyone thought it was a meteor – everyone except the man who called Paul Phillips.

Act 1

I, pod

MOST people don't wake up in the morning expecting a meteor the size of two city blocks to pass over their heads at low altitude and then crash a few miles away with a thud that rattles windows and makes pottery and dishes crash to the floor.

Paul Phillips, therefore, was startled when his morning coffee was interrupted by the screaming sound of something huge passing overhead, followed by a bone-rattling impact that sent heirloom dishes and a certain ugly green vase to certain splintering doom.

Oddly, while valuable Depression glass dutifully yielded to the forces of gravity meeting the hardwood floor and shattered into shards, the ugly green vase bounced and landed gracelessly on its side.

It had to land gracelessly; it was a graceless, misshapen thing with jewels dotted somewhat randomly around its surface and a rough painting of a red and golden bird emblazoned on its side.

"It figures you're indestructible, too," Phillips said, picking up the grotesque bit of pottery and tsk-tsking at the rest of the mess on the floor.

At that point the scene differed from your typical moment following a giant meteor strike or earthquake, in that the vase spoke back.

"How do you think I managed to survive all these centuries, smart guy?" came a voice that was somewhat masculine with just a tinge of androgyny. "I ain't as fragile as I look."

This was the Soulkeeper of Kiribati, the mysterious vase that somehow managed the exchange of Paul Phillips' body with that of Mychus, an ancient warrior whose soul had long ago gone to his final reward, creating the being that Paul named Myke Phoenix in a flight of fancy. How that exchange was managed remained a mystery to Paul for these 18 years Myke had watched over Astor City and fought off many a menace.

Paul, meanwhile, was either in his third career or still in the first, depending on your point of view. He had been a radio reporter and a newspaper reporter, and now he was the owner-operator-and-yes-reporter for the Astor City Beacon, a remarkably successful local news blog.

"So what is it this time, oh indestructible one?" Paul asked sardonically. He and the vase had an understanding – they didn't understand each other – and that was fine by each of them. "Plane crash? Another attack by the forces of evil?"

"Not necessarily evil," the vase said. "It's hard to read. But not a plane crash, either. It's more like something alien, as in not of this world. That was either a meteor or a spaceship."

"Something for a superhero to handle, I imagine," Myke said – Myke, not Paul, because he no longer looked like a middle-aged reporter. In place of Paul Phillips, but speaking with the same cadence as Paul Phillips, was a blond-haired Adonis. That's how quickly the change happened – even if you stared right at him and didn't blink, you couldn't see Paul change into Myke. One instant one would be standing in front of you, and the next instant the other would be.

"Or you could turn yourself back into yourself, kiss your wife and tell me why the house just rattled like an earthquake," said a sleepy-looking auburn-haired beauty in a robe who entered the room and apparently saw nothing odd about her husband talking to the pottery.

This was Dana Dunsmore Phillips, one of the top marketing and public relations professionals in Astor City and, for nearly two decades now, the loving partner of a reporter and part-time superhero.

Paul Phillips kissed his wife, but Myke answered the question. Although she had become accustomed to the admittedly attractive superhero who shared her husband's soul with the original, she preferred the familiar contours of Paul's lips and body when she needed a hug or a morning kiss.

"Well, hon," the muscular warrior said – because Paul was back inside the warrior's body – "as you might have heard the vase say, it was either a meteor or a spaceship passing overhead and crashing somewhere nearby. In case it's an alien invasion, I thought I'd check it out as Myke Phoenix."

"In case it's a meteor – which is more likely, you know – you might have better luck as Scoop, the crusading reporter," Dana replied with an impish grin, an endearing look that made Paul think his best option might be to stay home with her for a while. She had a good point; he changed back into the reporter. "Did you make coffee?"

"Yep; it's in the pot. I'd stay and help you wake up, but I'd better check out the scene. Who knows what the darn thing hit?"

"Go," she said, pushing Paul Phillips toward the door. "I'll just have some coffee and — WHAT HAPPENED TO MY MOTHER'S DEPRESSION GLASS?"

The look on Chief Deputy Arnie Rogers' face when he saw the reporter made Paul Phillips wonder if he should have appeared as Myke Phoenix after all. That is to say, he did not appear to be pleased to have a reporter snooping around.

"What are you doing here?" Rogers said, with an irritated tone that matched the irritated expression.

"Same as you," Paul said with a smile. "I heard the boom and followed the smoke."

Actually it wasn't smoke so much as dust. The flying thing had managed to land in the side of a small hill away from populated areas, kicking up a lot of dust and dirt and starting only small fires here and there. The top of the hill hung precariously over the gash where something large and roundish had buried itself and could be seen dimly through the dust. Given that there were homes and businesses in every direction, it seemed miraculous that no one was killed and no buildings were in the projectile's path – of course later it turned out to be no miracle, just good piloting, but I'm getting ahead of ourselves.

"Just stay out of the way and let the professionals do their job," Rogers sneered. Yes, it would have been better to show up as the superhero – although Chief Deputy Arnie Rogers wasn't a big fan of muscle-bound warriors intruding on police business, either.

The scene was reminiscent of a foggy morning except for the aroma of burning wood. Paul's heart gave a little jump when he saw a figure begin to lumber out of the fog, but then the figure formed into the more familiar shape of his friend Josiah Petri, the forensic pathologist for Astor County.

He almost said "Josie! What are you doing here?" but then he remembered that was something Myke Phoenix would say. Petri hated the nickname Josie, and for a superhero Myke was a notorious teaser.

Instead, Paul Phillips said, "Dr. Petri! What brings you here?"

Josiah Petri looked at Paul as if he didn't recognize him, but after a few seconds – as if a switch was thrown or a storage site accessed – "Hello, Paul," he said flatly. "I was called here in case someone was killed or injured by the impact."

"I take it no one got hit."

"That is correct," Petri said without emotion. "Nothing to see here except a big meteor."

"Well, that's something to see in itself," Paul said, taking a photo or two with his smartphone. "You OK, Josiah? You seem distracted by something."

Again, a blank look, then a slight smile.

"I'm OK, Paul," he said dully. "I'm just feeling a little – under the weather. Nothing to see here except a big meteor."

"Yes, you said that. I hope you feel better soon," Paul said, a little skeptically. He started to add something, but a rumbling sound interrupted the thought.

The top of the hill had begun to collapse into the gash. Thinking quickly, Paul activated the video camera on his smartphone. This would look good on the Astor City Beacon later that morning.

"Is anyone else down there?" Rogers called anxiously over the rumbling.

"No," Josiah Petri called back evenly. "It was – just myself."

Soil and rocks tumbled over the side for many seconds. For just an instant Paul could have sworn the big meteor looked round and shiny, like something that had been manufactured as opposed to a big rock, but then it disappeared under the small avalanche. Then the vast hole was filled and the rumbling subsided.

Josiah watched without emotion, then turned to go.

"Hang on a second, Dr. Petri, can I ask you for a quick comment?" said Paul, still running video on his smartphone.

Josiah looked back at Paul, saw the phone, and shrugged.

"Nothing to comment on," he said flatly. "Nothing to see here except a big meteor."

By now Paul was becoming convinced that there was, indeed, something to see here besides a big meteor.

"Josiah Petri was acting like a zombie? Well, honey, I don't blame him. It was before sunrise, after all."

The attractive auburn-haired beauty in a robe had been replaced by a beautiful auburn-haired professional woman most of the way toward dressing in sharp business attire. Dana was the president and CEO of Dana Dunsmore Agency, the biggest and best marketing and advertising firm in Astor City.

"There was something wrong besides being under the weather or not enough coffee," Paul said. "I know Josie – he'd usually be excited like a little kid over a giant meteor smashing into the side of a hill like an oldtime movie spaceship. He'd drive out there and be the first one on the scene. Come to think of it, he WAS the first one on the scene."

"Oh, and now he's been turned into a pod person by the aliens," Dana said. "And don't call him Josie."

"It sounds preposterous when you put it that way, but that's just how he was acting. OK, not exactly like that, he wasn't staring into space and inviting me to fall asleep, but –"

"Like he was dead tired and chasing after a meteor that woke up the whole town?"

The question hung in the air, and Paul was going to unwind from his unusual tension and say, "I guess you're right," when another flash of memory flashed.

"You know, when the landslide happened and the rest of the hill fell on top of the thing, I got a clear look at it – just for a second – and I could have sworn it was round and shiny, like it was made out of stainless steel or something."

Dana's eyes widened, but there was just a hint of playful light in her eyes, a glimpse of a smile around the edges of her mouth.

"Oh – my – gracious – you saw a flying saucer?! Why didn't you say so first? Call the National Guard! Call the governor! We have to stop them! Stop them, I tell you!" she said with mock horror, then let the playfulness take command of her face. "OK, Scoop, I'm already late for work because I had to clean up all that broken glass. You go hunt down the story and tell me when it's all online. Can't wait to read it. Love you."

"Love you, too."

A quick kiss and a rustling of sharp feminine business suit, and Paul Phillips was alone. He smiled to himself a little sheepishly. Flying saucers and pod people – she was right, his imagination was getting the best of him. Whatever was bugging Josiah, Petri would be his old self the next time he saw him. It was the crack of dawn, after all.

The phone rang. As he answered, Paul noticed it was darker than usual outside, like a rainstorm was about to happen.

"Paul Phillips, how can I help you?"

"Mr. Phillips? My name is Kevin Henderson. They're talking about a meteor crashing on the morning news, but it's just a big cover-up by the government."

"What makes you think that?"

"I was there; I was walking my dog along Batistoni Avenue and it passed right over my head," and here Kevin Henderson's voice shifted to a higher, more frantic pitch. "It was some sort of aircraft, like a spaceship."

In the dark recesses of his mind, Paul Phillips heard a theremin quiver.

Act 2

Warning from space

"OK, who is this really?" Paul Phillips said, attempting a wry chuckle to hide the fact that his heart had begun pounding harder.

"I tell you, my name is Kevin Henderson," the voice said. "I think we may be under alien attack."

"Even if that was a spaceship, I think you're jumping to conclusions. I was out there this morning, and the thing didn't even clip a power line. Maybe they're peaceful and had to crash-land and managed to avoid harming any – oh, what am I saying? It's a meteor, the county forensic scientist went down and looked at it."

"He told you it was a meteor?"

"Yes."

"What kind of meteor is smooth, round and battleship gray? Wait. You said he works for the county?"

"Yes."

"I'm telling you – it's a government coverup."

"You didn't get pictures, did you, Mr. Henderson?"

"I was walking my dog – it was over my head and gone before I could grab my phone. You've got to warn people about this! It's a spaceship, I tell you."

"Well, this is sure a part of the story. You said your name is Kevin – is that the common spelling of Henderson, H-E-N-D-E-R-S-O-N?"

Suddenly there was a long pause.

"You're going to quote me?"

"Well, of course. You knew I was a reporter when you called me."

"No. No, no, no, no. Can't I be like an anonymous source? I don't want the government and aliens coming to my door to shut me up."

"You'd have a lot more credibility if you go on the record."

"You don't believe me?"

"I didn't say I don't believe you, it's just that people are more likely to believe a story if names are attached."

"So it's about your credibility, not mine."

He had a point.

"Actually, you're right. I try not to be one of those reporters who hides behind anonymous sources," Paul said. "Over the years I've seen listeners – readers" (He still thought like a radio guy) "believe something more when there's a name attached to something that may be hard to believe."

"I understand," Henderson replied. "How do I convince you that I'm credible?"

"You went a long way to convincing me just by telling me your name," Paul said. "Now, anything else you can –"

"I don't remember anything," Kevin said firmly. "Not if you're going to use my name."

Paul Phillips sighed.

"OK, let me just ask you for background purposes, then. Anything else you can remember, did the thing have landing lights, or – hello? Hello?" The call was lost.

"Hey, Blanche. Rogers around?"

The police dispatcher in the corner cubicle looked through Paul Phillips. "You're not supposed to be back here."

"Come on, it's me, I've been coming back here for years," the reporter said.

"You came back here years ago," Blanche said, irritated. "That was when we had no security. I don't know where Rogers is."

"Who wants to know?" Chief Deputy Arnie Rogers appeared so suddenly at Phillips' elbow that he jumped.

"Oh! Hey, Arnie. I just was looking for an update on the meteor."

"No update," Rogers said flatly. "It was just a big meteor."

"Yeah, I'm getting that. I'm wondering if anyone is going to dig down and study it or anything. You know, archaeologists, space experts – who's doing the investigation?"

"No need for study," Arnie Rogers said. Paul noticed something: He wasn't trying to shoo the reporter out of the dispatch center, and he wasn't angry, like he'd been at the crash site. "The area is cordoned off. Too dangerous right now. It was just a big meteor."

"Dangerous?" Paul picked up on the word. "How do you mean?"

"The ground is unstable. You saw that landslide." Rogers' mouth went flat, as if attempting a smile. "Relax, Paul. It was just a big meteor."

"I'm relaxed," Paul said. "But that's the first time you've ever called me by name. You feeling OK?"

Arnie Rogers paused as if processing new information. "Guess I'm just getting used to you being around, that's all," he said finally. "I am a little under the weather, maybe."

"You're going to think I'm nuts," Paul told his wife when she came home for lunch. "First Josiah, then Arnie Rogers, not acting like themselves."

"I think you're nuts," Dana said. "No more old science fiction movies for you. Come on, Paul, there are lots of explanations short of space aliens. Maybe they found something big down there and they're not supposed to talk about it. You know, the old 'national security' routine."

"It could be some sort of spy plane that crashed, I suppose," Paul said. "But the way they were acting wasn't all 'I can't tell you about that.' It was more like something was suppressing their personalities."

Dana's laugh was always musical. "From what you've always told me about Arnie Rogers, I didn't think he had a personality to suppress."

Paul laughed softly, but he still was troubled. "Well, he was even less than his usual self. And you know, he snuck up next to me. I didn't know he was there until he spoke."

"That is something," she admitted. Ever since Paul and Mychus the Warrior began sharing bodies, he was more sensitive to his surroundings than he had been. Dana called it his "Mykie senses": Paul's senses of hearing, smell, all of them were enhanced.

"It sure is," he said. "And what about this Kevin Henderson?"

"Who's Kevin Henderson?"

Suddenly Paul realized he hadn't told her about the phone call from the agitated gentleman who swore he'd seen a spaceship fly overhead and crash into the hill. Now he had Dana's full and rapt attention.

"Oh my stars," were her exact words. Two public officials acting like zombies were a simple coincidence and perhaps not even that unusual, after all. But to add into the mix a man who claimed to have seen a flying saucer while walking his dog, well, now we were getting to a place where she could believe.

"You've been awfully quiet," Paul said, directing his attention to the display shelf that had this morning been crowded with Depression glass and now held one not-very-attractive ancient green vase. "I'm thinking it's not because you're lonely for company."

"I got nothing to say," the pottery replied. "This one stumps me, too. I don't recognize the emanations."

"That doesn't sound good," Dana said.

"Whatever is out there is not necessarily evil. Just – alien. I'm pretty in tune with stuff that this planet produces. Deinonychus, a talking dinosaur who radiates pure badness, hey, that one I can read like tea leaves," said the vase. "All I can tell you for sure is this thing isn't from this planet, which if it's just a meteor you could have figured out on your own."

"I'm going to head out there after lunch anyway," Paul said. "I'll see what I can unearth."

"Oh, I love it when you're punny," Dana said, rolling her eyes, then turned serious. "Be careful, Scoop. This one sounds too weird."

A funny thing happened on the way to the crash site.

Paul Phillips was driving out of the city on the route that took him past the big-box hardware and home supply center with the big orange sign. He glanced toward the parking lot and glimpsed Josiah Petri and Arnie Rogers getting out of a pickup truck. Although it's not unusual for the forensic pathologist and the chief deputy to be traveling together, 1) they usually came separately, 2) they usually would be driving a vehicle with municipal markings, and 3) they tended to bump into each other at places like crime scenes. There was no sign any mayhem had occurred in or near the big store.

Paul turned back toward the store. As he pulled into the lot, he could see the two men walking into the store. Another zombie-like attribute: The pickup was parked far out into the parking lot, but at a normal walking pace, they should have made it inside in the couple of minutes it took to turn around and come back. Oh stop, Paul said to himself, maybe one of them left something in the truck. Still, their shambling pace made for another clue.

It wasn't hard to spot Petri and Rogers once he got inside. He saw them down an aisle packed with metal fastenings and wire. They had a shopping cart and were loading it with, well, the kind of items you might need if you wanted to repair a damaged metal structure. When they stopped at the welding equipment, things really started to look like an aircraft fixer-upper project.

At one point Rogers glanced in Paul's direction and appeared to exchange a look with Petri. At first he thought they had spotted him trailing them, but they didn't act any differently or say anything to each other. They just went back to shopping.

The one thing that did happen is that the trail took them into a remote area of the store, where they disappeared around a corner. And when Paul looked tentatively around that corner to see how far up the aisle the two men had gone, he was startled to find them right there waiting for him with blank expressions.

"Yipes!" he said instinctively. It might again be noted here that he did not instantly become Myke Phoenix. One of the handy aspects of the relationship was that if the healthy but not-super-powered Paul Phillips were to blunder into a life-threatening situation, the force that recruited him into the service of truth, justice and good instantly transformed him into Myke so that he'd be ready to defend himself. Suddenly confronted with the apparently zombified Arnie Rogers and Josiah Petrie, Paul remained Paul, which gave him some assurance that he was not about to be blasted by an alien weapon or some such.

"Hi, guys! What are you doing here on a workday afternoon?"

"Are you doing an investigative report on public employees' shopping habits?" Josiah asked. That was odd because it wasn't odd; it was the kind of joke Petri would make. The problem was the expressionless way he said it.

"Ha, ha, no, Dana and I just have a project this weekend and I'm picking up some odds and ends," Paul fibbed.

"Stop following us," Rogers said abruptly.

"Beg pardon?"

"You heard me," Petri replied, which was odd in itself since the "Beg pardon?" had been addressed to Rogers. "You've been following us around to see what we're buying."

"Your friends are fine," Rogers said.

"I just need to use their bodies to move about in the community and gather supplies," Petri said.

"We will not stay long and then they'll be restored," Rogers said.

"So that's why you told me there's no need for a study. You don't want people to find out it's not just a meteor in that pit," Paul said. There was a long pause. The two men exchanged a glance, more like a meaningful look, then turned back to the reporter.

"Give us a day or so and everything will be back to normal," Rogers said.

"We don't want to hurt anyone," Petri said.

"We have no need to beat you," Rogers said.

"We just want to go our way," Petri said.

"What is this all about? You're saying there's a wrecked spaceship on that hill?" Paul asked. "What were you doing flying around here in the first place?"

"All we ask is that you leave us alone long enough to get away," Petri said.

"We don't want to cause a panic," Rogers said.

"No – no panic," Petri said.

"Sometimes it's not such a good idea to poke around," Rogers said.

"You might not like what you find," Petri said.

"We don't want to hurt anyone," Rogers said.

Act 3
Not quite friendly

"JUST so I understand this correctly," Paul Phillips said, his mind whirling, "you come in peace, you crash-landed, this is some sort of accident, you're controlling people to go shopping, and you want a little time to fix the ship before you put everybody back the way you found them. And you want me to shut up about it so people don't freak out."

"You understand this correctly," Josiah Petri said.

"Are you the real Josiah Petri and Arnie Rogers or some sort of robot clone or cyborg or something?"

The two zombified men exchanged a look, then turned to Paul. Their bodies relaxed visibly and they looked disoriented for a moment, then became far more animated than they had appeared seconds earlier.

"Hey. Hey! Paul, it's me," Josiah said. "They did something to us."

"It's like we're conscious but we can't do anything about what we do or say," Rogers agreed. "Somebody else is pulling the strings."

"Right!" Petri said. "And, say, listen Paul, don't for a minute tr –"

That was all they said. Both men stiffened again, and energy drained from their eyes.

"I believe that demonstration answers your question," the presence in control of Rogers' body said.

"That is all. Leave us alone, and your friends will be released unharmed," Petri-not-Petri said.

"What were you going to say, Josiah? Don't for a minute, what?" Phillips urged.

If there was an internal struggle going on behind Petri's blank eyes, the only clue was the extra-long pause before the reply.

"Don't interfere," Rogers said flatly.

And with that, they turned around and started pushing the shopping cart toward the cashier stations.

Dumbfounded, and without a clear idea of what to do next, Paul stood where the three of them had been talking and tried to absorb what just happened.

When he got out of the store, Josiah Petri and Arnie Rogers – or whatever energy had control of their bodies and minds – were climbing back into the pickup truck. Apparently they didn't need to shamble when they wanted to move more quickly. They looked across the parking lot at Paul Phillips for a moment, then started the vehicle. Rogers was driving, and Petri kept his eyes on Paul until they were out of sight.

"Hokey smokes," the crusading reporter and part-time superhero muttered.

Sheriff Rod Skjorte would not have believed the tale if it came from Paul Phillips, even though the reporter had more than two decades' worth of reputation for accurate reporting. That's why Myke Phoenix had chosen to deliver this unbelievable story as Myke Phoenix, with the added authority that comes from nearly 20 years of battling fantastic menaces.

Still –

"I don't believe it," Skjorte said. "You're telling me the meteor is an alien spaceship and they're using my chief deputy and the coroner as zombie slaves, but we should let them do it?

"It does sound ridiculous when you put it that way," Myke admitted. "But look, they told Paul they're not going to hurt them or anyone else, and they just want to fix their ship and be on their way."

"It wasn't the leaving them alone that I don't believe," the sheriff snorted. "It's the whole alien invasion thing. It's just too fantastic."

Myke let that statement float on the air for a few seconds. And then: "Sheriff, last month you and the National Guard were fighting a couple of giant spiders that spit flame. A few years ago we had a little run-in together with a talking dinosaur. Quincy Quackenbos, who happens to be half-man, half-duck, is due to be released from prison in a couple of months. Remember the week that the entire Big Top Paper Company mill just disappeared, leaving four empty city blocks, and we had to handle a gang of humanoid dinosaur things to get it back? What makes an alien spaceship landing too fantastic to believe?"

He knew he had a point. The obstinate look on Rod Skjorte's face showed that the sheriff also knew he had a point but didn't want to admit the fact.

"Those were earthly things," Skjorte said finally. "They happened for earthly reasons. You're trying to tell me there's something that came from outer space out there under that mound of dirt."

"Maybe they're just pretending to come from another planet, then," Myke said. "Let's say it's some secret organization that flies aircraft that look like flying saucers. Or it's some foreign power that was test-flying a spy plane. All I know for sure is that they have Petri and Rogers under their control, and they asked us to leave them alone until they finish fixing their ship."

"What happens to Arnie and Josiah after that?"

"They'll let them go. They said nobody will get hurt."

"Nobody will get hurt if we leave them alone," Skjorte said. "That sounds like a threat to me."

"Oh, come on, Rod –"

"We're done here. I got things to do," Skjorte said, turning his attention to the computer screen on his desk. "You go do whatever superheroes do."

"You going to leave them be?"

The sheriff looked up from his keyboard.

"I'm going to do my job."

Technically, it was Myke Phoenix's first visit to the crash scene, but Paul's psyche inside the warrior's body noticed that since morning a small camp had been established. The inevitable yellow tape surrounded the area where the earth had been disturbed, and mobile trailers bearing the insignia of State University and the National Weather Service were parked just outside the tape.

"'No need for a study,'" Myke muttered, repeating Arnie Rogers' original warning. "Even zombified, the guy lies to the press."

A team of scientist types was going over the site, taking soil samples, digging carefully here and there, collecting bits of debris. No, that wasn't right either – after a few moments Myke noticed that only two or three scientists were actually going through the motions of doing scientific things. The others seemed to be acting like a construction or repair crew. One or two at a time entered or emerged from what appeared to be a tunnel into the side of the hill.

Two things were odd as the large man in the white uniform with a crimson bird emblazoned across his well-proportioned chest strode up to the scene. First, when he called out "hey folks," the entire swarm turned to look at him at once. It wasn't that they each heard the call, registered that someone wanted their attention, and turned toward the source of the sound in their own time, either right away or after they finished whatever small task they were finishing. No, they all turned at once, as if the same intelligence were directing every one of them in unison.

Second, not a one of them started in surprise at the blond Adonis before them. Not that Myke craved attention. It's simply that in any medium- to large-sized crowd is someone who has never seen a superhero in uniform, and it can be a startling experience. Usually someone would say, "Wow, it's Myke Phoenix," or at least widen their eyes. This small swarm of scientists simply turned as one and stared at the new arrival, who just happened to be a large, strikingly powerful-looking man clothed in a superhero's uniform.

Finally, someone said, "Wow, it's Myke Phoenix," but without enthusiasm. Without sarcasm, either – without any emotion whatsoever.

"Hokey smokes," Myke said to himself. "It's a field full of zombies." But to the group he said, "How's the work going?"

"It goes well," said a nearby stocky middle-aged woman in overalls. "We should be finished processing the scene in a few hours."

"Great!" Myke Phoenix replied, but without enthusiasm – in the way that non-zombies speak without enthusiasm, that is, with a smile but a hint of anxiety as if trying to conceal the fact that he didn't feel great about the situation.

The woman stared at him without blinking. "You have spoken to Paul Phillips," she said after a few moments. As she spoke, most of the others turned back to their tasks.

"Yes, yes I have," said the superhero. "It appears you needed more help than you let on." There were perhaps a dozen swarming over the site, and who knows how many underground working on the unseen spaceship.

"Many hands make light work, as you creatures say," a young man said. "You are much better suited than we are to labor in your planet's conditions."

"But you'll let these people go when you're done," Myke said, more of a question than a statement. He heard vehicles approaching behind him, down the street.

"Letting them go was the plan all along," the stocky woman said. "But –" behind Myke came the sound of a large vehicle's engine revving and the machine's support system reacting to an impact and new terrain, and then smaller vehicles doing the same. Myke looked back. The sheriff's department emergency command center, an armored truck the size of a bus, had jumped the curve and started across the field toward them, accompanied by a small armada of pickup trucks.

The man in the white uniform whirled back at the stocky scientist.

"You were going to let them go, but –?"

"But these are very handy bodies for exploratory and other purposes," she said as the command center truck pulled up behind Myke and stopped.

"What other purposes?" Myke asked, but before she could reply the door to the large truck slammed and Sheriff Rod Skjorte jumped onto the ground holding a rifle. About 25 men emerged behind him from the pickups.

"All right," Skjorte called out loudly. "I need to talk with whoever's in charge."

"Any one of us speaks for the collective," said a man in a lab coat and holding a shovel. "What would you like to know?"

"You're holding my chief deputy and at least one other county employee, and I want to know if you're going to release them peacefully – now," the sheriff said authoritatively. Did I mention he was holding a rifle?

"I'm sorry, Sheriff Skjorte," the stocky woman said tonelessly. "I'm afraid I can't do that."

The sheriff pointed the rifle at the center of her chest. Even with the alien controls navigating her words and actions, her eyes widened in fear.

"You understand that your quarrel is not with these helpers?" she said as tonelessly as before.

"Right," Skjorte said, shifting his aim to between her eyes. "Take me to your leader."

Myke Phoenix lay a hand gently on the barrel and put gentle pressure on it until the sheriff lowered his aim. "I think they'll talk with us without the threats, Rod."

"You don't seem to be assessing the situation very realistically, Mr. Superhero," the sheriff said. "Looks like they've taken about a dozen people hostage without much of a fight. I've got double that number and I don't know if that will be enough. I do know I need to get through to whoever's controlling the hostages."

Myke looked at the captive scientists. "Will you – the leader – meet with us face to face?"

A grim smile from the man with the shovel. "To begin with, we don't have faces. I'm not sure you could handle that."

"Well, then," Skjorte replied, signaling to the group behind him. "I guess we have a problem."

Myke stepped in front of the sheriff. He turned and called back to the scientists.

"All right, folks, we don't want this to turn into anything ugly," he said, then back to Skjorte: "Come on, Rod, an interplanetary incident? Tell me you don't want to do this."

"What I want," Skjorte replied, his voice even but his face reddening, "is for my deputy sheriff and these other people to be de-zombified and get their lives back."

"Just a few more hours, sheriff," said the stocky woman. "Then we'll —"

"Not soon enough!" came a new voice from a group of four or five gun-wielding folks who had approached from the side while this conversation was going on. The leader lifted a rifle and aimed it where Myke had convinced the sheriff not to be pointing. "So! This is an alien invasion after all. I knew it! I saw your warship land this morning. You thought you could get away with this, did you? And you've recruited our 'super' hero to help in the coverup."

The voice was new but familiar to Myke. It was the frantic voice Paul Phillips had heard over the phone that morning: Kevin Henderson.

"This is not what you think it is, Mr. Henderson —" Myke began.

"HOW DO YOU KNOW MY NAME?!" an extremely agitated tone. This was not looking good. "I knew it! If you and the government have been tracking me since I called the reporter this morning, you know I'm serious about this. Release your prisoners!"

"We don't want to hurt anyone, but we will defend ourselves," said the man with the shovel, taking a step forward.

Henderson's rifle barked. The man dropped the shovel and grabbed his shoulder, where a red blotch had suddenly appeared. The sheriff and his posse raised their weapons but seemed unsure whether to aim them at the zombies or Henderson and his group.

A loud-and-getting-louder, high-pitched whine coming from the general direction of the buried spaceship got everyone's attention.

Act 4
The big reveal

FROM the earliest of stories about visitors from space, the aliens have had ray guns — awesome laser-type weapons that can zap a human being into oblivion or even level a city block. The devil ray that blasted out of the side of the hill was somewhere in between.

But it was not a disintegration ray; rather, it was a burst of light that seemed to possess a physical force of its own. Henderson, Skjorte and their gangs were blown off their feet and back several yards as if struck by a bowling ball. Myke Phoenix had planted his feet to prepare for anything, but even he was knocked down by the terrible blow.

When he scrambled back up — aware that the loud-and-growing-louder whine had culminated in the light blast and was building to another crescendo — he noted that most members of the two gangs were staying down, and a handful were not moving. In fact, not only were they not moving but their bodies were twisted in a way that suggested they would not be moving again, ever again. Among these clearly dead people was Sheriff Rod Skjorte, who had been the closest not-superpowered person to the beam.

For the moment no one except Myke Phoenix was able to rise back to their feet. Rise he did.

"What have you done?" the blond-haired man in the white uniform said incredulously.

"Nothing that they wouldn't do to us, given the opportunity, as you witnessed," said the man who'd carried the shovel, displaying his bleeding shoulder.

Myke took a step forward and then broke into a run for the tunnel. A couple of the white-coated prisoners tried to block his path, but they were too slow and Myke pushed them aside before they had a chance to brace for the collision. He stopped at the end of the tunnel with a gasp.

He was expecting to find a dug-out area where the side of a metallic craft was exposed, and a ramp leading up to a door into the structure. Even though that's exactly what he found, he still had to pause to process the scene.

"Hokey smokes, it's an alien spaceship after all," he muttered. "No wonder the vase was confused."

Arnie Rogers and Josiah Petri appeared in the doorway. It was a rounder door than our earthbound entryways, as if to accommodate something wider and not as angular as your basic human being. The two men were able to stand side-by-side and would have been able to go through the door together if that was their purpose.

"Can't let you in, Myke, sorry," Josiah said, but there was a fearful spark in his eyes, as if Petri's consciousness inside fully understood that if the phoenix-powered warrior wanted to get inside, no two men were going to block him for more than a moment.

"OK, folks, we're done here," Myke said evenly, struggling to keep his anger under control. "You lied to me about people getting hurt, and you lied to me about these people being released from your control when you're done. So you're going to let them go now and – AAAAaaack!"

The intense headache that burst into Myke Phoenix's mind was too sudden and too intense to be anything but some sort of assault on his brain. He could almost physically feel some sort of force invading and probing his cerebral cortex, wrapping itself around and through his spinal cord, and otherwise – well, before the force had a chance to do otherwise, Myke flexed a mind force of his own and, with an effort not unlike shrugging an 8-ton boulder off his shoulders, pushed the alien force back out of his mind.

He stepped back, breathing heavily. For the first time in many years, the superhuman abilities of Mychus the Warrior's body and, in this case, mind, had surprised its temporary occupant.

"So," Myke Phoenix said, "it appears you won't be adding me to your small army."

"A pity," said the force controlling Arnie Rogers' form, "if we had you, we wouldn't need so many of these others."

"Let them go," Myke said, beginning to seethe.

"We kind of like having slaves to do the tough jobs after all," Josiah Petri's voice said. "We've never encountered bodies quite this utilitarian. They'll do the jobs none of us really want to do."

"Step aside, gentlemen, I don't want to hurt you, I'm trying to help," Myke said to Arnie and Josiah, walking up the ramp.

Suddenly he was grabbed from behind, and the five white-coated scientists who had been working outside swarmed over his powerful body. Stupidly, he'd completely forgotten there was anyone behind him. They grabbed at his arms and legs – someone was conking him on the head with a heavy pipe of some sort – and the man with the gunshot wound in his shoulder was punching Myke in the solar plexus, ignoring his own pain.

The problem with five ordinary people trying to attack an invulnerable superhero, of course, is that he was invulnerable. He had been surprised early in his career with a blow to the abdomen that took his breath away, and from that moment forward he instinctively tightened his stomach muscles at the first sign of a physical assault.

He shrugged off the attackers and continued to stride up the ramp. Arnie Rogers and Josiah Petri drew close together and blocked his path.

"Sorry guys," Myke said. He clenched both fists and lashed out at both chins simultaneously. They crumpled in unison.

Stepping inside the alien spaceship was like stepping inside a steampunk greenhouse. The room was spherical. There was plant life everywhere and a collection of what appeared to be machines along the curving walls, but the purpose of each machine was not apparent to his humanoid eyes. The bank of machines, and the plants, continued up the sides and ceiling of the vast room, impossible to reach without a great ladder while the ship was on the ground but, Myke figured, easy to get to in the zero gravity of outer space. And we're talking impossible to access for humans; a blob of some kind clung high along the side of the far surface from the door.

Two other blobs stood – sat? lay? on a mosslike substance between one especially large grouping of machines and a cluster of plants that appeared to be a cross between bamboo and common wood ferns. There was no other word to use besides blob; as they'd already warned, the aliens had no apparent face – no eyes, nose, mouth, ears, or even limbs – but the steady throbbing of their bodies made it clear they were alive in our sense of the word.

Three men and a woman in sheriff's deputy uniforms stood in various spots around the room. Their belts and gun holsters were missing, and if there was any intent to continue the physical attack on Myke, it was not readily apparent.

In fact, almost immediately the humans relaxed, shook their heads as if to clear cobwebs, took a look at Myke Phoenix, turned to the blobs, screamed and raced for the door. They did stop to lift the groggy Arnie Rogers and Josiah Petri off the top of the ramp and help them flee.

"Go on out," Myke said to them as they departed behind him. "I've got some cleanup to do here."

For a few moments there was no sound beyond the soft whining of the machinery and liquid noises that seemed to be coming from everywhere – he guessed they were whatever system was servicing the plants and perhaps a different liquidy sound from the three blobs.

"I trusted you," the warrior snapped. "You said to leave this all alone and no one would get hurt."

"We acted only in self-defense," one of the two nearby blobs said. Without visible mouths it was hard to discern where the voice was coming from. "They wished to access the ship and perhaps to try to kill us."

"You said no one would get hurt, and now you've slaughtered a bunch of people," Myke shouted. "That's blood on my hands. I trusted you!"

"We have released our hold on your friends as a show of good faith," a blob said. "It became obvious that the mob was willing to hurt them to get to us. As handy as they have been in repairing our ship, we can't take them along with us after all."

"This unfortunate incident has demonstrated how fragile you all are," added the blob on the ceiling. "We did not realize our simple repulser ray could actually kill any of you. These beings would never survive in space, or in the hostile atmospheres of other planets. Even you, the mightiest of all, seem to need some sort of artificial protective covering. No, they make wonderful slaves in this atmosphere, but we can't take them with us."

"What makes you think I'm going to let you leave?" Myke said, and stepped toward the nearby blobs, fists clenched.

The intense headache returned, alien consciousnesses driving him to his knees with debilitating pain and the agony of attempted violation. He heard the whining sound of the killing light grow, there was a flash and he was hurled out the door and onto the ground of the tunnel.

Myke Phoenix scrambled to his feet but not quickly enough. The door slid closed and the ramp receded into the side of the craft. He swung a frustrated fist against the metal but failed to cause a dent, not even a dimple. A low hum and powerful vibration suggested the engagement of powerful engines.

The superhero made a judicious retreat. Out in the sun, emergency personnel had arrived and were tending to the injured and dead, but they had turned their attention to the shattered hill when the vibrations began.

"Get everybody back!" Myke shouted. "I think they're taking off."

Sure enough, small avalanches began to trickle down from the top of the hill, which bulged unnaturally, and then greater cascades of soil began to spill downward. Trees toppled as the hill popped and the great gray craft burst through toward the sky. It hovered a moment over the scene, and people scrambled for cover as they heard the now-familiar whining sound begin to build, but this time the powerful force of light was directed behind the ship and propelled it in the direction of the Shikaakwa River.

Fortunately, over the water was where the great ship imploded. The intensity of the implosion rattled windows and shook buildings for miles around, but the debris fell harmlessly into the river rather than onto people's heads.

"We didn't have time to finish calibrating the Shltemukereit," Josiah Petri said. "The Rquchlnic must have flurped the leaking Aplskereit. That was the problem last year over Chelyabinsk. We're going to have to resolve that before we try again." He paused. "What did I just say?"

"The repairs weren't finished and they took off anyway, which destroyed this ship, and the one last year developed the same problem," Chief Deputy Arnie Rogers said. "What did you think you said?"

"There must be some part of their consciousness, or at least their knowledge, lingering in my noggin," Petri said, tapping the top of his forehead. "I don't like that at all."

Myke Phoenix stood mute before the body of Astor County Sheriff Rod Skjorte. Kevin Henderson and two sheriff's deputies also had not survived the alien ray.

"This is my fault, Josie," Myke said as the pathologist came up beside him and placed a hand on the mighty shoulder. "I believed they would never hurt anyone."

"I tried to tell you, man, don't for a minute trust those guys," Petri said. "But it was us you trusted – they used us to pull off that 'we come in peace' malarkey."

"Wait, what do you mean by that?"

"Just what you think it means, Myke: This was a scout ship for a possible invasion. They tried to keep us from knowing them very well, but when someone is inside your head some of that stuff leaks out," Petri said. "And don't call me Josie."

"We're going to have to keep our eyes on the skies a little more from now on," Chief Deputy Arnie Rogers said. "It's a good thing we have Myke Phoenix on our side."

"I couldn't stop an alien invasion on my own," said the man in the white suit with the image of a red bird on his chest. "It's a good thing the ship exploded before it got very far."

Rogers swore. "That's right, I have another disaster scene to supervise," and he started to stride away, only to be stopped by a paramedic.

"That's quite a bruise on your chin, Arnie, let me check you for signs of concussion. What day is it?"

"It's the 12th of Tuesday, you idiot. Let me get to work." The paramedic took a firm grip on his arm and led him to the ambulance.

"Really, Myke," Josiah Petri said. "Thank you. You saved my life, again. You saved a bunch of lives."

"I didn't save Rod! I didn't save the others." Myke Phoenix himself was surprised at his own angry outburst. "Sorry, Josiah, I guess you're right. I don't know what I say to Julie." Rod and Julie Skjorte had three teenaged children.

"You say he died a hero, trying to protect his town," Petri said gently. "That's all there really is *to* say."

Myke Phoenix unclenched his fists.

"You're right," he said. "It's just that – wait. What did you say about last year?"

Epilogue

THE County Board appointed Arnie Rogers as the new sheriff until the next election. Homeland Security tried to close the Shikaakwa River "in the interest of national security" until someone pointed out the millions of dollars in shipping business that passed through the port every week. Then the agency sternly warned the public to stay away from the salvage vessels while they were pulling pieces of alien technology (and, ickily enough, alien flesh) out of the water. Some bits of metal did land on the shore, and a black market in alien spaceship fragments sprang up. Of course, customers had to be careful that they actually were buying extraterrestrial materials. One scam artist tried unloading fenders from a 1974 AMC Pacer as pieces of the alien wreck.

Of course, the Astor City Beacon had the best coverage of what actually happened at the crash site, although Paul Phillips wasn't able to offer any photos or video from the scene. He still hadn't figured out how to take pictures while Myke Phoenix was occupied saving the universe. One of the TV stations and several citizens got spectacular footage of the implosion.

For the second time, the aliens had maneuvered their craft during an emergency in a way that did the least damage to the human population below. So which was it: Did they mean us no harm or, as Josiah Petri, Arnie Rogers and the others insisted, was the craft a scout ship for a planned alien invasion? It was hard to argue with the people whose minds had been melded with the strange visitors, but for some actions spoke louder than words. And beyond that, there was the mysterious reference to another ship that had imploded over Russia a year ago.

"I'm buying that they're evil," said the misshapen vase on Paul and Dana's shelf, newly showcased in a spot he previously shared with fine Depression glassware. "The nature of evil is either to keep people ignorant or, if that fails, to put up a show of good intentions while you're plotting to kill everyone."

"I guess we have to keep our eyes on the skies, too," Paul said. "Especially if they've tried twice. 'Three times' the charm' may be a universal expression."

The skies would threaten Astor City in a different way just a few weeks later, when the storm of the century whooshed into town. Dana Dunsmore Phillips would find herself in the clutches of one of Myke Phoenix's earliest adversaries, while Paul sat at home sipping hot chocolate and wondering why his wife hadn't returned home from her business appointment.

But those troubles were still in the future. Tonight Paul and Dana held each other in a tight bear hug.

"Thank the stars you're all right, my love," Dana said, squeezing him with all her might.

"Protecting you from evil aliens and stuff is what I do best, doll," Paul Phillips said, putting on his best B movie façade.

Her hug softened considerably, but she did not let go.

"You protect me just fine," Dana purred into his ear. "But it's not what you do best."

What happened next is certainly none of our business.

Night of the
Superstorm

Prologue

IT was a dark and stormy night.

What?

OK, genius, you think you're so smart – you tell me how to describe the night. It was long after sunset, ergo it was dark outside. And the storm was hellacious enough to wake the dead – trees were crashing onto power lines, cars were getting swamped in high water, and the winds were howling. Howling, I tell you.

You know how the wind drives against your house so hard that it sounds like an oldtime movie about people trapped in a house on a dark and stormy night? That's how dark and stormy it was.

So don't roll your eyes at me when I tell you it was a dark and stormy night. Because it was dark, it was stormy, and it was night.

I'm sorry, I guess I'm a little touchy tonight. It's dark and stormy outside now, and it kind of reminds me about the night of the superstorm.

How about this: It was so dark and so stormy that even Myke Phoenix, the mighty protector of Astor City, looked out into the dark, poured himself a cup of hot chocolate, and closed the curtains. Well, technically it was Paul

Phillips, the mere mortal who occasionally became Mychus the Warrior, who decided he was going to settle in front of the television set rather than go out in the storm.

The television meteorologist grinned back at him and confirmed his instincts.

"Batten down the hatches and strap yourself in," she chirped. "It's going to be a bumpy ride. It's a dark and stormy night, just like a bad old novel."

"Bad old novel"? Everybody's a critic.

Twelve hours later, there was no grinning and no chirping in Astor City. But it certainly was a bumpy ride, which began when Paul realized his wife was not coming home that night.

Act 1

A three-hour tour

DANA Dunsmore Phillips wiped sweaty palms off on her skirt and sighed.

"This won't do at all," she said. "Come on, Dana, chill."

But she wasn't chilling and, yes, it wasn't doing. At all. She took another deep breath and tried to clear her mind. It would not be the end of the world if Gerald and Ginny Hallstrom decided not to market their products through the Dana Dunsmore Agency — but it would be the start of a new world of greater financial security. Every big new client meant a stronger and less unpredictable future for the company.

And truth to tell, the company's future was more unpredictable than it used to be. Oh, for so many years the sky was the limit; she still got goosebumps when she thought back on the day she first realized she not only needed to hire someone to help get the work done but could afford to pay that person a decent salary. And that happened more than a dozen times over the years, so that the agency was now comprised of 18 wonderfully creative and motivated people who were excited about telling their clients' stories.

In the rise and fall of the economy, clients tended to make the mistake of thinking they have to make do without marketing, not realizing that marketing is how they make do. "I have to cut the budget somewhere," they'd say apologetically, and although Dana made a convincing case that advertising and marketing is not the place to cut, the clients would cut anyway, and she'd be looking around for new clients again.

Gerald and Virginia Hallstrom were among the handful of the most pre-eminent entrepreneurs in Astor City. They had taken Hallstrom Professional Services from a mom-and-pop cleaning service to a regional economic force that included interior design and landscaping. The Dana Dunsmore Agency had a handful of clients that were Hallstrom's size and stature, and Dana knew how that kind of client can stabilize a business.

"Don't let them see how much you need this," Dana muttered to herself, and stopped. Wait a minute, she was right: The Hallstroms *couldn't* see how much she needed this. If she walked into this evening feeling like the future of the company depended on landing the client, her anxiety (desperation!) would be obvious and she'd blow her chances. The key was going to have to be convincing herself and the Hallstroms that it would be fun – and profitable – to work together. And it would be fun and profitable. She just had to project that message, not her fear of what might happen. That kind of acting came naturally to the marketing whiz: "I do it with Paul all the time," she said ruefully.

No, she hadn't had to act like she was having fun with her husband; he was her favorite person in the whole world and her best friend. But she did leave her work anxieties at work. Paul had worked his way out of more than a few rough spots with the smiling encouragement she projected when she was feeling nervous inside.

When they met two decades ago, he was a hot-shot radio news reporter, but local radio stations didn't have newsrooms much anymore. He got a job at the Astor City Tribune newspaper, but you know how newspapers are doing in the digital age, and a few years later he was out of work and exploring his options again. When they came upon the idea of the Astor City Beacon – an online local news source – she smiled and encouraged him and pledged the Dana Dunsmore Agency would help direct some advertising business to his site, but like any new business it had its fiscal ups and downs even though Paul was in fact the best and most experienced reporter in town. So she hesitated to tell him when the agency was having its share of the economic struggles everyone was working through.

Oh, and on top of that, Paul had a secret life as Myke Phoenix, the powerful and somewhat magical superhero who protected Astor City from the forces of evil, bad and just plain stupid. Sometimes the pressures on her husband made keeping the Dana Dunsmore Agency afloat seem trivial indeed, and although she didn't hesitate to seem anxious when he left to go fight killers and creatures from outer space and such, she did a decent job of acting to disguise when she was absolutely terrified.

Keeping a strong and confident face while spending a three-hour cruise with Gerald and Ginny Hallstrom shouldn't be so hard.

She was startled from her internal pep talk by a sudden and loud crash and clatter. Up near the bridge of the converted fishing boat, a woman stood with her hands on her hips looking displeased with a man at her feet, who was quickly gathering some scattered equipment he had apparently dropped.

"I swear, Gil, if you can't get the knack of holding things while walking in a straight line, I'm going to find someone who can," the skipper said, but Dana thought she sensed a trace of amusement behind the sharp words.

As Gil brought his gear back under control, he did a sudden double take and stared at the figure who had just arrived at the top of the boarding ramp. Dana understood his typical-male stare. She was a remarkably beautiful woman, wearing sunglasses and a white sun dress that flattered her body. Clutching a small purse with both hands, the woman looked around, decided Gil was staff, walked over and held her ticket to him. He still had a precarious hold of the recently scattered equipment, but he managed to scoonch his hand out and grab the ticket between his fingers.

"W-welcome aboard," he said, clearly a bit flustered. "Make yourself at home."

"Thank you, that's very kind," she barely whispered behind the dark glasses. Oh please, Dana said to herself, stifling the urge to roll her eyes, Marilyn has been dead more than 50 years and women still try to be her. Judging from the first mate's reaction, the allure still worked, however.

The next person up the ramp also seemed affected by the sex-bomb wannabe. His eyes followed the woman's slow but steady path across the deck to a chair near the railing. The conservatively dressed man was not wearing a tie, but he did have a sport jacket with patches on the elbows like a college professor from 40 years ago.

And just behind the scholar were the familiar faces of Gerald and Virginia Hallstrom, looking every bit as well-dressed as their millions could afford.

"Oh my stars," Dana said, looking around at the tour boat captain and her clumsy first mate, the millionaire and his wife, the woman with movie-star looks, and the professorial sort. "I'm Mary Ann."

"Dana!" Ginny Hallstrom squealed and threw her arms around the marketing maven. "I love that outfit. So good to see you."

"Yes, well," Gerald agreed, shaking her right hand and giving a half-hug with his left. "Hello, Dana. Looks a little nippy for a cruise today, don't you think?"

Dana looked over her shoulder at the dark storm clouds, which were still in the distance but appeared to be heading in their direction.

"The captain wouldn't take her out if it wasn't safe," she replied, as lightly as she could, trying not to think about what this meeting could mean for her company. "And what can happen on a river boat in three hours?"

"Ha, ha! Yes," Gerald Hallstrom grinned. "A three-hour tour." He whistled a little tune. "What could happen indeed?"

The Shikaakwa River is a broad, mighty stream, large enough to have a small handful of legitimate islands with homes and even businesses located on them. But the restaurateurs who hoped to make a go of exotic eating establishments accessible only by boat soon found it wasn't a sustainable business model after all.

The only successful business was the obviously named Island Resort, a collection of small cottages on Dog Island, the northernmost of the little chain of atolls just southwest of downtown Astor City. It was called Dog Island because over the years people decided its map resembled the head of a floppy-eared dog, right down to the round little pond where an eye would go. (Its name before maps were invented was long forgotten.)

Big Island, which lay a little south of Dog Island, was, well, the biggest, but paradoxically it was also the most remote, having been purchased in its entirety years ago by a reclusive millionaire who had since died. His stately mansion on the island's bluff facing the city was a landmark noted by boat tours like this one. The rest of the island was a bit of a wildlife sanctuary. There were three smaller islands south of Big, each with a cluster of small homes and docks.

Sarah Turner's river boat cruise began at the docks along the East Shikaakwa River, not far from the vast Quackenbos Laboratories complex, and passed under the city's three great bridges, down the Shikaakwa itself and around the five islands. The route gave passengers a pleasant view of the city and a glimpse at the surrounding countryside, which really was quite lovely. Although Astor City was an urban industrial center and its suburbs as suburbiastic as one might imagine, a few minutes' drive would bring you to a rustic, rural area, at least for now. Developers were starting to sense how much people enjoyed visiting Astor City and how many people might enjoy living there, and so the pockets of sub-division were starting to creep out toward the nearby farm fields and forests. Still, by the time the boat reached Big Island, the view along the waterfront remained fairly wild and free.

Dana Dunsmore had tried to steer the conversation toward promoting Hallstrom Professional Services, but the couple was enjoying the ride too much, and she did not want to get down to business too fast.

"Should we get down to how my agency can help you get your message out?" she asked finally.

"Oh, plenty of time for that," Ginny said. "I just want to bask in this lovely day."

The dark rain clouds starting to pass overhead didn't look lovely. But Dana had to concede that the contrast of storm clouds starting to creep overhead, with the sun shining in a blue sky on the other side of the sky, made for a beautiful contrast.

Wait. Storm clouds? Overhead? Uh oh.

Looking back, she couldn't remember if it started to rain before or after the sizzling crackle of light followed instantly by a deafening roar of thunder. In her memory the rain and lightning arrived all at once.

Sarah Turner immediately turned the boat toward a dock on Big Island, but the wind picked up and the waves were so rough she wasn't sure if they'd reach the dock or be hammered to shore.

"Where did this come from? There weren't any alerts on the –" she glanced at the weather radio, saw that the "on" light wasn't lighted, and pushed the power button ferociously. "GIL!!! When did you turn off the weather radio?"

"— This small craft advisory is in effect until 11 p.m. tonight," said a robotic voice. "Small boats should seek safe harbor immediately."

She wanted to glare at her first mate but was too busy struggling to keep the boat under control. "Never turn off the weather radio, Gil! How many times do I have to –"

The second lightningbolt struck with such ferocity that what came next remains a blur in Dana Dunsmore's memory to this day. Rain blowing sideways and stinging her face, soaking her clothes to the skin. A loud noise and sudden lurch that must have been the boat hitting the rocks. Shouting, the boat slowly spinning, waves like the ocean rather than the gentle river, more shouting, more crashing thunder, more rocking, and finally the strangely comfortable feel of solid ground on her back despite the continued pounding of angry raindrops against her face.

Her first clear memory after the crash was of sitting up and seeing her six companions scattered across the beach, and the tour boat listing in the shallow water, a gaping hole in her hull. As if to punctuate the scary sight, lightning flashed, a roar of thunder followed almost immediately, and a fresh blast of wind drove tiny daggers of raindrops full flush in her face.

Act 2
We're not alone here

"WE'VE got to get out of the rain!" Sarah Turner shouted to the others after a quick assessment revealed bumps, cuts, scrapes, scratches and bruises but no serious injuries to her flock. "Let's get up to the mansion!"

The reference to the big house was Dana's first realization that they had crashed on Big Island. This was good news. It would be an uphill climb to the huge estate, but the old house would provide safe haven to weather out the storm, no doubt. The bad news is none of the seven survivors made it onto the beach with a cellphone or any other means of communication, and no one was going to swim out to the half-sunken boat to try the radio in the middle of the storm. They were on their own for the night.

A loud crash not far away gave impetus to the need to find shelter; the powerful winds were going to be taking down more than one large tree tonight.

They pushed through the rain and wind and were at the mansion faster than they expected. They dove into the first door they saw, a side door quite some distance from the large front porch with its wraparound stairs and ornate columns. Fortunately (or perhaps not so, as it turned out), the door was unlocked and they staggered into a large kitchen.

Captain Turner fumbled for a light switch and flicked it. Electricity struggled to surge into the overhead light, but it was more of a pale glow.

"Brownout!" Gil barked, more authoritatively than one might have suspected he could. "Look for flashlights, candles, anything like that."

It was a providential suggestion, because after Dana found a drawerful of candles, with matches, and the professor opened a cabinet to find a stash of a half-dozen flashlights, there came another lightning flash and enormous boom from the outside, and the glow from the electric lights suddenly ceased.

For a moment the only sound was the clatter of rain against the windows and the howling wind outside. Then a click of light where the professor had been standing.

"Well, this is something," he said. "I think we might be safe here until morning."

As if on cue, a loud thump thumped over their heads, as if something large had been dropped on a second-floor floor. Something large but small enough to bounce, actually, for the sound was more of a "THUMP! thump-thump."

"What was that?" the stunning blonde said, a trace of anxiety in her voice.

"Hopefully, it was something that blew over near an open window," Gerald Hallstrom said with a glint of whimsy in his voice. "Of course, it could be a poltergeist."

"Jerry, stop, people are scared enough, thank you," Virginia teased with a light push.

"It's cold in here," Turner said. "And we're all wet. Let's see if we can find the great room. I think there's a big fireplace in there. Do we have enough flashlights for everyone?"

They did. The mansion was large but arranged fairly predictably. A door from the kitchen led into a big dining room. Double doors led into a hallway, but another set of double doors across the corridor led into a huge living room. The room was arranged as you might expect a wealthy family's great room to be arranged: Lightning flashes and flashlight beams revealed sumptuous couches and chairs, a grand piano in the corner, paintings and a great moose head on the walls. Facing the water – actually, it was so dark and stormy outside that you could only assume they were facing the water, which was a good assumption since despite the storm the Shikaakwa River probably wasn't going anywhere – were a pair of two-story-high windows flanking a massive fireplace. The natural stone of the chimney followed the windows up to the ceiling and beyond.

"Perfect," said the captain as seven flashlight beams played up and down the fireplace and around the room. "Let's see if we can get a fire going."

The home was built solidly, but on this night even those great windows rattled a bit from the ferocity of the storm outside. Still, it was not long before a cozy fire was crackling in the great fireplace, making the dark and stormy night outside seem more like it was outside.

Dana noticed something obvious: "We're all soaked to the skin. They left all of this furniture here; I wonder if there's clothing somewhere, too. Robes or blankets or something."

"Let's go looking," said the professor, perhaps a little too eagerly.

"Hang on, Romeo, we probably shouldn't be wandering all over this place," Sarah Turner said. She walked over to the great windows and started unhooking the huge curtains. "I think I see plenty of warm blankets right here."

A few minutes later seven figures draped in draperies were huddled around the fireplace, grateful for the shelter and slowly drying out while the howl of the raging storm howled outside. Wet clothes were spread out near the fire while everyone clung modestly to their allotted curtains. Sarah Turner, the captain, stared defiantly at the flames; next to her, the blonde who would be Marilyn's stare was more empty. The first mate, Gil, watched in awe as lightning flashed outside the window, each burst of brilliance revealing torrents of rain and trees thrashing in the gale. Gerald and Ginny Hallstrom leaned against each other with the confidence and comfort that comes from having weathered many a storm together. The professor's eyes danced around the room, alert to every small sound, taking in the many details of the ornate, well-furnished room.

Dana Dunsmore sat quietly under the great moose head. She had grown accustomed to being rescued by her superhero husband for nearly 20 years, but now she wondered if he even had a clue where she was.

"I would hate to be caught outside in this," Gil muttered.

"You *were* caught outside in this, nimrod," the captain said, but there was a trace of humor in her tone this time.

There was not much talking for the longest time. Rain rattled against the windows and windy noises, but they were wrapped in heavy curtains, the fire in the fireplace was crackling and warm, and the aroma of burning wood brought Dana Dunsmore's thoughts back to campfires and marshmallows. She began to feel safe and sleepy.

So, naturally, that's when all hell broke loose.

"I know what you're thinking."

Paul Phillips stood alone at the window to his living room, looking out at the ferocious storm. Now, if you or I was standing alone in our homes, we might be startled to hear a voice coming from the bookshelf. Paul Phillips didn't flinch.

He didn't even turn fully around to look at the shelf, where a frankly ugly old vase sat by itself. The green thing featured the crude image of a red bird and was dotted in seemingly random fashion by jewels here and there. Paul turned his head in the direction of the vase and said, "I'll bite. What am I thinking?"

"Something along the lines of 'Where in the holy Sam hill is Dana?'" The voice could have belonged to a female-sounding male or a male-sounding female, if it didn't in fact belong to an ancient, misshapen vase.

"Well done," Paul Phillips said with more than a trace of sarcasm. "You must have dug deep into your soulkeeper's intuitive powers to figure out I'm worried about my wife in the most horrible storm I've seen in years. Do you know where she is?"

The Soulkeeper of Kiribati – which is the formal name of the vase – did have a keen sense of when forces of evil were afoot nearby, and it knew when trouble was imminent. He was the link that linked the great phoenix, Mychus the warrior and Paul Phillips. But its powers were limited.

"Do I look like a GPS unit?" The soulkeeper also had a mouth. Well, all right, vases do not have mouths, but this particular vase did have a little bit of an edge, especially after 18 years of working with a mortal who sometimes seemed a bit thick to the average immortal being. "Best I can tell you is she's out there somewhere and not in immediate danger. But I should put a little emphasis on that word 'immediate' there."

"What does that mean?"

There was a short pause that, if the vase had lungs, could have been spent exhaling one of those sighs people exhale before delivering unhappy news.

"I get a feeling she's pretty close to a source of evil."

"What!?" Paul became alarmed. "Where is she?"

"Is there are part of 'Do I look like a GPS unit?' that wasn't clear? Where was she supposed to be?"

"She had an appointment with a couple of rich clients. They were going to –" and the alarm became something akin to horror. "They were going to take a cruise boat out on the river."

"A three-hour tour?"

"Spare me the pop culture jokes," Paul said, reaching for his phone. Good thing she told him which cruise boat. He looked up the number, punched "Call now" and held the device to his ear.

Voicemail. Of course it would be voicemail, it was after dark. He punched the number for police dispatch.

"Astor City Police."

"Hey Blanche, Paul Phillips."

"Criminy, Paul, we're kinda busy right now to talk to the media."

"Not why I'm calling. By any chance do you have any reports of a missing cruise boat?"

"I don't have a press release. I can't talk to you about that, you know that –"

"My wife might be on the boat! What's going on?"

Just enough of a pause for Blanche to register Paul Phillips' anxiety. "Yeah, sorry, Paul, you're the third call I've taken. Was she going to be on a Turner Cruises riverboat?"

His heart sank a little deeper and he closed his eyes. "Yes."

"It's late coming back. We've got some squads looking along the river with spotlights. It's way too choppy out there to put down the rescue boat right now. No sign yet." A longer pause. "Paul?"

Paul Phillips raced out into the storm.

First, there were footsteps. Then, there were voices. Then, three men entered the great room from the corridor. Seven people wrapped in draperies started from their places on the plush furniture.

"He's not going to be all nice and patient with us forever," a gruff voice was saying. "We gotta find the stash soon or – who the hell are these people?"

The speaker was a huge man with an ugly scar across his nose. He and his two companions carried flashlights, but he reached into his trenchcoat and hauled out an ugly-looking pistol.

"What is this?" the leader barked.

"I beg your pardon," the professor said. "We had no idea anyone else was in the house."

"We wrecked our cruise boat. Took shelter," Sarah Turner said.

For a moment no one spoke. The fire popped and crackled. The moose on the wall seemed to preside over the great room in silence.

"Well, ya can't stay here," the huge man said finally. This caused some general alarm, but being naked under their draperies and confronted by a firearm, no one did anything beside gasp and/or say "What?!"

"Where do you suggest we go on a night like this?" Dana Dunsmore said. As if to punctuate her question, a tree crashed to the ground outside, shattering the glass in a patio table outside the great windows. The chief thug flashed his pistol toward the noise but did not fire.

"Get the boss," the big man said, pointing to an underling.

"Awww, come on, Pookie, he said he wanted to get some sleep," the minion said.

"He said, 'Don't wake me up unless it's an emergency,'" the leader snapped. "What do you think this is, a bunch of pokes sitting around the living room with a fire?"

"He ain't gonna like getting woke up," the underling muttered as he left the room.

Pookie. Why did that name sound familiar? Dana Dunsmore frowned. It certainly was no common name for a gangster. Did Paul mention it after one of his adventures? You'd think I'd remember a name like Pookie, she told herself.

"OK, we're just going to sit here by the fire until the boss gets here to sort this all out," Pookie said, standing at the edge of the group brandishing his pistol.

"That's what we were doing when we came in, my man," Gerald Hallstrom said with forced friendliness. "Why don't you put that thing away? We're wet and tired and no threat to you now."

"Yeah, 'now' being the operative word," Pookie said.

"Oh come, we *all* broke into this house," Hallstrom persisted. "We could agree to leave each other alone. It's a dark, stormy night outside."

"Now you sound like a bad movie," the thug said. Everyone's a critic. "Let's say we agree to shaddup and just don't talk anymore."

The happy crackling of the warm fire contrasted with the chill in the air for several silent moments. Pookie did not put the gun away.

"Why are you here?" Gil asked. "Your clothes are dry, so you've been here since before the storm."

"Tell you what, Sherlock, it's none of your business," Pookie said. "We're here on business."

"We checked this room for it already, right, Pook?" the remaining underling said. "They couldn't have found it themselves, could they?"

A suspicious glint formed in Pookie's eye, but it faded. "We went through this room first. Nah, it ain't in here."

"What are you looking for? Maybe we can help you." Surprisingly, this was the Marilyn Monroe-ish woman who had kept to herself thus far.

"Maybe you can," the underling said, admiring the view as she shrank back a little. "I can think of a few ways you could help us out."

"Please. Is that all anyone ever thinks about?" The girl sounded unspeakably sad more than angry.

"Do you blame a guy? Maybe I'll just help myself to –"

"Knock it off, Sid," Pookie said. "Don't be rude. You know the boss hates rudeness."

Dana Dunsmore gasped. She remembered who Pookie was, and for whom he worked.

"What's wrong with you, lady?" Pookie said.

"Nothing's wrong," she stammered. "I – I just –"

"I think she's made you," the underling said.

"Is that it, lady? You know who I am?"

"No, no," Dana said, lying and getting a tad more anxious. "I just – stifled a yawn, that's all."

"Now we're putting you to sleep?"

"Nothing of the sort," Virginia Hallstrom said. "My goodness, we've been through a boat wreck, we've already told you, we're tired and wet and just want to be left alone."

"Why don't you just shoot us all and be done with it?" the professor said. "It's what you're going to do anyway, isn't it?"

"My, my, my, no, no," said a pleasant voice from just outside the door. "That's not our style at all, my friend."

Under other circumstances the little man who stepped into the room just then might have sent a bemused chuckle through the group. He was quite short, barely 5 feet tall, and had a bald, round head. His eyes, which could scarcely be seen, were huge behind thick glasses too large for his face.

"Greetings to all of you," the little man said. "I'm so glad you're safe from the storm, but you do complicate matters a tad. I would be pleased to introduce myself. I call myself –"

"Ladies and gentlemen," Dana Dunsmore interrupted, denying the newcomer his pleasure. "Meet Dr. Skull."

Act 3

Uncomfortable companions

"THIS is the world's nicest bad guy?" Captain Sarah Turner asked, her eyes wide.

The title seemed to make Dr. Skull wince while eliciting a slight smile of pride. "The same. Although I am not altogether comfortable with the appellation."

"You are one of the most evil thieves this city has ever seen," Dana Dunsmore Phillips snapped.

The little man looked genuinely hurt.

"Evil? I am merely an entrepreneur," he smiled, showing huge teeth. "I always make a point of donating 10 percent of my earnings back to worthy causes, God's tithe, if you will."

"I don't think that's what God had in mind," Dana said. "And entrepreneurs help people, they don't hold them up at gunpoint."

"Yes, well, perhaps I'm less subtle than the average businessman," Dr. Skull said. "Be that as it may, you are our guests and we will see to your comfort, but I must insist that you stay right here in this room. Jennings, if you would fetch – one, two, three," counting under his breath, "seven of those cozy bathrobes we saw hanging outside the sauna, that would probably be more practical than these draperies."

"Businessman? You're a common thief," Gerald Hallstrom muttered. "You wouldn't know a real businessman if he bit you on the nose."

Dr. Skull shrugged. "Let's not argue about semantics. The night is unpleasant enough."

As Jennings headed off, Pookie and Sid continued to hold their guns on the group.

"What is this all about?" Gil said. "What were you looking for anyway?"

"What *are* we looking for: We're still looking, I must say with some disappointment," said their smiling host. "I don't suppose any of you has seen a huge quantity of cash lying about?"

"We were shipwrecked," Sarah Turner said sardonically. "Not much time to look for cash."

"Yes, well," Dr. Skull said. "The owner of this house didn't completely trust banks, and we have it on good authority –"

"Are you sure this is a good idea telling them, sir?"

"Pookie, Pookie, Pookie, they're in no position to interfere," the boss said gently, and continued, "We have it on good authority that he left several hundred thousand dollars somewhere in this house when he died, maybe more."

"That's just an urban legend," the professor said. "The heirs made it clear they'd removed anything of real value from this house."

"The heirs don't need treasure hunters like us wandering the hallways," said the little leader. "You may have noticed they never put the house on the market, either. Wouldn't you want to cash in your inheritance – unless you had a feeling there still was something here that had never been found?"

"We're 'in no position to interfere,' you said," said Marilyn. "What does that mean? What are you going to do with us?"

"Oh, my dear, you've never examined my record," Dr. Skull said sadly. "You would find we never kill anyone, not even witnesses."

"You tied up Myke Phoenix and dropped him into the river, and you held a gun to a little old lady's head," Dana recalled. "And when you got out of prison, you held an entire paper factory and its workers hostage for a week."

"And yet all are still alive," he rejoindered. "Well, I can't speak for the little old lady; that was 18 years ago, after all. My point is, we're not going to kill you, no matter how much my friend Pookie argues with me. So everyone just sit tight right here and let us go about our business. Sid, stay with them."

"If you're not going to kill us, then –" the professor ran toward Sid with the intention of tackling him.

Dr. Skull withdrew a pistol from inside his coat jacket, took careful aim and shot the professor in the knee. And when I say he "took careful aim," I mean to say that despite the fact that the sequence took all of one or two seconds, Dr. Skull had time to take careful aim – that's how fast he reacted to the professor's lunge. It seemed this common thief had uncommon ability with a firearm.

"There are many ways to cope with a situation other than killing people," Dr. Skull said, playfully blowing imaginary smoke from the barrel of the gun as the professor writhed on the floor.

It was at about that time when Jennings returned with the robes, which allowed the naked professor to regain some semblance of modesty, not that he cared so much about his appearance with his knee severely damaged. Fortuitously, the thug grabbed a pile of about 10 guest robes, not bothering to count to seven, and so there was leftover material to form a makeshift tourniquet and bandage for Sarah and Gil to engineer and stop the bleeding.

"Boss, won't they be able to be witnesses against us?" Sid asked nervously.

"Think of it as an incentive not to get caught," replied the cheerful ringleader. "We are grand larcenists, not murderers, and that's that. Now, let's the rest of us get on with the search, shall we?"

Jennings took a seat near the door, and the seven refugees from the storm – who now felt a bit more like hostages – settled back into their exhaustion.

"Well, this is a fine how-do-you-do," Gerald Hallstrom said in a voice only his wife and their publicist-to-be could hear.

"My husband is going to be worried sick," Dana said. "That's actually a positive thing."

"How do you mean?"

"Well, Paul has – sources – and connections. If they can figure out where we are, help will be on its way soon."

"If they can figure out where we are," Virginia Hallstrom repeated.

The wind howled a lonely howl, and rain continued to pelt the big windows.

At that particular moment Paul Phillips was not feeling as confident as his wife that he would be coming to the rescue anytime soon. He pressed his face into the wind and peered across the wide Shikaakwa River. From shore he couldn't even see Dog Island or Big Island. The rain was pounding too hard, and the power outage left the islands in total darkness. He sensed more than actually saw the land formations in the middle of the great river.

What he surely did not see were the lights of a missing cruise boat.

Paul Phillips raised his hands in exasperation, but it was Myke Phoenix who lowered them to his side.

"This is going to be like finding a needle in a hay-STARGH," the great warrior said. The variation in the pronunciation of the word *haystack* was caused by a large tree landing with some force against the back of his head and shoulders.

You see, a handy side effect of the strange forces that made Myke Phoenix was that whenever serious danger is imminent, Paul Phillips automatically made the instant swap with the body of Mychus, the ancient warrior who once used the invulnerable body before his soul passed to the next life. Even though Paul did not see the oak tree that was leaning precariously and then being blown down on his head, the body swap occurred in plenty of time for Myke Phoenix to absorb the punishment and survive.

"I suppose if I'm going to venture out in a superstorm, the superhero's body is more appropriate attire," Myke said, rubbing the back of his neck. Although no known weapon had ever punctured his impregnable skin or broken the mighty bones or internal organs, Myke Phoenix did suffer aches and pains from various collisions with trees, bullets and the like – not so much pain as the average person who's been hit by a tree, but certainly enough to remind him to dodge trees and bullets when possible.

"I'm an idiot," he added as soon as he looked back out across the river, for with his warrior's sharp eyes instead of the fortysomething reporter's vision, the contours of the two great islands were a little sharper through the rain. He could make out the waving trees, as well as the vague shapes of homes and other structures. If he had switched to the superhero body sooner, the search would have progressed faster. "But now we're in business, more or less."

He scanned the river in every direction again. No sign of the cruise boat. Either it was wrecked on the shore of the river or one of the islands, or it sank. Because a forceful landfall carried a greater chance of survival than a sinking, Myke chose to believe they were on an island – and if they wrecked on shore, the police would have found them by now.

"Here goes nothing," he said, and took a running leap into the air toward Dog Island. Under normal conditions his incredible leg muscles could provide enough of a boost to make it across the water. However, as we've mentioned several times now, conditions were anything but normal this night. As soon as he was 50 feet or so into the air, a gust of wind smacked the superhero in the chest and threw him back to the shore again, where he landed unceremoniously on the rocks.

The trip to the islands was going not going to be made through the air this dark morning. Myke Phoenix waded into the choppy water and began to swim.

Dana Dunsmore was staring at a specific spot on the wall. She motioned to Sarah Turner, who made sure her work on the professor's injured knee was holding and walked over under Sid's watchful eye.

"Skipper, do you like old movies?" Dana asked under her breath.

"Sure."

"Did you ever watch a haunted mansion movie with Abbott and Costello?"

The captain followed the path of Dana's eyes to the spot on the wall. Her own eyes widened, but only just a bit; after all, there was a thug watching.

"Don't you think they would have checked that?"

"You would think so, but maybe they don't like old movies."

"I'll distract our little buddy, and you take a look when we're out of the room," Sarah said.

The captain sauntered over to Sid, who eyed her warily.

"What do you want?" he said, and shifted his weapon enough to remind her he was holding a gun.

"Your boss is quite the marksman to hit a moving target that neatly," she said.

"Oh yeah? Maybe he was trying to hit his head."

She chuckled as best she could. "Oh, I don't think so. The bullet hit square on the kneecap. You don't make a shot like that by accident." As she talked, she walked around so that Sid's back was to Dana. "He's going to need a few days in the hospital."

"After the guys and me are long gone, lady," Sid said. "You just sit tight now."

"Well, that's the thing," she said, shifting her weight from one foot to the other and back in nervous fashion. "Is there a rest room around here somewhere?"

"Hold it."

"What?"

"I mean, hold it. No potty breaks."

"You have to be kidding. I've been surrounded by water all day and night, there's a rainstorm going on outside. I have to go."

The henchman sighed and looked back into the room. Most of the group hadn't moved, and the other woman the skipper had been talking to was now settled into an easy chair underneath the big moosehead. Maybe for a couple of minutes ...

"OK, come here, there's a bathroom down the hall. Don't try anything funny."

Dana Dunsmore listened to the footsteps fade away, heard a door open and close, and leaped up to stand on the big easy chair. Her hands could just reach the dead moose's mouth, and she tried prying the mouth open. She was not surprised when the jaw moved easily.

She reached into the mouth and pulled out three packets of wrapped $100 bills. Banks normally wrap bills in stacks of 100. She was holding $30,000 in her hand. She reached up with the other hand and felt into the moosehead, withdrawing another fist full of five or six packets, and gravity brought three or four more out of the mouth and to the ground. She could tell by touch that there was plenty more inside the moosehead.

The reclusive millionaire had hidden his emergency cash fund in plain sight, using the moosehead to hold that —

"Grand!" Came a cheerful voice behind Dana. She turned with a start to find that Dr. Skull had quietly returned. "You have located our quarry for us. Thank you so much."

He motioned with the pistol for her to climb back down. Her shoulders and spirits sagged.

Act 4
Day break

"ONE for you, one for me. Two for you, one, two for me. Three for you, one, two, three for me." With a broad grin on his face, Jennings was motioning with his hands as if doling out cash.

"What in Sam's hill are you doing?" Pookie asked, not at all amused.

"Haven't you ever seen that movie? It's hilarious."

"Jennings, you mean to say you saw a movie where they hid the loot in a moosehead, and you didn't think to look until the broad did?"

"I –" The underling's face sank as he realized he'd goofed rather badly. "No, sorry."

The moosehead itself was bolted to the wall much more securely than need be, indicating that the millionaire always intended for the dead animal head to double as his cash stash. Once the head was emptied, Dr. Skull and his now-cheerful minions had taken possession of $770,000.

"Not bad for a single night's work," the little man with the thick glasses chirped. "All right then, let's pack up and get to the boathouse."

The refugees' clothes had dried by the fire, and they were dressed or in the process of getting dressed with the exception of the professor, who lay on the couch alternately glaring at the criminals and clenching his fists in pain.

The exotic blonde walked up and knelt beside him.

"Thank you for trying to stop them, that was very brave," she said, and placed a hand on his.

His grimace softened considerably. "Well. You're welcome. I – ow! – do wish I had thought it through a little more."

"I need you to know," she said, lowering her voice. "You saved my life. I've been thinking of killing myself, but this has showed me how much there is to live for."

"Killing yourself?" His eyes widened. "Why?"

"People think being beautiful is a wonderful thing," she said. "Well, of course it is, but the way I look is only part of who I am. And so many men think they can just – never mind. It's – it's complicated. I just needed you to know. I don't know how I can ever thank you."

"Dinner? A cup of coffee? And I promise not to mention that you're the most beautiful woman I've ever seen."

She smiled sheepishly, a quick smile that faded when she looked over his shoulder. Dr. Skull stood over them with the broad grin that seemed never to leave his face.

"I do want to apologize for the knee. I believe this will make your medical expenses a bit more manageable," he said, tossing two of the $10,000 packets onto the professor's chest.

A jumble of emotions and possible rejoinders rippled across the professor's face, and all he managed to say was, "Go to hell."

"Been there, done that," the cheery villain said, turning and waving a hand. "Hell is not at all what everyone says it is."

He gathered his henchmen at the door to the great hall and looked at the seven bedraggled shipwreck survivors.

"It has been a charming night, and thank you, Mrs. Phillips, for finding our earnings," he said. "The storm has subsided, and since you have all lost your phones, I believe it's safe for us to assume you won't be discussing this with the authorities for a little while. Have a lovely life."

And with that, the bad guys departed.

A few minutes passed, and in the distance they heard the sound of a boat motor starting. It was the mighty roar of a powerful speedboat clearing the mansion's boathouse. By dawn's early light they could see a number of trees that had been toppled and standing water in large puddles everywhere. Across Astor City, and the entire region, no doubt downed trees and power lines and high water were causing havoc.

"I'm afraid it may be a while before anyone comes to check this old place," Gerald Hallstrom said. "They have more vital things to worry about."

"I don't know, now that the water's calm, they're going to come looking for us," Sarah Turner said. "You probably can see the boat foundering from the west shore of the river."

The sound of the speedboat faded.

"I'm going to go out and take a look around," Gil said. "There's gotta be something we can signal the shore with."

"Good idea, I'll come with," Sarah said, scrambling to her feet.

Suddenly from the hallway came the sound of the front doors slamming open with a bang.

"DANA?" shouted a strong, authoritative voice. "Are you in here?"

"That's my – that's Myke Phoenix!" Dana cried, and shouted, "in the great hall! This way!"

Paul Phillips – whose soul was motivating the body of Mychus the great ancient warrior – wanted desperately to run to Dana and enfold her in his massive arms in relief. But the two of them had managed to hide his dual identity for 18 years, and to be honest she had survived quite a handful of more dire situations than this, so Myke Phoenix resisted the urge and looked around the big room as if assessing the situation objectively.

"Hello, Dana," he did say. "Paul will be out-of-his-mind relieved that you're all right. I was searching around Dog Island, and as the sun came up I saw the sunken boat on the shore over here. The wind has died down, so it was a quick jump over here. I saw your tracks in the sand heading up here."

"Hell of a wreck," Sarah said. "But Gil here helped me coax her close enough to the island that we all got out," putting a gentle hand on her first mate's shoulder that revealed something more than pride and affection.

"You're all OK, then?"

"Well, except for the professor here. He was shot in the knee," said Gerald Hallstrom.

"Shot? How?"

"Dr. Skull was here," Dana said simply. "He and his men left a few minutes ago. By boat."

The eyes of Myke Phoenix became narrow slits.

"I'll be right back," he said harshly.

The Shikaakwa River is wide as rivers go, but it is still only a wide river. It only took the speedboat a few minutes to reach its destination on the west bank. Dr. Skull jumped onto the dock with the satchel carrying the money while Pookie, Sid and Jennings secured the boat.

A helicopter was parked not far from the dock, facing the water. The little man waved as he ran up the small hill. The engine began to whine, and the big rotor began to spin slowly.

Dr. Skull saw the pilot's attention drawn to something high and behind him, which apparently descended quickly and landed with a loud "THUMP!" on the dock. He turned as he ran to see a large man in a white costume making quick work of a fight with his underlings.

"Myke Phoenix! How did *he* find us?" Dr. Skull said out loud, leaping into the passenger seat and shouting, "Get us out of here!"

We've established that Myke Phoenix had the strength to – well, if he couldn't leap tall buildings in a single bound, he could certainly cover the distance between Dog and Big islands, and he could jump from Big Island onto the west bank of the Skikaakwa River.

However, he couldn't leap high enough to reach a speeding helicopter above the ground. And although he could follow the chopper with great leaps and bounds, it wouldn't be long before the flying machine outpaced him. The wiser thing to do was to go back to the dock, corral the three now-unconscious minions for the authorities, and leap back to Big Island to rescue the group from the old mansion.

High in the sky and racing away, Dr. Skull pondered the events of the past few minutes while plotting the raid on the county jail that would take place a few days later, returning Pookie, Sid and Jennings to his employ.

"That dad-blamed superhero could not have known we were there, so he didn't come looking for us," he mused. "He had to be looking for one or more of those people. Which ones?"

If the evil villain drew any conclusions from his musings, he did not share them immediately. And four days later, 10 charities around Astor City were pleasantly shocked to receive cashier's checks for $7,700 each.

Myke Phoenix stopped at the sheriff's department long enough to alert them about the people stranded on Big Island, made a mighty leap back to the mansion, collected the professor for an emergency jump to the hospital, and told them help was on its way.

(Yes, he could have made seven round-trip leaps over the water, but even superheroes can drop passengers, and the landing does result in a bit of a jolt. Rescue by police patrol boat is a slower but safer and more practical solution except in emergency situations like getting care for a kneecap that was shattered by gunshot. And it also allowed for Paul Phillips to be waiting at the Turner Cruises dock when the rescue boat arrived with his wife and the others.)

As Paul Phillips unclenched the mighty hug that Myke Phoenix had yearned to deliver to Dana Dunsmore Phillips, Gerald and Ginny Hallstrom walked up to the relieved couple.

"Well, Dana, this has been one hell of a cruise," Gerald said with a wry smile.

"Yes, I'm sorry about that," Dana replied.

"Oh, no, it was quite the adventure, and we're all safe and sound now," Virginia said, patting Dana's arm. "All's well that ends well, eh?"

"I'll call in a few days and we can reschedule the appointment," Dana said. "I'd still like to have the Dunsmore Agency working for you."

"What's that? You thought we were still trying to make up our minds?" Gerald said. "My dear woman, we thought the cruise was to celebrate our new partnership. Of course we want to hire your firm. But do call in a few days and we'll talk about it."

As Dana watched the wealthy couple stroll away arm in arm, Paul reached over gently and lifted her dropped jaw back into position.

"Congratulations," he said. "Looks like you made the sale."

Sarah Turner and Gil walked up, perhaps not surprisingly also holding hands, although the skipper detached as they came up.

"You'll get your money back for the cruise, of course," she said to Dana. "I'm so sorry about this."

"I'm sorry about your boat."

"Insurance will cover it," Sarah shrugged. "The main thing is we got everyone to shore safe and sound, more or less. Hell of a storm."

"Thank you, Ms. Turner, you did a great job under the circumstances."

"I had a lot of great help," she said, looking at her first mate with something more than admiration. "You don't always realize what you've got until the chips are down."

Finally, the stunning blonde walked up timidly.

"Myke Phoenix seemed to know you, miss," said Marilyn's doppelganger. "Do you happen to know which hospital he took the professor to?"

Dana looked at her husband and back to the woman. "We surely do. Would you like a ride there?"

The blonde's eyes welled. "Yes, I would. Thank you so much."

"Where's your car, Paul?" Dana said, knowing full well that Paul had taken a flying leap to the dock but knowing somebody had to ask.

"I – got a ride here with the police," he said. "I guess we're all going with you."

"Let's get out of here, then," Dana said. "I've had all the water I can handle for a long time."

Epilogue

"A puppy?" Paul Phillips peered over the top of the Astor City Tribune comics section. "Let me think about that for a few months."

"The place just seems a little empty since Frick died," Dana said. Frick and Frack were the black-and-white cats that formed the rest of their blended family when they were first married. Frack lived until shortly after their 12th anniversary, and Frick had died at the ripe old cat age of 20, not long before the serial kisser became a problem in Astor City.

"Dogs are entirely different animals than cats," Paul said. "I'm not adverse to the idea, but give me some time to get used to it."

"OK," she said. "Oh, did you see this about a jailbreak?"

"I see someone hasn't been reading the Astor City Beacon," he said. "Pookie, Jennings and Sid all escaped somehow. They're still trying to figure out what happened. Dr. Skull had to be behind it; it was neat and clean and nobody got hurt."

"I see someone hasn't been telling me what happened at work," she reproached her journalist husband. "Don't you think I'd like to know when my hostage-takers break out of jail?"

"You have enough on your mind. And besides, Myke Phoenix will always protect you."

"You ain't immortal," came a voice from the ugly green vase on the bookshelf.

"Oh, thank you for your vote of confidence," Paul said. "I'm not planning on dying anytime soon, or do you know something I don't know?"

"I'm just saying don't get cocky, son," the vase said. "Always is a long time. And oh by the way, Quincy Quackenbos is getting out in a couple of weeks."

One of his oldest adversaries, the half-man-half-duck was finishing his second prison sentence, having not learned his lesson after Myke Phoenix ended his criminal behavior early in the superhero's career. Whether the lesson stuck the second time would be a matter of conjecture in the not-too-distant future.

"I think I'll worry about that when the time comes, if you don't mind," Paul said.

"I never mind," said the vase, and was silent for the rest of the morning.

"Do you want the comics section?" Paul asked his wife.

"I thought you'd never ask."

Duck Man Walking

Prologue

ONCE upon a time there was a little boy named Quincy who had a pet duck named Quacky. He and his family lived on Bikini Atoll until one day they blew it up. And they came back on other days to blow it up again. Unfortunately, one particular day and one particular explosion, no one realized the Quackenbos family was there, having returned to visit the site of their obliterated home for reasons no one has ever fathomed.

Mom and Dad died searching for their son, who had wandered away and delayed their departure. Quincy and Quacky did not die that day. Neither did they live. Instead, they merged, due to some fluke of nuclear power and radiation.

Quincy Quackenbos, the Duck Man of Astor City, grew up to be one of the community's foremost scientists and entrepreneurs, Quackenbos Laboratories becoming a major employer in town. Then Myke Phoenix appeared.

An invulnerable, superpowered man fighting crime in Astor City like some sort of comic book hero? Quincy had to know more. He broke the law trying to find the secrets of what made Myke Phoenix tick. Released from prison, he broke the law again, and he went back to prison.

The business soldiered on somehow. People sympathized with the half-man, half-duck, and they empathized with the honest men and women who worked at Quackenbos Labs, so they continued to do business with them. It wasn't their fault that their boss had turned into a pathological criminal.

During his second prison term, Quincy declared himself rehabilitated.

"The people who believed in me and worked for me, our customers, and the general public deserve better than the person I have been for the past 18 years," he said in a statement emailed to the media. "I don't know if the board of directors will have me back, but in any case I will devote the rest of my life to the cause of good."

And that brings us to the present day. Twelve days after his 64th birthday, Quincy Quackenbos was released from prison.

A limousine waited outside the gates of the state penitentiary, a limo with the well-known Quackenbos Laboratories logo emblazoned modestly below the windows on the driver- and passenger-side doors. The massive front gate rolled open, and a man carrying a small satchel walked through.

Wait: It was not a man after all, although it was as tall as a man and walking on two legs. His head and face – and indeed, his entire body – were covered with feathery hair, and he had a bill. Not a wide, flat bill like a cartoon character, nor were his eyes large half-ovals that took up most of the top half of his face. Have you ever seen a duck? That kind of bill, and those kind of eyes.

The back door opened, and a man in an expensive suit climbed out. He was a little taller than the duck man, with round glasses. He smiled a genuine smile at seeing an old friend free for the first time in a long time.

"Hello, Quincy," the man said.

"Duckworth," Quackenbos quacked, for his voice held a lingering tone of Quacky, the pet duck whose body and soul had merged with his when he was a child. "You came in person."

This was Brian Duckworth, president and CEO of Quackenbos Laboratories, the straight-shooting and honest man who was installed in that position to preserve the corporation when its founder lost his mind and veered into a life of crime.

"I told you once I would stand with you in whatever honorable venture you undertake," Duckworth said with a calm smile. "If what you've said is true, I'm with you all the way."

Quincy Quackenbos stared, and his eyes grew a bit watery. He extended a feathery hand.

"Thank you, Brian," he said. "You're the only friend I have in this crazy world. I won't let you down again."

The man and the manduck climbed into the back of the limousine, and the long vehicle drove away. Here is where I must draw your attention to another dark-colored vehicle, a sport utility vehicle with tinted windows, parked across the street.

A man and a driver sat inside watching the touching scene at the prison gate. Neither spoke until after the limo pulled away.

"OK, I've seen enough," the man said. "He's out. I just needed to make sure it happened."

"Want me to follow him, boss?" asked the driver.

"No. Nothing more to do today. Let's give him a few days on the outside before I recruit him."

"You don't want to get right down to business?"

"Myke Phoenix has been a thorn in our side for almost two decades," the man said. "I can afford to be patient for a little while longer before I get Quackenbos to kill him."

Act 1
Change never comes easy

PAUL Phillips and his wife, Dana Dunsmore Phillips, were having lunch at one of the middle-of-the-road restaurants in town. Dana often bought lunch for her clients at one of the upscale places like Parchisi's, but her husband was anxious about money these days, so they picked something less ostentatious.

"It's a remarkable opportunity, dear," Dana said. "You would be free to do your reporting thing without worrying about whether you have enough ads to pay the bills."

"I'd only have one 'boss,' that's for sure," Paul said, but without a lot of enthusiasm. "I'd only have one person to please instead of a lot of advertisers."

"That's the bottom line, though, isn't it? You *don't* have 'a lot' of advertisers."

Paul was the owner/proprietor/reporter/editor/ webmaster of the Astor City Beacon, a website he'd created after a long, distinguished career in radio news and then newspapers. The site allowed him to continue that career, only working for himself. The problem – one that most journalists cope with – was a shortage of income.

The item on the table this evening – besides the lasagna in front of Paul and Dana's whitefish – was the idea of applying for a grant from the Nelson P. Rodinske Foundation, a trust fund established by an extremely wealthy gentleman to support independent journalism organizations. Rodinske believed that the old media financial model – paying the bills by selling advertising and/or subscriptions – was on its way to extinction, and he handed out grants to new and existing news outlets that were willing to adopt a nonprofit status.

"You wouldn't have all those irritating pop-up ads and logos cluttering up your site," Dana said. "But don't you dare tell any of my clients I said they're irritating." As longtime owner of the Dana Dunsmore Agency, she had long ago outpaced Paul's earning prowess with her skills in marketing and advertising. She and her staff had also directed clients' ad budgets in the Beacon's direction, but it was a hard sell even in these connected times.

"A Rodinske grant could cover all my expenses and a decent salary, no doubt," he said. "But what if I unearth some dirt on someone he supports?" In addition to his media pursuits, Nelson Rodinske was a prominent contributor to politicians who shared a certain point of view. "He says he's just interested in good journalism, and let the chips fall where they may, but would he really keep his hands off?"

"If he jerks the funding, you just find another foundation," Dana replied with a straight face, then burst into the musical laugh that Paul adored. "I know – there are no other foundations that give out this much money. But then you get four or five smaller grants. There's always a way, Paul. The nonprofit route just seems simpler to me than dozens of advertising contracts. It opens up a whole 'nother brand of headache, but you'd have fewer moving parts."

"You may be right," Paul mused, and then he was distracted by the couple being escorted past their table. "Josiah Petri and Terri Travers! Hi!"

Petri was the forensic medical examiner for Astor County, and Dr. Travers was a natural science professor at the University of Astor City. Their paths first crossed when her expertise in arachnology was needed to deal with a pair of giant, fire-breathing spiders that menaced the community a few months earlier.

"Uh oh, Terri, we have to be careful what we say, the media is here," Petri smiled.

"Come on, Josie, I'm off-duty," Paul replied – and though he didn't let his face register it, inside his brain he said, "Oops."

"Don't you get started on that 'Josie' stuff," the examiner said, still smiling but without as much enthusiasm. "Your funny friend Myke Phoenix calls me that all the time because he knows I hate it."

"Sorry, Josiah, I guess I've been hanging around the guy too much," Paul said, which was more than true: Paul Phillips *was* Myke Phoenix. Only Dana knew that truth, and few suspected, because for nearly 20 years the now-middle-aged journalist had been occasionally using the body of an ancient warrior named Mychus in an exchange he admittedly did not quite understand. Mychus had long ago passed to the next life and had no further use of his mighty frame.

"How is your hand, Dr. Travers?" Dana ventured.

"Terri, please, and thanks for asking," the arachnologist replied. Her right hand and forearm had been horribly burned when her encounter with the fire-spitting giant spider got a little too up close and personal. She looked at the hand and made an obvious effort to flex it, but the fingers only twitched slightly. "To be honest, they don't have much hope that I'll regain full use of it, but I keep up the physical therapy. Good thing I've always done a lot of things lefthanded; I'm sort of ambidextrous."

"That is good, but it's a shame," Dana replied sympathetically.

"The spider didn't kill me, thanks to Myke Phoenix," Terri said. "Where there's life, there's always hope."

"Well, we don't want to interrupt your meal, and I'm hungry myself," Josiah Petri said. "Good to see you both."

As the hostess continued to escort the two scientists to a table, Dana raised her eyebrows at Paul with a smile.

"Josiah Petri and Terri Travers," she said in a knowing tone. "Who would have guessed?"

"It's a match made in a forensic laboratory," Paul smiled back. A ringtone from his pocket suddenly played the theme from "WKRP in Cincinnati." It was his dedicated cellphone for Astor City Beacon business. The little screen displayed the name and number of Quackenbos Laboratories. "I'd better get this," he said, his brow furrowing. "Paul Phillips, how can I help you?"

There was enough of a pause that Paul almost said "hello?" a second time, but then –

"Mr. Phillips?" an unmistakable quacky voice said. "This is Quincy Quackenbos."

"What is it, Paul?" Dana said, seeing the instant change in her husband's demeanor. He looked at her and mouthed, "It's OK." Of course, she put up her hands, palms up, and said, "I can't read lips," and he shushed her.

"How can I help you, Mr. Quackenbos?" Her eyes widened.

"It's urgent that I get in touch with Myke Phoenix," Quackenbos said. "I know that you and he are close, and he doesn't have an email address or cellphone."

"What is this about?"

"Ah, ever the reporter," Quackenbos said, attempting to lighten the mood. "I'm afraid that must be between Mr. Phoenix and myself, but I can tell you that I need to warn him about something."

"Why can't you tell me the warning? I can get him any message within minutes." Of course, seeing that Paul and Myke shared the same soul and consciousness, saying "within minutes" was stretching the point, but as you no doubt remember, his double life was a secret.

"The warning needs to be delivered in person and to Myke Phoenix. I don't think he'd believe me otherwise."

"You have to admit, you've made a habit of deceiving Myke over the years," Paul said. "How can he know he can trust you now?"

"That's all past tense," Quackenbos quacked patiently. "I want to help him now. Please, Mr. Phillips, it's in everyone's best interest that we meet. Please talk him into it. And say hello to your lovely wife."

"Don't you bring my wife into this." At that Dana began to look very alarmed.

"Oh, pish, I'm just trying to be sociable. Say hello to her or not, as you please. Just help me get in touch with your superhero friend."

Long pause.

"I'll do what I can."

"Splendid! That's all I can ask."

"What was that all about? What did he want?" Dana's questions started as soon as he broke off the call.

"Quincy Quackenbos wants to meet with Myke Phoenix. Says he has a warning for him."

She snorted gently. "Every time Mr. Quackenbos requests a meeting, Myke Phoenix gets a beating," she said. "Oh! I didn't mean that to rhyme." The laugh removed some of the chill from the air. "What are you going to do?"

"I'll meet him, see what he's up to," Paul said. "But not at his lab, I've learned that the hard way."

"You know, he's been out there talking about how he's rehabilitated and put the criminal stuff behind," Dana said hopefully. "Maybe he wants to be your sidekick."

"Myke Phoenix and Duckman, the Terrific Two. We could sell the comic book rights."

"There you go! I'll be first in line for movie tickets. Who do we get to play you?"

Quincy Quackenbos leaned forward at his desk, staring at the telephone he had used a moment ago. It was a small office, nothing like the ornate room where the chief executive officer held court. That was Brian Duckworth's job now; Quincy was the company founder, but his behavior over the past 18 years had disqualified the duck man from running the firm. And Duckworth had taken Quackenbos Labs to a new level of success. But we didn't change our perspective in this scene to discuss the corporation's success.

"I hope you're satisfied," Quackenbos muttered, looking up at the rather large man in a trenchcoat who was aiming a rather large pistol at his feathery chest.

"Oh yeah," the thug said. "You did fine."

When Myke Phoenix returned Quincy Quackenbos' call, he made arrangements for the meeting to take place in Waterfront Park.

"I just got out of prison," Quincy said. "Do you really think I'd do anything that would risk sending me back?"

"The first time I ever visited your company, you ran me through a series of experiments to see if I could be killed, and you endangered the life of Paul Phillips' wife," Myke replied. "And let's not talk about the second and third times, shall we?"

"Point taken. I am sincere about this. I do want to help," Quackenbos said. "I'll see you at the park."

Located at the fork of the Shikaakwa and (unimaginatively named) East Shikaakwa rivers, Waterfront Park was sometimes compared with New York's Central Park in its splendor, except that it was a mere 150 acres rather than 840. Once the site of one of a huge paper mill, the land had been reclaimed and turned into a grand natural area with an amphitheater that had gained a regional reputation for its musical and cultural events.

The spot where they agreed to meet was outside a pavilion with a grove of tall trees, one of them tall enough to house an elaborate treehouse where children could play. School was in session and the sun was shining when the two longtime adversaries met.

"You're looking fit," Quincy said. "But then you always look fit. You'll have to tell me how you stay so buff and young-looking someday."

"Maybe, but not today," Myke Phoenix said, a little more grim than usual. Their relationship over the years had not lent itself to small talk or friendly exchanges of workout information. "What's this about, Mr. Quackenbos?"

"I was approached shortly after my release by a gentleman who claimed to be representing a consortium of rather common criminals," the duck man also went straight to business. "They knew that through the years I have worked to develop a formula or technique that could penetrate that invulnerable skin of yours and injure or even kill you. They came to believe that I had succeeded."

"*Had* you succeeded?" Myke said.

"We'll get to that in a moment," Quincy said, walking around the superhero in such a way as to place Myke facing the pavilion with his back to the treehouse. "I just wanted to warn you that my formula seems to be in quite some demand among the underworld of Astor City and beyond, and I wanted to ask for your help."

"My help?" Myke sputtered. "What makes you think after all these years, and all your attempts to harm me and this city, I'd be willing to help you?"

"You're a good guy," Quincy quacked. "It's what you do. And after a while a person gets tired of breaking the law and spending time in prison. I'm ready to join your side."

"So I've heard," said the giant blond man with the image of a phoenix emblazoned on his chest. "You won't blame me if I say I have some trust issues with you."

"No, I don't blame you at all," Quincy said, a steely glint sparkling in his birdlike eyes. The ancient warrior and the half-man-half-duck stared at each other resolutely for a few moments and then, without turning his gaze away, Quincy said, "All right, Leonard. Do it."

From behind someone threw an arm around Myke Phoenix's neck. The superhero caught a glimpse of the assailant's other hand brandishing a syringe with a big ugly needle and a green substance inside.

"Gotcha!" said the newcomer, and he jabbed downward with the big needle.

Act 2

The Quakenbos Formula

THE needle snapped against the side of Myke's neck.

"Ouch!" yelled the superhero, reaching up to rub the spot where the needle failed to penetrate. Leonard the thug stepped back, a look of confusion on his face. Then he started to look angry and betrayed.

The thug turned to Quackenbos and was able to bark out "You tricked me!" before he was tackled by a flying feathered cannonball. Leonard fell back and banged his head, fortunately (for him) striking his noggin just off the asphalt onto the still-hard but somewhat more yielding soil at the edge of the grove. Quincy landed on Leonard's chest and began pummeling his face. The duck man's fists were covered with down, but the balled-up bludgeons were nearly as effective as any fists.

"There – is – *no* – *formula*, you – little – rodent!" Quincy shrieked, punctuating each word with a blow to Leonard's face. "Leave – me – alooonnne!" The howl of "alooonne" came after the duck man stopped slugging the thug with a left-right-left-right combination and switched his assault to wrapping the fingers of both hands around Leonard's throat, lifting back and forth so that the man's head wagged up and down as he choked.

Myke Phoenix plucked Quackenbos off the startled hoodlum, set him aside, and hauled the assailant up by the front of his jacket.

"All right, what the bejeebers is this all about?" Myke said, but then, "On second thought, hold that thought." He punched Leonard in the nose, which – in combination with the bang on the back of his head and the fowl pummeling, left the thug in a temporary state of unconsciousness. Then he turned to Quincy Quackenbos.

"Don't hit me! I'm on your side!"

"You lured me out to Waterfront Park and arrange for this jerk to inject me with some green stuff, and I'm supposed to believe –"

"He didn't inject you with anything! You know I knew the needle would break," Quincy said frantically. "I'm being straight with you, Myke. This guy held a gun on me and forced me to call Paul Phillips to set this up. He thinks I have some sort of secret formula that can kill you."

"Where is this secret formula?"

"It doesn't exist!' Quincy quacked. "I spent 15 years trying to come up with a poison, and there's no such thing."

Myke rubbed his neck unconsciously.

"All right. So why did he think you *did* have this formula?"

"My research was no secret. You know how rumors go: Someone must have decided I succeeded. I'm afraid this won't be the last attempt to force me to give it up, now that I'm out of prison."

"Sometimes," Myke said thoughtfully, "people come to conclusions because something is true. How do I know you haven't succeeded and you set up this guy Leonard to get me to relax my guard?"

"What motive would I have for not giving him the correct formula straight away? If I wanted you dead and knew how to do it, you'd be dead already, " Quincy said. "Listen, my friend, if I knew a way to kill you, I would have used it years ago. I'm not interested in that anymore. It was a fool's game, and I'm tired of being a fool. Being locked up makes a guy value his freedom."

"It also makes a guy angry enough to get revenge on who put him there."

"I'm not that guy," the duck man insisted. "I kill you – even if I could kill you – and sooner or later I go back to that lousy prison. Been there, done that. I'm out of the crime business."

Leonard started to come out of his stupor. Quincy Quackenbos slapped him across the face so hard that he sank back into unconsciousness. Myke suppressed a smile.

"You do seem to have some anger issues going on," the superhero said.

"Anger? Me angry? When did you notice?" the duck man said. "I'm angry that some mug pulls a gun on me and thinks that's all it takes to pull me back into being a criminal. But mostly I'm angry at myself, for wasted time sitting in prison when I could have been having a life – oh, and by the way, I'm still angry at myself for hiding from my parents when they were trying to get me out of a nuclear bomb zone. I have anger issues big time, pal – but I'm not. Interested. In. Killing. You. Anymore."

The last five words were punctuated by a feathered index finger jabbed into the eye of the image of the phoenix on Myke's chest. The ducklike eyes glared for several seconds of silent, uncomfortable eye contact, until the superhero blinked and attempted a wry smile.

"Quincy," said Myke, "I think this is the beginning of a beautiful friendship."

Dr. Terri Travers reached for the handle on the coffee mug and slipped three fingers through the space, leaving the pinky finger underneath. The fingers would not bend, and she couldn't bring her thumb to the top of the handle to steady it, but she was able slowly to lift the mug tremblingly to her lips and sip from it. But she made a frustrated face, grabbed the mug with her left hand and set it down.

"I hate this," she said. "I just hate it."

The lab at the University of Astor City was empty except for the professor and her beau. Josiah Petri looked at the professor with sympathetic eyes and rested his hand gently on her scarred right hand.

"It's going to take a long time," he said. "Hands are complicated tools, they take a long time to heal."

"And sometimes they *don't* heal," she said. "I'd give anything not to have grabbed that stupid spider web."

"You couldn't know it would be so sticky."

"Josiah, it was a spider web! The spider was bigger than an elephant! And I'm an arachnologist. Of all people I should have known how sticky it would be."

"You couldn't have known the spider would breathe fire."

A pause, and then the anguish in her face was invaded by a trace – just a trace – of amusement.

"All right. You got me there," she admitted. "That doesn't make this any easier."

"I just want you to stop beating yourself up as if you caused this," he said, moving his hand to her hair and drawing her close for a kiss. "How is your father doing?"

"Oh, he's obsessed with finding a way to repair the damage," she said. Dr. Jacob Travers was almost as renowned in the field of natural biology as his daughter. "I don't know why he is so intense about it – it's not his fault that the city was attacked by giant spiders."

"You're his daughter. You're hurting," Josiah replied. "Is his idea really practical?"

"Finding a way for people to regrow limbs like a reptile? I don't know," she said, finishing her coffee with her left hand. "Theoretically, yes. It would be groundbreaking, and obviously not just for me. I'm just concerned about possible side effects. I don't want to end up like some comic book experiment gone horribly wrong."

"But you'd make an adorable lizard," he replied, coaxing a laugh and a stuck-out tongue from the otherwise proper professor. "Come on, let's get you back to the lab," and he held out his right hand. She wrapped her left hand around it, smiled a grateful smile, threaded her right hand though the strap and tossed her purse over her shoulder.

"You're a wonderful guy, Josiah Petri," she said, wrinkling her nose like a teenager in his direction.

"Quincy Quackenbos wants to be friends." Dana's eyes were steely with skepticism. "You're kidding."

"I know. It's crazy," Paul Phillips said across the kitchen. "But he did take out the guy who wanted to kill me."

"And how do you know he wasn't in on it? He could have sacrificed one of his minions to gain your trust. He could have something bigger up his sleeve, something that kills you and accomplishes something even worse at the same time."

Dana Dunsmore could be forgiven for not trusting Quincy Quackenbos. When they'd first met, Quincy held her captive as bait to coerce Myke Phoenix into undergoing a series of tests – tests that the underworld believed had formed the basis for the Quackenbos Formula, whatever deadly potion or technique that may be. That was 18 years earlier, of course, but hard to forget.

"I admit I'm not always the best judge of character, Paul said. "But he seemed sincere."

"He seemed sincere when he threatened to blow up downtown if you wouldn't cooperate with his experiments," she said. "He seemed sincere when he – oh, you know all he's done."

"I do. And people do change. What do you think?"

This last question was not directed at Dana. It was almost as if Paul had turned to the bookshelf and asked a rhetorical question, like "Who is John Galt?" But then a voice came from the top shelf, where a badly constructed green vase sat like a weird party joke.

"I think the reporter's got a point." It was a lilting voice with a hard edge, the very definition of androgynous. The vase was neither male nor female, but it was some sort of life and it did speak. This was the Soulkeeper of Kiribati, which had some sort of tap into the currents of good and evil and mysteriously managed the switch that exchanged Paul Phillips' middle-aged body for the more durable Mychus model. "There was a time when I could sense an industrial-strength evil coming from Quackenbos Labs. These days it's just your common everyday ebb and flow of the universe."

"You're not as good at sensing good and evil as you are at calling forth Mychus the Warrior," Dana said, one of only two people in the world who could hear that voice. "You get confused."

"Well, sensing good and evil ain't an exact science, doll."

"I'm ready to trust him," Paul Phillips said. "I'll keep my guard up, I promise, but I really think I can trust him."

"I really am not sure I can trust you, Quincy." Brian Duckworth peered sternly over his round 1960s-throwback glasses. "Why didn't you inform me what you were doing?"

"I had to do it in completely secrecy," Quackenbos pleaded. "For one thing, the punk barely let me out of his sight after he first pulled the gun on me."

"But he did let you out of his sight for a while. You could have consulted me about this."

"I didn't even consult Myke Phoenix," the duck man quacked. "Look, I had to act like I was willing to go back to my old ways. The guy wanted the Quackenbos Formula and he wouldn't believe me when I told him it doesn't exist. We got the guy into jail, didn't we?"

"Is that true? There is no formula to kill Myke Phoenix?"

"No!" If the duck man could leave the ground, he would have done so at that moment as he flapped his arms in frustration. "I tried for years to figure out how to take the guy out. You can make him feel pain, you can knock the wind out of him, but you can't damage that body – not unless you're a talking dinosaur, and there's only one of those. There's nothing like Myke Phoenix in the world."

"So why do you think this man thought you *could* hurt him?"

An awkward moment. "I – might have once told his boss that I was close to success."

"Who's his boss?"

"She was more or less my boss, too, at the time."

"The dinosaur?"

"Yes. She was very insistent. Wasn't willing to take 'no' for an answer. But Brian, on my parents' grave, I didn't complete a working formula."

"All right," Duckworth said, his mood softening. "But Quincy, let's not have any more secrets from now on, OK? I don't need any more surprises."

"You have a deal, my friend," Quincy Quackenbos said, extending a feathered hand. "No more surprises."

"Perhaps one last surprise," said a voice from above them. A man wearing a ski mask and dressed in black dropped from the ceiling, took several steps and tackled Quincy Quackenbos. Another masked man in black stepped from a closet and tackled Brian Duckworth. Three other darkly clad figures emerged from hiding places, grabbed Duckworth, and tied him to a chair quietly and efficiently. The other two applied a makeshift muzzle to Quincy's bill.

"Don't contact the authorities when you get out of this, Duckworth," the first man said. "We need to ask Mr. Quackenbos a few questions."

"What are you going to do to him?"

"That depends on his answers."

With a rustle of ninja uniforms – that is to say, almost without a sound – the squad of dark agents was gone.

Act 3
The other side of the mirror

WHEN the blindfold was removed, Quincy Quackenbos found himself in an interrogation room. At least it looked like an interrogation room: the plain table in the middle with chairs on either side, a waste basket, a large mirror on the wall that had every appearance of being a one-way mirror where observers could watch the proceedings without being seen themselves.

Still wearing ski masks, two of the ninja-like figures settled Quackenbos in one of the chairs and left the room without another sound.

Minutes went by. Quincy Quackenbos got up, tried the door (locked, of course) and paced. He peered into the mirror to see if he could see anything in the next room. He paced some more. He sat back down at the table and folded his hands in his lap. Then he leaned on the table with his elbows on the surface. Then he rested his head on his feathered palms. Then he lay his hands on the table and pushed back with a sigh. Long story short, he was given a lot of time to fidget with nothing else to do.

After what seemed like a very long time (because it *was* a very long time), the door opened and a man walked into the room. He was wearing a well-tailored suit and a smile.

He withdrew from his coat pocket an old-fashioned egg timer, the kind with a little hourglass and three minutes' worth of sand to trickle between the two bulbs. He looked at it, displayed it across the table to the duck man, and set it with a bit of a flourish on the table between them, the sand in the bottom bulb.

"There's a marvelous little timer app on my smartphone, don't you know," the man said cheerfully. "But I do so enjoy the way we did things without all of the electronic toys, don't you agree?"

"I'm still learning how to work my smartphone," Quincy Quackenbos said in a ducklike, rumbling tone. "We weren't allowed to have them in prison."

"Yes, not a very jolly thing, that, prison," the man said, still friendly and sympathetic. "She was very sorry that you had to be incarcerated a second time."

"She?" The duck man shifted from being sullenly defiant to being curious and possibly angry. "Who are you talking about? If you're talking about who I *think* you're talking about, then –"

"We're going to do this in three-minute increments, more or less," the cheery man said, with just a hint of a glance over his shoulder at the two-way glass. "I will present a question, and you will have up to three minutes to answer the question satisfactorily. Each time the sand runs out without a good answer, I'm afraid, I shall be forced to make my questioning a bit more, shall we say, aggressive."

"What is this about?" Quincy Quckenbos said sharply.

"Oh, you know what it's about," replied the man who would be questioner.

"No, I don't, but I have an idea," Quincy said, pushing away from the table. He walked to the door and tried the latch again. (Still locked, of course.) "I have nothing to tell you that would be any use to her, so you may as well disembowel me now and get it over with."

The interrogator's eyes widened. "Disembowel you? Oh, sir, no one is going to disembowel you." His eyes narrowed. "Although at some point in these proceedings, you may wish to be disemboweled and put out of your misery. Your choice."

Their eyes locked for a moment, Quincy standing and irritated, the interrogator calm and coldly reassuring. Quincy sat down.

"What's the first question?"

"Jolly good!" He took hold of the timer – "When did you start working on the formula to kill Myke Phoenix?" – and turned the timer over so that sand began to flow downward.

Quincy sighed. "I knew it. The blasted formula."

"There, see? I *told* you you know what this is all about."

"If you followed my trial, you know it's on the public record how long I tried to kill Myke."

"Yes, yes, but I thought we'd start with an easy-peasy question."

"Why do I have to play this game? I don't want to answer *any* of these questions."

"Oh, let's not go there just yet," the man scolded. "You'll want to save that attitude and that energy for later, no doubt."

"Right. I started trying to figure out how to kill Myke Phoenix from the first time I met him. Invited him to my labs and ran a series of tests on him."

"What did you learn from that first experience?"

"Is that another question?" Quincy said, and gestured toward the egg timer.

"Oh, quite right." He picked it up and saw that the first three minutes was not up, not by a long shot. "Well, if I just turn this over, you won't have the full amount of time, will you?" He reached into his coat pocket and withdrew another egg timer, placed it on the table and turned it over after repeating, "What did you learn from that experience?"

Quincy Quackenbos stared at the two egg timers for 30 seconds.

"Mr. Quackenbos. What did you learned from that first experience examining Myke Phoenix?"

Quincy Quackenbos stared at the two egg timers for another 30 seconds.

"Mr. Quackenbos?"

The sand in the first timer ran out.

"You only get one answer every three minutes. That's the setup, right?" Quincy said finally. "I learned that Myke Phoenix can't be killed. You can't penetrate his skin with a needle, so you can't get a blood sample or inject him with anything. You can't crush him, you can't blow him up, you can't use poison gas with any hope of success."

If the interrogator was miffed by Quincy's passive-aggressive response to the egg timers, he didn't signal it. Indeed, he said, "I see. Very good," and then waited for the sand to run out in the second timer.

"That first experience didn't go so well, I know," the man said. "But I happen to know that at some point in the ensuing 18 years, you did obtain a blood sample from Myke Phoenix."

"How would it be possible to get a blood sample?" Quincy scoffed. "I just told you you can't penetrate his skin."

The questioner just raised his eyebrows.

"No point in denying it. I know you were provided a blood sample."

"OK, you got me," the duck man said. "Yes, that's because the only thing that ever cut him – the *only* thing – was Deinonychus' claws. Maybe you should find her." He glanced at the window.

"Right. Now we're communicating, don't you see? So, the next question is: In what ways did examining Myke Phoenix's blood provide you with what you needed to create the formula?"

He turned the first egg timer over. As the sand began flowing, the man and the duck man locked eyes.

The screen on Paul Phillips' phone identified the caller as "Quackenbos Laboratories."

"Oh boy, here we go," he muttered, and pressed the button. "Paul Phillips, how can I help you?"

"Mr. Phillips, this is Brian Duckworth," said the voice at the other end. "We have a problem."

"Oh boy," Paul said. "Is your boss stealing factories again?"

"Technically speaking, I'm *his* boss," Duckworth said testily. "And no, the opposite – Quincy's been kidnapped."

One beat. Two beats. Three.

"Oh." A few more beats. "What happened?"

Duckworth quickly explained the conversation he'd been having with Quackenbos, the sudden appearance of the five ninjas, and the warning not to go to the authorities.

"We need to get hold of Myke Phoenix," he concluded.

"Don't you think Myke Phoenix counts as one of the authorities?"

"Well, yes, of course," Duckworth said. "But we need to rescue Quincy. We'll need more than just the police for that."

"I'll have Myke meet you at police headquarters."

And sure enough, 20 minutes later the CEO of Quackenbos Laboratories and a white-clad superhero were sitting in the office of Detective Captain Fredricks of the Astor City Police Department.

"Don't you have surveillance cameras around that joint?" Fredricks barked.

"Of course we do," said Duckworth. "And before you ask, here's a recording from outside the administration building about an hour ago."

He handed a flash drive to Fredricks, who inserted it into his own computer. Moments later the image of a back entrance was on his screen, complete with the scene of five dark-clad individuals packing a half-man-half-duck into a plain white van and driving off.

"Not bad. If only we had traffic cameras in this city, we could follow them right to wherever they went."

"No traffic cams?" Duckworth sputtered.

"Some wiseacres on the city council said something about invading people's privacy and how the whole thing was just a way to write more tickets and raise revenue for the city budget."

"Where did they get *that* idea?"

"Well, it's true, for one thing," Fredricks said. "But this is one of those rare occasions where it'd be nice to have 'em."

Myke was watching the kidnapping unfold over and over on the computer screen. He hit the space bar to halt the action and said, "From that angle, do you think anyone could read the license plate?"

Fredricks scrutinized the picture. "Might be able to have the techies enhance that. We'd at least know where the van belongs, if it ain't stolen."

"Meanwhile, I'll do some hoofing and see if I can find the van the old-fashioned way."

Myke Phoenix was able to do an "old-fashioned" search much faster than an ordinary human being, given his ability to run faster than – well, no, not faster than a speeding bullet, but faster than the average electric golf cart, for example. And given routine traffic, he could outpace someone who was driving around town in a squad car. Still, finding a single white van in a city of 175,000 souls was going to be a search for the proverbial needle in a haystack.

"Um, Paul Phillips loaned me the Astor City Beacon cellphone," he told Fredricks as he raced out the door. "Call me on that if you find the van first."

The man in the suit was holding Quincy Quackenbos' head under water in a large bucket. Quincy was flapping his arms and screaming at him to stop. A torrent of air bubbles spluttered to the surface.

After a short time the man released his hold and Quincy came up for air, coughing and gagging.

"Well, well, well, it seems ducks can drown after all," he said. "I never would have imagined."

Quackenbos glared as the interrogator pulled a chair over and sat down next to him. He put a sympathetic hand on the duck man's shoulder, which was angrily brushed away.

"This doesn't have to go this way," said the man with all the questions. "I can't comprehend why you're being so obstinate about this. What has Myke Phoenix ever done for you?"

"Let me try this again, you – cough! hack! – insipid little toad," Quincy Quackenbos said. "There is no formula! I failed – cough! cough! cough! – he can't be wounded. He can't be poisoned. Even if it were possible, he has some sort of healing process beyond anyone's understanding."

"And yet, you reported that you had found 'the holy grail,'" the interrogator said, turning the egg timer over with a bit of flourish. "Why would you say such a thing, knowing the cost of lying about it?"

Not for the first time that day, Quincy Quackenbos was dumbstruck.

"Is that what this is about? When I told her I found the formula just before I went to prison? Yes, I told her I was closing in on a solution, but I never completed the project. Oh my great-grandfather's boney bones." He looked at the two-way glass. Peering into the mirror, he screamed, "Is that you? You're back? Is that you in there? You filthy little reptile, I'm telling you, there is no formula!"

He banged a feathered fist against the glass, which wobbled but did not come close to cracking.

The sand in the egg timer ran out once again.

"All right, then," the man said wearily, taking a firm grip on the scruff of Quincy Quackenbos' neck. "Let's give it another try."

But just at that moment, somewhere from not far away inside the building came a hellacious crashing sound.

Act 4

An exchange of information

THE interrogator obviously did not expect a sudden crash. He turned his head in the direction of the sound, more or less toward the door, stood up and pressed a button on some sort of intercom device.

"What was that?"

"Nothing," said a voice from the speaker. "One of the boys accidentally tipped over a shelving unit."

"Well, do tell them to be more careful. I'm trying to work in here," said the man with the questions, visibly relaxing.

He smiled in Quincy's direction.

"Now. Mr. Quackenbos –"

"You can't get blood out of a turnip, my friend," the duck man said quietly. "I'm telling you, I never solved the problem. I got nothing for you."

"If that's true, then I'm afraid to say that you're useless to me," said the very polite man. "But I happen to know you're lying, and therefore –"

There came another hellacious crash, followed by a clattering sound and footsteps running past the door. The interrogator tensed again in irritation and was about to say something about how hard it is to hire good help these days when an incongruous shout suggested that this time, it was not one of the boys accidentally tipping over a shelving unit.

The precise words everyone heard were: "Police! Freeze!"

Quincy heard a "clunk" behind the two-way glass but nothing more from that direction. The interrogator raced to the door, opened it a crack, peeked, said a single word we won't repeat here, and burst into the hallway outside, running down the corridor away from the clattering sounds.

The duck man eased himself up from the table, walked across the room awkwardly and leaned against the door, still winded from being dunked several times. He looked down the hallway and saw a large man in a white uniform running toward him. The uniform had gold trim and red buttons up the left side of the torso and securing the pants. The red symbol of a phoenix was emblazoned in the center of his barrel chest.

For almost 20 years Quincy Quackenbos had reacted with a sense of dread when Myke Phoenix ran toward him. Usually it meant the game was up and he was about to flee or be arrested. He felt something different this time – relief. He was rescued.

Myke took him by the shoulders and looked in his eyes the way athletic trainers do when they're looking for signs of concussion.

"You all right?"

"I think so," Quincy said. "I'm a little –" Myke started up the corridor where the fleeing man had disappeared. "Wait! Be careful! She's here! She may still be back there."

Myke stopped and turned.

"'She'?"

"Deinonychus."

For almost 20 years Myke Phoenix had reacted with a sense of dread when he heard the name Deinonychus. And it had been a long time since last the word was connected with the phrase "She's here!"

"How can she be here?" he said, denying the possibility.

"I don't know! Just be careful. I think she was in the observation room."

"You *think*?"

"I didn't actually see her."

The door to the observation room was right next to the superhero. Forgetting the fleeing man for the moment,

Myke pushed on the door roughly with his palm. The latch and hinges yielded and the door flew into the room beyond.

A table. A lamp, not turned on. A laptop computer. A bookcase. One large book on the floor, next to an unconscious man. Whoever had been in this room with him had clunked him on the head and fled.

"Little help here, Mr. Superhero?" Fredricks' voice from the entrance area. A shot. Several more shots. "Never mind."

"What's down this hallway?" Myke asked the duckman.

"I have no idea, they didn't exactly give me a tour."

The superhero dashed down the corridor, followed closely by Quincy Quackenbos, and burst through a door that led to an alleyway outside. A limousine was starting to pull away. The interrogator's face was visible in the rear window.

Myke Phoenix started running toward the long car. Behind him, a gunman stepped out from behind a dumpster and took careful aim at the man in the white uniform.

"Look out!" Quincy yelled and hurled himself at the thug. He collided with enough force to jar the gun loose and topple both of them to the ground. He grabbed the hoodlum around the waist and hung on for dear life while the man thrashed and pushed and beat with his fists.

Myke turned around and saw the struggle, then shot a longing glance at the departing vehicle. He broke off the pursuit and ran back to extract Quincy and the thug from one another.

Seven gang members in all were taken into police custody that day. Four of them eventually were identified as operatives who had some training in special forces – and by *some* training, we mean that they had washed out and did not complete the training. That explains why they had the ability to surprise Quincy and Duckworth with ninja-like efficiency but were caught flat-footed when Myke Phoenix and Fredricks' team raided the warehouse.

The fifth ninja had apparently been the interrogator, who did slip away. Oddly, the seven men in custody fell in two categories: Five did not know their well-spoken colleague's name, and the other two refused to identify him with frightened looks in their eyes. All seven appeared to fear him.

An eighth thug decided to shoot it out with the police and managed to wing one officer in the shoulder. Funeral services were held for the hoodlum five days later.

To the best of anyone's ability, only the man who questioned Quackenbos and the mysterious leader escaped the raid. And Quincy was convinced the person behind the two-way glass was not exactly a person at all, but a criminal mastermind who also, impossibly enough, was a talking dinosaur.

"Once we had a license plate number, it was just a matter of legwork to find the van, which was conveniently parked down the street from where they had you," Fredricks told Quincy Quackenbos. "Pretty sloppy of them, but then crooks are often dumb as bricks."

"It could be she wanted you to find me," Quincy said. "She and my interrogator obviously had planned an escape route. She liked to make the authorities think they had won a victory from time to time, but as you know she's usually one step ahead of you."

"You mean Deinonychus," said Myke Phoenix. "What makes you so sure that she's behind this?" The two men and a man-duck were seated in Fredricks' office, the captain of detectives behind his desk and the others facing him.

"The interrogator knew things that only she would know."

"For instance?" Fredricks was more skeptical than Myke. Quincy squirmed in his otherwise-comfortable easy chair.

"Shortly before you captured me the second time, I reported to Deinonychus that I had succeeded in developing the formula," he said, raising his hands when Myke Phoenix straightened up. "I *didn't* - succeed. But she wasn't taking no for an answer. So I told her I just needed to run some more tests to be sure. She was the only one I told about completing the formula. But this guy knew."

"How do we know that you *didn't* complete the formula?"

Quincy Quackenbos stared back at Captain Fredricks with something approaching open disdain.

"I had a lot of time on the outside," he quacked. "If I had a way to stop Myke Phoenix, don't you think I would have used it?"

"The guy the other day, Leonard - he believed you finished the formula, too," Myke said. "Obviously she got the word out. Anybody she told could have been behind the kidnapping; it didn't have to be Deinonychus herself."

"The interrogator said that I reported finding 'the holy grail,'" Quincy said. "Those are the exact words I used when I told her about it."

The fine hairs raised on the back of Myke Phoenix's neck and forearms. If this was a movie instead of a conversation in the captain of detectives' office, ominous music would swell at this point.

"But you didn't see her," Fredricks said.

"I've never seen Deinonychus in my life," said Quincy Quackenbos. "That's how she worked – works – behind the scenes. She doesn't want to be recognized, as if being a talking dinosaur isn't enough of an identifier."

"You never met." Now Myke looked skeptical.

"She was always just a voice at the other end of a telephone. First time I saw her was in the TV coverage after you flushed her out."

"Frankly, the way we left things with Deinonychus, I don't know how she could possibly be behind this," the warrior said. "I think now that we've busted up this gang, you're safe. Or as safe as a former criminal can be."

"Thank you," Quincy said.

"Hey, rescuing people is part of the job," Myke said.

"No. Thank you for calling me a 'former' criminal." Quincy reached out a feathered hand. Myke took it and they exchanged a grip.

Dana Dunsmore Phillips had looked uncomfortable during the entire meal. Even when Quincy Quackenbos stood up and carried his own dinnerware to the kitchen sink, an anxious look played about her face. The duck man even mentioned it.

"I really am sorry that you can't relax in my presence, Ms. Dunsmore," he said. "But I can't blame you. I gave you no reason to relax when we've met in the past."

"It's not you," Dana fibbed, just a little, and glanced over at her husband. "I've had too much on my mind lately."

"I appreciate your coming over," Paul said.

"My pleasure, I appreciate the opportunity to be heard, get a fresh start," Quincy said. "After that amazing dinner, shall we get down to the interview?"

"Well, I do want to do the interview at some point, but to be frank, that's not the main reason I asked you to come tonight."

Quincy Quackenbos looked a bit crestfallen and perhaps a bit miffed. "What is this?"

"I want to talk to you about something. I want to tell you something –"

"And I want to clear my name! What do you mean, you don't want to do the interview?" The duck man opened up his mouth to say more, but caught himself and instead crossed his arms in front of his chest. "This better be good."

"Oh, it's good. It's something I haven't told anyone else except Dana."

"And I'm not sure you *should* tell anyone else –" she said.

"Please, love, the Soulkeeper suggested –"

"Soulkeeper? What *is* this?" Quincy insisted.

"Oh, just tell him."

That last statement was not made by Paul Phillips, nor by Dana Dunsmore Phillips, nor of course by Quincy Quackenbos. It was an entirely different voice.

"Who said that?" Quincy said, looking around the room.

"You heard that?" Dana asked.

"Of course I heard that. Somebody said, 'Oh, just tell him.' Tell me what? Who said that?"

"Well, you're only the third person it has allowed to hear that voice in 20 years," Paul said. "And it's a good judge of character, so I guess it's time to trust you with the secret."

"Secret?"

By way of reply, Dana picked up a misshapen vase from a display shelf in the dining room, held it in both hands and lifted it over her husband's head.

"I still don't think this is such a good idea, but I've been wanting to do *this* all night," she said with feeling. And she crashed the vase down.

Two remarkable things happened. Actually, one thing *didn't* happen, and that made in itself made it remarkable: The vase did not shatter when it struck. And the other remarkable thing: The vase did not strike Paul Phillips' head. Instead, it struck Myke Phoenix's head with a rather impressive BONGing sound.

"Ouch!" said Myke Phoenix, for although he could not be harmed or debilitated by a blow, he still could feel a twinge of pain if you conked him on the head (or anywhere else, for that matter).

It was impossible for the naked eye to see the switch. All Quincy Quackenbos knew was that Paul Phillips was standing there one instant and Myke Phoenix occupied the same space an instant later.

And the duck man reacted as anyone would. He freaked out.

"What are you doing here? Where did Phillips go? What did you do with that vase? Where did that voice come from? *What are you doing here?*"

After a few minutes of explanation, Quincy Quackenbos – once one of Myke Phoenix's deadliest foes – was in on the secret of the Soulkeeper of Kiribati and the link between Paul Phillips and Myke Phoenix.

"Why are you telling me all of this?"

Myke Phoenix and Dana Dunsmore Phillips looked at the ugly vase, which was now back on the shelf.

"I'm not sure, Soulkeeper," Myke said. "It seems like the right thing to do, but why *are* we telling him all of this?"

"Things ain't gonna get any easier from here on out," said the voice from the vase. "You're going to need some friends, Mychus. You're going to need some friends."

The man, the woman and the half-man-half-duck exchanged an uneasy glance.

"I'm not sure I like the sound of that," said Quincy Quackenbos.

Epilogue

FLAMES licked a sheaf of papers that Quincy Quackenbos was feeding, one page at a time, into the grand fireplace in his small mansion on Astor City's outskirts. The man-duck stared wistfully into the cozy fire.

"I guess I'm going to have a secret or two from Duckworth after all," he said softly, then chuckled a ducky chuckle: "Wak, wak, wak."

He watched for several minutes as the papers turned black and fragile, and then he took the poker and poked around until the fragile black charrings were broken apart and scattered about the firebox, slowly turning into ashes.

Quincy Quackenbos sighed.

"That's that," he said, turning next to his personal computer, a special device that he had never connected to the grid, where he could store his most private files. He navigated around until he found an encrypted file folder.

The folder was named "PEST EXTERMINATION." It contained several documents of some considerable size. He dragged the entire folder into the Trash. Then he emptied the trash. Finally, he took several steps to ensure that the deleted folder could never be reconstructed.

"Brian, on my parents' grave, I didn't complete a working formula," he had told his dear friend Duckworth. He had chosen those words carefully. His parents had no grave; they had been obliterated without a trace in a nuclear explosion. The formula had never been tested on an actual superhero, so he was not absolutely certain it would have worked. But a very promising formula had indeed been completed. He wouldn't dare lie to Deinonychus in those days.

And now all physical traces of the research were obliterated. No doubt he could start over and reconstruct the research. But he wasn't going to. Not now.

Quincy Quackenbos had three friends now. Brian Duckworth. Paul and Dana Phillips. This crazy world was looking up.

But the idyll was not destined to last long. In the weeks and months ahead, he and his new friends would be pulled into a struggle that threatened their very lives.

If this tale were going to end with a "happily ever after," they would have to earn it with sweat and blood and tears.

The Second Warrior

Prologue

RICK Mahoney hadn't been called Rick in a long time, not since somebody in the gang asked him about the scar on his face and he foolishly answered truthfully.

The scar came from a run-in when he was 7 years old with a golden retriever – a friendly golden retriever who had not been trained not to jump on little kids. The big pooch needed a nail trimming. In his boy-oh-boy-is-it-good-to-meet-a-new-friend-let's-be-friends-OK-please-please-please enthusiasm, one of the retriever's nails cut a deep scratch down his left cheek.

It stung, but not as much as it stung after he told the story to a bunch of tough guys, who thought it would be the funniest thing ever if they called him "Scarface."

And from that day on, Rick was Scarface Mahoney.

The appellation never really fit. Scarface was not a mean or a tough character. He liked puppies and kittens and hung around on the fr inges of the criminal underworld, picking pockets and shoplifting to gain some extra cash here and there. Someone named Scarface ought to be feared and powerful; Scarface Mahoney was not much more than a skinny kid with good hands.

His greatest claim to fame was his role in the apprehension of the so-called Serial Kisser. It felt surprisingly fulfilling to have played the role of crime fighter rather than crime perpetrator, and though he hadn't met Myke Phoenix, the superhero who finally stopped the Serial Kisser, Scarface Mahoney thought of himself as something of an aide or assistant to Phoenix.

Picking pockets and procuring valuables off of store shelves had not held the same appeal since his brush with heroism, and he had begun the process of finding a real job.

"I'm going straight," he told himself and any of his colleagues who cared to ask. "As soon as I get a job, I'm going to start making money the honest way."

And he secretly hoped that his path would cross one day with Myke Phoenix, that he could work side by side as an actual assistant, not just someone who happened to help point the hero in the right direction.

The opportunity came in the form of an offer that, in the end, was not exactly what it appeared to be.

Act 1

Storm clouds gather

"HOKEY smokes," said the barrel-chested man in the white uniform. "I know where the boy is."

"Impossible," said the man in the green suit crouched on the ground. "You'll never find him until I get my money."

"You're not getting your money, and I'm taking you in," the larger man said with a toss of his blond hair. "But first I'll tell the police to go get Bobby in the old abandoned manager's shack at Big Top Paper Company."

The green-suited man's jaw dropped. He might have stayed to chat and find out how Myke Phoenix had figured out where he had stashed the kidnapped child, but discretion being the better part of valor, he knew it was time to try to effect an escape.

He sprang from the crouch 100 feet into the air in the direction opposite of the white-clad superhero.

"Oh, I hate when they run," Myke quipped and made a prodigious leap of his own.

For about 30 seconds Ultra-Frog and Myke Phoenix hopped enormous hops across the badlands outside Astor City, but Myke possessed greater stamina and mightier legs, so it was only a matter of time before he caught up. He tackled the froggy man about 50 feet off the ground on the upswing, then twisted so that they would land with his own invulnerable back absorbing the shock of landing. Ultra-Frog was a bad guy and a kidnapper, but Myke Phoenix was not interested in harming him, just bringing him to justice.

"You may stop me this time, Phoenix, but there will be another time," Ultra-Frog said as he squirmed in the superhero's vise grip. "And those who come after me will be legion."

"Yeah, right," Myke Phoenix replied. "Where have I heard *that* before?"

A right cross to the frog man's jaw, and the kidnapper/supervillain was subdued.

"Now," Myke Phoenix said firmly, "let's go get that kid."

Now that our hero has brought the leaping supervillain into custody and retrieved young Bobby Koosman from captivity, we turn our attention to a corner of the basement of the Astor County Justice Center, specifically the morgue and its adjacent Office of the County Medical Examiner, where forensic scientist Josiah Petri was staring at a computer screen and filling out a death certificate.

But it's not the end of life that concerns us at the moment; it's an ongoing beginning, which becomes clear with the arrival of an attractive woman of approximately Petri's age, whom he was clearly pleasantly surprised to see.

This was Terri Travers, professor of biology at the University of Astor City whose expertise in arachnology led to her involvement in the incident of the firespiders some months earlier – and whose right hand was severely burned in the encounter. The drama also brought her into contact with the county forensic scientist, where biochemistry began to come into play. That is to say, they were becoming quite fond of each other.

"Dr. Travers the younger," Josiah said with some delight (Dr. Travers the elder being her father, also a professor at the same institution of higher learning). "What brings you to my lair tonight, milady?"

"One grows weary of studying the mating habits of fruit flies and arachnids," she said with a smile, bringing her face up close to his with a brilliant smile. "A person longs for the comfort and familiarity of her own species after a while."

They exchanged a friendly kiss. Well, let's be honest: They exchanged a kiss on a level that would lead any reasonable witness to conclude they were developing into something much more than just friends.

"If you are quite finished with your work for today, I have a pork loin roast that's been simmering in the slow cooker all day, and a bottle of wine with your name on it waiting at home," Dr. Terri Travers said in a low, husky voice that suggested something about dessert.

"Pork loin – sounds – absolutely – GaaaahhhhH!" the forensic scientist said, first matching the urgency of his companion's hunger and then reacting to the large man in a white uniform who had entered the room and was standing behind her.

He had the silhouette of a red phoenix emblazoned across his barrel chest and a sly smile on his face.

"Sorry, was I interrupting?" the newcomer asked with that innocent tone that indicated he knew very well he was interrupting.

"Myke," Terri Travers exhaled. "You scared us both half to death."

"Sorry," Myke Phoenix repeated as if he was more amused than sorry, and, turning to Josiah, "I just wanted to thank you for helping me find Bobby Koosman. He's safe and sound, and Ultra-Frog is in custody."

"Thank goodness," said Terri.

"All I did was identify the stuff in the frogman's footprints. You were the one who linked it to that shed at the paper factory," Petri said. "You connected the dots."

"I didn't have any dots to connect until you did that analysis," Myke said. "Anyway, hi guys. How's the hand?"

Terri Travers raised her scarred right hand, and her fingers twitched slightly. That was all she could muster in an effort to make a fist.

"Not good, I'm afraid," she said. "I'm learning how to do more and more with my left hand, and my father has some interesting ideas about some experimental treatments."

Her father was Dr. Jacob Travers, himself a brilliant biologist who knew a thing or two about biology.

"He thinks he can help her grow a new hand like a lizard," Josiah interjected. "Very comic book-type stuff."

"I wish you wouldn't make fun of Dad," she said, touching his shoulder with her good left hand. "He means well, and who knows? He's accomplished some amazing things. If he succeeded, think what it could mean for amputees and anyone who's lost the use of a limb."

"Just don't get your hopes up, Terri," he replied tenderly. "You've been hurt enough."

There was a long pause, and then Myke Phoenix said, "Well, OK. I've got to get going to – where I've got to go – thanks again, Josie. We'll see you around."

"Don't call me Josie," said Josiah Petri, forensic scientist, but the superhero was already gone.

"It was kind of sweet watching Josiah and Dr. Travers mooning over each other like kids," Paul said as he opened the door to Parchisi's Supper Club for his wife, Dana Dunsmore Phillips. "It reminded me of when you and I were starting to date."

"You still moon over me all the time. It's one of the things I love about you," she replied with a smile.

"I try, my sweet," he said. "But when it's all brand new, there's something, I don't know, urgent about the whole thing. It's like they just can't live without each other."

"Oh, and you can live without me?" Dana looked at him askance, still smiling.

"You know what I mean," he protested. "After you've been together a long time, the fire is still there, it's just simmered down to a warm glow."

"Nice recovery, Scoop," she said, she said, gliding up to the hostess' station with her husband. Dana was the only one who called him "Scoop," and he preferred it that way.

Parchisi's was the finest restaurant in Astor City, and since they were meeting with the richest man in Astor City, it seemed appropriate to meet him there. But when Nelson Rodinske walked in wearing a casual short-sleeve shirt and high-end blue jeans, they started to wonder if that was such a great idea.

"Are you sure you can afford this place?" the multi-multi-millionaire asked as they sat down around the table. "I thought you wanted to talk about a grant for your struggling news site."

Paul and Dana looked at each other a little sheepishly.

"It was my idea," Dana said, taking responsibility for the tactical error. Mrs. Phillips was the president and owner of the Dana Dunsmore Agency, the most prestigious advertising and marketing firm in Astor City, and spent more time smoozing with spenders than her news reporter husband – at least more time with spenders who spent their own money. As a news guy, a greater percentage of Paul's time was spent with politicians.

"Maybe that's an example of why I could use your support," Paul interjected, attempting to salvage the faux pas. "I'd like to believe the Beacon provides an important public service, but my expertise is in journalism, not money management."

"So you're arguing you need the money because you can't handle money," the millionaire philanthropist said with a twinkle in his eye. "I'm not sure you're helping your cause here." An awkward pause, and then Rodinske laughed. "I'm yanking your chain, Paul. Lighten up."

The Astor City Beacon was the website that Paul Phillips operated to provide local news to the city and county. He had run it on a shoestring for more than two years now, paying fees and putting food on the table by selling advertising, but that financial model was not sustaining itself. Paul had applied to the Nelson Rodinske Foundation for a grant that would essentially turn the Beacon into a nonprofit organization.

"Why are you doing this?" Nelson Rodinske asked, his gray eyes flashing. The best word to describe Rodinske was "chiseled." He had solid square features, not a silver-gray hair out of place, his body was fit and firm, and even his casual wear was neat, clean and perfectly fitted.

"It's a departure from the traditional methods of funding local news, but I think it's the wave of the future," Paul said.

"No, that's not what I meant." The square jaw jutted even a bit farther. "You spent a decade reporting local news on WACR Radio – I listened to you all the time – and then you went to work at the Tribune for a few years. When they laid you off, you started a local news website."

"That's my career in a nutshell."

"And now that the site is in trouble, you're asking me for funding to keep it going," Rodinske said. "So I ask you, why are you doing this? When the radio station closed down its newsroom, when the paper downsized you, and even right now, you could have – I don't know – gone to work for your wife, picked up a public relations job at any number of companies here or anywhere in the world. Instead you keep searching for ways to keep reporting Astor City news. Why?"

For a few seconds the only sound was the low murmur of conversation from around the room and the clinking and tinking of silverware against plates and coffee cups. Paul Phillips took a deep breath.

"It's important work. The people who run the city, and the county, and the little burbs, are making decisions every day that affect the rest of us. When the city decides to fund a homeless shelter or pave the streets or buy a new playground set for Waterfront Park, they're spending our money, our tax dollars. If the police are trying to track down an armed robbery suspect or some other bad guy, people need to know there are bad guys on the loose. I'm kind of old school. I think the public still wants to know these things, still *needs* to know these things, and just because the radio station or the newspaper doesn't want to emphasize that information doesn't mean it's still not important to people."

"And why you? Why does it have to be Paul Phillips?"

"Because he's the best reporter in town," said Dana Dunsmore Phillips, not with the proud smile of a spouse but with the firm conviction of someone stating a simple fact. "The city needs him to keep doing what he does, in more ways than one."

That last turn of phrase was a reference (which she would not be sharing with Nelson Rodinske this day) to the other part of Paul Phillips' life, the part where he served as a powerful superhero named Myke Phoenix, whom we have already met.

The well-groomed multi-multi-millionaire smiled a broad, disarming smile that made Dana think of a popular movie star, the one who charms all the girls and gets to walk off with the heroine at the end of the film.

"I believe," Nelson Rodinske said, "you have both given me the right answer to that question." And the rest of the meal would be spent discussing how his foundation would administer the grant to the maximum benefit of the Astor City Beacon.

Except for one little detail –

"Mr. Rodinske," Paul said before the relationship became too etched in stone, "I do want to ask about my journalistic independence. I mentioned that I'm old school, and that means especially that I'm going to follow a story wherever it goes, whatever the consequences."

"I thought this might come up," Rodinske said, still smiling but with a trace of steel in his eyes. Dana held her breath.

"You're a big player in this town –"

"Probably the biggest."

"Probably. I need to know that you won't interfere with my ability to follow those stories," Paul said.

"Understood."

"Are you sure you'd be OK if, oh, for example, what if I uncover some scandal involving Senator Bobcat or someone like that?"

"I donate more money to Ted Bobcat's campaign fund than anyone else I support, and you know I support a lot of politicians," Rodinske said. "Ted Bobcat is a good friend of mine."

"That's what I mean," Paul said firmly but not without a touch of trepidation.

Nelson Rodinske sighed. "If Teddy Bobcat were a crook – and he's not – I would be the first one to tell you the public has a right to know. Don't worry, Paul, I'm as committed to the Beacon's independence as you are. I'd appreciate it if you covered some of the senator's initiatives, and," with a wink, "I understand you'll also have to give coverage to the fools who disagree with him."

The square-jawed man seemed earnest and sincere enough, and Paul wanted to believe him. Time would tell if he really could.

From the very beginning, humanity has created tools to make life easier, or more efficient, or safer, and almost immediately found ways to use those tools for harm. The laser is a fine example of such a tool. In the right hands a laser can save a life or create a remarkable work of art.

On this night in Astor City, this particular laser was not in the right hands.

Sparks flew from molten metal as a focused beam of light cut through the hinges of a vault door as if they were made of butter that had been sitting on a kitchen counter for several hours. The beam was coming from an instrument strapped to the forearm of an oddly garbed man.

He was wearing welder's goggles and a red leather jacket with, of all things, a cape dangling from his shoulders – a gaudy yellow cape. Over his heart was a round patch with the image of a sailboat.

After a few swipes of the laser, the door groaned and fell inward, revealing rows and rows of safe deposit boxes. Our scene is the interior of the Fourth National Bank of Astor City.

"Quickly, boys, an alarm is going off somewhere and we'll have company soon," said the man in the goggles. "The world will meet Laser Master soon enough, but not tonight. Not tonight."

Act 2
The second soulkeeper

THE rain was coming down fairly heavily in downtown Astor City. In the window of the dimly lit storefront was a yellowed temporary sign with several missing letters.

CARLSON'S PRETTY NEAT ANT Q ES

NOW OPEN

GOOD DEALS   CLAS IC ITEMS

A young man pushed open the door and entered, squeezing between a suit of armor and an early 20-century reading lamp. The ancient wooden floorboards creaked under his weight, even though he was a skinny lad. A thin scar crossed his face.

He glanced around at the shelves and boxes piled high with vintage memorabilia and junk: A rotary dial telephone, a rubber duck, a hand-crank meat grinder. It was all scattered here and there with what at first appeared to be no apparent rhyme or reason, but then here was a box of porcelain electrical insulators, and there were several crates of dusty Bakelite 78 rpm records. There had been a sorting, of sorts, after all.

"Anything special you're looking for?" came a cheerfully crotchety voice seemingly from out of nowhere. A very old man with a smile hobbled out from behind a stack of wooden milk crates filled with books.

"No," said the young man, his eyes passing over a row of glass pitchers and flower vases. "I just wanted to come in from the rain and look around, I guess."

"Well, I'll be around if you see something you want to buy."

"Guess I'll know it if I see it."

The young man had finished walking past the row of glass containers when he heard a new voice behind him.

"Buy *me*, Scarface."

"Huh? What?" said the young man, spinning around.

"Buy me."

No one was there.

"Who said that?" the young man called.

"Eh? Did you say something?" came the old man's voice.

"He can't hear me, Scarface," the new voice said.

"Who's talking? Why do you keep calling me that?"

"It's your name, isn't it? Scarface Mahoney?"

The voice seemed to be coming from the direction of a black vase sitting on the shelf among a motley collection of 1930s-style glass and porcelain. This vase was a strikingly bold Art Deco piece, or perhaps it was Art Nouveau – Rick Mahoney was not an expert on antique glassware styles. In any case he was more concerned about the fact that the glassware appeared to be speaking to him with a distinctive bass voice.

"What's going on?" he said, not without some nervousness at having a conversation with a fancy flower pot.

"Buy me, and I'll tell you all about it when we get home. Are you ready to save the world?"

"Save the world? What are you talking about? AAHH!"

Rick Mahoney had been startled by the grizzled old man who poked his head around the corner, casually holding a baseball bat, perhaps a little warily.

"Are you all right, son?" the man asked in all sincerity. "It sounds like you're talking to yourself."

"Yeah, yeah, yeah," Scarface replied. "I was, uh, I was just trying to decide whether to buy this Art Deco thing here."

"I think it might be Art Nouveau," the old fellow said. "But I can never get those straight, either. I can give it to ya half-price tonight – 10 bucks."

"Buy me, Scarface," the black vase said. "We can continue this conversation at home."

"Only if you tell me my real name."

"I don't know you from Adam," the old man said. "How would I know? Are you adopted or something?"

"Richard Dennis Mahoney," said the vase. "But everyone calls you Scarface."

The young man with the scar gave the old man a small portrait of Alexander Hamilton in exchange for the black vase, plus several coins for the sales tax, then retired back into the rain.

Home was a one-bedroom apartment on the second floor over what used to be a hardware store but now was a storefront church in an area of Astor City that had seen better times. Scarface Mahoney trudged up the stairs, unlocked the door in the dimly lit hallway, went inside and bolted the door behind him.

He placed the black vase on the round kitchen table and sat down on the couch.

"Are you still there?" he asked, hoping whatever he'd imagined had stayed behind at the antique store.

"Oh, my man, yes I am," came a voice from nowhere that he knew was the vase. One side of the young man's heart sank, and the other two chambers filled with adrenaline.

"What is this? What's going on."

"Oh, most fortunate of humans, you have been selected to be part of one of the most select corps of warriors in the world," intoned the strange voice. "Are you aware of the being known as Myke Phoenix?"

"Well, duh, everyone knows about Myke Phoenix."

"What you may not know is that he once was a mighty warrior named Mychus, who lived hundreds of years ago but whose body is still preserved through powerful forces no mortal can understand. Through the power of the Soulkeeper of Kiribati, a normal human being exchanges places with Mychus and together they fight the Forces of Evil in the World."

"The Soulkeeper of Kiribati."

"A vase molded at the beginning of time to hold the user and contain the forces that effect the transfer."

"Mychus is dead, and Myke Phoenix uses his body?"

"Oh! No wonder you have been selected," said the voice from nowhere. "You have divined with clear understanding."

"And what are you, then, telling me all this?"

"I am the Second Soulkeeper, and you shall be the Second Warrior, fighting side by side with Myke Phoenix."

"What?"

"Mychus had a powerful ally named Coronius. All these years while Mychus has walked the Earth again, the powers that formed this miracle have been preparing the second ancient for this moment, the moment when evil in the world is becoming palpable and a worthy holder is needed to bear Coronius' standard."

"Why me?"

"Why not you? You have crossed the divide between evil and good. You helped capture a bad man and have abandoned your life of dire depravation."

"He was just a sick pervert who liked to kiss women who didn't want to be kissed. And all I did is do some shoplifting and pickpocketing, I'm not depraved."

"There are no degrees of evil. You take one path or the other. And now you have been chosen for the purest path of them all."

There was no sound in the room for a few moments. In the distance a siren echoed against storefronts, a lonely, distant whoop and chatter.

"So Myke Phoenix is really some normal dude like me? Who is he?"

"Never you mind, young man," the vase spoke, sounding more like a great-grandmother. "Under the warrior's code it is better not to know each other's alter ego, lest the knowledge fall into the wrong hands. Never, ever talk about such things with your, colleague, Myke Phoenix, where other ears can hear. Let's just get you started on your journey."

"I'm tellin' ya, the evil-o-meter is spiking off the scale," said a voice that appeared to be coming from a shelf in Paul and Dana Phillips' dining room.

The vessel sitting on Paul and Dana Phillips' dining room shelf did not in any shape or form resemble the sleek, black vase that had been talking to Scarface Mahoney in recent days. If I may be so rude, this vase was butt-ugly.

Its only distinction was its antiquity. This crudely formed, pale green creation was dotted with jewels in no clear pattern. Its maker obviously had attempted to make it smooth and round but did not possess the knowledge or technology to do so. An image painted on its side seemed to depict a bird flying up from the ashes, like the legend of the phoenix.

The only thing this bit of pottery had in common with the one in the Mahoney household was that it talked. It spoke with a voice that could have been male or could have been female. It spoke with a voice that seemed to materialize from nowhere, except that it was coming from the vase's direction. Oh, and it first spoke to Paul one day, 18 years ago, from a shelf in Carlson's Pretty Good Antiques. But our hero, his wife and vase were not yet aware of that particular connection.

"You're not saying Ultra-Frog's appearance was a harbinger of a new surge of evil in this part of the world?" Paul Phillips said calmly, as if talking pottery was the most normal thing in the world.

"That lame little leaper? Nah," came the reply. "This is something much bigger and much more ominous than that. And it's something new, something familiar."

"Something new and familiar? Something old, something new? Do we need to find something borrowed and something blue, too?" Dana asked.

"It ain't a marriage, doll," said the vase with its voice that sounded somewhat masculine but somehow feminine at the same time. "Something new for you, as in you've never seen it before, and something familiar, as in it reminds me of something."

"Something like what?"

"I just read the temperature of the wind," the vase said, somewhat cryptically. "I can't say precisely what or who is sending out these signals – whoa! Whoa! WHOA!"

Speaking of something new, Paul and Dana Phillips had never heard the vase interrupt itself and then shout, "whoa! Whoa! WHOA!"

"What the bejeebers does THAT mean, Soulkeeper?" Paul Phillips queried.

"This is coming from the darkest corner of existence," the vase said as emphatically as a disembodied voice can say. "Whatever or whoever is responsible for this latest uptick in the darkness, be careful."

"We talking Deinonychus-level carefulness?" Dana asked, referring to the talking dinosaur who was Myke Phoenix's most dangerous foe to date.

"Yes and no."

"You're being unusually not helpful today," Paul noted.

"Yes, Deinonychus level. This is extremely bad stuff in the air right now. But no, it's not Deinonychus. It reminds me of someone else."

"Someone else? I thought you said you can't say precisely who we're dealing with."

"I can't. It just feels like the same feeling I got when this one guy walked the Earth, but he's been gone a couple, three thousand years, so it's only somebody or something like him."

"This one guy, he was pretty bad?"

"Just about the baddest. He could almost match Mychus blow for blow. But of course he's gone now."

"Tell me about him anyway."

"He was a warrior for the other side, the forces that hate the Phoenix. He showed up a few times during Mychus' second and third incarnations. Tough guy, they fought to a draw a few times before we got the best of him."

"How?"

"He got old," the vase said. "The advantage you have is that you might get old, but Mychus doesn't. This guy was the closest thing to an even match Mychus ever faced. His name was Coronius."

Shortly after Baxter's department store closed a few nights later, an armored car drove up to the employees' entrance. Two guards went inside while the third man, the driver, kept the engine idling, and then the others returned, one carrying a big bag with the day's receipts, and the other keeping a sharp eye on their surroundings.

They made it safely back and drove off. But two blocks away, a concentrated beam of light flashed from atop a bus stop and struck the hood of the truck, separating the front of the vehicle from the cab. Momentum carried the two pieces forward about 100 feet, seemingly still together, before gravity did its work and the truck folded in its tracks like a giant accordion, crashing to the ground.

"All right, boys," said a man at the side of the road wearing goggles, a red leather jacket and yellow cape. "Let's do this."

The guards made to reach for the pistols at their sides but were dissuaded by the four gunmen who surrounded them, so they reached dejectedly for the sky instead. The man with the goggles walked to the vehicle's back door, aimed the instrument on his forearm, and shot a blinding beam of light. Seconds later there was a hole big enough to climb through, which a fifth henchman accomplished. Money bags began to fly out through the hole. Two gunmen kept their weapons trained on the guards while their colleagues started carrying money bags to a waiting truck.

Rick "Scarface" Mahoney watched the unfolding scene from the shadows of a nearby alley, sizing up the situation.

"Well, what are you waiting for?" he muttered to himself. "Do it, Scarface. Just do it."

The black vase had briefed him on what to expect: superstrength, lightning speed, just like Myke Phoenix, but unlike Mychus, he would not be invulnerable. The late Coronius instead had an ability to generate a defensive force field, and the energy could also be directed in an offensive fashion. Even six men against one, the odds would be on his side.

"OK, this is it," the young man said, and then paused. "Wait. How do I turn into the superhero? He didn't tell me how – Oh!"

The exclamation at the end was a result of discovering that he already had changed dramatically, just by thinking about it. The figure in the dark alleyway was no longer a skinny 19-year-old.

Out on the street, the Laser Master had jumped on top of the disabled truck in order to keep a sharp eye in every direction.

In a third-floor window he saw a man cradling a telephone in his hands and speaking furtively into the device. He pointed his forearm instrument at the window and launched a beam of light that cut a hole in the glass and struck a television set on the wall, which erupted in a shower of sparks. The man dropped the phone and scurried to cover.

"No delays – chop chop," the goggled man encouraged his men. "People are calling 911. We'll have company soon."

"You got that right." A large figure emerged from the alley across the street. Tall and dark-haired, he was wearing a loose-fitting uniform that appeared to be black, although everything appeared black in the soft glow of the streetlights. By day it would be more obvious that the uniform had a dark purple hue. On the man's chest was emblazoned a white symbol that resembled a bird of prey. He held his fists at his side but placed himself into a stance of defiance and readiness. "You boys aren't going anywhere tonight."

"It's Myke Phoenix!" one of the henchmen gasped.

"No," the dark-haired newcomer said firmly. "Call me Cory Hawke."

"I'm afraid I'll have to call you dead," came a voice from the roof of the armored truck. A bright beam of light cut the darkness.

The light stopped about five feet in front of Cory Hawke and dispersed into jagged angles, like a rock striking a frozen pond.

"Cool!" the big man exclaimed, for the soul of young Rick Mahoney was inside the mighty body. He began to walk forward. The Light Master was still directing the laser beam toward the white hawk on his chest, but it was not reaching its target. "Let's try the other thing," Cory Hawke said softly.

He raised his hand and pointed at one of the gunmen. The thug was launched backward as if slugged by a powerful, invisible fist and fell clumsily on the asphalt. At this stage the two moneybag carriers dropped what they were doing and sprinted for the getaway car. Cory Hawke pointed at them, and they stumbled to the ground as if shoved.

The goggled man on the truck's roof changed his aim, directing his beam of light at the edge of a manhole cover in the street. The heavy metal flew into the air toward the dark-uniformed superhero. The makeshift weapon struck something invisible five feet away from Hawke, but the collision knocked the new superhero off his feet, and he hit the ground with an "Ooooof!"

"Hasty retreat, boys!" The Laser Master jumped off the truck and sprinted for the getaway car, a black sport utility vehicle. The guards, who no longer had guns trained on them, drew their own service revolvers and aimed at the running thugs.

"Hold it right there!" one of the guards shouted, but the other guard just started shooting. His aim was not true. Under fire, everyone piled into the SUV and started to speed away.

Suddenly another figure arrived on the scene, running so fast it appeared he would be able to catch the SUV. This figure was a blond, barrel-chested man in a white uniform. Cory Hawke raised his hand toward the newcomer.

"Holy cow, it's Myke Phoenix!" Hawke exclaimed.

He raised his hand to greet the more experienced superhero. Suddenly the man in white bounced off an invisible wall and clattered to the ground. The SUV disappeared in the dark as Myke Phoenix picked himself up and turned toward the dark-uniformed man.

"Did you do that?" the veteran superhero said angrily. "Why?"

"No! I mean, I don't think so. I – I don't know," the rookie superhero replied. "I'm sorry, this is the first time I've used these powers, I don't know exactly how they work yet."

"Who are you then?"

"I'm Cory Hawke," he replied, extending a hand that looked like a hand of friendship – until a powerful force threw Myke Phoenix backward and to the ground. "I'm sorry! I'm sorry!" the rookie yelled and started to run away.

"Wait a minute, buddy," Myke said, picking himself up again. "Who are you? Where did you get these powers?"

Cory Hawke remembered what the black vase had said – "Never, ever talk about such things with Myke Phoenix where other ears can hear" – and so he called over his shoulder, "You know who I am! Ask your soulkeeper!" and disappeared into the night.

Act 3
The jewel heist and the menace

"ASK your soulkeeper?!"

"'You know who I am, ask your soulkeeper,' that's what he said," Paul Phillips said. "How did he know you even exist?"

"*Your* soulkeeper," Dana mused. "It almost sounds like he has one, too. How many soulkeepers are there?"

"Just the one," insisted the Soulkeeper of Kiribati. "I am the only one there is."

"You're the Soulkeeper of Kiribati. Is it possible there's, I don't know, a Soulkeeper of Maui or a Soulkeeper of Tennessee?"

"Only. One," said the voice that was neither male nor female. "I was made to execute the transition of a soul into the body of a warrior. That's you, that's Mychus. Only one man at a time gets the power."

"What about that man you mentioned the other day, Coronius?" Dana said. "Didn't you say this superhero called himself Coro something?"

"*Cory* Hawke. You have to admit the name's similar."

"What did he look like?"

"Talk, dark hair, I didn't get that good a look at him."

"Could be Coronius, except for the part where he's been dead for centuries."

"So has Mychus," Dana pointed out.

"That's different. When Mychus' soul passed to the next realm, steps were taken. His body was transformed."

"Who did all this anyway? You've never actually said."

"And I never actually will. The Phoenix oversaw the process for a righteous purpose, as you've seen and fulfilled through the years. That's all you need to know."

"If a good man could undergo the process, why not a bad man?"

"The thought has occurred to me, doll, but I'm telling you, Coronius' death was not as peaceful as Mychus' death, and let's just say his body was not as well preserved. You're better off treating this like a new menace. It can't be Coronius."

"Are you sure?"

Paul Phillips' question lingered over the room for several more seconds than the vase was usually prone to wait before speaking.

"No. I really hate to admit it, but I'm not sure."

"Stupid, stupid, stupid," Rick Mahoney said as he paced his living room. "Why did I run away?" He paused in front of the mirror hanging on his wall. "That was your chance to meet Myke Phoenix and forge the alliance, dummy."

"You bid a strategic retreat," said the mysterious black vase on the kitchen table. "You correctly sensed the time had not yet come."

"I have to learn to control the power better. He probably thinks I'm a dork or an idiot – or worse, a bad guy. What else would he think I am? I did knock the guy off his feet twice."

"Yes, yes you did. Good, that shows Coronius has been reborn with his full strength. It is just as well that you left the scene when you did. Myke Phoenix and – what was that name you chose?"

"Cory Hawke."

"Hmph. Yes. Cory Hawke and Myke Phoenix might be better off working separately. Two heroes spread across the world can accomplish more than fighting in one place."

"I want to meet him, though," Rick said. "He's been doing this for years, he could teach me how to use the power, show me the ropes, you know."

"Are you sure that's advisable? You knocked him down twice –"

"And apologized for it! I'm new at this."

"Next time he'll have his guard up. He may even attack."

"I've got the force field, don't I? I'll be fine. I just need to meet him and make him understand!"

"Your paths will cross again, and when it does, you will have the interaction you seek. Time to rest now, superhero. You stopped the forces of evil tonight, and tomorrow is ahead of you."

Laser Master is still loose in the city, and Myke Phoenix probably thinks I'm some bumbling amateur, Rick Mahoney said to himself. But the black vase had one thing right: He was tired. The whole thing probably would make more sense after a few hours' sleep.

Dr. Jacob Travers could have played Santa Claus if the Astor Community Players ever staged a Christmas pageant. He also bore a strong resemblance to the befuddled insect pathologist professor in a certain 1950s movie about giant ants. Right now he was befuddled himself, because a white rat with a burned paw was lying stiff and lifeless in its cage.

"Oh, I do hate sacrificing animals for the greater good," he said, muttering as he prepared the little guy for proper disposal. "It certainly didn't do *this* one any good."

He was going to have to tell his daughter that another serum derived from his experiments on limb regeneration had ended in disaster.

"Disaster just seems to be my middle name lately. Jacob D. Travers, that's me," he said, puttering about the lab at the University of Astor City.

He stopped and gave a double-take at a terrarium filled with tiny spiders. Their mother, a large yellow and black garden spider, lounged in a web in the corner of the terrarium. His eyes widened.

"They hatched! Now this is a breakthrough indeed," he said, fluttering about for his pad and pen.

All of his attempts to breed a more efficient predator of garden pests had been failures, some of them more dramatic than others – one of them most dramatic of all. The birth of these baby spiders was his first possible success in months.

"Perhaps it is a good day after all," he said, shuttering the window. He had one important measurement to make before declaring victory.

The mother spider was .97 inches long. The day before she had been .86 inches long. This, Dr. Travers believed, was in the realm of acceptability.

It would be two months before he realized his mistake.

"If only I could help Terri the way I'm going to be able to help gardeners everywhere," he mused.

In two months he would realize how fortunate his daughter was that he couldn't.

The security at the J.D. And Emily Astor House Historical Museum had been tightened over the years, but it had never reached the level it had this week. A fabulous jewel collection exhibit had opened.

Armed guards were stationed at each entrance and roamed the grounds, passing each window at irregular intervals so that burglar couldn't time his entry to a pattern. Even if the burglar got inside, there were additional guards in strategic locations and, in the old house's grand room, laser-guided alarms that were set when the museum closed every night, ensuring that anyone who tried to reach the featured exhibit in the dark would be detected before the magnificent jewelry collection could be stolen. And finally, with a villain calling himself Laser Master loose in the city, another layer of security had been added to the laser alarms – simple motion detectors.

Just before dawn on this particular day, it appeared that all the hard work designing the security system was paying off. Suddenly the laser alarms blinked off and their guidance system erupted in a shower of sparks. Simultaneously the motion detector alarm starting beeping, and the guards converged on the exhibition of Emily Astor's most priceless jewels.

They were fated to find nothing amiss. The alarm at the Astor House turned out to be a misdirection.

Across town, the Laser Master and his henchmen waited outside of Henry's Diamond Vault, the city's largest purveyor of, well, diamonds and other expensive jewelry. In addition to his smart red leather jacket and welder's goggles, Laser Master's attire now included a pair of unobtrusive wires leading from a smartphone in his pocket to ear buds.

About 23 seconds after the commotion began at the museum, the police scanner app in his phone chirped with an alert tone.

"All units respond to an alarm at the Astor House Historical Museum," a dispatcher's voice intoned.

"All right, boys, there's the signal. Let's get ready," Laser Master said, and a thug with a pair of wire clippers turned toward a box on the outside wall. "NO, you fool! We wait five minutes. First every police unit must respond to the alarm. Once they do, all of the police will be at least twelve minutes away from us. Plenty of time to stage our little seven-minute operation. Take your places!"

"You thought of everything, didn't you, boss?"

"That's why I'm the boss," Laser Master chuckled. "That, and my brilliant expertise with lasers."

Of course, dear reader, as you no doubt have already imagined, Laser Master had not thought of quite everything.

Five minutes after the police alarm went off, after the sixth and final officer on duty at this time of night reported "10-23" – radio code for "I've arrived at the scene" – Laser Master said, "Now, boys," and the thug with the wire clippers clipped the wire to the alarm system. That interruption of electric current, they all knew, would set off an alarm at police headquarters.

In less than 30 seconds, the scanner alert tone sounded again.

"Cars 242 and 245, divert to Henry's Diamond Vault for a burglar alarm."

"242, 10-4."

"245, 10-4."

"They're coming, boys," said the Laser Master as he carved a man-sized hole in the back door of Henry's Diamond Vault.

But they were twelve minutes away, and the burglars planned to be gone in seven minutes.

The door gave way. The thugs streamed inside. They reached Henry's safe. Laser Master sliced the safe open and systematically began to generate holes in the glass cases. One thug began to pull shelves of diamonds and emeralds and other valuables out of the safe and pour them into bags, while two other thugs emptied the display cases. A fourth thug and the Laser Master watched the front and back doors. A sixth man, of course, was behind the wheel of the idling SUV near the back door.

Four minutes and 16 seconds after the henchman with the wire clippers had clipped the wires, the flaw in Laser Master's plan presented itself.

"Hello, boys," a voice said in the back hallway.

A large man in a white uniform stood there. It was a well-tailored but not skin-tight uniform, and the image of a bird rising from flames was emblazoned on the man's chest. The Laser Master's next words were a tad redundant, because everyone recognized the man.

"Curse it all to the infernal regions! It's Myke Phoenix!"

Two minutes later, the whoop of police sirens began to sound in the distance, but they were still nearly six minutes away. Just as Laser Master had predicted, officers would not arrive at the scene until about twelve minutes had passed, and everything would be all over by then. Of course, it was a different "everything" than Laser Master had planned.

Three thugs were unconscious, and Laser Master's weapon was proving to be ineffective against Myke Phoenix's invulnerable body. The amazing thing was that the laser directed at the superhero's chest wasn't even scorching the image of the bird, although the fiery patterns from the deflected laser made the image of the flames more lifelike.

"Come on, friend, the jig's up, as they say," Myke said. "Let's make this easy."

At that moment came another heroic-sounding voice.

"Yes! It's time to give yourself up, Laser Master."

"Boss! It's that Cory Hawke guy," called the thug in the SUV, who had nobly stood by waiting for any survivors rather than drive away and save himself – if "noble" is a word that can describe a miscreant thief.

A tap on the jaw from the man in the dark uniform, and the question became moot, as the crooked driver was neither noble nor ready to drive away, merely oblivious to his surroundings.

"All right, Laser Master, give up, you can't beat two of us," Cory Hawke said firmly.

Laser Master's response was to turn the weapon on his other arm toward the newcomer, but the sharply focused light that burst from both arms diffused harmlessly against Myke Phoenix's chest and Cory Hawke's invisible shield.

"Don't you hate when that happens?" Cory said, reveling in the safety of his superpowers as the two heroes closed in.

He pointed at Laser Master, intending to knock out the goggled supervillain with an invisible slug to the jaw.

Instead, it was Myke Phoenix who flew backward through the air and slammed into a glass display case with an awkward and spectacular crash.

"Oh, this is ridiculous," Cory Hawke muttered, and he sent another blow toward Laser Master, more precisely this time.

But instead of striking and felling the man in the red leather jacket, once again the invisible force barreled into the man in the white uniform. Laser Master took advantage of the distraction to duck out the back door, toss his flunky driver aside, and jump behind the wheel of the SUV.

"Stop it, kid!" Myke shouted. "If you can't control your power, don't use it."

He started to run after the sport utility vehicle, and Cory Hawke raised both hands to the sides of his head in frustration. In synchronization with those hands, Myke Phoenix's path was deflected into the side of a building.

"What the bejeebers do you think you're doing?" Myke Phoenix yelled. "Knock it off!"

"I can't!" Cory Hawke cried. "I've lost control of the power."

He thrust both hands to his sides so that he couldn't make a move again. But that action drove Myke Phoenix to the ground.

He blinked in dismay. The blink sent Myke Phoenix flying through the air against another building.

As the SUV disappeared around the corner, it dawned on Cory Hawke that the greatest immediate danger to Myke Phoenix and the community was not Laser Master and his gang.

"I'm the menace," he whispered.

Act 4
The choices people make

MYKE Phoenix climbed out of a pile of rubble, dusting himself off, and walked cautiously up to the man in the dark uniform. Rick "Scarface" Mahoney, who up until a few moments ago had believed he was the one animating the body of Cory Hawke, tried not to move, breathe or blink. The whooping police sirens in the distance were still about three minutes away.

"I'm going to take a wild guess here," Myke said quietly, his voice and eyes filled with menace. "Coronius, right?"

"Yes! Well, it's the body of Coronius. My soulkeeper told me about you and Mychus and said the same process puts me inside Coronius. I just want to help, but there's something wrong with my power."

"Because you act like you're surprised to be trying to kill me, I'm going to take another wild guess. Whoever gave you this power didn't tell you that Mychus and Coronius have been mortal enemies for a couple millennia."

Cory Hawke's eyes widened. "No! My soulkeeper said they were mighty warriors. It said we would be superheroes together. I want to be your partner. I'm the Second Warrior!"

"There's only one soulkeeper, the Soulkeeper of Kiribati, and there's only one warrior. You don't have a soulkeeper, you're being manipulated by some sort of fake, and the fake has harnessed the power of one of Mychus' worst enemies."

"I don't understand!" Cory Hawke said with the frantic cry of a confused 19-year-old pickpocket. "I don't understand any of this!"

"I don't either, kid. But let's get back to this later," Myke said. "Laser Master is getting away."

With that, the warrior leaned back, made a fist, and sucker-punched Cory Hawke with the full force of his strength. This time there actually was contact between fist and chin, because Myke Phoenix crashed against the invisible force field with such might that it yielded.

As a result Cory Hawke was already unconscious as he flew into the sky and over a seven-story building. Myke heard a crash like the crumpling of a parked car's roof, and a car alarm began its urgent whooping. The police sirens were now about a minute away.

Officers were handcuffing thugs and packing them into the back seats of squad cars when Myke Phoenix walked back to the scene, holding Laser Master by the upper arm with a vise grip. The devices strapped to the villain's arms were crushed and inoperative. He meekly consented to the removal of the weapons and the cuffing of his hands.

"I'll let you guys handle these gentlemen," Myke told the officers. "I have one more loose end to tie up."

A block away, Myke Phoenix encountered a crowd surrounding a late-model car that looked as if a large boulder had been dropped on it. But there was no sign of a boulder or, for that matter, any sign of a man in a dark uniform with a hawklike image on his chest.

There were a couple of people in the crowd, however, who had seen such a man climb off the roof of the ruined vehicle and sprint from the scene.

"Anybody follow him?"

"I did," one man said. "But when I went around the corner he was gone."

"Really? He disappeared?"

"All I saw was some skinny kid, and the guy looked at me like I was crazy when I asked about the guy in the hawk suit."

That clue seemed to spark a note with the superhero.

"Describe this kid."

Most people thought of Scarface Mahoney as a mild-mannered young man, if a little askew of the law, so they probably would be surprised at the look of cold fury in his eyes as he entered his apartment and stood over the black Art Deco (Art Noveau? It didn't matter) vase on his dining table.

"Tell me about Coronius," the young man said.

For several ticks the clock on the wall made the only sound.

"I'm waiting," insisted Rick Mahoney.

"Coronius was the mightiest warrior of his time," the vase said.

"And an ally of Mychus, you said."

"Well."

"Well?"

"I may have exaggerated about the depth of their alliance."

"Exaggerated their alliance?! Myke Phoenix said they were mortal enemies! I couldn't use his power anywhere near Myke Phoenix without striking him by accident."

"Oh, that was not by accident."

"You never intended me to work with Myke Phoenix, did you?"

"The power of Coronius is strongest when used in proximity of Mychus and against Mychus. You were recruited for perhaps the most important role of your life – the fight against the Phoenix and his superhuman pet."

"The fight *against* –? You have some serious explaining to do. What made you think for one minute that I would help you?"

"The threat was too great. Myke Phoenix must be stopped one way or another. It never occurred to us that you would assist us willingly."

"It should have occurred to you that I would never assist you at all."

"Well."

That awkward pause again.

"Well – what?"

"Do you want this power, now that you have held it in your grasp?"

Rick Mahoney thought about the rush of emotion he'd had when he, as Cory Hawke, stopped a laser beam in its tracks. He rubbed his chin in the spot where he had taken a punch thrown by Myke Phoenix with all of his might – and lived to tell the tale.

"Well ..." said Scarface Mahoney.

"The power is yours to wield as you wish," said the black vase. "But you must understand that the power of Coronius will always want to crush Myke Phoenix. That is our most basic purpose. Anytime you are near Mychus you will lose control of the power. Your best option is to join us in crushing Mychus. After he is defeated once and for all, you will be free to use the power in whatever fashion you desire. If you want to do good, if you want to be a superhero, you may. First help us destroy Myke Phoenix."

Rick Mahoney stared at the black vase for many moments.

"Well, this one's a no-brainer," he said at last.

He picked up the vase, held it by one hand high above his head, and opened the window to the alley.

"No! You'll lose the power you've dreamed of," the vase intoned. "Think what you're doing."

"I think," said Scarface Mahoney, "that if you lied about Coronius, you're probably lying about everything else."

He looked up and down the alley to make sure no one was in harm's way, and then he heaved the vase with all of his might from his second-story window.

The Soulkeeper of Kiribati cannot be destroyed. The vessel that sat on Paul Phillips' dining room shelf was as unbreakable as the warrior once named Mychus.

The faux soulkeeper that Rick Mahoney found in Carlson's Pretty Good Antiques, however – well, it was a fake. The black vase struck the brick wall about four feet off the ground, so hard it shattered into tiny fragments and dust.

The young man went for a walk in a park down the street from his apartment. There was a small hill in a clearing and a rocky outcropping. The rising sun turned the sky purple and gold. Rick Mahoney reached his arms up to the sky and stretched back.

He didn't know where the vase came from.

He didn't know how he managed to exchange bodies with a dead warrior from two millennia ago.

He didn't know if he would ever be inside Coronius again.

He didn't know if he would ever encounter Myke Phoenix again and, if so, whether it would be as friend or foe.

He didn't know a lot of stuff.

But he knew he had made the right choice.

And that was good enough for now.

He noticed the sky was beautiful.

Epilogue

"WITHOUT the digital ad you used to have on the side, the Astor City Beacon logo can be displayed bigger," Paul Phillips pointed out to Dana.

The redesigned website had cleaner lines and sharper graphics, and just a single line of anything that looked like advertising copy on the front page: THE ASTOR CITY BEACON – "sponsored by the Nelson Rodinske Foundation." The lead story was Paul's analysis and explanation of the Astor County Board's latest planning initiative, with photos and graphics.

"It looks old school, but optimized for the screen of any device," he said.

"It looks good, Scoop. I'm proud of ya," Dana said, giving her hubby a proud hug from behind. "So what's next?"

"I'm going to keep doing what I've been doing, only I'll have more time to report the news because I won't be hindered by having to sell ads on the side."

"You don't seem to be worried that the big corporate investor will interfere with your journalistic freedom and all that," she said.

"He said he was committed to the Beacon's independence, in those exact words," said Paul Phillips. "I'm going to take him at his word for now. I sure hope this works."

There was a little headline under the header "Courts and Crime News" about an elaborate jewelry theft plot that had been broken up by Myke Phoenix and a mysterious new superhero.

"I see you gave that Cornelius Hawke person a pretty sympathetic writeup. What was that all about?"

"Cory Hawke. I don't know; he really did seem completely surprised that Coronius and Mychus were enemies. I got the sense that he was just some kid who wanted to be a superhero like Myke."

"Do you think you'll hear from him again?" Dana asked. "Could he figure out a way to use Coronius' power as a good guy?"

"What do you think about that, Soulkeeper?" Paul turned to the pottery on the shelf. "We going to hear from Cory Hawke ever again?"

"I should let you know that not long after your little soiree the other morning, the aura of evil in town took a sudden dive as if something nasty was snuffed out suddenly," the vase admitted.

"Hokey smoke! You don't think the kid got killed?"

"Actually, no, I don't," the vase said. "There's still a residual from what we interpreted as being Coronius, and it's ambivalent. I think your kid might have smashed that phony soulkeeper thing he was blabbing on about."

"If someone tricked me into doing something the opposite of what I wanted to do, I'd be mad enough to smash something," Dana said.

"You didn't answer the question, Soulkeeper," Paul said. "Will Cory Hawke be back?"

"If the thing was acting like a real soulkeeper, it was the conduit for the exchange. It's possible for you to switch bodies if I'm not in the picture, but you need to know how to manage it."

"I thought you were unbreakable."

"Everything's breakable if you try hard enough, mate. Nobody's ever tried that hard."

"And I could still make the switch if I had to?"

"If you knew how. And you do. There have been a few times over 18 years where you and I were separated by a long enough distance that I wasn't much help, and you did fine."

"This kid was having trouble managing the basics. If something happened to his soulkeeper-thingie, he's probably done."

"Just one little flaw in your logic, son."

"Yes?"

"A soulkeeper, or a phony soulkeeper-thingie like this one, has to be built. There's only one true soulkeeper, but if you can build one fake, you can build another."

"That's right. We still don't know who or what was behind this."

"I can think of a FEW possibilities, if you take my meaning," the vase said. At that particular moment, Paul Phillips did not take its meaning.

A small, energetic bundle of white fur bounded into the room with a look of triumph on its face. Running the whole way, the little creature deposited Dana's left slipper at Paul's feet and leaped into his lap.

"Goombah! Noo," Dana protested as Paul rubbed the little dog about the ears and shoulders. It squirmed back so that Paul could turn his attention to her chest and belly. "Paul, that's my slipper. I don't want her chewing on my slippers."

"Well, you wanted a puppy," he replied with a grin. "Oh, what a naughty little puppy!" he said as he played with the little thing, using a tone of voice that in no way, shape or form, transmitted a message that the puppy had been naughty.

"She's just incorrigible," she said. "How are we going to get her to behave?"

"This is why God invented puppy classes," Paul said calmly, wrestling with the enthusiastic bundle in his lap. "Ow! No biting, Goombah. The Astor City Dog Club has obedience classes, we can probably look those up and get her in."

Goombah sat up in Paul's lap and looked into his eyes, her tongue hanging out as she panted. It looked like she was smiling.

"Oh, my little Goombah, the stories we could tell each other if you could only talk," Paul Phillips said to his puppy.

He had no idea.

The Puppy Cried 'Murder'

Prologue

THE shock of being shot in the chest would follow Benny Parsons into his next life.

He forgot everything else in that moment. He didn't notice the person who shot him running away, and he couldn't remember if anyone was with him. Come to think of it, he lost track of exactly where he was.

All he could think about was the hole in his chest where, for 30-odd years, his heart had been faithfully beating along, circulating his blood and keeping him alive.

He gasped for breath and found air, but his lungs were not the problem. Without his good old heart, he would not be able to function much longer. His eyes widened in astonishment; it felt so strange that his heart was not beating – so very strange.

Benny Parsons' eyes stayed open as he lost consciousness.

And then, like anyone whose heart had been struck dead-on by an exploding bullet, Benny Parsons died.

"Goombah! NO!"

Our scene: A pleasant middle-class home on the outskirts of Astor City, a pleasant middle-class community in the heart of the United States. An attractive woman with auburn hair is addressing a white golden retriever puppy who has been on this Earth about four months and a member of this household approximately 10 weeks. (Actually, the woman at the kennel didn't call it a *white* puppy – it was "English Cream," la-ti-da, thank you so much.)

A man of approximately the same age as the woman – they are in their forties – glances up from his reading to watch the woman chase the small canine. He is amused; she does not appear to be.

"You wanted a puppy," he said.

"This is not a puppy," she said. "This is some sort of alien parasite or a terrorist infiltrator of some kind."

The puppy sat at the living room entrance, wagging her tail expectantly, chomping on something, and staring at the reading man with an expression that might have been playful, or it might have been pleading, or it might have been playfully pleading, as in, "Won't you play with me, please?"

The man happened to be Paul Phillips, who often worked late by virtue of his career choices. He was a reporter and, for the past 18 years, moonlighted as Myke Phoenix, a powerful superhero. The newcomer in the house was an effort to provide his wife with some companionship on those work nights.

"Oh, Goombah, what are you chewing on now?" he said with exasperation, or it might have been great amusement.

"Why on Earth did we name the dog Goombah, anyway?" the woman said. "What does that even mean?"

"Are you kidding? Look at that puppy," he said. "She looks just like a little goombah." The little dog jumped up and ran to the man, who picked her up onto his lap and started rubbing the top of her head.

"Paul. What's a goombah?"

"You *are* kidding," he laughed, "Look at her, Dana. Look at her! *This* is a goombah. She's a little goombah if I ever saw one."

Dana Dunsmore Phillips rolled her eyes as the puppy continued to chew on something. "We should have named her Roomba, the way she sucks up everything in the house."

"Wait a minute, wait a minute," Paul Phillips said, prying open Goombah's jaws and running his fingers inside. "What *does* she have in her mouth?"

Act 1

Scenes from before I was born

I don't know how much longer I'm going to remember all of this. Even now the memories are starting to fade away. I'm just glad I managed to - OH, there's Daddy! Where's that thing? I'm going to grab that thing and play tug of war with Daddy! Hey! Hey, Daddy! Hey! Hey!

"No bark, Goombah, not in the house. And gimme dat thing," he told me as we fought for the orange thing. Grrr! Daddy is so much fun. I still can't believe he's also Myke

Phoenix. Wow! I wonder if I'll still remember that when I'm all dog. Boy, I hope so.

Now that it's settled, maybe it's just as well if I don't remember my old life. Nothing more I can do about Benny Parsons, so I may as well enjoy being Goombah.

I guess I'm getting ahead of myself.

The whole adventure started a few days after I was born, even before my eyes opened for the first time. I actually was surprised to find out I was a puppy, because the last thing I remembered was being shot in the chest. Mowed down. I was dead! I remembered the hole in my chest and everything going black. Why wasn't I dead?

I'm still ahead of myself.

It all happened in a jumble, so I may turn out telling it that way. After all, I'm a puppy.

You can call me Goombah, everyone else does. I thought my name was No for a long time, and I think my full name is Goombah-no, but I'll come if you call me Goombah. I'm a good dog.

The very first thing I remembered was whimpering because I was so hungry. My eyes were closed, and I was too young even to know that it was possible to open them. I just knew I was hungry.

A big warm something nudged at me and moved me closer to a big warm wall or something – it wasn't really a wall because it was soft – and I sniffed and sniffed and jostled around until I found a faucet that gave out milk. Ooooh, that tasted good! I lived for that faucet. I would drink and drink and something warm would stroke my head. When my eyes woke up a few days later, I saw that it was Mom, and the jostling was caused by five little bundles of fur. When I saw one of them go get a drink from Mom, I figured out that I must be one of those bundles of fur, too.

Every so often these familiar-looking two-legged animals would come over and make a fuss over us. The little two-legged animals we met on the street especially seemed to like us. Daddy would attach a string or something around my neck, and we'd run around the block together. (OK, I would run, Daddy would walk and pull at my neck.) The smaller two-legged animals would come up and say, "Hi, Goombah! Can we pet her?" and I would wag my tail and sniff them while they ran their hands over my back and rub my belly and scratch my ears and, oh! They were so nice to me.

I had my first bad dream a few days after I opened my eyes. In the dream I was one of the two-legged animals, and I could understand the sounds they were making.

"Sorry, Benny," somebody said, and there was a flash, and then there was like a hole in my chest. It was so real that I woke up with a yip and it took me a few seconds to remember I'm a puppy. The weird thing is I every time I had the bad dream, I'd wake up better able to understand what the two-legged men and women and boys and girls were saying. See? I even remembered that they're called men and women and boys and girls.

I started to wonder if something had happened to me before I was born – which you have to admit is an odd thing for a puppy to be wondering – and if I'd lived life as a boy and then a man before. I thought that was a silly idea, but then I remembered a dream that Benny had when he was a kid.

In *his* dream Benny would be flying around looking for food and land on a big juicy plain of dark grass. He would sink his proboscis into it, not noticing a dark shadow above, and before he could take off again, everything suddenly went splat! and went black.

And another memory: Benny sniffing around looking for fallen nuts on the ground, noticing the big bird standing stark still in front of him, and then it grabs him in its bill, picks him up and flies over the lake, and ouch! everything goes black again ...

Was it all stuff that happened to Benny before he was born? Benny had past lives as a mosquito and a chipmunk? And was I Benny? Or were they all just goofy dreams? It really was a lot of heavy thinking for a puppy.

Now I know that of course I was Benny, remembering past lives. And now I'm Goombah, and for some reason I remember being Benny more than I remembered being the mosquito or the chipmunk. I think maybe it has something to do with being murdered and then trying to bring my killer to justice. If it wasn't for everything that happened, maybe I'd have passed them all off as bad dreams.

Oh! The ball just went rolling down the hallway. Hang on a second, I have to get it. Where's that ball? I'm gonna get that ball!

Got it. Now bring it to Daddy. Here it is! Here it is!

"Give me the ball, Goombah."

No, it's fun making you tug at it. Heeeee hee!

"Drop the ball."

Oh, all right. Here.

"Good girl. What a good girl you are, Goombah."

Oh, that's another thing. I came back as a girl. That took some getting used to. But I like it.

I think the day with the newspaper was the first time I connected the dreams with the real world.

I was playing my usual game with my two-legged mom. She would sit in an easy chair holding a wide piece of paper in front of her face, and I would jump up on top of the paper so I could see her again. It was like hide and seek.

"Goombah, stop it! I'm trying to read!" she would cry out, which I interpreted at the time as "Oh, you sweet thing! You found me!" I still hadn't figured out the nuances of tone of voice.

On this particular day I sat there in her lap on top of the paper, smiling and wagging my tail at her, and I glanced down and suddenly realized what the writing on the paper meant.

"POLICE BAFFLED BY PARSONS CASE"

Astor City police detectives say they have no new evidence that could lead to an arrest, six months after the brutal murders of city auditor Benjamin Parsons and —

That was all I was able to read, because she pushed me off her lap with a great big "Goombah, NO!" and got up.

"I can't even read the morning paper anymore!" she said. I tried to get back in her lap to see the paper. She pushed me off and held a stern index finger inches from my face. When she picked the paper back up, I jumped again and tried to paw back to the story I had seen. She stood up, scattering me and the papers on the floor, and stalked away.

"You wanted a puppy," my daddy said. He loves to tease her.

I sniffed and sniffed around the pile of papers, but I couldn't get back to the story I had seen. Something about the name Benjamin Parsons sounded familiar.

As if the universe and I and daddy were on the same wavelength, he said, "I see they still don't know who killed Benny Parsons."

Benny.

"I don't even care anymore," she called from the kitchen. "I can't read the paper without Goombah jumping up. What happened to those puppy classes we were going to take her to?"

Benny.

"I'll make the call today, maybe we can get her in starting next Wednesday night," he called back. "I think I'll talk to Captain Fredricks about the Parsons case today. I haven't bugged him for a while. Oh, that's right, that bridge dedication is Wednesday morning, and I should cover it. That'll make it a busy day, but we have to get her started. Right, Goombah? You're going to learn how to be a good dog, instead of a little goombah terrorist."

Benny.

"Sorry, Benny."

Staring at the muzzle of a gun.

"Please, I won't tell anyone."

"Can't take that chance."

The flare of the shot, the deafening noise, the hole in the chest.

I can't breathe. The long sleep.

Waking up as a dog.

The night of the first puppy class, Daddy burst through the door in a rush, and Mommy came home in a rush a few minutes later.

"Are we going to be on time? Don't forget the leash," she said.

"It was great, and how was *your* day, dear?' he laughed back. "We have plenty of time, the school's just 10 minutes from here and we have 25 minutes to get there. The new bridge is open finally, so we'll be there in no time."

"It'll be nice to get across the river on German Street instead of having to go all the way downtown," she said. My little puppy heart skipped a beat but didn't know why.

"So Goombah, do you want to go for a RIDE?" Daddy said with a happy bounce to his voice. He's always fun when his voice has that happy bounce, so I wanted this ride, whatever a ride was. My tail started wagging for no reason. "A RIDE! Yes! We're going for a ride!" I was so excited I didn't mind when he clipped the long string to the collar around my neck.

He opened up the door to the car, and Mommy said, "We're going for a RIDE in the CAR-CAR!" I couldn't help it; I barked and ran around in circles in the back of the car.

"What a good Goombah you are!" Daddy said as he pulled himself behind the steering wheel. How did I know that was the steering wheel? I really did know more than a puppy usually knows, I thought to myself. But how does anyone know what a puppy usually knows? All I knew for sure is I shouldn't know how a car works. But then we pulled out of the driveway and down the street and I didn't care how it works anymore, I just knew it was fun! fun! fun!

"Put down the back windows a crack," Mommy said, and Daddy pushed the magic button that opened a piece of the outdoors to me. I love the feel of the rushing wind against my face. It's wonderful! Until you try it yourself, you'll never understand.

"Well, here it is, ladies: The brand-new German Street Bridge! Are you ready to give it a try?" Daddy said with an overblown tone of drama. Mommy said, "oooooh!" but I just froze, and my little puppy heart skipped several beats.

I started whining as we approached the big brick road that carried itself over the big river below. There was a little bump in the road as the bridge started, and I started yelling "No! No! No! NOOOO! No! No!"

"Goombah, no barking!" Daddy shouted back. And he sounded like he meant it. But I couldn't help myself. I ran back and forth from one window to the other window as we crossed over the Skikaakwa River (How did I know it was called the Skikaakwa River?) and I tried to stop myself, but the sound kept coming out of me. "No!" I shouted, and held myself back as best I could, but the fear was so deep and overriding I had to let it out. "No! No!"

"Don't make me come back there," Daddy growled, then started laughing. "Listen to me, I sound like my dad."

Mommy laughed and looked back at me. "I think she doesn't like the new bridge." She reached out her hand and scratched the side of my face gently. "It's OK, Goombah, we'll be over this mean old bridge in just a few more seconds."

When we reached the other side, relief washed over me like a bath. I sighed and lay down.

"What was that all about, I wonder?" Daddy said.

"I don't know. I've never heard of a dog being afraid of bridges."

"We've taken her into town before, and she never barked on the river."

No, I hadn't. But we never came over THAT bridge before. I was just as confused as Daddy. What was that all about? It had been way too scary, but I didn't know why.

We pulled up to a big, sprawling, one-story building that I recognized as Astor West High School. There I went again: How did I know what Astor West High School was? Daddy stopped the car in front of one of those funny flat things on sticks poked up along the edge of the grass. I surprised myself again when I looked at them and all of a sudden I knew that there was writing on them that said "Visitor Parking," even though I didn't know what a visitor was, or parking for that matter. Just as suddenly they were just flat things on sticks again.

Other dogs! Other puppies! Oh boy! They were all on strings and running (or trying to run) into the big building. I was gasping for air as I tried to join them and Daddy and Mommy walked behind me at the other end of the string. Why were they going so slowly!?

We went through the doors and into a big open room with mats and rug runners all over the floor. A lady with a big smile and a clipboard walked up and said to Daddy and

Mommy, "Welcome to puppy class! Is this your first time?"

While they were talking with the nice lady, I looked around and wagged my tail. There were all sorts of puppies here, black ones, white ones like me, multicolored ones, brown ones – I could tell this was going to be fun!

One of the brown ones came walking over, straining against his string, and started sniffing me. I started sniffing back to say "Hi!"

"Paul, good to see you," came a voice behind the brown dog and above us. "I didn't know you had a new puppy, too."

"Oh, hi, Tony! Yes, welcome to puppy class, I guess. This is Goombah, and this is my wife, Dana."

"Hello," Mommy said, shaking the man's hand.

"Tony Washburne. He works for the city," Daddy told Mom. "He's the public works engineer in charge of bridges and roads. That's his baby we just went over the river on."

A growl started in the back of my throat. Where it was coming from, I didn't know for a few seconds.

"Oh, that's a beautiful bridge, Tony," Mommy said, "although little Goombah here wasn't happy about it for some reason."

Bridge. Public works. Engineer.

"She's a goofy dog," Daddy said. "All of a sudden she's scared of bridges."

"Oh, poor little puppy," the man named Tony said, and he stooped down to pet me on the shoulder. Now I could see his face better.

"GRRRRRRRrrrrrr," I said. Sorry, there's no translation for that. "GRRRRR!!!" Tony pulled his hand back suddenly, just in time because I snapped my jaws at it.

"Goombah!" Daddy said in shocked surprise. "I'm sorry, Tony, she's never done that with anyone –"

"NO!" I shouted. "No! No! No! No! No!"

"Goombah, no! No barking! Get down!" Daddy said, and this time he meant it. But I meant it, too.

"No! No! No!" I shouted, lunging forward. "GRRRrrrrrrr. No! No!"

Daddy yanked at my chain, but I just kept on shouting. I wanted to go for the man's throat and rip out his lungs. Why? What was wrong with me? I forgot for a second.

But then I remembered again. I remembered it all.

I was looking into the face of the man who killed Benny Parsons. That is to say, I was looking into the face of the man who killed me.

Act 2

Blanks for the memories

AND just as suddenly, I forgot again. It had to do with Daddy holding my snout and staring into my eyes with a dark look on his face.

"You behave, little girl," he said. "I know this is a new experience with lots of dogs, but it's especially important to be a good dog here."

Of course, it sounded like "Blah blah blah blah" to me. I heard his anger more than I understood the words. I don't know how it all happens: One minute I could have held a conversation with Daddy and Mommy if I knew how to talk, and the next minute I was all doggie again. As he lectured me, I sat like a good little Goombah, panting so it looked like I was smiling like golden retrievers do.

Most important, I just didn't remember that I had ever been anything except a little dog. The past memories came and went, and as time went on they have stayed away longer and longer.

"Sorry about that, she's usually a great little puppy," Daddy said.

"When she's not terrorizing the household," Mommy added. "I think all these other dogs may have spooked her a little."

"Not a problem, I know how puppies are," Tony Washburne said.

"The new bridge looks great, we just went over it on the way over here."

"Thanks, Paul, it did turn out nicely, didn't it? Good architect, solid contractor."

Blah blah blah. What was that delicious aroma?

A handsome poodle puppy pranced over. I have to admit my girly instincts kicked in when I saw him. We sniffed each other and strained against our leashes to get a little closer. I wanted to play with him – just play. I mean, yes, he was hot! I wasn't used to feeling the way he made me feel, but mostly I just wanted to play and be friends. We were puppies, after all.

"Well, they seem to like each other," Daddy said to the man holding the poodle puppy's string. "What's her name?"

"She's a he. My daughters couldn't agree on whether to call him Prince or Buster, so we named him Prince Buster."

"I like it. This is Goombah."

Prince Buster had a sparkle in his eye, and he licked the side of my face like nobody's business. If it weren't for those silly strings attached to our necks, we would have run and run and run and run around the room. And what was it about his scent? I was ready to throw my arms around him and surrender to his charms, except I don't have arms. Oh my, he was a handsome dude. And he smelled so familiar, so – comfortable. It reminded me of – what did it remind of? Or who?

Suddenly a lady in the middle of the room called us all to attention and started saying stuff about sitting and staying and coming and getting down and whatever. For the next 45 minutes we all walked in circles and practiced sitting and staying and coming and stuff.

And then we went back to the car.

I was pooped! That was a lot of activity for one hour. I kept thinking about Prince Buster. If I wasn't a puppy, I'd swear I was in love or something. He seemed to like me, too. Did he have the same sense that we knew each other somehow, even though we'd just met? It was the weirdest sensation.

"Look at that, she's just lying down in the back like a pooped pup," Mom said. I *was* a pooped pup! "She doesn't even seem to care that we're about to go over the new bridge again."

What? The new bridge?

"No!" I shouted. "No! No! No! No! No!"

"Goombah, calm down," Daddy barked from behind the wheel, then glanced over at Mom. "You had to mention the bridge."

"Right, like a puppy knows what the word 'bridge' means."

"NOOO!" I howled. That made them both look back at me.

"Maybe she *does* know what it means."

Despite my insistence, they started going over the bridge. I began to feel silly for making such a commotion, but then a horrible grinding sound filled the air just as we reached the top of the bridge. It sounded like someone groaning under the weight of a package that was heavier than they could carry, only louder and deeper than any human voice.

"What in heaven's name is that sound?!" Mom said.

And suddenly I knew. I knew why I was barking, and I knew what the noise was.

"Noooooo," I whined. "No! No! No."

"Oh, for crying out loud," Daddy said. "No barking, Goombah!"

"I don't blame her," Mom said as the groaning continued. "This bridge sounds scary."

And then the noise stopped. You could see other drivers looking around, so we hadn't imagined the loud, crackling, groaning sound, but it was gone now.

But the bridge! And Washburne! And –

"Maybe the ball will calm her down."

Ball?

"Is that right, Goombah? Do you want your ball?"

Ball! I couldn't help it; my tail started wagging despite myself.

"There's your ball. Now sit and play until we get home."

I licked and chewed the ball in the back of the car, completely forgetting about the bridge and Tony Washburne and Benny and – something else. I thought about that nice Prince Buster and how warm he made me feel. At that point I didn't realize why those terrible memories triggered images of the handsome poodle I'd just met.

There's just something wonderful about a ball. Whatever it was about that jumble of emotions just vanished while I had my teeth wrapped around my ball.

"I'm going to call Tony Washburne in the morning and ask about that sound we heard on the bridge."

"Good idea. That was so scary," Mom said.

I was curled up on the couch next to my ball while Dad and Mom sat at the dining table not far away. I tried falling asleep with the ball in my mouth, but it was more comfortable just putting my nose against it so that I knew it was right there if I needed it in the night.

"See? You *can* sit still." Daddy's voice made me open my eyes just a slit. "And you were very good in class. Well, mostly good."

"She was horrid to Mr. Washburne. I wonder what that was all about?"

"Who knows what evil lurks in the heart of a puppy? You do gotta wonder. And going over the bridge – hokey smokes, I bet she would have jumped out of the car and bitten the darn bridge if she could." He sounded more amused than unhappy with me.

"Maybe the bridge is a source of evil in the universe," Mom said.

"Don't be so sure it isn't," said a third voice, which made my ears perk up. I was suddenly fully awake and tipping my head to hear where the voice came from.

"What? I suppose that noise was the groaning of some arcane demon or something?"

"You really oughtta be more respectful about demons and the forces of evil in the world," the strange voice said. I say the voice was strange because, for one thing, there were only two people in the room and this was the third voice, and for another, there was something about the tone of the voice that I couldn't figure out if it was a boy or a girl talking. It was weirdly – what's the word? – not a boy, not a girl – androgynous! The voice was androgynous. That's strange, too: How does a puppy know a big word like androgynous?

"Grrr," I said, not liking the voice out of nowhere, and Daddy laughed.

"It's OK, Goombah girl," he said. "It's just the Soulkeeper of Kiribati." He got out of his chair, picked up a pale green vase off the shelf, and carried it over to me on the couch. It was an ugly piece of pottery, with red, blue and clear jewels embedded in it kind of randomly, not in any pattern, and a painted picture of a bird. I sniffed. It smelled old and musty.

"Knock it off, doggie," the voice sprang out of the vase, and I jumped off the couch, ears perked at full attention. For some reason this made my daddy laugh hysterically. "What's so funny, Scoop?"

"Don't call me Scoop, only Dana can call me Scoop," Daddy laughed. "I just think it's sweet that Goombah wants to protect me from you."

"Is that what this is?" the vase said, and that was enough for me.

"Hey!" I shouted. "Hey! Hey! Hey! Hey! Hey!"

"Oh, Goombah, stop it," Daddy said patiently, but I was having none of that.

"Hey! Hey! Hey! Hey! Hey! Hey! Hey!"

"Goombah!"

"Hey! Hey! Hey!" No talking green pot was going to invade my territory if I could help it. "Hey!"

"Goombah, that's enough!" Mommy chimed in. "No!"

"No! No! No!" I agreed with her. "Hey! No! No!"

"OK, puppy, you asked for it," Daddy said, and all of a sudden he wasn't Daddy anymore.

The transformation struck me dumb. Instead of the slightly gray-haired, semi-pudgy guy who fed me, a big-chested blond guy in a white costume stood in front of the couch. The costume shirt was buttoned up the side and it had a big image of a bird on the front – a better-designed bird than the funky image on the green vase, I might add. There were sort of stylized flames under the bird's picture, like it was a – what was the word? – like it was a phoenix.

A phoenix!

Daddy had turned into Myke Phoenix!

"That's better, little girl," the big man said, with a deeper voice but using the same tone that Daddy did when he was talking to me. "You just be quiet and be a good dog, now, OK?"

"You're not going to believe this," the boy-girl voice said from the vase. "I think she recognizes you."

"Well, she's not a complete goombah," Myke said. "I'm her puppy daddy, after all."

"No, you don't get it, as usual," the vase said. "I think she knows who Myke Phoenix is."

"How could she know that?" Mommy broke in. "She's a puppy."

"I don't know, but I'm definitely getting a different reading from her than a minute ago. First she was madder than a winter hornet about a talking vase, and then she was all awestruck, with a glint of recognition. I know a glint when I feel one."

Myke Phoenix, the mysterious superhero who captured crooks and battled the super villains who popped up from time to time in Astor City – yes, the name of the town was Astor City – was my daddy. Or at least he replaced my daddy and talked like my daddy only with a deeper voice. Myke Phoenix would know what to do about Tony Washburne.

And I remembered again. I was Benny Parsons. No, I was Goombah, but whatever it was that made me Goombah used to be what made me Benny. And Tony Washburne killed me – killed Benny –and it had something to do with the German Street Bridge. What a stupid thing to kill somebody over. Why? And there was something else, worse than killing me, worse than whatever it was about the bridge, it was –

Oh. Oh, no. Oh my goodness. It was the worst thing of all. It was –

"There's more to that dog than meets the eye, I'm telling ya," the vase voice said.

"Oh, that much I agree with," Myke Phoenix said, and he reached down to rub my head, just like Daddy. "This is no dog, this is a wild goombah."

And just like that, I forgot what the worst thing of all was.

Act 3
It all comes back to me

I didn't forget for long. In fact, I remembered, and for a very long time after the next puppy class. Well, I guess it wasn't really a very long time, but it was long enough. I suppose I won't remember it all much longer, either. But that's OK. It's all better now.

I'm getting ahead of myself again. Sorry about that.

For the next week my brain kept bouncing back and forth. For a while I would be all puppy eyes and flowers, and then something would remind me about Benny and the bridge and whatever it was I still couldn't remember. I guess I probably drove Daddy and Mommy a little cuckoo, one minute being the playful puppy and the next the excited murder victim running around trying to get their attention. On the other hand, maybe those two things looked the same on the outside.

Every day I would jump into Mommy's lap while she was reading the newspaper to see if there was anything new about my murder, but there wasn't, not that week.

"Goombah, get off!" Mommy shouted when I jumped up to see the paper. "Why doesn't she jump on you when you're reading the newspaper, Paul?"

"Oh, she does, she jumps on me sometimes," Daddy said. He was right: I would check the paper when he was reading the news section. Usually he was reading the comics or the entertainment section, though. I suppose as a news reporter himself, he didn't need to read the paper to know what was happening in town.

"Does anybody really play bridge anymore?" Mommy said.

"What makes you say that?"

"Oh, this column 'The Bridge Tender,' I think it's been in the paper for 100 years and I never read it, but sometimes the headline grabs me: 'Bob and the mystery of the poisoned slam,' 'Lucky Lily cashes in with risky finesse.' They draw you in with the headline, and it's only about some silly card game."

"Don't call bridge silly," Daddy said. "The people who read that column take it very seriously. Back when I was working at the paper, we forgot to run it one day, and the office was flooded with angry calls."

Of course, all I heard was "Blah blah blah BRIDGE blahbidey blah BRIDGE blah blah blah blah BRIDGE blah," and I couldn't remember why the word filled me with dread. But later when I *did* remember, it gave me an idea.

Every day Mommy or Daddy would give me a little drill about sitting or staying, and they would hook me up to the leash and we'd walk around the yard sitting and staying some more. It was like puppy class only more boring, but at least I got treats out of it.

When I wasn't chasing the ball or playing tug of war or cruising the back yard looking for sticks and rocks to eat, I was trying to figure out how to tell Daddy and Mommy about what Tony Washburne did to Benny Parsons and – those other things he did that I couldn't remember yet.

I remembered that $100 bills have a picture of Benjamin Franklin on them, but if I brought Daddy a $100 bill, I wasn't sure how to help him make the connection between "Benjamin" Franklin and Benjamin Parsons. I also figured he wouldn't notice anything except a puppy chewing on a $100 bill. And then there was the little detail that he didn't carry $100 bills very often, if at all.

"Sorry, Benny."

Staring at the muzzle of a gun.

"Please, I won't tell anyone."

"Can't take that chance."

The flare of the shot, the deafening noise, the hole in the chest.

I can't breathe. The long sleep.

Waking up as a dog.

Then one day it happened again. Daddy burst through the door in a rush, and Mommy came home in a rush a few minutes later.

"Are we going to be on time? Don't forget the leash," she said.

We all piled into the car, and a few minutes later I was screaming as we crossed the German Street Bridge. A few minutes after that, we were at the school and lining up with the other dogs and their owners for puppy class.

The brown dog walked by, and I looked up behind him to see Tony Washburne, who just waved and didn't come over this week.

"GRRRRRrrrrrr!" I said. "No! No! No! No!"

"I don't know why, Tony, but she loves everyone except you," Daddy called over. "Sorry about that."

"Did you ask Tony about that weird sound on the bridge?" Mommy said. "I forgot to ask last week."

"Oh yeah, he said it probably was just normal settling of the piers or some such. I can't say I ever heard anything like that before on a new bridge, but he didn't seem worried."

"It didn't seem very normal to me, either. Oh, here's Prince Buster, Goombah's boyfriend."

If I didn't like every inch of Prince Buster's poodly body, I would have been embarrassed by Mom's remark. But it was true. My tail started wagging as soon as I saw him walking up with his owner, and by the time we actually met and started sniffing each other, my whole body was wagging. This big poodle just drove me crazy, I loved everything about being near him.

I jumped on his back, and he jumped on mine, and we strained against the leashes. I sniffed along his neck and the scent reminded me of how Sophia smelled when I wrapped my arms around her in the morning and kissed her neck.

Wait a minute.

Sophia?

Who the bejeebers was Sophia?

And then ...

Then I remembered.

I remembered it all.

And I remembered the worst thing of all.

The very worst thing ever.

SOPHIE! NOOOOOOOOOOOooooooooooooo..........!!!!!

"Tony? You got a minute?"

Tony Washburne looked up from his computer to see his visitor.

"Oh, hi, Benny. Sure. What's up?"

"Well," Benny Parsons said, pulling up a chair and sitting uncomfortably on the other side of Washburne's desk. "I've been looking over the expense reports for the German Street Bridge project."

"Uh oh." Washburne's tone was light but there was a sudden darkness in his eyes that Parsons didn't notice. "We're not going too far over budget, are we?"

"What? Oh, no, no, not at all," Benny replied. "In fact, it's kind of the exact opposite."

"We're too far under budget?"

"Right. I've been adding up the receipts and the expense reports. The materials purchases are way under what we budgeted, and there are a few 'miscellaneous' categories that are more or less unaccounted for. It's only a few dollars every day, but this is a long-term project so we're talking more than 700 days so far."

"So what are you saying?"

Benny Parsons took a deep breath, then exhaled. "I have a feeling the contractor is buying lower-quality materials than the specs called for, and pocketing the difference. It looks like about a half-million dollars."

If he had been paying attention, Benny might have noticed how long it took Tony Washburne to say, "Oh, my goodness. Are you sure?"

"I'm sure. Tony, you've been inspecting the work all along, right?"

"Right."

"You haven't noticed whether the steel or the supports or any of the concrete was substandard?"

"No, of course not. Everything looks fine."

"Except it's not fine. I think I'm going to have to report this to the state, and see what they think."

"Good idea," Washburne said, and Benny did not notice that Washburne didn't seem to think it was a good idea at all.

That night, Benny Parsons arrived home and was greeted as he walked into the kitchen with a passionate kiss from an exotic, olive-skinned beauty with jet-black hair.

"Benjamin Parsons, what took you so long?" the woman breathed huskily in his ear. "I've been dying for this since I got home from work."

"Sophie, Sophie," Benny said with a sigh and a huge grin. "What did I ever do to deserve this?"

"You married me, silly," she smiled back, tossing her hair.

After dinner they went for a walk through the neighborhood. Their path took them through a wooded park. They would be found the next morning in the most secluded area of that park, almost the only place along their path where no houses were in sight. It was just after sunset, and no one else was in the park. Well, almost no one else.

They were holding hands and not speaking as they walked along with contented smiles on their faces.

"Benny."

A man stepped out of the woods in front of them. Benny and Sophie jumped.

"Oh my gosh, Tony," Benny laughed after a few seconds. "You scared the life out of me. What are you doing here?"

"Sorry, Benny."

It took a few more seconds for Benny to realize he was staring at the muzzle of a gun. Sophia gasped.

"I'm sorry you're here, Sophie," Tony Washburne said. "I'm sorry you figured out the bridge gimmick, Benny. I really wish you hadn't done that."

He cocked the gun.

"Please," Benny said, looking around for help and breathing heavily. "I won't tell anyone."

"Can't take that chance."

The flare of the shot, the deafening noise, the hole in the chest.

A second flare, a second deafening noise, Sophia's black hair flying as she toppled back, a horrible red flower blooming in her chest.

I can't breathe.

I can't breathe!

Sophie!

The long sleep.

Prince Buster and I looked into each other's eyes. Was he feeling the absolute shock that I was feeling? Could it really be true? I came back as a girl golden retriever, and Sophie came back as a gorgeous male standard poodle?

The scent couldn't lie. The scent had crossed with us from one life to the next. It was like no other scent in the world. Now the scent had more of a male tinge, and a canine tinge, but there was no mistaking: This was my soulmate. When we stood on two legs, our names were Benjamin and Sophia. Now we stood on four legs, the spark of recognition charging the air like a lightningbolt, and our names were Goombah and Prince Buster.

My tail began to wag again, and if dogs cried like baby humans I would have been sobbing like a woman who thought her man was dead until he walked up the sidewalk and took her in his arms and said it was all a horrible mistake. Oh, my love! It was her! him! whatever!

And then I saw Tony Washburne across the room.

What happened next is a blur. I remember Daddy yelling my name sharply as I pulled the leash out of his hand. I remember running as fast and as hard as I could toward Washburne, growling like an angry and perhaps rabid dog. I remember screaming "NO! NO! NO!" and running and running, until my neck jerked back violently as something grabbed the end of my leash when I was 20 feet from ripping out Tony Washburne's throat.

I remember how shocked I was when I looked back and saw that Prince Buster was holding the other end of my leash in his mouth, his chest heaving from running as hard as he could after me.

I remember how angry Daddy was, and I remember him apologizing to everyone all around for scaring their dogs. I remember Mommy being upset and saying, "Let's just go home. I don't know what's wrong with her."

I remember lying in the back of the car, exhausted and panting hard, and Mommy looking back with worried eyes. "What's wrong with her? Why did she act like that, all of a sudden?"

I remember my growing anger about Tony Washburne fighting with my growing joy about Prince Buster, the love of my life – the love of my lives.

I remember Daddy driving back over the German Street Bridge again, and how the bridge groaned louder and longer than it had a week earlier, and how I knew now that I was listening to the sound of inadequate steel and stone trying to hold up more weight than it was designed to hold.

I remember whimpering, wondering how to tell Daddy - Myke Phoenix - before the bridge fell into the river.

Act 4
Daddy to the rescue

MOMMY took me to the vet the next morning.

"What a sweet little Goombah you are!" the vet said as she looked into my ears and pried my mouth open to check my teeth. "She's just adorable, Mrs. Phillips."

"You wouldn't have said so last night," Mommy said. "I thought she was turning into a little pit bull for a minute there."

"Pit bulls are sweet, gentle dogs when you treat them sweetly and gently," the veterinarian replied in what sounded like a soft scolding. "The people who raise them to be mean have given them a bad name."

"I know that, I'm sorry," Mommy said. "She seems vicious only when she gets near this one man. When she took off across the room after him, I was afraid that she would – I don't know what she would have done."

The vet turned me over on my back and pressed against my tummy, which was very fun. I wanted her to scratch my chest, but she just held a cold metal disc against me instead.

"I don't know how to explain that, but you'll be happy to know it's nothing physical. This is one healthy puppy – and adorable, too!" she said, squeezing my face between her hands and rubbing playfully. "There's no sign of rabies or any other disorder."

"So she just had a psychotic episode," Mommy said.

"They *are* animals. We're never going to completely understand why they do what they do," said the vet, and she rubbed the top of my head. "So long, Goombah! See you next time."

During that next week, I remembered that I used to be Benny Parsons almost all the time. There were some short times when I completely was a puppy, when Daddy or Mommy would throw the ball or wrestle with me or make me chase the flying disc, but when everything calmed down I'd remember Sophia and Prince Buster and Tony Washburne and the bridge and the gun all over again.

I paced the house looking for a toy bridge or a toy gun or something I could use to talk to Daddy or Mommy, but they didn't have kids so there weren't any toys. It would be so easy if dogs talked.

The vase! The weird, talking Soulkeeper of Whatever. It knew when I recognized Myke Phoenix; maybe it knows how to communicate with dogs. But it was no use. I put my paws on the second shelf from the bottom and looked up, but I knew I'd never be able to reach it or even shake the shelves enough to knock it to the floor. Anyway, I figured it would shatter and I'd just get in trouble. I didn't find out until much later that it's thousands of years old and unbreakable.

I kept jumping up to read the paper with Mommy when I could, but there was nothing there. No news. With no new evidence, our murder was easing itself onto the back burner of the police files.

I thought about Prince Buster a lot. Did he remember as much as I did about the night Benny and Sophie went for a walk in the park? He had to have some memory of who we were, because of the way he chased after me and kept me from attacking Washburne.

I wondered if I would ever see him again. Now that I knew who he was, I wanted to be with Prince Buster even more than I wanted to live with Mommy and Daddy. I couldn't wait for another puppy class, and because most of the time I didn't know how to count anymore, I wasn't sure when seven days would be going by. Being a puppy with fading memories of being human was awfully frustrating.

And then, that last day, which turned out to be the day of the third week of puppy class, everything fell into place.

The morning started the same as every morning – Daddy let me out of the house while Mommy was still sleeping, and I ran around the yard for a while, same as always. When I came back in, Daddy was drinking his hot drink, same as always. Mommy woke up, same as always. There was a "pop!" sound against the front door that made me bark, same as always. Daddy opened the door, picked up the morning paper, and walked it over to where Mommy was sitting down with her own hot drink, same as always.

Something different happened then, but Mommy and Daddy didn't realize it at first.

When Mommy unfolded the paper and started looking at the front of the newspaper, I saw something on the back page that I'd been hoping to see for a long time.

I jumped into her lap.

"Goombah! NO!"

I pulled the paper out of her hands and ran across the room, leaving behind the inside pages and taking just the sheet of paper that had the front page and the back page.

She chased after me, and when she grabbed the paper out of my mouth, I held on so part of the back page ripped off.

"Oh, you!" she said, picking up the rest of the pages and stalking back to her chair. I dropped my piece of paper and looked to make sure I had the right piece. I did! It was perfect. I picked it up again.

"You wanted a puppy," Daddy teased Mommy.

"This is not a puppy," she said. "This is some sort of alien parasite or a terrorist infiltrator of some kind."

I sat in the corner of the room with the paper in my mouth, my tail wagging in excitement, but they stopped paying attention. I decided to risk chomping on the paper a little bit to make them notice, and it worked.

"Oh, Goombah, what are you chewing on now?" he said, sounding tired.

"Why on Earth did we name the dog Goombah, anyway?" Mommy said. "What does that even mean?"

"Are you kidding? Look at that puppy," he said. "She looks just like a little goombah." He wasn't in any hurry to come get the paper scrap, so I jumped up and ran over to him. He picked me up into his lap and started rubbing the top of my head.

"Paul. What's a goombah?"

"You *are* kidding," he laughed, "Look at her, Dana. Look at her! *This* is a goombah. She's a little goombah if I ever saw one."

Come on, Daddy, look at what I brought you. Look! In my mouth!

Mommy rolled her eyes. "We should have named her Roomba, the way she sucks up everything in the house."

"Wait a minute, wait a minute," Daddy said, prying open my jaws and running his fingers inside. "What *does* she have in her mouth?"

Finally! I couldn't get my tail to stop wagging. He saw me! He saw *it!*

"I guess I should turn on the TV," Mommy said, walking over to the flat screen against the wall and pressing a button.

"It's part of the paper," he said, withdrawing the fragment from my mouth and rubbing the top of my head. "You're just a little silly, Goombah."

He smoothed the paper out and saw what I wanted him to see.

"It's the Bridge Tender column, dear," he said. "Oh, and it's got one of those fun headlines: 'Tony makes a killing.'"

Tony makes a killing.

Tony makes a killing. See, Daddy? See?

He didn't see. He was looking at something on the screen.

"– about 10 minutes ago," the news anchor was saying. "You're looking at a live shot from the Astor City traffic cam system, and as you can see, at least two or three cars are dangling over the river at the edge of the part of the roadway that's still intact, where if you've just joined us, part of the new German Street Bridge has collapsed, sending several vehicles into the Shikaakwa River and threatening several more. Now we're told police and rescue crews are on their way, but –"

I spilled onto the floor when Daddy jumped up, and a split second later he wasn't Daddy anymore. I didn't blink or anything, but one instant Daddy was standing in front of the TV, and the next instant Myke Phoenix was running across the room toward the door.

"Be careful, dear," Mommy said.

"I always am," Myke called back and he was gone.

Five seconds later the anchor said, "Is that – I think, yes, that's Myke Phoenix. Myke Phoenix has arrived on the scene and just dived into the river. He must be checking the vehicles that fell in."

Mommy and I sat in front of the TV for a long time after that. Daddy found all of the cars and a couple of pickup trucks that were underwater, and he pulled everyone out and up to the surface. It was too late for two or three people, but he got the others out safely.

People were still on the bridge and you could hear that horrible groaning sound like we had been hearing when we crossed it, and the roadway jerked downward. But Daddy – I mean, Myke Phoenix – got underneath and pushed up on the bridge, giving it support while police officers and firefighters ran toward the last stranded cars and helped people get out and onto solid land.

"Is everybody off the bridge?" you could hear Myke shout from underneath.

The police officers shouted back "yes!" and gave the thumbs-up sign, and Myke let go and jumped out of the way. Daddy is amazing; he jumped from the middle of the bridge all the way to the river bank.

That big groaning, crackling noise was louder than ever, and the rest of the bridge fell into the water with a big monster splash.

"We have inspector Anthony Washburne on the line, he's the city manager responsible for bridge construction and safety," the TV anchor said. "Mr. Washburne, thank you for coming on with us right now, this is a terrible tragedy."

"Yes, it is, just terrible. Tragic," the voice on the phone said. A photograph appeared on the big screen, and I growled.

"Hush, Goombah, I want to hear this," Mommy said.

I ran over to where Daddy had been sitting, picked up the piece of paper with the bridge column headline and ran back to Mom.

"No, we had no idea this could happen," Tony Washburne's voice was saying. "None of the inspections showed anything wrong or inadequate. We had some routine settling of the piers, but nothing that could be called alarming."

I put my right paw on Mommy's hand. She looked at me and said, "Oh, Goombah, you're just a sassafras," and pulled the paper out of my mouth.

She looked at the screen again, so I pawed her again. When she looked at me, I glanced down at the paper. And so did she.

"'Tony makes a killing,'" Mommy said, and looked back at Tony Washburne talking on TV, and then back at me. "*Tony makes a killing. Oh, my stars.*"

Right in the middle of puppy class that night, a bunch of police officers came marching in, and the leader went right up to Tony Washburne and said, "Mr. Washburne? I'm Detective Capt. Fredricks of the Astor City Police Department. I need to ask you some questions about the German Street Bridge construction project, bribery and, oh yeah, the murder of Benjamin and Sophia Parsons. These ladies and gentlemen are here to escort you safely to the police station for me."

I ran in circles, jumped on Daddy and Mommy, and shouted "Yes! Yes! Yes!" I looked over at Prince Buster, and he was licking his master's face.

"Did you know he was going to be arrested?" Mommy asked, and Daddy nodded.

"I couldn't tell you until they had him in custody. Fredricks questioned the contractor, and it turns out the guy gave Washburne $75,000 in exchange for giving him a pass on the substandard materials he used on the bridge. He was buying cheap stuff and keeping the difference, something like $500,000. The idiot honestly figured the bridge would hold up anyway."

I couldn't stand it anymore. I pulled free from Daddy and pranced with the leash trailing me over to Prince Buster. We nuzzled each other in celebration, ran around each other and jumped up and down, yipping with happiness. It was the best time of my puppy life so far.

"Wow, they really like each other," Prince Buster's master said.

"I guess so!" Mommy agreed.

Prince Buster put his paw on my neck and licked my face over and over. I couldn't do anything but wag my tail.

"Honey," Daddy said, putting his arm around Mom, "have you ever seen a golden doodle? They're the most adorable dogs you ever want to see."

So that's how it happened, as best as I can remember. And the older I get, the harder it is to remember. I'm almost 10 months old now, and sometimes days go by before I get a flash of Sophie's face or even remember the name of the big guy in the white suit who changes places with Daddy every so often.

Myke Phoenix! That's his name, that's right. I think I'm probably not going to remember his name when I grow up to be a complete dog, but I'll always know how wonderful he is. Wait, what am I saying? His name is Daddy! I'll always remember that.

Prince Buster comes over to visit a lot; Mommy and Daddy and his owner are getting to be really good friends. We run around in the back yard and play and stuff.

After Prince Buster leaves, Mommy always teases me and says, "Are you going to have puppies, Goombah? Do you want to be a puppy mama, little Goombah?" I don't know why Mommy says stuff like that, but I do know that Prince Buster makes me all tingly like nobody else ever. If making me feel happy all over gives me puppies, then I guess I want to be a puppy mama. I love Prince Buster.

We graduated from puppy class together. Yes, we still kept going even though it was a longer ride after the bridge fell into the river. And I never was a bad dog again, but that's because I never wanted to rip anybody else's throat again after that one guy – what was his name again? I don't even know what got into me that day. All I know is I have the best Mommy and Daddy in the world, and they let me see Prince Buster.

Daddy and Mommy are so nice to me. They throw the ball and the disc so I can chase them around the house and the yard. Mommy and I always play the game where she holds up the paper and I jump in her lap, and she shouts my full name – "Goombah-no!"

When I think of everything about my life, I think I must be the luckiest puppy of them all. I have Daddy, and I have Mommy, and I get to play with Prince Buster and sleep on the couch and run around the yard and chase stuff. Daddy says I fulfill my purpose in life because I retrieve like gold, and I think that's really good even though I don't know what it means.

Hi! My name is Goombah. Let's be friends!

Epilogue

"HAVE you noticed Goombah doesn't bark and growl anymore when they show Tony Washburne in court on TV?"

"Really? I guess you're right." Paul Phillips was reading a book on the couch with the big white – that is, English cream – golden retriever's head in his lap.

"It's almost as if she was a spirit who fulfilled her duty to Benny and Sophie Parsons and passed on to the great beyond," Dana Dunsmore Phillips said, reading the paper.

"If life was a movie, I'd probably agree with you," Paul said. "But I don't see it. She's just mellowing out as she grows up."

"I don't know, for a while there I thought she was developing some real intelligence, even as if she could understand English," Dana said. "And remember that 'Tony makes a killing' thing?" The young dog stretched, got down on the floor, and walked toward her. "But you're right. Lately she just acts like a dumb old goombah again."

"I disagree – GOOMBAH!" he shouted as the dog started to jump into Dana's newspaper. "Stay!" Goombah stopped and looked back at Paul. "See, Dana? She understands English better than ever."

"I guess you're right. What a good Goombah! Yes, you are!"

Paul looked across the room and out the bay window, which had a lovely view of a small forest. He sighed a big sigh.

"This has been a heck of a year," he said. "I've had to deal with petty criminals like the Serial Kisser, and common murderers like Washburne, and on top of that there've been giant spiders that breathe fire, an alien invasion, Dr. Skull, Ultra-Frog, that kid Cory Hawke, Laser Master, and whoever it was who kidnapped Quincy Quackenbos – Quincy is sure it was Deinonychus, back again, which would be all we need."

"I remember you complaining about how it was too quiet around here, too," Dana said with the smile that always made Paul melt.

"I remember that," said a third voice that made Goombah look up and bark once. "Still too quiet for ya, smart guy?"

"No," Paul Phillips replied, glancing up at the ugly green vase on the shelf. "No, I think I have enough to keep me busy and then some, thank you."

"For what's coming next, you're going to need some extra help," the vase said.

Paul set his e-reader down. "Why? What's coming next?"

But the Soulkeeper of Kiribati spoke no further.

"Oh, I hate when it does that," Paul said. "If you want to warn me about something, spell it out. No, it's, 'For what's coming next, you're going to need some extra help,'" he said, assuming a mocking androgynous tone of voice.

"Whatever it is, it'll happen soon enough," Dana said. "Come on, let's get ready for work."

They walked into the bedroom to get dressed, leaving the morning television news show on, so only the dog was present for the next story.

"The Astor City Beacon reports that police are dismissing as a prank a report of spiders the size of small dogs wandering a neighborhood near the University of Astor City," the news anchor said. "But responding officers found nothing suspicious in a sweep of the area. And Sheriff Arnie Rogers downplayed the report."

The sheriff appeared on the screen with a microphone poked near his face.

"I know people are nervous after what happened in this community a few months ago," Sheriff Arnie Rogers said. "I just want to remind people that making a false report can result in a stiff fine."

Daughter of Mychus

Previously

Spiders of Fire (Episode 7):

EVERY spring the Astor City Service Club held its Philanthropists' Ball on the luxury cruise ship *River Girl*, which operated on the Shikaakwa River during the warmer months of the year. This year's ball was the biggest yet ...

The furnishings were festive. The food was festive. The mood was festive. It was quite the festive night until the giant spider spit flame and set everything on fire.

+ + + + +

"Myke," Josiah said in greeting. "This is Dr. Travers from the University of Astor City, and this is –"

"Dr. Travers," the attractive woman said, extending a hand. "Dr. Terri Travers."

"Are you related by marriage or –?"

"She's my daughter, the best arachnologist in the country, and that's not just a proud papa talking," the bearded professor said with a grin. He almost had a Santa Claus quality about him. "Jacob Travers. A pleasure to meet you, sir."

"Arachnologist? As in somebody who studies spiders?"

"Yes, I taught her everything she knows, and she took it all to the next level," Travers said with a wink.

"Stop it, Dad, he's going to think I'm Wonder Woman or something," his daughter said. (If you think this is not a throwaway line but a foreshadowing of a plot element that I'm tucking away for years from now, you may be right. But it works as a throwaway line, too.)

+ + + + +

Terri Travers screamed in fear and pain as the flames raced over her hand, still stuck to the web. The good news is that the fire poked a hole in the web so she was able to pull her hand back; the bad news is that the fire first had to strike that portion of the web with her hand still attached

+ + + + +

If only he could enlist his daughter; her talent and knowledge of arachnids were far beyond his. But she had too much respect for spiders as they exist in nature; she would not approve this tinkering with the design. No, he would have to carry on the experiment as he had begun – by himself.

Dr. Jacob Travers sighed, took one last look around the lab for the night, and turned out the lights.

+ + + + +

Duck Man Walking (Episode 10):

"How is your hand, Dr. Travers?" Dana ventured.

"Terri, please, and thanks," the arachnologist replied. Her right hand and forearm had been horribly burned when her encounter with the fire-spitting giant spider got a little too up close and personal. She looked at the hand and made an obvious effort to flex it, but the fingers only twitched slightly. "To be honest, they don't have much hope that I'll regain full use of it, but I keep up the physical therapy.

Good thing I've always done a lot of things lefthanded; I'm sort of ambidextrous." ...

"I'm learning how to do more and more with my left hand, and my father has some interesting ideas about some experimental treatments." ...

"He thinks he can help her grow a new hand like a lizard," Josiah interjected. "Very comic booky-type stuff."

"I wish you wouldn't make fun of Dad," she said, touching his shoulder with her good left hand. "He means well, and who knows? He's accomplished some amazing things. If he succeeded, think what it could mean for amputees and anyone who's lost the use of a limb."

+ + + + +

The Second Warrior (Episode 11):

"Disaster just seems to be my middle name lately. Jacob D. Travers, that's me," he said, puttering about the lab at the University of Astor City.

He stopped and gave a double-take at a terrarium filled with tiny spiders. Their mother, a large yellow and black garden spider, lounged in a web in the corner of the terrarium. His eyes widened.

"They hatched! Now this is a breakthrough indeed," he said, fluttering about for his pad and pen ...

The mother spider was .97 inches long. The day before she had been .86 inches long. This, Dr. Travers believed, was in the realm of acceptability.

It would be two months before he realized his mistake.

Prologue

ANY day that begins with a stolen dinosaur claw is bound to be unusual. And so it was.

The "OMG! Dinosaurs!" exhibit was already the most controversial ever to be booked into the Astor City Museum, a previously staid and proper establishment that began its life as a massive mansion, built by Jefferson Davis Astor in 1877 for his bride, Emily. For more than 70 years now, it had quietly hosted exhibits about the history of Astor City – lovely old photographs, lovely old clothes, lovely old artwork, lovely, lovely, lovely.

As attendance waned, the brash new members of the board said it was time for something exciting and bold and family friendly.

What did they have in mind?

OMG. Dinosaurs.

Shockingly to the old guard, the exhibit was a smashing success. Moms, dads and kids alike flocked to the grand old manse to see lifelike reproductions of prehistoric beasts and fossils of their actual remains.

More than one kid said, "Ooooh! Coool!" when they saw the grim foot with its massive claw in the front, like some mutant can opener, and read the inscription that said the claws were razor sharp, making their owner the most feared beast in the plains even though it was barely four to six feet tall.

"Deinonychus," a visitor inevitably would say, "Wasn't that the name of the evil crime lord who ran the Astor City underworld for many years?"

"Yes," the docent would explain patiently, "and her claw is the only weapon ever known to wound Myke Phoenix, the powerful superhero whose base of operations is this city."

"Why would someone name their child after their own species?" sometimes people would ask, and perhaps a companion might tease, "Yeah. What kind of a name is Homo Sapiens for a kid?"

"No one had seen a deinonychus for millions of years – the deinonychus didn't even live in the same era as our ancestors," the docent would say. "As the last of her kind, she probably chose to go by the name of her species."

William Lumpkin, the kindly old soul who worked the overnight shift for museum security, walked into the "OMG! Dinosaurs!" exhibit early one morning and noticed nothing amiss until he came to the place where the deinonychus claw was displayed. The sign was still there, but there was no sign of the claw.

If the disappearance of a razor-sharp dinosaur claw wasn't forboding enough, then there were the spider sightings.

Arnie Rogers was still getting used to being the sheriff of Astor County. He had been perfectly happy being chief deputy and letting his old boss Rod Skjorte handle all the administrative stuff, but then Rod had to get himself killed when aliens invaded town. That fact in itself was very difficult to accept.

It had been a weird year anyway, starting with that nutbag who walked around kissing women. That goofy superhero Myke Phoenix had to break up a fight when a bunch of angry boyfriends and husbands surrounded the kisser. That was nothing next to the giant spiders that spit fire, the aliens, the big storm, the bridge collapse – what was happening to his sleepy little town?

When the phone rang in the middle of the night, it was never a good sign.

"Rogers," he muttered into the phone, hanging onto the last shreds of a dream where he was on a Hawaiian beach with his wife 25 years ago, when they both were young and lean.

"I'm sorry to bother you, sheriff, but it's the spiders again."

That woke him up. Even the sound of the ocean waves stopped abruptly.

A few minutes later Arnie Rogers was in uniform and pulling up to a home near the University of Astor City, where several other squad cars were parked and stabbing the early-morning dark with red, blue and white flashing lights.

"Hey, Carson," Rogers greeted the first uniform he spotted. "What do we got?"

"Well, sir, Mr. Thompson over there says he was walking his dog –"

"Pretty durnfangled early in the morning to be walking his dog, don't you think?"

"Says he goes into work at 4."

"Yep, sure. OK, he was walking his dog, and?"

"– And he sees this pack of little wolves or something cross the road over there, just scooting from the Lemens' house into the woods across the street," Carson said.

"Except when he looked closer, they weren't wolves, they were big spiders. At least he thought that's what they were."

"Carson, I've seen big spiders. There's no mistaking."

"Right. Well, they weren't as big as the firespiders. More like puppy spiders, or whatever you call a pack of baby spiders."

"It's a cluster," the sheriff said.

"It sure is," Carson agreed.

"No, you idiot, it's called a cluster of spiders. I don't know why I remember that."

"Right. Well, we've been going through the woods, but there's no sign of a – cluster of spiders."

"OK, well, get a statement from Thompson and keep looking for a while. Sounds like you all have it under control," Rogers said. "I'm going back to bed."

"Sir? What should we tell the media?"

"Tell them to go back to bed, too."

"Well, all of the television stations and a couple other reporters are here asking for a statement," Carson said. "I told them they'd have to wait for the sheriff."

"Fudge, a duck, and her 12 sisters," Rogers spat. "OK, I'll deal with the press."

"Sheriff Rogers! Sheriff Rogers!" the pack seemed to cry in unison.

"That's my name, don't wear it out," Arnie Rogers shot back as he walked up squinting against the lights. A cluster of young men and women with perfect hair huddled in the darkness behind the lights.

The money sound bite that was reported in the paper and played on every radio, TV and Internet newscast for the next 24 hours was Sheriff Arnie Rogers looking grim and perhaps a little sleepy, saying, "I know people are skittish after the events of several months ago, and maybe they see things that look like something they're not. We also remind people that making a false report can result in a stiff fine."

"You're not saying that Mr. Thompson made this whole thing up?"

Arnie Rogers thought for a second before replying, "No, I think he saw something that made him think of little firespiders. I just don't want people getting ideas that it'd be fun to tie up the police by reporting other sightings."

Be that as it may, for the next three days and nights, the police and sheriff's dispatchers were flooded with reports about giant baby spiders. Most of the reports were indeed pranks.

Most of them.

Act 1
Something goes horribly wrong

"ON a scale of 1 to 10, where 1 is almost nothing and 10 is the worst pain you've ever felt ..."

Terri Travers' mind often wandered back to the day in the emergency room when the doctors and nurses were treating her for the burns left when she grabbed a gigantic spider web with her right hand and got stuck, unable to let go until the giant spider who'd made it breathed fire and melted hand and web.

The moment had given her a new scale. It was as if the worst pain she'd ever felt before was a bump on the elbow and now she had accidentally plunged her hand into a river of molten lava. For the rest of her life, normal aches and pains would not bother her, for now she understood what real pain felt like.

She stared at the wreck of a misshapen hand that the firespider had left. These many months later, it still refused to do much more than twitch when she commanded it to touch and grab and grip and all of the things a right hand is supposed to do. Most doctors agreed she would never regain full use.

A bearded, white-haired man interrupted her reflection. He fussed about like the absent-minded professor that he was, but so often he reminded her of some impossible Santa Claus. Today he was carrying a beaker, a white lab rat and – a syringe?

"I've done it, daughter," the man said. "Look here, George's paw has regrown with no apparent side effects. He's perfectly fine."

"You shouldn't carry all that stuff at one time, Dad," she scolded, taking the squirming rat out of his hands. The animal did seem to be absolutely normal, except perhaps that one of his paws was pinker and covered in fresh down rather than coarse fur, as if the hair was newly grown. "What in the name of good sense did you do to this animal on my behalf?"

"Eh, perhaps you needn't ask," Jacob Travers said. Both father and daughter were on the biology faculty of the University of Astor City, so actually she did not have to ask what pain he might have wrought on the little animal. She even had a sense regarding what his recent experiments might have entailed, and what was in the beaker and syringe.

"That's remarkable," she said despite herself. "It looks like a brand-new paw."

"It is indeed brand new," the elder Travers replied gleefully. "It works, too, Terri. I can now say unequivocally that I can give you back your hand."

She stared at her useless appendage. "How long since you treated him?"

"Four days," he said. "Think of it – four days! Think what this means for anyone with an injured or even a severed limb. Absolute restoration."

"It looks a little early to say *absolute*, Dad. George is still favoring that paw."

"He didn't even have the paw four days ago, limping around like a sad little boy," Jacob Travers said. "I think we can call this an unqualified success."

"Oh, Dad, really. It's a little early for that, but this does look promising."

The older professor opened his mouth in surprise.

"'Promising'? My dear, don't you see what this means? You can have your hand back in four days, perhaps five. Don't you want that?"

"Of course I do, but are you sure it's safe?"

"I'm here to offer the treatment to my own daughter," he huffed. "Do you think I would do that if I didn't think it was safe?"

"No, I suppose not," Dr. Terri Travers replied. Of course, in her defense, she wasn't aware of a number of things her father had done, thinking it was safe, that in fact were not safe. On the other hand, one would think as a scientist she would know better than to reach out her injured hand to accept a treatment that had never been attempted until four days earlier, and then only on a lab rat.

But sometimes, when life dangles something shiny in front of us, we simply forget that we know better.

"All right," she said. "Put George away and let's do this."

As her father puttered off with the white rat, she examined the contents of the beaker and the syringe. The beaker contained a thick gray substance, and the syringe was filled with a reddish, orangeish liquid. A flicker of fear may have passed over her eyes, which she attributed to the excitement of leaving her comfort zone for a new adventure in science. Her father was right: This could revolutionize the treatment of burned and mangled limbs. The sooner they confirmed its potential, the sooner the treatment could be applied to real and suffering people.

By the time he returned from placing George in his cage, Terri Travers was ready to do what it would take to get her hand back.

Few words were spoken as he dipped a latex-gloved hand into the beaker and scooped out the gray substance, which he spread like an ointment (because it *was* an ointment) over her hand, covering all of its surfaces and nooks and crannies.

Then he picked up the syringe and looked her in the eyes.

"Are you sure, daughter?"

In response, still holding his gaze, she rolled up her sleeve.

A few minutes later, Astor County Sheriff Arnie Rogers strolled through the doors of the outer room of the UAC biology labs.

"Should have thought of this before," he muttered. "If anyone can figure this thing out, the Traverses ought to."

The city had turned to Terri and Jacob Travers for help when one giant fire-spitting spider, and then its offspring, had terrorized the community a few months earlier. Although the great creatures were destroyed by mere brute force – a giant fly-swatter wielded by the superhero Myke Phoenix, and a tumble off a cliff to the rocks and river below – the biologists had helped devise a strategy and later consulted in the removal of what appeared to be a number of spider egg sacs – at least everyone thought they had all been removed.

"Anybody here?" Rogers called. He heard someone moving in an adjoining room, and Jacob Travers scurried out.

"Yes, yes, hello –Sheriff Rogers!" the man said cheerfully enough. "What brings you to our humble laboratories?"

"I don't know if you've been watching TV lately, but a bunch of people who live in the neighborhood swear they've seen a pack of big spiders wandering around."

"It's a cluster."

"I know, with all of these stupid reporters having to get something to fill their durnfangled shows –"

"No, no, no, I mean it's not called a *pack* of spiders. It's a cluster."

"Right. I knew that," Rogers said. "Wait – you mean there *are* little big spiders wandering around?"

Jacob Travers waited a beat too long to break into reassuring laughter.

"What? Oh, no, no, no, no, no," he laughed. "I just meant if there were this large group of giant spiders, it would be called a cluster of spiders. No, I can assure you, sheriff, we've seen the last of the giant spiders in this town."

The sheriff looked thoughtful.

"You're not, like, working on anything or doing any research related to the firespiders of a few months ago?"

"Heavens, no," Travers said. "Well, of course, I've studied my daughter's injury in relation to the fire and the venom, but we're not growing giant spiders here. Oh, my! Wouldn't that be silly of us? Ha ha ha."

"Your daughter, right. Is she here? I'd like to get her thoughts on this, too."

"I don't blame you!" Jacob Travers seemed far too jolly now. "Teresa is the real arachnologist between us. You can't imagine how proud I am to see my daughter advancing and exceeding my poor knowledge of the spider kingdom," but then, suddenly, "but she's not here now. Good to see you, sheriff, off you go."

Jacob Travers closed the door behind Rogers and watched the sheriff amble back down the corridor and out the door. He looked back once, and the white-haired professor gave a grim grin and waved. Once the sheriff was out of sight, Travers crossed the lab to a locked door.

"I'll be right there, daughter," he called to the other room. "I just need to check, eh, on some samples."

He unlocked the door, opened it, and gasped. Instead of the orderly row of spider cages he had left the night before, chaos. The row of cages with their crippled white rats was undisturbed, but where he had been keeping his spider specimens all he saw was glass broken, screens torn, shorn bits of wood scattered on the floor.

And no sign of spiders, puppy-sized or otherwise.

A window was broken, and part of the wall punched out around it, as if something too big to squeeze through the window had forcibly burst through.

And – around the edges of the exit hole – scorch marks.

"Oh my goodness," said Dr. Jacob Travers, looking helplessly around the room. Where were they? Where were they all? "Oh, my goodness gracious me."

Just that moment, a blood-curdling scream came from the other lab.

"Terri," he whispered. Carefully locking the door to the room behind him, he rushed to where his daughter sat, bent over, holding her right forearm with her good left hand, squeezing to keep the pain in her right hand from escaping to the rest of her body.

"It hurts, Dad," she said with an effort, sweat streaming down her face. "It really hurts."

"On a scale of one to 10 –"

"Oh, please, stop it! It burns. It's like a vise. It's – Aaack!" This time her whole body shuddered, as if the struggle to contain the pain had failed.

Through his panic he noticed that her hand was still red and blistered but not as badly as it had been, and in her thrashing she was flexing the joints better than she had in months. He was about to point out the improvement when she screamed again.

"What did you do to me?!"

"This didn't happen to George at all, I don't understand."

"Oh! Oh. OHHH!"

"Try to breathe, Terri. Breathe. In, out, in –"

"I'M NOT HAVING A BABY!" For just an instant his mind flashed back more than 30 years, to another beautiful woman who had screamed at him, "YOU DID

THIS TO ME!" Terri looked so much like her mother, never more so than this moment.

He shook himself back to the present moment. This moment, his daughter was wracked with pain. And it was getting worse.

She seemed to be holding back an even more blood-curdling scream, beads and streams of sweat covering her face now and soaking through her clothes to her lab coat. A groan began in the back of her throat, the scream trying to force its way out, and then, when it would not be denied anymore:

"AAAAAAAAAAAAAAAAHHHHHH!!!!!!" And her eyes widened in horror as she watched a thick stream of flame shoot from her mouth and ignite the blinds on the window.

"Oh, my," Dr. Jacob Travers whispered.

"What the – what the –" Dr. Terri Travers stammered, and her next words were not a frantic scream but a cold accusation. "What did you do to me?"

The bearded professor yanked a fire extinguisher off the side of a lab table and rushed to the window, dousing the flames while they were still melting the blinds and before they could spread to the walls.

She gripped his arm with her left hand, hard enough that he winced.

"Father," Terri Travers said darkly. "What did you do to me? What was in that syringe?" Neither of them noticed that she was not writhing in pain as much, having discharged the flames.

"I – I – I – I mixed the serum with a firespider's blood," he said quickly, detaching from her grip and running a cloth under cold water to apply to his daughter's forehead, and as he pressed the cool compress to her head, added, "I thought that would act as a vaccine to reverse the effects of the original injury."

Terri nodded, but then a confused expression crossed her face.

"Where did you get the firespider blood? One of them was squashed, and the other's body was never recovered."

"Well, um, errr," her father said. "I have been trying to replicate my experiment without the gigantic side effect."

"Your experiment? *Your* experiment? OH!" she said, as a new wave of pain began to build. "What are you talking about?"

Jacob Travers hesitated, looked one way, then the other, and made a decision. He opened his palms apologetically.

"I meant well! I've been breeding a bigger, better garden spider –"

"WHAT?!"

"– and something went horribly wrong. I didn't know how to tell you, or anyone, daughter, I thought you'd make me stop just as I was making progress –"

"YOU – made – the – FIRESPIDERS?! ARE YOU – AAAGH – INSANE?!" Her hand burned, her whole body ached, and jolts of searing pain jerked through her like lightning.

"But it's all right, Terri! I've succeeded. This batch isn't at all as huge as the last. They'll be a boon to gardeners and agriculture –"

She looked at him with an expression that could have been shock or anger or physical pain or emotional hurt or despair or accusation but was really a combination of all of those emotions.

"YOU – CREATED – the – Firespiders?" Terri Travers screamed, and then there was nothing left in her universe except the most excruciating pain, pain that once again completely redefined her concept of what exactly is meant by the word *pain*.

And, crumbling to the floor and writhing, she unleashed a scream that would not only curdle blood but congeal it into a solid brick. Another burst of flame escaped from her mouth with the shriek.

"OOOOOOOOOOOHHHHHH! AAAAAAAAHHHHHHH! EEEEEEYAAAAA –"

Blip!

Silence struck the room like a slap.

One instant Dr. Terri Travers was squirming on the floor, unable to sit or stand. The next instant she was simply not there, and instead another woman was standing in the exact same spot.

The woman was tall, with long red hair flowing over her shoulders and partly down her back, and lithe and toned muscles. She was wearing a powder-blue tunic with white trim on the collar, at the edges of the short sleeves, and around the bottom of the skirt that extended halfway down her powerful-looking thighs. A white belt girded her waist.

In the center of her chest, the silhouetted image of a phoenix stood in black contrast to the light blue. She looked down at her clothing and perfectly sculpted body as if for the first time – mainly because it *was* the first time – then met Jacob Travers' eyes with a look lacking comprehension.

"Wh – What happened?" Jacob Travers said, his anxiety heightened almost beyond reason. "Who are you? What have you done to Terri?"

The square-jawed woman stared at the bearded professor, looked down at her strong hands – flexing them in unison, especially the right one – and stared back at Jacob Travers.

"Dad," the woman said with a firm, powerful voice that belied the confusion in her eyes. "I *am* Terri."

Act 2

Daughter of the Phoenix

"YAAAAAAAaaaaaaaaaahhhhhhhh!!!!!"

Paul and Dana Phillips jumped apart as if a water balloon had squeezed into the narrow space between them and burst. What had been a romantic hug in front of their big bay window looking into the quiet woods behind their home switched to an alarmed alertness. The four-month-old puppy that had been curled on the easy chair behind them leaped up and started barking.

In a blink, it was no longer Paul Phillips standing next to his wife of 18 years. Instead, a large man with a shortish but wild mane of blond hair stood warily looking toward the dining area of the open-space ranch home, hands balled into powerful fists, ready for whatever adversary had made that terrifying sound.

But he saw nothing out of place. Or did he?

On the top shelf in the dining room rested an (I don't know what other word to use) ugly green vase. It was pea green and not especially symmetric in design, with jewels embedded seemingly at random about the surface and a crude image of a bird rising from flames emblazoned on the side.

The vase sat in its usual place of honor in the center of the top shelf. It used to sit among a collection of valuable Depression glass, but the glass had all fallen and shattered when the house was shaken by an alien spaceship crash-landing in the general vicinity. (That's another story.)

The reason I bring up the topic of the ugly vase is not to criticize the Phillipses for their odd taste in home decor, but to point out the one thing that seemed to be out of place in the scene that greeted the huge, blond warrior.

A puff of white smoke had puffed out of the vase and was lingering over it, dissipating quickly. The smoke left no apparent odor.

"It's OK, Goombah," the big man told the puppy, which immediately broke off its barking with a little whine, and he asked, "Soulkeeper?" You might ask why someone was asking the vase a question, but then a moment later you would be asking how it was that the vase answered the question.

For there came into the room a voice – an androgynous kind of voice, neither male nor female but somehow both – and there was no mistaking that the voice was coming from the vase. The voice was frantic.

"She – she must have changed. The first time always is intense. Why did she change? We always tell them they've been picked before the change; that way the change doesn't upset them so much. She must have been in mortal danger. I don't sense danger now. *Why did she change?*"

Normally – if there can be anything normal in a discussion about a talking vase – the vase was a bit of a wiseacre. Nothing wise was emerging from the vase at this time, beginning with the unearthly scream a few moments earlier.

"What are you talking about, Soulkeeper? Was that you that screamed?" For this was the Soulkeeper of Kiribati, an ancient vase presumably from the Phoenix Islands that somehow guided and aided the transformation of Paul Phillips, who made his living as a reporter, into Myke Phoenix, who made his living as a crusading force for good, battling criminals and more exotic villains who threatened Astor City and/or the universe at large.

"Myke Phoenix" was the name that Paul flippantly had chosen for Mychus, an ancient warrior whose soul had long ago passed to the great beyond but whose powerful body was preserved for use in the battle against the forces of evil in the world. The body was impervious to harm and possessed of an incredible strength that enabled him to leap higher, run faster and, well, punch the lights out of an opponent at a scale unknown to any mortal. Paul Phillips was the latest in a line of people chosen over the centuries to employ Mychus' body by a mysterious phoenix, whom he had only ever seen once before (Also another story – oh, the stories to be told!) in more than 18 years.

"She's here. She's definitely here. I can feel her strength," the Soulkeeper of Kiribati said. "But why is she here now? I can tell she's as confused as I am. You have to talk to her, Paul."

"There's nobody here."

"Not here-here, dummy." Being called *dummy* was actually a relief to Myke. It was the first sign of the vase's normal personality since the scream. "She's here in the world. Mychala."

"Who's Mychala?"

"It's a long story. Well, not that long." There was a pause that, in a human being, might be accompanied by fidgeting and a grasping for words.

"Go on."

"Mychus had a daughter."

"A –"

"I keep her soul, too. She inherited many of Mychus' abilities and traits, and the Phoenix watches over her, too. When the big bird finds an appropriate hostess, well, it works just like you and Mychus."

"Wait, what? Back up to the part where Mychus had a daughter and you keep her soul, too." Dana broke in. "You always said only one person at a time could have the power."

"No, I didn't."

"Oh, yes, you did," Dana insisted with a firm toss of her auburn hair.

"No. I didn't."

"What is this, Monty Python? Yes. You did. You said only one person at a time can have the power."

"I said only one *man* at a time could have *Mychus'* power."

"No, you didn't," she insisted.

"You want to go back and check the canon, lady?"

"Like someone is writing down every conversation we ever had."

"Maybe I misspoke once," the vase conceded. "But this is the deal. There's an opportunity for only one warrior man in a generation, that's what I remember saying. But there's also an opportunity for only one warrior woman."

"Anything else you've been lying about?" Myke Phoenix asked.

"I never lied!"

"Fine. Anything else you've been hiding?"

"Probably."

"So you can keep both a man's and a woman's soul in there? How?"

"After 18 years you're asking how I keep souls? Room in here for one, room in here for two."

"But a woman? I always assumed you were a guy."

"Why? You ever listen to my voice? Am I a male or a female?"

"I never thought about it, but I guess your voice is sort of" – and Myke paused as the realization sank in – "androgynous."

"There ya go," the vase said. "But she changed. She changed into Mychala before we had a chance to tell her. She has to be completely disoriented and frightened. We have to find her."

"OK, so who are we looking for?"

"We're looking for Mychala! Who else would we be looking for?"

"Get a grip, Soulkeeper," Dana said firmly. "The chosen person. Who got picked to be Mychala?"

"I told you already!"

"No, I think we would remember a name," she said.

"I know I told you, but whatever. It's Teresa Travers!" blurted the vase.

"Stop saying that, I'm sure you didn't tell us," Myke Phoenix said. "And – Hokey smokes! Dr. Travers?!"

Most of what Spencer Jones would remember of his wedding day had nothing to do with how gorgeous Molly was in her white dress, but right this minute he was convinced the most beautiful woman in the universe had plopped down on Planet Earth and swept him off his feet. She looked resplendent passing through the arbor at the back of the crowd and walking up the aisle on her father's arm, glowing in the sunshine and drinking in the flowery aromas.

The University of Astor City gardens were one of the most popular wedding sites in the entire region, and for good reason: An army of volunteer gardeners worked hard each spring to make the gardens an explosion of color and sweet aroma. Many a bride chose to be married in this setting, and on a sunny day like this, the setting was everything Molly Franconi and Spencer Jones had been hoping for. All the fussing and heated discussions about the plans melted away from Spencer's memory as he watched the woman he loved walk through the sunshine toward him.

Papa Franconi offered his daughter to Spencer, who held out the crook of his arm to her. She took it with the biggest smile he'd ever seen –she always had a big smile for him, but this was the biggest ever – and his heart melted into a pool of mushy mush. Spencer had never felt a happiness this happy, a joy this joyful, or a peace so peaceful. He was getting married to Molly Franconi! And they surely were going to live happily ever after.

The smiling couple turned to the pastor, who himself was smiling in the sun. Everything was perfect.

"You may be seated," the pastor said, and behind them they could hear the rustling of 150 of their most intimate friends being seated.

"Dearly beloved – Great Halls of Montezuma!" the pastor said. The first half of his opening words were said with a smile, looking around, and the second half were said after his smile evaporated into confusion as his eyes came to rest on something at the back of the clearing.

Everyone turned as one, and it was not immediately clear what had caused the pastor's outburst. Then the spider that had formed a web across the arbor moved slightly enough for everyone to notice: The yellow and black arachnid was at least three feet long, hanging suspended in the seven-foot-tall arbor and ready for any prey that might fly through the vicinity.

The sight of the big spider caused a collective gasp among the dearly beloved. But when several dozen – some people later would say it was several hundred – yellow and black spiders, also three or four feet long and two or three feet high, poured from behind and over the flowers on either side of the arbor, collective screams roared forth and people began to stand and run, toppling over the chairs that had been so carefully placed for the wedding of Spencer Jones and Molly Franconi.

The spiders began to climb over the chairs, slowly like spiders tend to move, but in sufficient numbers that the gathered crowd was alarmed.

One brave soul took a program and stepped forward, waving the card to shoo one of the spiders away. The big little spider – it was no larger than a medium-sized dog, but that is bigger than spiders are supposed to be – reared back on its haunches and spit a stream of flame that set the program on fire.

That was all it took to shift the alarm one step farther into full-fledged panic.

"FIRESPIDERS!" screamed everyone who was not simply screaming wordlessly. And the panic descended into chaos.

The lovely, powerful-looking red-haired woman stared into the mirror in the lab and touched her face with her right hand. Then she stared at her right hand – her large, long-fingered, more than perfectly healthy right hand – and flexed it into a fist, then opened it, several times.

"Is this a reaction to the serum?" she asked.

"Surely not," said her father.

"What's happened to me, Dad? I was in pain – it hurt so bad – and now I feel fine, better than I have for years, and my hand is healed. But I'm not me!"

"Calm down, daughter," Jacob said feverishly. "There has to be some explanation."

As sometimes happens in stories like this, at that very moment Terri Traver's cellphone began to chirp. The statuesque woman reached toward the phone with her left hand – the hand that had been the only hand that could grip a phone for the last seven months.

She pressed the "Talk" button and held the phone to her ear.

"Terri? Do me a favor and if someone is with you right now, don't say my name out loud. This is Paul Phillips."

Terri Travers looked at her father. "It's – a reporter."

"Good, thank you," said the voice at the other end. "I understand something unbelievable may have just happened to you."

"How do you know about that? What's going on?"

"Can you come over to my house? Alone?"

"Now?!" she said.

"It's kind of important. It's about what just happened. I think I can explain."

"On my way."

She cut off the conversation and tossed the phone on a lab table.

"I have to go," she said. "And I'm sorry, Dad, I have to leave you here."

"What? Who was that? Terri! What reporter? What did he say?" Jacob called after her, but she was running away, and faster than his daughter had ever run.

I'm sure I mentioned that the lab was on the campus of the University of Astor City. As you no doubt have guessed by now, her path off campus was to take her through the UAC gardens, where the wedding of Spencer Jones and Molly Franconi had just been disrupted by a cluster of giant garden spiders.

Act 3
Along came a cluster

"UH oh," said the Soulkeeper of Kiribati.

Several minutes had passed since Paul/Myke had called Terri Travers. The Phillipses' home was not far from the University of Astor City.

"Now what?" Myke Phoenix said.

"Something's wrong," the vase said.

"It hasn't been that long," said Dana. "She needs a little time to get here."

"That's not the problem. I'm feeling some kind of disturbance in the air, and not just because Mychala is here. Got your police scanner on?"

"We were having a romantic evening that didn't include listening to the police scanner," Myke said, striding over to the kitchen counter, where Paul's cellphone was charging. His police scanner, like most of the other tools of his reporter trade, was on an app, which he now called up.

"There must be a hunnert of 'em," were the first words they heard. "Little spiders – I mean big spiders – but littler than the ones from last winter – and some of them are spitting fire."

Firespiders.

"Hokey smokes," Myke muttered. "Where is this happening?"

"This is 47, I'm just pulling up to the UAC gardens now," a new voice said. "Where do you want me."

"10-4, 47," said the voice of Blanche, the county sheriff's dispatcher. "Arnie said we need someone at the northeast exit."

"Are you seeing this? There's some woman in the middle of the spiders, fighting them off, I think she's trying to herd them or something – Great goslings! She just spit fire at them!"

Myke looked in shock at Dana. They both looked in shock at the vase.

"That's new," the vase said.

"I'm getting over there," Myke said.

"Please do," Dana said. "Be careful, Scoop."

Myke Phoenix had speed and stamina on his side. He had barely broken a sweat when he arrived at the University of Astor City gardens seconds later, and when he did, he repeated: "Hokey smokes."

Terri Travers didn't know why she decided to run to Paul Phillips' house. If she had grabbed her purse and hopped into her car, she probably would have gotten there faster.

Or would she? Her body suddenly appeared to be in magnificent condition, even supernaturally so. She was not breathing hard, nor was she breaking much of a sweat, despite running in the summer sunshine faster than she had ever run before. The full mane of red hair was bouncing and flowing in the breeze created by her speed. Despite her concern about what had happened to her, she was enjoying the run. After writhing in agony from the effects of the serum that was supposed to heal her, after discovering her father had created the menace of the firespiders, and after having suddenly become a powerful amazon-like creature, the sprint was clearing the cobwebs from her mind. Terri realized she had never felt better in her life, all of a sudden.

She was not actually off campus yet when she stopped herself in her tracks. A commotion was underway in the university gardens.

In point of fact, a full-scale riot was in progress. Well-dressed people were running from the garden, which was being overrun by spiders as big as medium-sized dogs. Folding chairs were tipped over in disarray, and a frazzled groom was leading a beautiful but equally frazzled bride down what was left of the aisle.

She dashed up to them.

"What's going on here?"

After having their wedding ceremony interrupted by a cluster of giant spiders that spit fire, being accosted by a tall, remarkably fit woman with flowing red hair and wearing a powder-blue tunic with a phoenix on her chest seemed downright ordinary to Spencer Jones and Molly Franconi.

Still, all the response they could muster was to scream in unison, "FIRESPIDERS!!" And, as if to punctuate the scream with an extra exclamation point, one of the little big spiders shot flame and ignited the tattered remains of Molly's bouquet.

That was enough. Bride and groom ran for the hills.

"We're all gonna die!" shrieked Spencer Jones.

"Spencer, wait for me! A little help here?" Molly Franconi lifted the hem of her dress off the ground and cursed herself for her choice of shoes. The long veil trailed after her.

Fortunately for their future marriage, Spencer stopped in his tracks, turned and ran back to his bride. He kicked at a big spider that was showing some interest in nibbling the bride's train.

"I'm so sorry, I'm so sorry," he said, gathering up his bride and grabbing the trailing parts of her dress so the two of them could run up the hill more easily.

The last words Terri Travers heard before the couple ran out of earshot were, "We're eloping!"

Terri stood watching the chaos and realized she must be partially responsible for this. It wasn't 100 spiders, but it was more than a dozen – perhaps two dozen or more, and of course this was probably not all of them. Besides the one busily setting up shop in the arbor, the spiders were crawling around the turned-over chairs or into trees surrounding the garden, spinning webs or partaking in other spidery-type activities.

"Oh, Dad, what have you done?" she said. She wished she had asked her father more about his statement that he had created the firespiders, apparently in some sort of experiment gone wrong. Time enough for that later – the best thing to do with these things would be to round them up and get them back to the lab. At least none of them were bigger than an elephant, like the ones her father had apparently bred months ago. On the other hand, back then there were only two monstrous spiders, as far as anyone knew.

What of Paul Phillips and his odd telephone call, promising answers as to why she was suddenly taller, stronger, faster and definitely not the Terri Travers who had been staring out of the mirror at her for nearly 35 years? That would have to wait. There were spiders to catch, and she was one of the world's leading arachnologists, although herding spiders as big as dogs was in no one's realm of expertise.

She reached down and picked up the nearest one. Two things happened in quick succession: First, she gasped at how easy it was for her to pick up the large beast – it was if she had picked a feather off the ground. Second, the spider attempted to bite her with its jaws that easily wrapped around her forearm – but it was as if it had tried to bite a rock. Terri Travers felt a pinch, but her skin did not break. Between her strength and her apparently invulnerability, she dropped the spider in surprise.

Forgetting the present trouble of rounding up a cluster of firespiders for the moment, she wondered what else this body was capable of. She had already run faster than any human being she'd ever seen, except for Myke Phoenix. Now she saw that she was strong like the superhero, and her skin could not be punctured, like his.

There was one other feat she had watched him do. She tried jumping, and leaped to the top of a 20-foot-tall tree.

That settled that. The phoenix on her tunic's chest definitely was no coincidence. Terri Travers was now endowed with powers similar to those of Astor City's resident superhero.

"How is this happening?" she said out loud. Did it have something to do with her father's serum? It couldn't. Myke Phoenix had been around for about 19 years. Her father had only just developed the formula to rebuild her injured hand. No, some other force was at work here.

And then she realized she was clinging to the tree trunk without wrapping her fingers or arms around anything. Something about her fingers was helping her stick, like a spider. Strength and stamina like Myke Phoenix, with some kind of spidery power as well? She needed to explore this.

A distant scream from the now-scattered wedding crowd brought her back to the present. First things first. There was a spider cluster to round up.

How does one herd spiders?

"Same way you eat an elephant," she heard her strong new voice say – "one bite at a time."

She started running around the outer edges of the spider infestation, pushing the creatures back into a group. They didn't come easily, and like an amoeba once she got one side of the cluster penned in, another corner would ooze out.

Suddenly she felt a warm flush in her chest, and an idea occurred to her.

"Of course."

Still spreading her arms to warn the spiders in front of her not to make a break for it, Terri reared her head back and spit a wall of flame across the garden in front of the spiders that were beyond her reach. They jumped back from the fire. There – that did it.

Or not.

"Uh oh."

The spiders turned toward her, and she sensed alarm and (uh oh) anger behind the multifaceted spider eyes. No longer a scattered cluster, they began to stalk toward her with – I can't resist – fire in their eyes.

"These are firespiders. Idiot, idiot, idiot," she muttered, banging the side of her head with the ball of her hand and looking around for cover.

Too late.

About a dozen streams of fire shot toward her at once. Terri Travers screamed without thinking, her mind flashing back to the wall of flame that destroyed her right hand.

But as the flames licked at her body, hot but not painfully, she realized that she was not melting horrifyingly the way her hand had.

Before she could fully assimilate this information, a powerful figure jumped between her and the streams of flame. He was dressed in white, with longish blond hair, and while his back was to her, she knew the image of a phoenix was emblazoned in red and gold on his chest, too.

"Oh, no you don't," Myke Phoenix said as the fire licked harmlessly against his barrel of a chest. "Are you all right?" he asked over his shoulder, keeping himself between the spiders and the woman.

She looked down at her unburned tunic, held out her intact arms and hands and examined her strong and untouched legs.

"I'm fine," she said, a little surprised and a little empowered. "Let's round up these spiders. They – well, they escaped from the university lab."

It's often said that something is easier said than done, but in this case, two superheroes – one of them fire-breathing, both of them invulnerable, faster than the wind and stronger than any mere mortal – were able to gather the spiders together in a matter of minutes and began urging the eight-legged monstrosities back toward the UAC science building.

After the first attempt Terri knew better than to spit more fire at the firespiders, who did not fight the herding efforts as much as they might have expected.

"This is easier than I expected," Myke Phoenix stated the obvious as he policed one side of the group, running forward and back to make sure all of the big little spiders were moving in the direction the two spider herders wanted.

"These seem to be younger animals, still somewhat docile, although the people at the wedding couldn't have known that," she called back, giving one especially curious little one a firm push back into line and getting a pouty burst of fire in return.

"Are you all right?"

"I'm fine," she said again. "I know spiders. Well, I don't know how these got so big, but I know spiders in general. You see, I'm –"

"I know. You're Dr. Travers."

She looked over at the blond superhero, who met her eyes, and something clicked into place in her mind.

She looked around to ensure no one else was near, then said, "Paul? Paul Phillips?"

Myke Phoenix looked startled, but he said nothing to deny the question.

"Let's talk after we get these little buggers back to your lab."

"It's not my lab – I mean, these aren't my firespiders."

They were nearing the science building, and Jacob Travers ran out the door to greet them, carrying something that looked like a large water gun – a light green water rifle, to be precise.

"Is this all of them, Dad?" asked the statuesque red-haired woman in the powder-blue tunic.

The white-haired, bearded man looked over the field of big little spiders, moving his lips as he counted. "Yes, I think so. Well done. I've done some quick repair work in the spider lab if you want to bring them this way."

"SCREEEEEEEEEEEEEEEE-eeeeeeeee-eeeeeee-EEEEEE-eeeee."

Three heads jerked at once in the direction of the UAC gymnasium. Before anyone could speak, even to say "What the bejeebers was that?" a huge spidery leg wiggled over the top of the gym building, and then another, and then six more legs, carrying an enormous spider body.

When the monster reached the roof, it stood defiantly looking down at the two athletic figures, the older bearded scientist and the cluster of little firespiders between them.

"SCREEEEEEEEEE!" screamed the firespider – the one the size of an elephant – the one last seen toppling off a cliff into the river – the one that was the mother of all firespiders, back from the seeming dead and as angry as any arachnid could possibly be.

Act 4
The Soulkeeper explains

"SCREE! Scree! Scree!"

The little firespiders began to jabber together and break ranks.

"Oh, no, you don't," the woman in the blue tunic said, moving to round up the youngsters. She had to grab one by a leg, then lifted it up bodily and dropped it as gently as she could but awkwardly back into the pile.

"SCREEEEEEEEEEE!" said the huge firespider on the gymnasium roof.

"What do we do now?" Myke Phoenix asked. Over the arachnologists' objections, months ago he had splattered one giant firespider with a hastily constructed giant fly swatter, but this one was larger, and the fly swatter wasn't handy anyway.

"Get the little ones into the lab!" Jacob Travers said. "Come here, babies – don't worry, they listen to me." He waved the spiders toward the door with his water rifle contraption, and amazingly they did seem to follow him.

"We're going to have to talk about this," said the red-haired woman.

"I know, I know!" he said. "One thing at a time, daughter."

Myke Phoenix and his companion turned together, looking up at the eight-legged monster on the roof.

"Any ideas, doc?"

"Something that doesn't involve squashing it," she replied. "But right this moment, I don't know what that is. I want to take a closer look at it, at least."

She took a running start and jumped before Myke had a chance to say, "Hold on just a minute!" and she was on the gymnasium roof.

"What do you think you're doing?" Myke called up in alarm.

"Are you kidding? A chance to examine a firespider up close and not get hurt? I'm not going to pass up this opportunity."

Myke Phoenix rolled his eyes. Dr. Terri Travers' confusion over being converted into a superhero had sure worn off in a hurry.

"Will you think about being careful, for cryin' out loud? You're not immortal."

That was a point.

"Can the spider hurt me?" She called down, walking cautiously toward the giant arachnid, which was eyeing the smaller newcomer warily.

He had to admit: "I don't think so. But you're not me. I'm coming up there."

"NO!" she said. "I don't think I'm in immediate danger – she's calmed down for a moment. Let me take a look."

She instinctively reached down to where, under normal circumstances, her cellphone would be resting in her lab coat pocket. She had to get photos of this thing, and in an invulnerable body she'd be able to approach closer and get angles no one else could dare. But her hand met skirt, not lab coat.

"Where did my cellphone go? I need a camera!"

"It's probably with your body."

"My body?! This isn't my body?" She had been growing accustomed to the idea that her body had changed in an impossible instant. It hadn't occurred to her that her own body was somewhere else and she was borrowing someone else's.

"Like I said, we need to talk. First let's handle the giant spider, you think?"

"Right." She remembered then that she'd tossed the phone on a lab table. No photos, then, but she could make observations. The yellow-and-black markings suggested that she was looking at a ridiculously mutated common garden spider. What had her father done to make it grow to such enormity? The good news was that for his experiments he had selected a species that was not particularly aggressive. On the other hand, this thing, or something very much like it, had caused massive destruction in downtown Astor City. She would have to be careful until –

SPLOT! The messy blotch of web caught her full-on and pinned her to the asphalt roof.

"Stupid, stupid, stupid," she muttered. "Pay attention to the arachnid, Terri."

Reacting to the splotty sound, Myke Phoenix jumped up onto the roof, landing not far from where a big white blotch of web was wriggling. He rightly figured that the wriggle was caused by a woman in a blue tunic.

"Hang on, I'll get you!" Myke said, knowing that he had the strength to tear the web.

"I got this," came the voice from inside the web, which suddenly burst into flames.

"SCREEEEEE!" said the spider.

"Hokey smokes!" said Myke Phoenix.

The blue-clad woman stood, brushing off smoldering bits of web.

"How did you do that?"

"Like you said, we need to talk. What about her?" she said, nodding toward the firespider.

"You go over there, I'll go over here, and we'll see if we can flank it."

"And then?"

"I don't know. Gotta any ideas?"

"Hello!!" came a voice from below.

"Dad." Dr. Terri Travers looked over the edge and saw Dr. Jacob Travers waving his water rifle.

"This is filled with a mixture of pyrethrum and deltamethrin! If you spray the spider in the face –"

"That would probably kill it, Dad, I don't know if that's –"

"First off, Terri, you might not want to be calling your father 'Dad' at the top of your lungs when people could hear," Myke said. "And second, killing it is the idea."

Before she could object, Myke Phoenix bounded down to her father and accepted possession of the water rifle. As she shouted, "No! Wait! Hold on a minute!" Myke ran a few steps and leaped back onto the roof.

She waved and ran toward Myke Phoenix, who stood in front of the giant eight-legged creature with the toy-like device.

"We don't need to kill it!" she cried – and was blasted by a wall of flame from the firespider.

"SCREEEEEEEE!" the creature scolded.

Myke Phoenix looked the big beast in the eyes, said, "Sorry, big girl," and sprayed it in the face with Jacob Travers' chemical concoction.

"SCREEEEEEEEE?!" said the firespider in a different tone of voice, one that spoke of surprise and pain. It staggered backward, shook its head and pawed at the substance with one of its forelegs.

Myke gave it another dose, and was rewarded with another "SCREEEEEEE!?!" that had more surprise and more pain.

The firespider blasted Myke Phoenix with a fiery blanket and followed up by pinning him to the side of the roof with a webby SPLOT. Then it staggered over the side and jumped awkwardly to the ground.

Faster than any chemically sprayed monstrous-sized spider could possibly move, the firespider ran away from the science building and into the gardens, knocking Jacob Travers roughly to the ground as it passed.

Jacob did not stir.

"Dad!" cried the red-haired amazon in the blue tunic, leaping over the side of the building to the ground before the nearby blotch of web could ask, "A little help here?"

She knelt at the side of the white-haired professor, who blinked his eyes open, started to get up, winced and said "Ouch!" and lay back on the ground.

"Just lie there, we'll get an ambulance," she said.

"I put the little ones back in their pens, I think they'll be safe there." He looked up at her sorrowfully. "I'm sorry, daughter. I don't know how they could have escaped, or where the giant spider came from."

"It's OK," she said. "We'll sort that out later."

From the underbrush came a reptilian hissing sound, and she looked over in alarm –but saw nothing. The hiss was not repeated, and neither the spider nor any other animal appeared.

"That wasn't the firespider," she said to herself.

"Thanks for the help, sir," said a man in a white uniform who stepped in front of the sun as she knelt by her father. The sound of approaching sirens echoed across the campus. "Where did the spider go?"

"My father's hurt," she said.

"I'll be all right. I don't think anything's broken – famous last words, eh?" the old man chuckled. "You go after the big one. They'll find me soon enough."

And as Myke Phoenix and his new partner combed the campus as only two impossibly strong, impossibly fast superheroes can, paramedics did indeed find Jacob Travers sitting on the ground outside the science building, where they found no broken bones but carted him off to St. Valentine's Hospital for a checkup just in case. Being slammed to the ground by a rampaging firespider is not to be shrugged off indifferently.

The search was unsuccessful. There was no further encounter that day with the giant firespider. And with everything else that had happened, Dr. Terri Travers forgot about the strange hissing sound she had heard from the underbrush, until later events jogged her memory.

After it became apparent that the search for the firespider was fruitless, and Dr. Terri Travers checked the lab to make sure her father had indeed secured the baby firespiders, she and Myke Phoenix stood in her office and each took a deep breath.

"OK," Myke Phoenix said. "Let's go have that talk."

"Oh my stars," said Dana Dunsmore Phillips when she first set eyes on the tall, lithe, red-haired woman in the powder-blue tunic with its short skirt. She looked at the tall, barrel-chested man in the white uniform with a questioning look and perhaps a twinge of jealousy.

"Relax, doll," came a voice from the top shelf. "Remember, she's his daughter. And he loves you to death anyway."

She looked back at the two heroic figures, the one that talked with her husband's speech patterns and the one who had just whirled toward the strange new voice and then glanced in surprise at Myke Phoenix.

"Yes," Dana admitted. "The square jaw, the eyes –I can see the family resemblance."

"It's time to tell me what's going on here," the tall woman said. "Way past time, actually."

"Well, we had a cluster of firespiders to deal with first," Myke said.

"I heard about that on TV," Dana said. "Where did they come from?"

"Put that thought on hold, if you don't mind," said the androgynous voice from the vase. "Terri Travers, I am the Soulkeeper of Kiribati, I carry the essence of two mighty warriors –"

"Just two?" Myke said.

"Just two, I promise," the vase said. "Don't interrupt."

"We interrupt you all the time," Dana said.

"This time it's important! Knock it off. Terri Travers, I am the Soulkeeper of Kiribati. I carry the essence of two mighty warriors, Mychus of Kiribati and his daughter, Mychala, who were protected by the phoenix over the years. Every so often, when the big bird decides humanity needs heroes, he makes sure the right people end up with the essence. Nineteen years ago he decided it was the right time, and Paul Phillips was infused with the essence of Mychus. Now the need is even greater, and the phoenix has selected you for Mychala's role. We were supposed to have this conversation before the conversion actually happened. Otherwise a person tends to freak out."

"Why did I turn into – this – prematurely, then?" the red-haired woman asked.

"I think I know," Myke replied. "You were in mortal danger, and –"

"I'm telling the story, big guy," the vase interjected. "But he's right. You were in mortal danger. That stuff your daddy worked up was going to kill you. There are two ways the switch works. Either you make it voluntarily, or when you're in imminent danger and don't realize it yet, the switch occurs automatically."

"But why? Why me? Why now?" she asked.

"Why you, because there's no one better suited. The phoenix decides, and it's a pretty good judge of character. Why now, because it's the right time."

"The right time? What does that mean?"

"She asks better questions than you did, big guy. All you did was make with the wisecracks about being some guy in spandex named Myke Phoenix."

"I don't wear spandex," Myke said. "And it's still a good name."

"Right. So what makes this the right time is because so much is wrong. You may have noticed that in the last 19 years, there's been a lot more evil in the world, especially around this town. The whole shebang has kicked up a few notches in the last few months. Mychus can't be everywhere, and some situations he won't be able to handle alone. We need Mychala."

"What if I don't want to be a superhero?" said the woman in Mychala's body, which drew a laugh from Dana.

"You're sort of drafted, girl. You don't have a choice. It's your destiny," Dana Phillips said, putting air quotes around the word *destiny*.

"You sort of get used to it," Myke said. "And what I found is that something inside of me was prepared for it, wanted to make a difference."

"I see," Terri Travers said, and she did see. An indefinable something in her heart knew that fighting the forces of evil in the world was something she wanted and was willing to do. That she would do it as some sort of superhero, well, that would take some getting used to.

An important something occurred to her.

"Did Mychala have the ability to breathe fire or climb like a spider?"

Myke and Dana looked at her as if she'd asked why bananas are so purple.

"Because I can – spit fire, that is," Terri said. "That's how I got out of the web on the roof. And I guess you didn't see me shoot fire at the little spiders just before they turned all their fire on me."

"No, they were blasting you when I got there," the big man said incredulously.

"What happens is that the best of you blends with the best of Mychala," the Soulkeeper said. "Myke Phoenix is a better investigator than some of the past Mychuses because Paul Phillips was a good reporter already. But he didn't have any superpowers, so the enhancement was more subtle. You'll probably find that Mychala is an even better biologist than Dr. Terri Travers has been up to this point. And, of course, whatever abilities that serum gave you carried over – without the lethal side effects."

"I'm not sure I'd use the term abilities to describe them," she said. "And what about Dr. Terri Travers? How do I get back?"

"It's easy," Myke Phoenix said, except in less than the time it took to say those two words, Paul Phillips was saying them. The transformation happened so fast that Terri didn't see it happen. "Is it safe for her yet?" he asked the vase.

"What does that mean?"

"Some sort of healing process happens while you're gone," Paul explained. "It works better for Mychus – I once was mortally wounded and it fixed all the wounds completely, but if I cut or bruise myself as Paul, the wound remains when I come back. Something like being poisoned, though, would be cleaned up."

"What about my –" she began to ask, and held out her good right hand, flexing the fingers.

"I'm afraid that won't –" the vase started to say, but Terri Travers had already replaced Mychala and was staring at her burned and twisted hand. "Like Paul said, the process works better on the superpowered bodies."

"I'll get used to it," she said. "And my father's serum did do some good. I can move the fingers more easily than I could before. Just not as well as I can as a superheroine."

"I'm sorry, Terri," Dana said, touching the scientist's shoulder.

"I'll get used to it," she said again, more firmly. "Why is the time right for there to be two superheroes, Soulkeeper?"

"I'm glad you asked," said the odd voice. "There's this dinosaur. But first there's the alien invasion."

Epilogue

TWO women and a man walked into the reception area outside the Astor City mayor's office. If anyone had been paying attention, they might have noticed a stiffness in their gait, as if they weren't used to walking in these bodies. But everyone was caught up in the everyday business of working for the mayor, so the trio walked up to the reception desk mostly unnoticed.

"Hello. I am Ivana Christanova and these are my colleagues," one of the women addressed the receptionist. "We are from Popeysk, Russia, and we are here to discuss a sister city relationship between Popeysk and Astor City."

"Oh, how nice, I didn't know you were coming," the receptionist chirped, turning to her computer screen and calling up the mayor's calendar. "Your appointment isn't listed here, I'm sorry – are you sure you have the right time and day?"

"We do not need an appointment," Christanova said. "We will see the mayor now."

The receptionist's head snapped back as if she had been punched in the jaw. She put her hands to her head as if an impossibly bad sudden headache had descended over her, but then she shook her head and looked up with a blank smile.

"Of course you do not need an appointment," she said blankly. "I will take you to see the mayor now."

The four of them exchanged a sly look of triumph as the receptionist led the visitors to see the mayor.

And the dinosaur claw was still missing.

March of the Alien Dead

Prologue: 1975

THE girl just wanted to spend a little time kissing her boyfriend and stuff. She had washed her hair with Yucca Daisy shampoo because she knew he loved the scent. She'd touched her neck and wrists expertly with perfume to encourage him to sniff there. She put on the jeans that were torn several strategic inches above the knee, and the halter top that was fastened by a string so that her entire back was visible from her shoulders to her wide vinyl belt.

"You, girl, are going to get kissed tonight," she said to the girl in the mirror with the long, straight, jet-black hair.

As he drove them to the county park along the Shikaakwa River, "When Will I Be Loved" came on the radio, and she cried out "Stop the car!" and when he pulled over, she said "Turn up the radio" and jumped out. She danced in the setting sun in the ditch under the big electric towers that stood along Park Road, waving enticingly to him to come out and join her.

"I've been made blue – I've been lied to – WHEN will I – be – loved?!"

As the jangling guitar solo burst from the little speaker in the middle of his dashboard, she she raised her hands over her head and bounced to the beat, her hair flying to and fro. She caught a glimpse of his admiring, approving eyes and said to herself, "Oh yes, girl, you're going to get kissed."

And she did, just a few minutes later along the stream that raced through the park and into the mighty Shikaakwa. He ran his fingers up and down her back approvingly and kissed her like there was no tomorrow.

She closed her eyes and melted into the kiss, then felt a sudden shift in his attention as he broke off the embrace. When she opened her eyes, he was looking at something along the banks of the brook.

"What the flurp is that?" he said.

Plopped on a big rock next to the water was a blob of some kind. No other word but blob would do – it was just a shapeless mass that appeared to be made of some kind of flesh. Almost as quickly as it takes to say this, her young man straightened up and groaned as if fighting some internal struggle, then relaxed – but the fire in his eyes disappeared.

"Do not worry about the blob by the brook," he said without emotion. "It is nothing to worry about."

"Charlie? Are you all right? What is that thing?" she asked fretfully.

"It is nothing to worry about," he repeated. And he turned and started walking away.

She ran in front of his path and said, "I'm not kidding. What's going on? You're freaking me out a little here."

"It's nothing to worry about. Let us go back to town," he said.

Hoping to regain his attention, she threw her arms around him and gave him a big hug. Her long, full hair flew into his face.

"WHOA! Holy flurp. Wow!" he said, shaking his head as if waking from a dream. "What IS that thing? Let's get out of here."

"What's going on, Charlie?"

"I don't know. It's like it reached into my brain and started giving me orders," Charlie said. "When I smelled your hair, it broke the connection."

"What? What's wrong with my hair?"

"Nothing –your hair is great. But the monster doesn't like it."

Not every girl would think to do what came next. But this was no ordinary girl.

She reached into her purse and grabbed her bottle of shampoo. Running down to the water as Charlie shouted, "Whoa! What are you doing? Get away from that thing," she unscrewed the bottle cap and poured it over the strange blob.

Sure, enough, the misshapen creature screamed and started to smoke. After a few seconds of writhing and smoking, it became still. She hadn't noticed that it was sort of throbbing as if breathing until the throbbing stopped.

"I think I killed it," she said.

"What the heck is in that bottle?"

"It's just my Yucca Daisy," she said, showing him the label. "It must be lethal to this thing."

"Whoa."

"But what IS it?"

"I have no idea. But it's dead now. Let's get outta here."

"What if there's more of them?"

"Then we should REALLY get outta here. Come on."

She climbed into his car, staring at the motionless blob as they drove away. Charlie was very quiet until they were about two miles away.

"I think you stopped an alien invasion with your Yucca Daisy."

"What?! What are you talking about?"

"It started merging its mind with mine. I think I was going to be its slave or something. I couldn't move for myself until you hit me with your hair," he said. "It was an advance scout, all alone. Don't worry, there weren't any more of them. I just had to get outta there."

She stared at him. If she hadn't seen the blob herself and killed it with a splash of shampoo, she'd have slugged him for coming up with such a goofy story.

"Let's not tell anyone about this," he said. "It's too crazy."

"You're probably right," she agreed. "But if we ever do get an alien invasion, we'll have to tell people about Yucca Daisy."

"Yeah. Who knew?" he said. "We'll have to keep a supply of killer shampoo on hand at all times."

They laughed and drove back home.

She and Charlie broke up a few months later. She never forgot that night, but neither did she tell anyone else about what had happened.

Late in the 1970s, Yucca Daisy was purchased by a mysterious group of investors who quietly closed down production.

The shampoo has been off the market for 40 years.

Act 1
Secrets are shared

TWO inhuman figures faced each other in Paul and Dana Phillips' living room.

One was dressed like a human being, and he stood like a human being, but his head was covered in feathers, not hair, and all over, not just on top and back. His eyes were set farther apart, toward the sides of his head, and where his mouth should be protruded a ducklike beak. Also, his hands, although shaped like a human's, were covered with a soft brown down.

The other sat on its haunches, covered in white (excuse me, English cream, thank you very much) fur, floppy ears hanging down the sides of her face, her mouth open and tongue languishing off to the side. She looked very much like she was smiling.

"Woof," she said, wagging her tail.

Quincy Quackenbos, renowned chemist and industrialist despite being half-man and half-duck, scowled at Goombah, the five-month-old golden retriever.

"I don't like dogs," the duck man said. "Do you know what dogs do with ducks? It's humiliating."

Goombah licked her chops and resumed panting with the same vacant smile-like expression.

"Just have a seat, Quincy," Paul said. "She'll leave you alone."

Quincy sat in the big easy chair next to the bay window that showed the Phillipses' lovely view of the woods. Goombah put her front paws in Quincy's lap and hovered inches from the duck man's bill.

"Goombah! Off!" Paul said with a commanding tone. The golden retriever looked at him, whined and plopped her feet back on the floor. Paul gave his guest a sheepish smile. "She's friendly."

"All dogs look hungry to me," Quincy said. "What's up, Scoop? Why did you want me to come over?"

"Please don't call me 'Scoop.' It's Dana's nickname for me." Paul Phillips had been a reporter in Astor City for two and a half decades, first on WACR radio and then at the Astor City Gazette. When first one and then the other found themselves (shall we say) less committed to full staffing, Paul struck out on his own and created the online Astor City Beacon, which competed with the more traditional newsrooms, fueled his journalistic passion, and more or less kept food on the table and kibble in Goombah's bowl. "It doesn't sound as endearing coming out of someone else's mouth."

"Touchy about it, are we?" and Quincy Quackenbos seemed to smile just a little, the way friends do when they realize they've learned a new way to tease a friend – or the way former supervillains might do when they've learned one of a hero's weaknesses. Quincy liked to think he had been a thorn in Myke Phoenix's side on more than one occasion, until his second stint in state prison taught him that being a bad guy tended to limit one's freedom too excessively. "I'll keep that in mind. Really, what's up, Paul? You sounded mysterious on the phone."

"We wanted to introduce you to a friend," a lilting feminine voice said from the door. Dana Phillips, owner of the Dana Dunsmore Agency marketing and advertising firm as well as wife and partner of Paul Phillips, swept into the room as only an attractive, auburn-haired beauty can sweep. She had such a way of dominating a room that – had her companion not been almost equally attractive – Quincy might not have seen the lovely woman who walked in with her. "Or have you met Dr. Terri Travers from the university?"

Terri Travers was gorgeous in more of a geeky, biology professor way. She did not go to any lengths to style her hair or otherwise prepare her looks in what is generally accepted as a feminine way, a trait that made her all the more attractive to a geeky chemist like Quincy Quackenbos, who held out his left hand to shake hers, because he knew her right hand had been rendered useless in an attack by a giant spider some months earlier.

"Yes, of course I know Dr. Travers," he said, making contact with her impossibly blue eyes and feeling more than a little twinge of attraction. But he knew it wouldn't be reciprocated, so he shook off that feeling and added, "Is Josiah Petri coming, too?" because he knew Terri Travers and the Astor County forensic examiner were what they call an item.

"No, not today," Terri said. "That's one of the reason we wanted to talk with you this afternoon."

"OK, not following," Quincy replied, looking from Terri to Paul and then Dana and back to Terri –who wasn't Terri anymore.

"Wak!" quacked Quincy Quackenbos, who only quacked when he was surprised or amused. This was the former.

For Terri Travers was not Terri Travers anymore. In her place was a somewhat taller, red-haired woman with cascading red hair. She was no longer wearing the conservative business dress and lab coat of a biology professor but a short, powder-blue tunic that cinched at the waist, the red and gold image of a phoenix on her chest.

"There have been some developments since I saw you last, Quince," Paul Phillips said.

"Yeah, I knew about the puppy," Quincy said, looking at the powerful-looking beauty with awe. "What is this, are you Mrs. Phoenix or something?"

The newcomer who had replaced Terri Travers laughed with Terri Travers' laugh. "Well, there is a family connection, but that's not it."

And they told the tale that had unfolded a few days earlier, in which the Soulkeeper of Kiribati had informed Terri Travers that she had been chosen to inhabit the superpowered body of Mychala, daughter of Mychus, the ancient warrior whose body was shared by Paul Phillips and who was known colloquially in Astor City as the superhero Myke Phoenix.

The Soulkeeper of Kiribati, of course, was the crudely formed ancient vase sitting on a top shelf in the Phillipses' dining room, which now spoke.

"They figured since you know the secret of Mychus, you ought to know the secret of Mychala, too," said a voice that may have been male, may have been female, but clearly was emanating from the bit of pottery on the shelf. If Quincy Quackenbos had not heard the vase speak in the past, he might have been further disoriented by this development. "I'm not sure 'The more, the merrier' necessarily applies to secrets that have been preserved for centuries."

"So are you Mykala Phoenix, then?" Quincy said, recovering some of his wits. "I've read this comic book. Somewhere you're hiding Myke Phoenix Jr., and if we really look around maybe you'll find a batty old Uncle Phoenix who makes believe he has super powers, too." He paused a moment, then laughed a quacky laugh. "I guess I'm the talking tiger! Except I'm a duck."

"No, nothing like that," laughed Paul Phillips, who also read comic books once upon a time, while the women smiled half-smiles at each other and humored them. "But we do have a bit of a conundrum. I shared the secret of Myke Phoenix with Dana very early in my career as a superhero, but I'm not sure that Terri should tell Josiah about this."

"He's my boyfriend," said the woman in Mychala's garb. "I don't see how I could keep something like this from him. And it seems to be OK to share the secret with one of your most bitter foes. Didn't you concoct a formula to kill Myke Phoenix?"

"No, that's an urban legend," Quincy said, although Paul noticed he cast his eyes downward as he spoke. "Well, yes, I did try to come up with an anti-Myke serum in the old days. But it never worked, and I don't do that stuff anymore."

"Paul trusts Quincy," Dana said. "And I think you should trust Josiah."

"I seem to remember you bursting into the room while Myke Phoenix was having a showdown with an evil genius," Paul said.

"I remember that," said Quincy, who was the evil genius in question at the time. "I remember wondering why this frantic woman was putting herself in harm's way."

"Yes, but I always would have rather known why you were rushing off all the time," Dana said. "How would I have known it was so you could save the world? If you're serious about Josiah, he deserves that."

Terri's phone rang. She looked at the caller screen.

"It's Josiah," she said. "What are the odds?" The red-haired woman was replaced by Dr. Terri Travers in the blink of an eye. "Hello, you."

"Terri, you're going to think I'm crazy," said the anxious voice at the other end.

'What's wrong?" That response drew concerned stares around the room.

"Do you remember just after we first met, I was grabbed by those aliens who borrowed people's bodies?"

"Of course."

"I think it's happening again," Josiah said. "Only this time they've got people like the mayor and city council."

"You think the aliens are back?" The concerned stares turned darker.

"Yes." Josiah didn't hesitate, and his voice was firm and maybe a little wavery. "I think the aliens are taking over the city government."

"What?! How could they do that?"

"The mayor and a couple of the aldermen were here at the county building with some folks from Russia, and they just weren't acting like themselves," he said. "Terri, I remember how it felt from the inside. They reminded me of me when I was possessed."

"OK, well, hang tight, I happen to be with Myke Phoenix. I'll let him know."

"What are you doing with Myke Phoenix?"

"Uh, he wanted some more information about the firespiders," she lied. It was a good lie. Only a few weeks had passed since several dozen large, fire-breathing spiders had swarmed the University of Astor City campus and the first firespider – the size of an elephant – had made a brief appearance before disappearing again.

"Oh, yeah, gotcha. Well, tell him about this. I think it's serious!"

They ended the conversation, and Terri shared Josiah's concerns with the three others.

"The aliens are back. Great Godfrey, isn't it always something around here anymore?" Quincy said. "If I'd known there was going to be so many villains available to help, I'd have stayed on the evil side." The others stared. "Wak! Can't a guy make a joke anymore?"

Moments later the phone rang in the Astor County Sheriff dispatch center. "Astor County Dispatch, Blanche speaking," said a late-middle-aged woman in a dark blue uniform.

"Hey, Blanche, how are ya? It's Paul Phillips."

Her eyes narrowed. "Nothing going on, Paul. Slow day," she said, using her best "Leave me alone, you crummy reporter" voice.

"Actually, I was just calling to check on something," Paul said, using his best "Please don't hang up on me" voice. "You see anyone acting funny today, especially important people?"

"Besides you?" she asked sardonically. "Don't you have anything better to do than call up three times a day and ask if anything's going on in town?"

"Yeah. Actually, I was wondering if you saw the mayor and City Council guys who were visiting this morning."

"What about 'em?"

"Probably nothing," Paul said. "But I got a call from a guy who swears they've been acting like those body-borrower aliens have grabbed them."

"Oh, come on."

"I know it sounds nuts, and if nobody else has reported it, well, I'm sorry to bug you."

"It must be a slow news day if you're calling to waste my time with an alien invasion story," Blanche said hotly. "Go chase stupid stuff somewhere else."

She clicked off the connection angrily, but alarm bells were ringing in the back of her mind. Blanche reached for her purse, opened it up, and unzipped a seldom-unzipped side pocket.

She pried it open and reached inside, feeling for something at the bottom of the pocket, her heart beating quickly.

Yes, it was still there. She exhaled and realized she'd been holding her breath. As long as it was still there, she felt a little safer.

Blanche zipped up the pocket, put the purse back on the corner of her desk, and went back to work. But she kept looking around the room and over her shoulder the rest of the day.

Act 2
Bad things happen

IF the truth were told, Mark Fielding was tired of being a colonel in the National Guard. His military discipline contributed to how far he had advanced in business, and he did enjoy the camaraderie of the troops, but he was ready to start using his weekends like an average citizen does. And he was saying as much to the mayor of Astor City.

"A guy reaches the point where he wants to stand in a stream and cast a fly on a Saturday morning, not report to the training center," Fielding said. "You know what I mean, Dan?"

"Yes, that would be nice," Mayor Dan Adams said without enthusiasm. "Would you like to come to the sister city ceremony when we cement our relationship with Popeysk? They are very nice people."

"No, thanks, Dan," Fielding said, suddenly wary. "I'll be at the training center, as I said. Who else will be there?"

"I will, my secretary, a few council members. It will be nice."

"No doubt. Well, good talking to you. I'd better go."

"Stay, Mark," said the mayor. "There's something I'd like to show you."

"Nope, gotta go. Leaving now, thanks, maybe next time," Fielding said, throwing open the door a little too enthusiastically and marching out.

"Yes. Maybe next time."

Mark Fielding didn't know why, but a chill was going up and down his spine as he walked briskly to his car, got in and drove away. He did a quick search for the Astor City Beacon phone number and made the connection.

"Hi, Paul, it's Mark Fielding," he said when Phillips answered. "Look, I know you have some kind of connection with Myke Phoenix. I need to talk with him right away. There's something odd going on at City Hall."

Dan Adams loved to talk about fishing. He wouldn't change the subject when it came up unless something was very wrong. Mark Fielding aimed to find out what it was, but if his suspicions were correct, he needed the superhero's help.

Terri Travers had mixed feelings about the basement of the Astor County Government Center. Visiting the morgue was not generally a pleasant experience, but visiting the forensic examiner was a pleasure. She and Josiah Petri had become extremely fond of each other since they'd met during the first firespider invasion.

She popped into the office to find Josiah on the phone. Terri gave him a broad smile. He did not return it.

"I will call you back, thank you," he said into the phone and hung up. "Hello, Terri."

She threw her arms around his neck and gave him a kiss. He put his hands on her size and received the kiss.

"Everything OK?" she asked, knowing at once that it wasn't. As I mentioned a moment ago, they were extremely fond of each other, and their greetings were usually enthusiastic.

"Everything is fine, I am just – tired," he said. "Nothing to worry about here."

"You sounded pretty worried a little while ago," Terri said. "Myke Phoenix is going to look into it."

"Oh, I wish he wouldn't," Josiah said. "I feel so silly, I was just imagining things. There's nothing to worry about here."

"Are you kidding? You sounded so upset before. That's one of the reasons I came right over," Terri said. "What could make you change your mind like that?"

Unless – oh no.

"They didn't borrow your body again, did they?"

"Don't be silly. I was just imagining things," he said. "I went to Dan Adams and he explained the whole thing. You said that was one of the reasons you came to see me. What were the others?"

"I was going to tell you something, but it can wait," she said, backing toward the door. "You know, I just remembered, Dad's spider colony needs to be fed."

"Stay for just a minute, Terri."

"No, I –" but she didn't finish the sentence. Suddenly her senses were blasted by the most intense headache she had ever felt.

"I am so sorry, Terri," Josiah said.

"Astor City Sheriff, Blanche speaking."

"Hey, Blanche, it's Paul Phillips."

"Paul! Hi, how are you? It's good to hear your voice."

The intrepid reporter removed the phone from his ear and stared at it.

"Blanche?"

"Not much is happening in the county right now," said the normally sour dispatcher. "But if you swing by here on your rounds, I have something to show you."

"A press release?"

"No – sure, let's say it's a press release," she said. "Just come on by when you have a chance. As soon as you can. So nice to hear from you."

Paul switched the call off but continued staring at his phone.

"What's wrong, Paul?" Dana asked from across the living room.

"I'm not sure," he replied. "Josiah and Mark say the mayor isn't acting like himself, and now Blanche is acting cheerful. Whatever it is, it's contagious."

Somewhere not far from Astor City – but far enough away and in a secluded enough area that no one had seen it land – a spaceship lay in a small clearing in the middle of a forest.

Inside the spaceship were five blobs and another, furtive figure. "Blobs" is not intended as a pejorative term; the beings were formless, shapeless, and breathing, so "blob" is the most accurate word to describe them. Stationed at each of the room's three entrances was a tall, copper-colored sentry, each kind of reptilian in an insectoid sort of way.

"We now control the mayor and a majority of the city council," one of the blobs said, although not a sound was heard. Having no mouths, they spoke directly into their companions' minds.

"Exccellent," said the furtive figure, stretching the "sss" sound in the word. "You will be able to control the entire city government now."

"The customs of this planet are very odd," the blob replied. "It should not be so easy to seize a city."

"Humanss are a very strange lot," the furtive figure said. "They are built with a thirst for freedom and the ability to fend for themselvess, but they inevitably assk ssomeone elsse to think for them and take care of them. In effect they voluntarily accept sslavery and congratulate themselvess for choosing their own masterss."

"Very strange indeed," another blob said. "Good for us, though. All we need to do is seize the minds of the chosen masters."

"Like the mayor, yess," said the furtive figure.

"We have a problem," said a blob attached to the ceiling. It was monitoring an electronic monitor of some kind. "One of the humans rejected our seizure."

"You didn't overextend the range again, did you?"

"No, we're well within tolerance levels. There's room for at least a dozen more before we stretch the system," the monitor blob said. "And there's more. This felt just like what happened when we attempted to assimilate Myke Phoenix."

Terri Travers leaned back against the wall of Josiah Petri's office to steady herself. Except it wasn't Terri Travers.

"What just happened?" she said, holding her head – except it wasn't her own head anymore. A long mane of untamed red hair flowed over and around her hand.

Josiah Petri stared. Even in his zombified condition, he seemed startled.

"What just happened?" he echoed. "Where is Terri? Who are you?"

She looked down and saw that she was wearing a powder-blue tunic with white trim, with a skirt that ended a couple of inches above her knees. She didn't need to look carefully to know the image of a phoenix was embroidered onto the tunic's chest.

"Maybe I should be asking questions," she said. "Why did my head just explode? Were you trying to take me over, too? I think you need to be letting go of Josiah now, whoever you are."

"Who are you?" Josiah repeated.

"My name is Mychala, daughter of Mychus," the red-haired woman said. "Or rather, this is her body. And you people are in a heap of trouble, especially if you don't let go of Josiah."

"I don't understand," he said.

"I'll tell you all about it later, honey," she said. "First we have to free you from the aliens' clutches."

"Easier said than done, I am afraid," Josiah said and slugged her with all of his might.

His face crumpled in two kinds of pain: First, he was aghast that the aliens would force him to punch his girlfriend, even if she suddenly looked more like a superheroine than his girlfriend. Second, his hand hurt like bejeebers from striking the jaw of an invulnerable, well, superheroine.

"Alien mamas don't tell their kids never to hit a girl, I guess," she said. "And especially not this girl. Serves you right. It's OK, Josiah, I know that wasn't you doing that."

"Who are you?"

"Oh, lover, I want to tell you," said the beautiful woman who did not resemble the beautiful woman who called him "honey" and "lover" most of the time. "But I can't explain" – and with this she grabbed him by the shoulders and barked into his face – "UNTIL THE ALIENS LET GO OF YOU. YOU HEAR ME??!! GET OUT OF THIS MAN!!!"

Josiah Petri smirked. Well, it wasn't Josiah Petri smirking. Josiah Petri was not a smirker, so we must assume that the alien who was controlling most of his brain and all of his actions was the one who was smirking.

"Honey, or whoever you are, we're not letting go of your lover until we're ready to let go."

And with that, they tried to seize her brain again. That was the agonizing headache that ripped behind her eyes, the pain that felt like something had reached under her skull and started squeezing her brain, the pain that would not stop until it controlled her – except she had the power to resist. But it took all of her willpower to fight the pain. She crumpled to the ground in the effort to drive the aliens out of her brain.

And when they stopped trying and released her from the pain, Josiah Petri was no longer anywhere in sight.

Mayor Dan Adams called the emergency session of the Astor City Council to order.

"All right, you have before you a resolution setting a temporary curfew of midnight to 5 a.m. for reasons we discussed in closed session. I assure the public that we are establishing this curfew for reasons related to public safety and, indeed, for reasons of national security. But as a result we cannot disclose the reasons for the curfew at this time."

Sitting at the media table, Paul Phillips considered raising an objection. He was well within his rights if he stood up and questioned whether the closed city council session was legal under the state open meetings law. He decided not to for two reasons: One, the call to public safety and national security meant that he'd have to go to court to try to establish whether they had a right to close the meeting, and they might win. Two and more important, he was pretty sure he was watching aliens who had seized the minds of the mayor and a majority of the council, and to fight THAT kind of City Hall, he probably needed the power of Myke Phoenix, not mere mortal Paul Phillips.

Three of the 12 aldermen, however, did raise objections.

"Why weren't we informed about the closed session? Why haven't you told us what's going on, Dan? This is nuts," said one of the aldermen.

"All those in favor say 'aye,'" said the mayor, and nine aldermen said "Aye."

"Opposed."

"NAY!!!" shouted the other three aldermen.

"The ayes have it. No one is allowed on the streets of Astor City between the hours of midnight and 5 a.m., effective immediately and until further notice. The police are instructed to apprehend and hold anyone in violation.

"Trust us, folks," Mayor Dan Adams said to the small group watching from the gallery and, more important, directly into the camera for the public-access channel that streamed the council meetings live. "When this is all over and we explain what's going on, this will all make sense."

After publishing a short story about the mysterious curfew on his Astor City Beacon news site, Paul Phillips swung down to the Astor County 911 Dispatch Center.

"Hey, Blanche," he said cautiously to the late-middle-aged and usually very grumpy woman at the corner desk.

"Paul. Good to see you," Blanche replied tersely but still a lot more cordially than she ever did in the past. She grabbed her purse and stood up. "Marge, I'm taking my break. Come with me, Paul."

"Always good to see you, too, Blanche," Paul said as he followed her down the corridor to a break room. "To what do I owe the special attention? You said there was a press release?"

"Stick the press release somewhere," she said, sounding more like good old curmudgeonly Blanche and pulling him over to a table in the corner of the deserted break room. "Sit down."

He sat.

"What is it, Blanche?" She was beyond grumpy, but her agitation wasn't aimed at him for a change. "What's wrong?"

She sat for a moment looking across the table at him with her purse on her knees, as if she was trying to make a final decision whether to talk to him.

"I'm telling you this because you're friends with Myke Phoenix," she said at last, the second person today to make that statement. "Remember those aliens that landed a few months ago and killed the sheriff and all?"

"Of course I do."

"I seen them before, a long long time ago," Blanche said. "And I'm pretty sure they're back again."

"OK, I have to tell you a lot of people are starting to think the same thing."

"But I think I can help stop them." She started rummaging in her purse.

"Really?! How?"

"It was a long time ago, must have been 1975 because that's when I was dating Bruce Powell and that was the year we were together," Blanche said. "We went out on a date in Griswold Park and we spotted these blobs. From what you wrote about the things that killed the sheriff and took over all of those people, I think it was the same blobs."

"1975? We're talking almost 40 years, Blanche."

"You don't have to tell me that, I can do the math," she said. "Anyway, they took over Bruce for a few seconds, until he sniffed my hair. That broke the spell, so I sprayed the blob with my shampoo and I'm pretty sure I killed it."

Paul Phillips looked at Blanche for a very long moment, and suddenly he couldn't help it: He burst out laughing.

"It ain't funny, Paul! I'm serious."

"I know, I know," he stifled a giggle. "It's just – the aliens can be killed by shampoo?"

"Not just any shampoo," she said, unzipping the special pocket in her purse. "I've never gone anywhere without this in my purse ever since."

She whipped the bottle out of her purse and slammed it on the table, label facing Paul Phillips.

YUCCA DAISY.

"Hokey smokes," Paul said. "I haven't seen a bottle of that stuff since –"

"– Probably since about 1975," Blanche said. "Actually, more like 1978. I Googled it. That's when the company got bought and went out of business. I think the aliens bought the company and shut down production."

"That sounds ridiculous," Paul said, but admitted – "but not *that* ridiculous when you think about it."

"I don't know why I kept this stuff," she said. "I guess I figured I'd have something to defend myself with if they ever came back."

"And they came back," Paul agreed. "But you can't stop an alien invasion with one bottle of old shampoo."

"I know. You'd need to make a whole bunch of the stuff all over again, and who knows where the formula is anymore?"

"Maybe we don't need the formula," Paul said thoughtfully. "I happen to know a chemist."

Act 3
Lines are drawn

"WAK! Reverse engineer a bottle of shampoo?" Quincy Quackenbos laughed a quacky laugh. "I can do that in my sleep. Give it here."

The orangey-yellow plastic bottle still retained some of its original shine, and the paper paste-on label looked almost new except for the 1970s-style hair style on the model. "Yucca Daisy" was emblazoned in old-fashioned hippie lettering across the top of the label.

"I forgot this stuff ever existed," Quincy said nostalgically. He unscrewed the cap and took a sniff. "Still has a little aroma. Good. This may have broken down some in 40 years, but not as much as you'd think. I should be able to guesstimate the original ingredients."

"Is guesstimating enough? Don't you need the exact combination to be lethal to the aliens?" Terri asked.

"You'll have it," the duck man said, looking directly into her eyes with confidence. He waved the bottle. "We can rebuild this. We have the technology."

"If you need any ingredients, let me know," Paul said.

"This label said it was made with an extract of the yucca plant," Quincy said. "Might need a few hundred plants. I think I could get Duckworth's assistance to round some up." Brian Duckworth, of course, was CEO of Quackenbos Laboratories, having assumed the reins and guided the company through the awkward times when its founder was incarcerated for crimes against humanity.

"OK, but if I can do anything –"

"Paul," Quincy said, laying a feathered hand on the reporter/superhero's shoulder. "I got this. Formulas, playing with chemicals in the lab, it's what I do. I take to it like a duck to water – Wak! Wak! See? I do have a sense of humor. I'm telling you I got this. You go save the mayor from the aliens."

"Could you use a lab assistant?" asked professor Terri Travers.

"Not this time, young lady, but thanks for the offer," said the duck man, turning on his mass spectrometer and preparing a sample of Yucca Daisy for testing. "I think Myke Phoenix is the one who's going to need another pair of hands this time."

The delegation from Popeysk, Russia, was working alongside Mayor Dan Adams and nine members of the Astor City Council to set up chairs and erect a banner behind the podium in the council chambers. The sign said "Astor City-Popeysk: Sister Cities." A news conference was scheduled in a half-hour or so.

They went about their business quietly. One might be reminded of the eerie silence that hung over the work site several months earlier when an alien craft crashed and was buried in a hillside outside of town, to be rebuilt by a crew of humans whose minds had been seized and their bodies borrowed. The aliens communicated telepathically, so conversation was extraneous. This was also helpful when a group of Russian-speaking Russians was working side-by-side with a group of English-speaking Americans. Talking to each other with their minds didn't require language with its resulting barrier.

They got some help hanging the banner high on the wall from two of the tall, copper-colored, reptilian-insectoid sentries who had guarded the doors of the alien spacecraft when we visited there last chapter. These two now retired to an inconspicuous place elsewhere. The city officials looked like city officials; the otherwordly sentries would be a little harder to explain to anyone whose body hadn't been borrowed.

"Hi folks," came a cheerful voice from the back of the room. As one, almost as if the same consciousness was controlling all of their actions, the dozen or so people turned to the source of the voice.

A tall, barreled-chested blond man in a white uniform emblazoned with a red-and-gold phoenix stood in the doorway. Next to him was a red-haired woman in a powder-blue tunic with white trim. The same image of a phoenix adorned her chest.

"Myke Phoenix, welcome," Mayor Adams said with a welcoming-enough expression on his face but no expression in his voice whatsoever. "And you must be Mychala, hello, pleased to meet you."

"How do you know who I am?" said the woman with a mane of red hair.

"Your exploits corralling the firespiders were well documented," Adams said. "And Josiah Petri told me your name."

"Where is Josiah? We wanted to talk with him while we were here," Myke asked before his partner could respond.

"He's not here," the mayor said.

After a pause, Myke asked, "So what's the curfew about? Gotta move some big pieces of alien equipment and don't want the common folks to see?"

Adams smirked. Well, it wasn't actually Dan Adams smirking. The smirk reminded Mychala of the smirk on Josiah Petri's face a few hours earlier.

"Of course I don't know what you're talking about," the mayor lied. "And even if I did, I couldn't speak of it. It's a matter of national security."

"So you said," Myke said. "Well, you know, I've been given a little clearance now and then over the years when my help was needed. What can I do to help fix this 'matter of national security'?"

"Nothing, thanks," said Dan Adams. "Let me be clear, Myke: There's nothing you can do about this, and I'd appreciate it if you stayed out of it."

The mayor stood in front of the superheroes, looking up as if daring them to try sticking their noses into his official business. The two costumed figures looked down fully aware Mayor Dan Adams had been possessed by an alien intelligence with evil intent. Mayor Dan Adams looked up at the two heroes fully aware that they knew. The alien consciousness wouldn't stop smirking. Long moments passed.

"Well, OK, then," Myke Phoenix said finally, turning to go. "Have a nice news conference. Come on, Mychala."

She looked at him a bit incredulously, looked back at the possessed officials, and followed Myke Phoenix from the room.

"This is a bit of a problem," Dan Adams said when the superheroes were out of earshot. "We'd better mention this to our powerful little ally."

Outside the building, Mychala touched Myke on the sleeve to get his attention.

"What was that about? Why did we just leave? I don't get it."

"Aliens have taken over the city government, and there's just the two of us," Myke said. "We're going to need the National Guard."

Dana Phillips peered at the screen with a practiced eye, trying to determine whether the logo her graphic artist had designed for their client really matched the message of good food and great pizza that they were trying to convey.

This was the inner sanctum of the Dana Dunsmore Agency, Astor City's leading marketing and advertising firm. Dana tried to concentrate on the pizza logo while reflecting on the developments of the past few days. A new partner for Myke Phoenix, the return of the aliens – what next?

The intercom buzzed.

"There's a Josiah Petri here to see you," said the voice at the other end.

Josiah? He was upset because he thought the aliens had taken over the city council. And Terri was trying to decide whether to share the news about Mychala with him. Which brought him here now?

"Send him in," Dana said, emerging from behind the desk to greet him near the door to the office.

When Josiah came in, he didn't look troubled at all. Neither did he look agitated or angry or any of the other emotions that might come with suspecting an alien takeover of the city government. He just looked blank. She worried about what that might mean but smiled at him anyway.

"Hey, Josiah," she said. "What brings you to my inner sanctum this afternoon? Does the coroner's office need a marketing campaign?"

"Ha, ha," he said without laughing. "Actually, it is something like that, Dana."

An awkward pause.

"What's up?" she said.

"They need your help."

"My help? Who needs my help? Why?"

"They need your help," he repeated.

"All right, we've established that. Who are they?"

"They need your help."

"Josiah, you're being a little scary. I – *oh my stars!*"

She held her hands to her head to try to fend off the pain that squeezed her brain, just for a few seconds. That was all the time it took for the alien mind to damper her personality and seize control of her body.

Dana Dunsmore Phillips had been absorbed into the aliens' collective consciousness. As she stood blankly before Josiah Petri, she felt her secrets and knowledge being assimilated. Behind her blank eyes was waged a fearsome battle for control of her mind, just for a few seconds.

"See? They need your help," Josiah said.

Mark Fielding was startled when two people with phoenixes on their chests walked into his office as the sun set. The big blond man in the white suit had been a familiar figure for almost two decades, and Fielding's National Guard troops had fought unusual menaces side by side with him several times over the years.

But the shockingly attractive red-haired woman in the light blue tunic was a surprise. The phoenix figure on her chest matched the bird on Myke Phoenix's chest, suggesting a connection.

"Is this the mystery woman who fought the firespiders with you the other day?" he asked, extending a hand and getting a firm shake in return. "Mark Fielding."

"Mychala," she said.

"Your name is Mykala Phoenix? Really?" Fielding seemed amused. Mychala did not.

"No. There's a family relation, but I'm just Mychala," she said, pronouncing the "ch" with a slight gutteral Germanic that, if it were more pronounced, would sound as if she were preparing to spit.

Fielding looked at her, and then at Myke Phoenix, and back to Mychala.

"It's a long story," Myke said finally.

"What have you learned?" Fielding asked, shrugging off the name game.

"You were right," Myke Phoenix said. "Something – I'm guessing the same set of aliens that landed here earlier this year – has taken control of the mayor and city council."

"And Josiah Petri," Mychala said anxiously.

"Oh, schmitt," Fielding said. "They got him last time, too. Do you think they grabbed Arnie Rogers again?" Then chief deputy, Rogers was named sheriff after Rod Skjorte, the old top guy, was killed in the confrontation with the aliens.

"Hard to say, I haven't seen Arnie since before all of this started," Myke said. "They've definitely changed tactics from last time. They were just grabbing folks randomly to borrow their bodies, but now they've targeted specific influential people."

"And used their influence," Mychala said. "What possessed them to call that midnight curfew?"

"That's why we're here, Mark," Myke said. "Do you think you could get us some help with reconnaissance?"

"Sure. I need more information before I can convince the governor to do a general call-up, but there are a few people I can bring in for some discreet looking-around. I'll make some calls."

"Meet you here around 11:30?"

"Make it 11. We should spend a little time coordinating our efforts."

"Alrighty then," said Myke Phoenix. "We'll see you then."

They walked out, and Mychala grabbed Myke by the arm.

"That's it? We're going to wait until 11 o'clock before we do anything?"

"What do you suggest we do?"

"Josiah's out there somewhere, being manipulated by alien creatures to do whatever it is they want him to do. We can't just sit around and wait!"

"Terri – Mychala – we have to. We don't know where they are."

Back at the home of Paul and Dana Phillips, the Soulkeeper of Kiribati was working overtime.

"Hoo boy. Hoo boy. Hoo boy," said the ugly green vase. "I wish Paul was here. Hoo boy. Hoo boy."

Suddenly the green vase started talking in Dana Phillips' voice.

"Oh my stars! What's happened to me?"

"Your body has been borrowed by the aliens."

"My body? What am I doing here?"

"I'm keeping your soul."

"You separated me from my body?!"

"Well, yes. Hoo boy. Hoo boy."

"Why?"

"Think about it, doll. If they grab your mind and body, then they know everything – hoo boy – that you know."

"Oh! You mean like how Paul is Myke Phoenix and uses the body of an ancient warrior named Mychus with the help of the Soulkeeper of Kiribati, which is you, and the whole thing is overseen by the Phoenix, an ancient mystical bird that can live for 500 years?"

"Exactly! Hoo boy."

"Why do you keep saying 'hoo boy'?"

"Paul and Terri are in their warrior bodies, and I nabbed you on the side. You think it's easy keeping three souls at once? Hoo boy!"

"Soulkeeper, how do we know what's happening to my body if my soul is inside this green vase?"

"Well, that's the one flaw in the whole plan. I don't have the connection to your body that I have with Mychus and Mychala and Paul and Terri. When the aliens let go of your body, you'll snap back in there, but in the meantime we can't track you."

"Hoo boy," said Dana Phillips' soul.

Paul Phillips called Dana to tell her he'd be working late. And he called her again, and he called her again. He kept reaching her voicemail, and this worried him a little bit. But he was not as worried as Terri Travers was. The difference was that Terri knew that her loved one was being used by the aliens.

But now the required hours had passed, and Myke Phoenix and his new red-haired partner returned to the office of entrepreneur/National Guard Col. Mark Fielding. A group of five men and two women, all looking grim and seriously fit, were gathered with Fielding.

"This doesn't look like much of an army," Mychala said as they entered the room.

"Maybe not, but it looks like a great reconnaisance squad," the colonel said. "Our goal tonight is to assess what we're facing and only engage if necessary."

"That makes sense," Myke said.

"Maybe to you," Mychala said. "I'm ready to do what we need to do tonight."

"We don't know what we're facing yet, how many numbers they have, and how many people they've – recruited," Fielding said.

"He's right, Mychala," Myke said. "What about 'Know thine enemy'?"

Her eyes flashed, fiery as her long flowing hair. "I know they mean us harm. I know they're in control of – people who are very important. I know they need to be taken out."

"First we need to know who 'they' are and and something about their intentions," Fielding said. "We're going to spread out around the city and see if we can find what they're up to. They must have set that curfew to hide whatever movements they plan to make. When you find them, do not engage. Contact the rest of us and keep them in sight until we can determine their moves."

"You'd better hope I'm not the first to find them."

"Come on, Mychala, let's work together on this," Myke said.

"If I see J – someone in danger, I'm not waiting."

"Fair enough," Fielding said. "But if you do engage, the rest of us who aren't bulletproof will hang back. Just call us when you find them. Let's go."

Leading the way out, Myke Phoenix opened the door and stopped abruptly, greeted by an inhuman figure in the hallway.

Quincy Quackenbos stood, there, holding two flasks plugged by stoppers. He held them out to show the syrupy, yellowy substance inside.

"As promised," the duck man said. "Here's your Yucca Daisy."

"That was quick," Myke said, looking surprised.

"I'm good. Actually, I'm the best in the world at this. You always did underestimate me," Quincy said. "Looks like I didn't bring enough to go around, but that's OK," he added, looking at the small group of soldiers. "I have one of the lines at the Labs running a mass supply of the stuff now."

Myke and Mychala each took a flask.

"I recommend you two wash your hair before you go out there," Quincy said. "Don't forget to rinse and repeat."

Act 4
The battle is waged

IT didn't take long for the small squad to find the aliens. In fact, as soon as they emerged on the street shortly after midnight, they heard a rhythmic sound that seemed to be coming from several blocks away.

Clop – clop – clop – clop –

It was the sound of marching. And it sounded like a lot of marchers.

"Change of plans," Col. Mark Fielding said. "Let's check out that sound together."

Stealthily –because after all, the curfew was still in effect – the group moved in the direction of the marching sound.

"It sounds like they're moving toward City Hall," Myke said. "Why don't we go on ahead of you and meet the head of the line?"

"OK, we'll flank them as best as we can."

One of the reasons Myke and Mychala went ahead of the others was simply that they could run faster than any other human being. Another was that if the aliens or their puppets did something violent, like shoot at them, bullets would bounce off of them. The eight non-super heroes did not have that kind of natural armor, so they would stay back in reconnaisance mode.

They positioned themselves at the top of City Hall's stairway entrance, between the two pillars that straddled the main doorways into the building. They arrived when the line of marchers was about two blocks away. It was dark, but they could see about two dozen people walking normally while a force of taller, uniformed beings marched in lockstep behind them. These were the tall, copper-colored, reptilian-insectoid sentries that you and I encountered earlier when the possessed politicians were conferring with their furtive adviser.

"What are those things?" Mychala said.

"I'm not sure, let's get behind cover and see what happens before we try confronting them."

They each ducked behind a pillar to watch the strange entourage approach.

At the front of the group were the humans – the mayor, most of the City Council, a number of random police officers, Josiah Petri and Dana Phillips.

Dana Phillips?!

Myke Phoenix and Mychala gasped in unison.

Myke began to step forward.

"Don't you dare," Mychala said. "Remember? 'Let's see what happens first?'"

The group arrived at the base of the stairs, and the humans began to walk up toward where they were hiding, with four sentries accompanying them, one at each corner of the human group. The other sentries spread out around the perimeter of City Hall, positioning themselves equidistantly and then turning to face the outside. They clearly were setting up a massive guard around the building, unaware that two superpowered beings were already inside their perimeter.

Myke got his partner's attention and mouth the words "The guards first." She nodded.

The humans were almost at the top of the stairs when Myke and Mychala nodded to each other and stepped out. All other motion stopped. The sudden silence was unearthly.

"Hi folks," Myke said. "We broke the curfew."

Nothing happened for several beats. And then Myke flashed to his right and struck the tall sentry with an uppercut that lifted the alien being off its feet and sent it clattering down the steps. Mychala flashed to her right and struck her sentry full in its reptilian nose, the result being identical. Before the two rear guards could react to their clattering companions' fate, the two superheroes moved to the back of the small group and dispatched the third and fourth guards.

"All right, I know you're all under the aliens' spell, and we don't want to hurt you," Myke said.

"That's your disadvantage, Myke," smirked Mayor Dan Adams. "Because we want to hurt you." And the group started to surround the two heroes.

"Come on, Dan, that's the alien controllers talking," said Myke Phoenix.

Dan Adams tilted his head to one side, still smirking: "Well, yes, of course."

Josiah Petri walked up to Mychala with an angry look on his face that seemed to be a combination of alien control and personal vendetta.

"Where's Terri? Where are you holding her?" he said, pushing at the red-haired heroine's shoulders.

"I'll tell you all about it once your head clears. Right now we've got to get you to safety."

He pushed her again, as hard as he could, and they were both surprised when she tripped to the ground, sprawled on the steps. She wasn't hurt, of course, but it turned her around, and when she looked up she saw the four sentries picking themselves up and aiming themselves at the superheroes again. The guards around the perimeter of the building also began marching up the wide stairs and toward the commotion.

"Myke, we have a problem," Mychala called.

"Everyone into the building," one of the Russian delegates said without a trace of an accent, for after all it wasn't a Russian speaking but an alien controller. "The Zembella will take care of the superheroes."

"Dana!" Myke Phoenix shouted. His wife looked back with a blank look in her face, turned and rushed up the stairs. He looked around to see if he could follow Dana, but three copper sentries – the Zembella, apparently – were grabbing Mychala, and he went to help her.

As the people herded themselves into City Hall and the sentries surrounded Myke and Mychala, shots rang out from eight different directions, and bullets struck several sentries at the bottom of the stairs. The force of the projectiles changed the direction of the sentries' bodies, but they quickly straightened out and kept marching upward.

"Cease fire! It doesn't help!" Mark Fielding's voice shouted from the darkness.

"The bullets don't stop them," Mychala said. "Maybe they're robots or something."

At that the nearest sentry rudely belted her in the back of the head, which knocked her off balance but mostly made her angry.

"I don't think they're robots," Myke said. "I think they're being controlled just like the people are, by the alien blob things."

"We'd probably better find out where the alien blob things are, then. Wulllfff!" she said as a sentry grabbed her from behind and picked her up with his arms wrapped around her abdomen.

The action pushed her thick, flowing hair into the tall soldier's face, which had an immediate and bizarre effect: It screamed, dropped her and clattered lifeless to the steps. The other sentries stopped in their tracks. Everyone looked at each other in surprise.

"The shampoo," Mychala said softly, and then said it again more loudly: "The shampoo!"

She ran headlong toward another one of the tall sentries, ducked her head and leaped, swinging her hair so the alien was struck full in the face by a mane of hairy red fury. The same result: A scream and a clattering to the ground.

"Why does this kill them?" she said. "Blanche said the stuff only broke off the psychic connection between her boyfriend and the blob."

"I don't know. Maybe these guys are already dead," Myke called back. He tried charging into the arms of an alien sentry and pushing his blond head toward its face. Although he did not have the ample hair of his female compatriot, the effect was the same –the aroma seemed to turn off the sentry like throwing a switch, and it fell to the ground.

"Yucca Daisy do!" he cried triumphantly, surveying the advance of the tall creatures. "But how do we get to them all?"

As if on cue, headlights appeared in the distance as one tanker truck, then another, then a third, turned the corner and started racing up the street toward City Hall. The robotlike Zembella kept coming at the two costume-clad warriors, who alternately pasted the tall aliens with fearsome punches and, when they got close enough, rubbed their hair into their faces, which was much more effective. When they connected with their fists, the aliens went down, picked themselves up, dusted themselves off, and started coming all over again. When they encountered the superheroes' shampoo-laced hair, they fell down and stayed down.

The three tanker trucks climbed onto the sidewalk and came to a screeching halt at the bottom of the City Hall steps. The door to the lead truck opened, and in the glow of streetlights could be seen an eerie, feathery man with a duck bill, wearing a lab coat and leather work gloves, who jumped to a compartment in the rear, opened it up and started yanking a hose up the steps. Another man, who looked more like a man, jumped out from the passenger side and stood by a valve in the compartment.

"Hi guys," Quincy Quackenbos shouted as he dashed up the stairs more quickly than you'd expect a duck man in his sixties to dash. "I hope I'm not late."

"Just in time," Myke called as two sentries tackled him, one high and one low. He kicked at the low alien, who fell backward but caught himself and started coming again. He leaned his head into the face of the high alien, who clattered lifeless to the ground.

The duck man braced himself and pointed his hose into the center of the melee, calling down to the truck, "OK, Gus, go for it!"

The man spun the wheel-like valve and moments later a thick, creamy substance rushed from the nozzle of the hose, showering the guards and superheroes.

The effect was instantaneous. The tall, copper-colored sentries shrieked in unison and toppled to the ground like puppets whose strings had been cut.

"Holy enchilada," Quincy said. "Wak! That works better than I expected!"

"Is that hose long enough to reach into the building?" Mychala asked after the duck man twisted the nozzle to cut off the flow of newly brewed Yucca Daisy.

"Give us a couple of minutes to hook up a couple extensions," said the duck man.

The foyer of City Hall was much more quiet than they expected. Emergency nightlights cast an eerie glow over the scene, and it appeared that the City Council Chambers, up a short flight of stairs, was the only room with its full complement of lights on.

They raced up the steps and threw open the doors to the council chambers to be greeted by a weird sight. The mayor, council members, and Russian delegation stood along the front of the room facing Myke and Mychala, in front of the raised mayor's desk. Josiah Petri and Dana Phillips stood in the aisles with their backs to the other possessed humans. They all had blank expressions on their faces, but several had more than a hint of anxiety in their eyes. Myke couldn't help but be anxious himself, because Dana looked completely calm, with no sign of her soul even in her eyes.

Nestled on top of the mayor's desk was a pulsing, alien blob. Some sort of electronic device blinked next to it, and wires led to two electrodes attached to the blob like the heart or brain monitors that medical personnel use on humans.

"As I expected, the amplifier works like a charm," the voice of the blob spoke into their minds. "By ourselves, we can only control a dozen or so humans, but the amplifier gives just a few of us the power to take over the entire city. And perhaps I can even do – this."

Jolts of psychic energy burst into Myke and Mychala's brains as the alien made an amplified attempt to borrow their minds. They fell to their knees and held their heads as they fought to resist the invasion.

"Hang on, Mychala," Myke said through gritted teeth.

The doors burst open and Quincy Quackenbos appeared, dragging a great hose that was clearly charged and full of lethal shampoo.

"OK, blob, get a load of *this*," Quincy shouted, reaching for the nozzle. "AAAGH!" he added, dropping the hose and holding his head. A moment later he shook his head, straightened himself up and smirked. "Well, that was anticlimatic."

"Hokey smokes, they have Quincy!" Myke cried.

"And once I have the two of you under control, the rest will be easy," the blob's voice said into their minds. They could feel it wrapping itself around the control centers of their brains and squeezing.

But –

Through the pain and the brain squeezing, Myke Phoenix and Mychala stepped inexorably toward the back of the room where the hose lay unattended.

Seeing the problem, the blob sent its possessed humans to the rescue. Dan Adams and Josiah Petri led the charge to leap onto Myke Phoenix's back. Dana Phillips and the leader of the Russian delegation approached to try to tackle Mychala.

Myke shrugged the puppets off. Mychala reared her head back and a stream of flame shot from her mouth, not long enough to ignite anything but intense enough to make her two attackers think twice.

Quincy Quackenbos stepped in front of Myke Phoenix.

"Sorry, Quince," Myke said, and swatted the duck man aside.

"You fools!" the blob shouted into their brains, knocking them psychically to the ground. But they got up.

Mychala pushed off the advancing human puppets while Myke raised the hose and turned the nozzle.

A thick stream of lustrous sheen sailed over the city council's desks and splotched in a direct hit onto the alien blob.

The scream of agony felt like an explosion in their cerebellums and knocked every human in the room to the floor, including the two superpowered warriors – especially the superpowered warriors, who cried out in pain simultaneously.

And then all was quiet in the City Council chambers. For a moment.

People began to moan as they regained control of their own bodies and staggered to their feet. The two warriors, even though they had been hit hardest by the alien's death scream, were the first to rise.

"Hokey smokes," muttered Myke Phoenix. "That hurt."

"Not as much as it hurt that thing," Mychala replied, indicating the lifeless blob on the mayor's desk.

"What were those tall reptiley-insecty things anyway?" Myke asked Dan Adams as the mayor straightened his tie and drew himself up to his full mayorly self again.

"Dead aliens," Dana answered, trying with all her might not to throw her arms around Myke Phoenix, since after all public displays of affection might suggest to the others that Myke was her husband's alter ego. "Since the attempted invasion in Astor City and Chelyabinsk, they encountered a race of alien warriors who were even better suited than we are to doing their menial work as they journeyed through space. The bad news was that the Zembella all died for various reasons because the work involved going outside the ship in a vaccuum or in poisonous atmospheres. But just because they were dead didn't mean their bodies couldn't be controlled. In fact it was even more convenient than controlling live beings, because they didn't need to be fed or anything."

"And you know all this because ...?" Mychala asked.

"When they borrow a mind, they share a lot of knowledge with each other," Myke said. "They have any more of these amplifier things?"

"No, that's the prototype. I suppose they have the ability to make new ones, but this is the only one they've made so far."

"Where's the rest of the blobs?" Mychala said.

"Outside town somewhere," Dan said. "They never gave us a good view of where their ship is hidden. We shared a lot of knowledge through the psychic link, but they blocked a lot of information from us, too."

Myke took Dana aside and asked softly, "You shared all this information –did they kidnap you because of your connection to me?"

"No, thank goodness," she laughed. "Believe it or not, they wanted me for my marketing knowledge. They figured they'd need a P.R. campaign for the curfew."

"They didn't find out who you are, who Myke Phoenix is, who Mychala is? Hokey smokes, Dana!"

"No, they didn't," she said. "I completely lost track of my body until I woke up in the council chambers just now. I don't remember much of anything that happened tonight, but I had a weird dream where someone kept repeating, 'Hoo boy. Hoo boy.'"

"Hoo boy, indeed!" Myke said, giving his wife a quick hug. "I'm glad you're safe."

"I have a more important question," Josiah Petri said, walking up to Mychala and planting himself in front of her, hands on hips. "Where's Terri? What did you do with her?"

The striking red-haired beauty looked around the room and back into his eyes with a grim smile.

"She's safe, Mr. Petri," she said. "It's a long story that I'll tell you – and only you – as soon as we're done here."

Epilogue

"HAVE you seen this?" Terri Travers barked as she walked into Dana Phillips' office waving a copy of the Astor City Gazette in her good left hand.

"Good to see you, too, Terri," Dana said as the newspaper was flung onto her desk.

"'Mykala Phoenix steps into action,'" Terri said as Dana read the headline. "The TV people are doing the same thing. 'Mykala Phoenix.' As if Mychala is some sort of junior partner in the Myke Phoenix Corps. Paul is the only one who spelled it correctly."

Paul, of course, being both the editor of the online Astor City Beacon and the alter ego of Myke Phoenix, knew that Terri's preference was just to call herself Mychala, the actual name of the superpowered being whose body she borrowed when a superpowered being was needed.

"I don't know if they're calling you a 'junior' partner. You looked pretty co-equal out there on the street the other day," Dana said. "And that fire-spitting trick is something a little more than Myke can do."

"That's not the point. That name makes me sound like some sort of sidekick," Terri said. "Don't I get to define my own identity?"

Dana looked at the headline and back up at the university professor and newly minted superheroine.

"That's the thing about celebrity, you can't always control what the media is going to do," she said. "The best you can do is manage it. My advice? Roll with it. 'Mykala Phoenix' is kind of catchy, it ties you right in with one of the most well-known and respected figures in Astor City, and face it, girl, there's a phoenix on your chest."

The wind went out of Terri Travers' sails.

"Mykala Phoenix," Terri said. "It's a silly name."

"So is Myke Phoenix, when you come to that," Dana said. "Mychus the Warrior sounds much more dignified. The phoenix emblem ties him back to the Soulkeeper and the Phoenix itself, but to be honest, he came up with the name Myke Phoenix as a joke. The Soulkeeper liked it, and it stuck. You can call yourself Mychala with that hint of a Germanic "ch" sound all you want, but the tide is going to carry you along as Mykala Phoenix. Just roll with it."

Terri Travers sighed.

"All right," she said. "I guess in the general scheme of things, it's a small difference and not that important."

"Right. If you're the only thing standing in the way of rampaging aliens and giant spiders, nobody's going to care how to spell your name."

And from that moment on, the name of Astor City's newest champion was Mykala Phoenix.

Somewhere outside of Astor City in the hidden alien spacecraft, a regrouping of sorts was in progress.

"This was a defeat. You losst thiss battle," said a furtive figure in the corner. "But you have not losst the war."

"We have lost our leader," the voice of an alien blob entered everyone's minds. "You do not understand our culture. This is a moment of devastation."

"Have you lost leaderss before?" the furtive figure said. "What do you do at those timess?"

A murmuring of minds echoed around the room.

"Exactly," said the figure. "You move on. You start over. You get a new leader, and you win the war."

"Surely," said another blob, anticipating the figure's next words, "you are not proposing to lead us yourself?"

"You foolss," the furtive figure said, drawing herself up to her full height of about 4 feet and stepping from the shadows. Her reptilian eyes darted around the room, she clenched and unclenched the deadly claws on her smallish hands, and her tail lashed back and forth. "I have been leading you for weekss. You ssimply did not understand. Yess, I shall lead you, and I shall lead you to victory. Thiss planet will be ourss, or my name is not Deinonychus!"

The room was silent except for the triumphant laughter of a small but lethal dinosaur. But in the consciousness of all present, the sound of supportive cheering echoed around the walls.

And the deinonychus claw stolen from the Astor City Museum was still missing.

THE END

Claws of Death

Prologue

THE dinosaur muttered to herself as she walked toward an alien spacecraft in the woods outside Astor City, a medium-sized city built on the fork of two rivers. Behind her strolled an elephant-sized presence.

Excuse me?

Why, yes, I did say, "The dinosaur muttered to herself." Why do you ask?

No such thing as a talking dinosaur? You're new here, aren't you?

Let's just say that when your species has been around for several million years, you pick up a few things along the way. Speech and language, for example.

Our modern-day birds are said to be descended from dinosaurs, and you hear them talking all of the time, chattering away in the trees or calling to each other as they fly through the air.

Yes? Well, of course you can't understand what they're saying. They don't speak English, after all.

So: The dinosaur muttered to herself as she walked toward an alien spacecraft in the woods outside –

What is it now?

Yes, as a matter of fact, she *was* muttering in English. That was her first tongue. And, I might add, a story for another day.

When you hear that story – on another day! – you will see that it's perfectly logical she learned English first. For now – because the fate of Astor City, and perhaps the world, depends on my telling *this* story rather than *that* one – please accept that the dinosaur was muttering to herself in English as she walked toward an alien spacecraft in the woods outside Astor City. Behind her strolled an elephant-sized presence.

"Enough of this infernal skulking in forests," is what she was muttering to herself, if you must know. "It's time we regrouped and took our final action."

It wasn't a large woods, but it was thick – thick enough that you could hide a dinosaur and an alien spacecraft in it. Deinonychus – for that is her name, this dinosaur – approached the spacecraft as if she owned it, and perhaps she did own it after spending weeks essentially in charge of the aliens inside. This fact became clear when the roundish door to the craft opened at her approach.

Inside were four bloblike, demoralized creatures. She knew they were demoralized not because of any obvious body language – for the body language of a blob is hard to read – but because she had been with them recently when they suffered a major loss. Their leader, who had ventured into Astor City and taken control of the minds and bodies of several key individuals, had recently perished at the hands of the superpowered warrior named Myke Phoenix and his new partner, whom the media were calling Mykala Phoenix.

The humans had a chemical compound, which they used to wash their hair, that had proved deadly to the blobs. Knowing its lethal qualities, years ago humans under alien control had purchased the company that manufactured the compound – "Yucca Daisy" – and quietly closed it, but the Phoenixes' half-duck, half-man ally named Quincy Quackenbos had retro-engineered the compound and mixed a new batch.

The blobs had adopted Deinonychus as their leader in part because their late, lamented leader had acted in consort with the dinosaur and in part because – let's face it – they were afraid of her.

She stood only 4 feet high, a mere 1.2 meters, but she had razor-sharp teeth as well as claws on all four extremities. The claws at the ends of her short arms were for shredding, and the massive, angry-looking claws on her feet were for tearing. Her name – the name of her species – came from the Greek *deinos onukh*, meaning "terrible claw."

Deinonychus looked around the control room of the ship, which some might consider festive and natural, being covered in plant life to sustain the blobs over long journeys through space.

"Are you all sstill moping?" she snarled. "No wonder the humanss have defeated you twice."

"Perhaps we should let the humans have their planet," a voice spoke into her mind, for the blobs (having no mouths) spoke with their thoughts. "There are easier worlds to conquer that would suit us just as well."

"Oh, buck up, matiess," the dinosaur said scornfully. "This world iss worth dying for, and exterminating the humanss will be a favor to the universssse."

"Why do you hate the humans so? They seem like a pleasant enough species when not provoked," asked another blob.

Deinonychus stalked over to the blob who had "spoken" up until she was hovering over it with clear menace. Dinosaur body language usually is much easier to read than blob body language, but not so this time: The blob began to quiver.

"'A pleasant enough species when not provoked,' you say? Why, yes, I suppose that's true," she spat – not hissing as much when she was agitated. "But they rise in arms at the tiniesst provocation, especially when their foolish rulers tell them to."

"I believe you are jealous," a third blob said. "There are billions of humans on this planet, and you are the last of your species. Exterminating the humans would even the score. You call them foolish, but destroying the humans is a fool's errand. We value our lives more than your craven plans. Why should we follow you?"

The deinonychus is a swift and vicious creature. Before any of the other blobs could react, Deinonychus raced across the room and slashed the third blob to pieces.

"Because I demand it!" she said as she slashed and dissembled the questioning alien.

At that moment the elephant-sized presence that had been strolling through the woods with Deinonychus appeared at the door. It was a massive spider.

As the remains of the murdered blob twitched at her feet, the spider spit a stream of fire and ignited the pieces of dying flesh.

For a few moments there was no sound in the room except the crackle and sputtering of the small fire. Deinonychus rose to her full height and looked around.

"We can accept that reasoning," one of the blobs said at last. "What would you like us to do?"

Act 1
Jurassic Journey

PERHAPS we should back up a bit. After all, the last time anyone had a clear view of the talking dinosaur, she was disappearing into the sky in the talons of a phoenix, nearly 10 years ago. Actually, not "a" phoenix, but "The" Phoenix, a mythical bird – which as we now know is not a myth at all – with a life span of 500 years that, upon dying, erupts into flames and rises reborn from the fire.

Through means that you and I may never understand, the Phoenix erased Deinonychus' memories and left her to fend for herself in a forest in Bavaria.

Now, when you hear the phrase "a forest in Bavaria," you may think of something exotic, perhaps a mysterious stranger or an arcane monster mystery involving vampires or experiments gone horribly wrong. Or perhaps you think of a motor works that makes fine automobiles. Or maybe you anticipate the taste of an elegant lager.

Bavaria may not be the first place where you expect a dinosaur that has lost her memory to be wandering through a forest, hunting, eating, and trying to remember who she is.

And yet our story begins quite some months earlier in that Bavarian forest, and there is that lost dinosaur, dining on the remains of a deer that wandered too close to the river and did not hear the hissing of the velociraptor over the gurgle of the water.

For years now the rumors of the deinonychus creature had flown about the region. It was said that one day a great bird singing an unspeakably beautiful song had soared overhead, a strange reptile clutched in its talons, and dropped the little beast into the heart of the forest, there to live out its days as a soulless predator with no mind. Every once in a while a man or a boy would claim to have seen the small dinosaur, but just in a glimpse, because the terrible animal was as afraid of being seen as we were afraid of seeing it.

Today is the day that would change, to the detriment perhaps of all humanity.

The two hunters walked carefully and as silently as they could, hoping to raise up the huge buck that also was known to haunt these woods. They had scouted this area for weeks and were certain this time they would take him down.

"Rudy, shush," one said as the other stepped not-so-gently into a crinkly mass of fallen leaves. Rudy cringed and looked up sheepishly.

"Sorry, Hans," he said. (Actually, he said "Es tut mir leid, Hans," but your humble narrator is translating for you. You're welcome.)

There came a rustling and a stir ahead. Hans held out his hand for Rudy to remain completely stock still. Both men readied their weapons.

The rustling had come from the direction of a small outcropping of rock not far from where they were standing. They saw a movement at the base of the outcropping and raised their rifles in hopes of spotting the great buck.

But instead of the majestic antlered animal they anticipated, they were shocked to see a smallish, hairless creature walking upright on two muscular legs, with a long reptilian snout baring razor-sharp teeth, and a long tail. At the ends of its limbs were sharp claws – an especially lethal-looking claw protruded from the angry thumb-like toe on each of its three-toed feet.

It was the dinosaur of local legend. And it snarled at them.

That was enough to startle Rudy into shooting. The bullet whizzed past and over the dinosaur, striking the rock outcropping and knocking loose a stone, which flew through the air and struck the dinosaur in the side of the head.

The beast – perhaps 1.2 meters high – was knocked over by the blow. It stood back up, shook its head and, impossibly, spoke.

"You dare to shoot at me? Do you know who I am?" the beast snarled indignantly, then tilted its head to one side. "Wait. *I* know who I am! The spell is lifted."

Hans and Rudy looked at each other in confusion.

"It speaks?!"

They turned back and began to raise their guns again, but it was too late. The dinosaur had quickly closed the distance and was upon them with razor-sharp teeth and terrible claws of death.

"I am not some helpless creature of the forest. I am Deinonychus!" the dinosaur shouted over Hans and Rudy's pitiful remains. "I have scuttled about this forest in fear and ignorance for years, thanks to the Phoenix and its feeble human servant. They shall pay for this! They shall pay."

The two hunters' bodies were found a couple of days later and a massive hunt was launched for the creature who had killed them. After a while, a mountain lion was cornered, and if it could speak, the great cat's final words may have been a plaintive, "What'd I do? What did I do?!"

For a time the talking dinosaur stayed in the Bavarian forest, biding her time and plotting her return. In later conversations she would refer to this as her time in exile. But it wasn't long before she was ready and, with no great love of Bavaria and what it represented in her life, she departed.

In the days that followed, a series of dinosaur sightings was made between Bavaria and the coast of France. Here and there a farmer reported the gruesome death of one of his animals as the beast had a meal. The attacks remained a mystery to the local authorities, but you and I know it was a small dinosaur, raised from extinction and making its way west.

The details of the journey across the Atlantic Ocean and half of the United States are less interesting than you might expect. It should have been very interesting indeed – after all, this was a dinosaur, alive in the present day, and if truth be told it was the very dinosaur that had nearly killed the superhero Myke Phoenix a few years earlier after serving as the crime boss of Astor City for many months, ruling the underworld with the terror of those claws of death – but it seem she crossed the ocean and half of a huge country without anything interesting happening at all.

In point of fact, saying she "nearly" killed Myke Phoenix is not quite an accurate phrase: The great warrior's heart had stopped beating altogether after a deadly fight with the talking dinosaur, and he returned only after weeks of a strange, unexplained absence. As for the dinosaur, a great mysterious bird singing an impossibly beautiful song had swooped down and grabbed the beast in its talons, soaring away with the struggling dinosaur on a fateful mission to a Bavarian forest.

But as I said, nothing especially noteworthy happened on Deinonychus' furtive journey back to Astor City until one night weeks later, when she at last was approaching the city limits, walking along the banks of the Shikaakwa River just south of town.

She could hear a great commotion, shooting and explosions far above her on the cliffs, and as a result the dinosaur was walking slowly and carefully and out of sight.

As she turned a bend in the river under the highest cliff, a great mass suddenly dropped from the sky and landed on her back with a rude plop.

"Whoof!" said Deinonychus.

It was a spider the size of an elephant, and it was wounded and dazed. Only the fact that the spider had shot a web out to break its fall prevented the little dinosaur from being squashed.

The giant creature's eight eyes flickered. Spotlights from above darted onto the water but failed to reach the two impossible figures along the river bank.

"What happened to you, my pretty?" asked the talking dinosaur, studying the gunshot wounds and bruises and burns that the firespider had sustained during its rampage through the city.

The only response was a whimper of physical pain and spidery sorrow. The giant beast had no way of telling Deinonychus that Myke Phoenix had just killed her offspring with a humongous fly swatter, but that act did cause a psychic scar.

"Such a mighty weapon you could be," the dinosaur said, petting the side of the giant spider and looking it over admiringly as if it were some majestic horse. "Such a mighty weapon you are."

It was a month or so later, as Deinonychus camped in the woods west of Astor City, that a rumbling and crashing sound came from a distance.

"Stay here," the dinosaur instructed her giant spider companion and went off to follow the sound.

The woods opened into a farm or two, which became a residential area, and on the side of a hill in an open field in the middle of the suburban homes something had crashed and buried itself into the ground. About an hour after leaving the spider, the dinosaur watched from some bushes as the area was cordoned off. She saw that infernal reporter Paul Phillips talking with a man she did not know who had emerged from within the crash site, then a small landslide covered whatever was under the soil and debris.

Biding her time for a few hours, she crept into the dug-out site and discovered a spaceship. The door was open.

The inside of the ship was described as a "steampunk greenhouse" in a report about those events colorfully titled *Invasion of the Body Borrowers*. Plant life covered the spherical main control room, and unearthly machines lined the walls and ceiling. Five beings that could best be described as blobs tended the flora and devices.

"You appear to be a native animal of this planet, and yet we sense sentience," a voice with no sound spoke into Deinonychus' consciousness.

"Ah, you communicate with your minds," the dinosaur replied out loud. "Intriguing."

"You could be useful," came a different soundless voice, and she felt a heavy pinch in her brain. It was like a sharp headache, and Deinonychus felt a tug at her willpower as if someone were trying to seize control of her brain.

"You fools! Mind control cannot work on me," she said. "You need not conscript me into your plans by force. I will gladly help you conquer this wretched planet."

"How did you know – that is to say, what makes you think we're here to conquer you?"

"You shall never conquer me personally, but I offer my services in the pursuit of our mutual aims."

"Why should we work with you?" asked the blob nearest to the talking dinosaur.

We have already seen an example of Deinonychus' persuasive abilities. Suffice it to say, an alliance was born.

Over the next few days, Deinonychus helped map out a plan to repair their crashed ship using the enforced labor of human puppets – men and women were far more susceptible than she to having their bodies borrowed!

Deinonychus was back in the woods when accursed Myke Phoenix interfered and her allies made a premature effort to fly their ship away, exploding over the Shikaakwa River. But that wasn't the end of the alien invasion.

The blobs had shared that another scout ship had landed more safely, albeit more dramatically, in Chelyabinsk, Russia, and taken possession of several high-ranking officials in a nearby city called Popeysk.

"Good, good," Deinonychus said. "Taking over government operatives is a stroke of genius."

"How so?" the blobs asked.

"The government rules everyone else," the dinosaur said. "People will listen and obey no matter how absurd the orders are – their leaders are the perfect puppets for your purposes."

Deinonychus and the aliens arranged for that ship to make its way to Astor City at a later time, and she suggested that the ship land in the more inobtrusive wooded area where she and the spider were hiding.

But first, a flashback within a flashback –

Act 2
The Quackenbos Formula

QUINCY Quackenbos never did get used to working with a talking dinosaur, which was ironic, because he was a talking duck.

Not exactly a duck, of course. When he was a little boy, he got caught in a nuclear explosion while holding his beloved pet duck, Quacky. The radioactive blast should have scattered the atoms of his body to the four winds, but – as frequently seems to happen in tales of superhero fantasy – instead the explosion worked in the other direction, fusing the minds and bodies and souls of the two young creatures into a single, once-in-a-lifetime being.

This was a fortunate arrangement for Quacky, because the average lifespan of a duck is far fewer years than 60. It was not such a fortunate arrangement for Quincy, who had been the only half-man half -duck in existence for more than six decades. For a few years this drove him mad, and he devoted his life and energy for evil intent. This is a scene from that insane time of his life.

It is several years ago and the duck man – considerably taller than you'd expect a duck to be but somewhat shorter than you'd expect a full-grown man to be – is working in a lab coat surrounded by the equipment and accoutrements of a fully equipped chemical research laboratory. His work has been interrupted by the arrival of a fearsome-looking but small dinosaur – perhaps four feet high, or a tad taller; hard to say because she always crouched as if ready to spring and removed chunks of your body from your body.

With the hubris born of madness, she had given herself the name befitting the last of her kind. That is to say, she named herself after her entire species, reasoning that as the last of her kind she *was* her entire species. As we've already established, she was called Deinonychus.

"I don't have it," Quincy broke the silence, answering the only question he ever expected her to ask. "I don't know if I'll ever have it."

"That iss not an acceptable answwer," the grim dinosaur replied.

"Wak!" A small puff of smoke or steam rose from a test tube, and Quincy Quackenbos made a notation on his computer. "Look, your mightiness," saying this with a trace of sarcasm in his voice, "Myke Phoenix can't be wounded, or I didn't think so until you found a way to cut him and get me a healthy sample of his blood. But the blood has the ability to neutralize every poison I've managed to throw at it. And even if it were possible to wound him or poison him, he has some sort of healing power beyond anyone's understanding."

"That iss why I have turned to the greatest chemist of thiss generation to find the answwer," Deinonychus hissed. "Do not disappoint me, duck man. The Forcess of Evil in the World are counting on you."

"When you put it that way, how can I not succeed?" Quincy said, now fully sardonic as he typed another observation into his computer. "Every time I think I'm getting close, I hit a dead end. I've never seen blood react like this. The guy's human but he's something more than human. But you already knew that from the bullets bouncing off him and the super strength and all."

Deinonychus paused as if considering this information, then turned to go.

"All right," she said. "But I would like to see results ssoon, Quackenbosss. Very ssoon."

"Yeah, yeah, yeah," the chemist said, waving a feathered hand in dismissal and peering into a microscope. The door closed with a slam.

When the door opened a few minutes later, Quincy Quackenbos did not look up.

"I still don't have it," he said. "Did you really think I'd have results in 10 minutes? Oh!"

The reason Quincy said "Oh!" was that when he he did look up, instead of a small, vicious-looking dinosaur, he saw a tall, blond-haired man in a white costume. The image of a red-and-gold bird was emblazoned on his barrel chest – the image of a phoenix, in point of fact.

"Hello, Quincy," Myke Phoenix said, grabbing the fowl chemist by the shoulders with a firm grip before he could make any other moves. "It's over."

When Quincy Quackenbos was released from prison, she arranged for him to be kidnapped by a ninja squad and questioned about his long-ago assignment to develop a serum that would assassinate Myke Phoenix. Her squad installed a tracking cookie in his personal computer in the event his publicly-stated reformation was real and he was no longer willing to cooperate.

And he did refuse to cooperate. Oh, what a pitiful sight he was, feigning indignation and quacking like a duck as her assistant tried to reason with him, then shouting into the one-way window at her.

"Is that you? You're back?" the duck man quacked. "Is that you in there? You filthy little reptile. I'm telling you, there is no formula!"

A short time later, police raided the facility accompanied once again by the infernal superhero.

Her assistant dashed from the interrogation room and into the adjacent observation cubicle.

"I suggest we tallyho," he said.

"Take me with you," begged a henchman who had been watching with Deinoynchus. The well-dressed assistant knocked him out with a sudden blow.

"Sorry, old chap, there's only room in my car for one person and one dinosaur."

As they sped away from the scene, Deinonychus vowed that the superhero's days were numbered.

"How many timess do I have to sssay that Myke Phoenix musst die before he actually diesss?" she hissed in frustration.

Time passed. The dinosaur had taken refuge in an abandoned cabin she and the spider found in the woods where she had suggested the aliens land, anticipating their eventual arrival. The spider's wounds had healed, leaving scars.

For the sake of making a long story shorter, I have passed over the moment when Deinonychus discovered this was no mere giant spider, but a firespider – a creature that spit fire in addition to the usual spidery things that spiders do. The commotion that had been in progress not long before the firespider dropped on the dinosaur's head was a showdown with Myke Phoenix and other local authorities after the huge arachnid rampaged through the streets of Astor City like a baby daikaiju.

The two creatures, the small talking dinosaur and the elephant-sized firespider that only occasionally made a sound, became unlikely companions, not unlike you and I with our canine and feline companions. One day Deinonychus asked a question that perhaps she should have considered many weeks earlier.

"Are there any more creatures like you, my pretty?"

The giant spider furtively led Deinonychus into the city, or more precisely to the campus of the University of Astor City, and even more precisely to the sciences building and a specific locked laboratory, where the dinosaur discovered cages full of dozens of spiders the size of a small dog.

She broke all of the cages. Going to the window, she summoned her eight-legged companion to break a hole in the wall to let the creatures out. And out they scampered, some of them shooting streams of fire through the hole on their way to freedom.

"Come here, my little prettiess," she hissed cheerfully, but the critters did not yield to her will. Dozens of little arachnids scattered into the woods and would not come when she called. Deinonychus beckoned her giant firespider companion in hopes the little ones would respond to the mother of all firespiders, but the willful puppy-sized spiders had minds of their own.

And so Deinonychus and her ward watched from the underbrush as the little monsters disrupted a wedding in the nearby arboretum.

"Thiss will at leasst have the advantage of attracting the attention of Myke Phoenix," said the talking dinosaur.

But much to her surprise, it was not the white-clad superhero who arrived first. Instead, a tall, red-maned woman in a light blue tunic burst from the science building and began to sprint at blinding speed away, only to be diverted by the screams of the wedding party.

Deinonychus watched in awe as the woman attempted – with greater success – to round up the firespiders. Most astounding of all was the moment when the mysterious woman herself breathed fire!

And then Myke Phoenix arrived, and the two of them used their superpowers together to corral and tame the outbreak.

"This won't do," Deinonychus said, turning to the elephant-sized companion and saying, "Sic 'em!"

What happened in the next few minutes was transformational for the talking dinosaur. The giant spider climbed on the roof of the UAC gymnasium and the two superheroes prepared to combat her.

But then a professor came out brandishing a weapon filled with spider poison. For a university professor he bore a strong resemblance to Santa Claus.

"If you spray it in the face –" the man called up to the superheroes on the roof.

"That would probably kill it, Dad," the red-haired woman called down.

"Dad"? Deinonychus snarled from her hiding place.

In quick succession, Myke Phoenix jumped down and grabbed the lethal device, which looked like a child's water rifle, and jumped back up on the roof.

"We don't need to kill it!" the female phoenix hero said, but just then the big firespider spit fire at her, and Myke Phoenix responded by squirting it between the eyes, twice.

Howling in pain, the great creature retaliated by blasting the hero with fire and webbing him to the roof, then jumped to the ground and ran into the woods, knocking Santa Claus aside as it staggered away.

Instead of chasing the spider, the superwoman cried "Dad!" and knelt at the professor's side.

Deinonychus hissed in anger from her hiding place. The woman (who she would later learn was named Mykala Phoenix) looked up, and the dinosaur would swear they made eye contact, but Mykala stayed with the man – her father?! – and the dinosaur turned to chase after the giant spider. After she caught up, the unlikely pair furtively made their way back to the woods outside town to wait for another opportunity.

The spider would take some time to recover from the chemical spray while Deinonychus continued to aid the aliens from behind the scenes, waiting for her opportunity to make a final attack on Myke Phoenix and his new partner.

Now our attention finally begins to shift back to the present day. A well-dressed man with an elegant accent knocks on the cabin door, and she lets him in.

"We've had a spot of good luck," the man said. "The I.T. people have finally broken the encryption on the materials our ninja team collected from Quincy Quackenbos' computer."

"Ssix months," she replied. "It'ss about time."

"Well, if I may, if you hadn't slain our best woman for failing to decrypt the files after three months, we might have had this information a tad sooner."

She looked at him sharply, and he smiled serenely.

"I should have killed you a long time ago," she muttered.

"And I am grateful every moment that you choose to let me live," the well-dressed man said. "The important thing is that Quincy Quackenbos succeeded long before he was captured and rehabilitated."

"What?!"

"Yes. He developed a formula that broke down the sample of Myke Phoenix's blood rather effectively. Goodness knows why he chose not to tell you. We found it among the deleted files. He must have tried to remove it after we planted the tracking cookie."

"You're right, Smothers. This is 'a sspot of good luck,' indeed," the dinosaur said. "It meanss I can come out of the shadowss and confront my old enemy directly at lasst. How soon can we recreate the formula?"

"I imagine it will not take very long at all. I took the liberty of delivering the pertinent files to our labs."

"Very good, very good." She stared out the window at the bright fall colors and falling leaves. "Finally, finally, it'ss time for Myke Phoenix to die."

Act 3
Before the storm

JOSIAH Petri had been the Astor County medical examiner since a few months after the Phoenix flew off with Deinonychus and erased her memories, all those years ago. It seems Josiah's predecessor had gone to prison for doing errands for the talking dinosaur, including collecting and delivering a vital sample of Myke Phoenix's blood to Quincy Quackenbos.

The new medical examiner was a fairly straight shooter and definitely had no inclinations toward consorting with bad guys as his predecessor had. He knew his business, too. Dr. Petri wasn't just a discoverer of what went wrong when a person died; he was a full-blown forensic scientist who routinely helped authorities, and a certain superhero, in finding the most interesting clues at crime scenes and the like.

He did have his quirks, which led him to become a good friend to Myke Phoenix and – not so coincidentally – to Paul Phillips, the crusading reporter who happened to be Myke Phoenix's alter ego. Through the course of that friendship he had met and fallen in love with Dr. Terri Travers of the University of Astor City, one of the world's foremost arachnologists who was called in when giant fire-spitting spiders began to appear here and there.

You hear tell of unrequited love, where one person is incredibly attracted to another who barely knows he or she exists. This was definitely not one of those cases. Dr. Terri Travers requited Josiah's love in a very big way. They were on track to living happily ever after until she was chosen to be Astor City's second superpowered protector.

Mykala Phoenix had emerged unexpectedly a few weeks earlier while Terri Travers was busy testing her biologist father's attempt to restore her right hand, which had been badly damaged when it got in the way of a firespider's fire – not just any firespider, mind you, but the very elephant-sized firespider that had recently been keeping company with a talking dinosaur.

Much as Paul Phillips assumed the mighty body of the ancient warrior Mychus through machinations which he never completely understood, Dr. Terri Travers had begun sharing the body of Mychus' daughter, Mychala, who was similarly empowered. Actually, Mykala had the added benefit – if superpowers can be considered benefits, and they usually are – of being able to spit fire like the firespiders, a side effect of her father's experiment that carried over. Did I mention that her father accidentally created the fire-spitting giant spider? He just had a knack for accidents.

Myke and Mykala exchanged bodies but not souls with the ancient heroes, whose souls had long ago passed to the next level of existence, according to the Soulkeeper of Kiribati, the mysterious vase who facilitated the exchange and somehow kept in psychic touch with the Phoenix and the flow of good and evil in the world. How these magnificent ancient bodies were preserved for this process is a mystery as complete as how their bodies were healed of their rare injuries while they were away from this plane. In fact, Mychus was brought back (again) from apparent death after being brutally slashed by Deinonychus just before the

Phoenix intervened those years ago, just before Josiah Petri became Astor County medical examiner.

Josiah had wrapped his head around many a shock through the years. But he was having a bit of trouble wrapping his head around the greatest shock of his life: the idea that his beloved was a superhero.

"You're having trouble – listen to what you're saying, Josiah," Terri said as the two of them stood in the kitchen of her apartment. "You've been working with Myke Phoenix for years. In the last year you've fought firespiders, you've had your mind and body confiscated by aliens twice, and you've accepted a duck man as your friend and colleague. What is different about *this?*"

"I don't know," he admitted. "Maybe it's the idea that Myke is always running into danger. I don't like the idea of you running into danger with him."

"That's because it's not as dangerous to us. Mykala's body is bulletproof, she's super-strong and fast, and oh by the way, she spits fire," she spat back. "And did I mention – " she paused to send a stream of fire from deep down her throat into the kitchen sink – "Mykala got that flame trick from me?"

It was true. Dr. Jacob Travers had given his daughter a potion concocted from the venom of a firespider, in hopes it would help restore her crippled right hand. Instead it would have killed her if not for the mysterious healing power of the Soulkeeper, and it had the additional side effect of passing the spider's flame-throwing habit along.

"OK, maybe it's the opposite," Josiah stammered. "I'm a guy, my instinct is to protect you. Maybe I need to get used to the idea that you are suddenly the physically stronger one. You don't need me for that anymore."

"But I still need you," Terri smiled, and suddenly the extremely attractive, oval-faced scientist was six inches taller, her face was square and still extremely beautiful, and her hair was a red mane that cascaded wildly around her head and halfway down her back. She reached her arms around his neck. "Doesn't this just make everything more interesting?"

"OK, you're freaking me out a little here," he said, taking a step back and holding a hand up defensively. "Can I have Terri back, please?"

She sighed loudly and was normal again.

"Thank you," Josiah said, and he reached out and stroked her plain, straight hair. "I didn't fall in love with a super heroine, Terri. I fell in love with you."

"She's still me! It's me in that body."

"I know, I guess," he said, drawing her close and kissing the top of her head. "But I like this body. Like I said: I fell in love with you, not Mykala Phoenix."

"Awww," she said, snuggling in and returning the hug. "You always say the right thing." The hug continued for a moment, and then she looked up. "You're not just saying that, are you?"

"No," he laughed. "Let's use Mykala's body for saving the city and this body for saving my soul from utter loneliness."

"It's a deal," she said.

"Where are they?"

Dana Dunsmore Phillips looked up from her reading at her husband, Paul, who was peering out the window into the woods behind her home. He was standing next to a young, white – excuse me, English cream, if you please – golden retriever, who leaned into his leg until he started scratching the top of her head.

"Where are who?"

"The aliens," Paul said, turning toward her. "They took over the mayor and city council and went marching through the city with those creepy reptile-insect looking soldiers, and when we killed that one blob the spell was broken and the soldiers scattered. But where did they go? The blobs don't travel alone." He stopped petting the pup, but she pawed at his leg and looked up at him with pleading eyes. "I'm sorry, Goombah," he said, dropping to one knee and gathering her into his arms.

"Where did they go after you beat them the first time?" Dana said. "They were trying to go home until their spaceship blew up over the river. Maybe this bunch just went home."

"That would be great. But given the last year, I'm not counting on it."

"And you shouldn't," said a third voice from the top shelf in the dining room. A green and not-very-attractive vase sat on the shelf, seemingly minding its own porcelain business except for the voice impossibly emanating from it. This was the afore-mentioned Soulkeeper of Kiribati. "They're still somewhere in the neighborhood. Not literally," it said as Paul looked sharply back at the window. "I mean I can sense an alien presence somewhere in the general area of the city. Probably outside the city, out in the country."

"How do you know?"

"Because if it was inside the city, their spaceship would get noticed," replied the voice, which sounded like a male but sounded female at the same time. "Eighteen years of this and you never got any smarter."

"Sit and have your coffee, dear," Dana said, motioning to the easy chair and the steaming cup on the table next to it. "If the aliens come back, you'll be one of the first to know."

"You're probably right," Paul said, but the dog jumped into the easy chair before he reached it. She looked up at him and her tail wagged loudly against the arm. "Off, Goombah." She complied, and he sat down.

"She was just keeping it warm for you," his auburn-haired wife smiled.

"I know," he said, and scratched the canine behind the ears gently. "Such a good Goombah you are. Such a good dog. I guess you're right, hon. Short of conducting a search over the countryside for an alien spaceship that may or may not be there, I guess it's hurry up and wait."

A rap came at the door of a certain cabin in the woods.

"Enter," said Deinonychus, the talking dinosaur, who was reclined in a chair poring over documents on an electronic tablet.

The door opened and in walked Smothers, her meticulously groomed assistant.

"I've never quite grown accustomed to the giant spider lurking in the woods just beyond the clearing," Smother shivered. "But I don't suppose I'd notice it if I didn't know to look."

"The spider is harmless – to you," Deinonychus said. "Like any creature, it just wants to be left alone and makess a willing ally if you treat her gently."

"I have never thought of you as gentle," the assistant observed.

"You have never given me a reason to be gentle," the dinosaur snapped. "Why must you alwayss insult me, Smotherss?"

"For some strange reason, it seems to keep me alive."

"You have a point there," Deinonychus laughed mirthlessly. "You do amuse me, Smotherss. Why have you come?"

"The lab has finished production," he said, and held out a small bottle by its thin neck. "May I present the Quackenbos Formula?"

The serum had an odd color that was not red and was not pink, a much lighter red than the color of blood but a deeper pink than a flamingo. It was a heavy liquid, perhaps the consistency of cooking oil. It shone in the dim light.

"Very good, Smothers, very good," the dinosaur said, extracting the bottle from his assistant with her claws.

She uncapped the bottle and set it on the table. One by one she dipped her claws into the container and made sure the serum coated them completely. She carefully poured the substance over her larger feet claws, paying special attention to the large claw that protruded from her big toe – the *deinos onukh* that gave her species its name.

Deinonychus flexed her deadly hands. "And you're confident thiss exactly replicatess Quackenbos's work?"

"I knew you would accept no less," Smothers smiled.

"Well, then." She showed her teeth in what no doubt was meant as a smile. "Thank you, Smothersss. Stay here. This next part will not require your servicess."

Deinonychus stalked through the forest to the alien spaceship, followed by the great firespider. The craft's door opened and she walked in among the blobs.

"The time has come," she declared without preamble. "Releasse the Zembella!"

Act 4
The lethal scratch

THE Zembella are a proud race who live on a planet far, far from here, but not so far that it is out of the range of the spacecraft our strange blob friends operate. (And perhaps "friends" is not the most appropriate word, seeing as they seem to be intent on seizing our world and disposing of us.)

One day said blobs landed on the Zembellan planet and used their manipulative powers to kidnap and control several dozen of them. After their experience with having humans repair their ship – insufficient as those repairs proved to be – the blobs caught upon the idea of keeping a group of workers with them in space to take care of odd jobs, such as maintenance and repair. Humans, however, were deemed too fragile for such work.

The Zembella, on the other hand, appeared to be hale and hearty, so rather than release their captives the blobs took them along for the ride. Their insect-reptilian nature did indeed keep their bodies more intact than humans would have been, but the poor things died anyway working out there in space. The good news for the blobs was that the Zembella's exoskeleton-protected bodies did not deteriorate very much after death, so the animated corpses were still useful for a variety of purposes.

This rather ghoulish arrangement led to the Zembella marching one night through the streets of Astor City. After Myke Phoenix, Mykala Phoenix and Quincy Quackenbos thwarted that attack, the blobs and Deinonychus put their heads together to come up with an alternative plan – the one that involved dipping the dinosaur's claws with a serum that Quackenbos himself had devised back when he used his genius for evil rather than good.

And that brings us to today.

Hank Gosling liked to take a walk by himself through the neighborhood before going to bed. The neighborhood wasn't quite what it used to be, but most nights it was perfectly safe to stroll a block or two under the streetlights. He usually walked down to the University of Astor City entrance and back. That gave him a good half-mile of walking, which at his age was plenty.

That was how Hank Gosling came to be the first person to witness a strange procession: A four-foot-high reptile that looked very much like the nasty dinosaur critters he had seen in four different movies over 20 years, followed by several dozen tall uniformed creatures that appeared to be a cross between a reptile and an insect, shuffling along as if they were marching puppets but still making a brisk "clop-clop-clop-clopping" sound with their boots as they marched in unison. And behind all of them, a box truck driven by a well-dressed man.

Hank fished his phone out of his pocket and dialed 911.

Dr. Terri Travers was working late in the UAC science building. Her conversation with Josiah had continued for some hours after we left them, but then she needed to check on a number of specimens at the university. Oh, let's admit it: The cluster of firespiders that her father had raised was in a locked room in the biology labs, her father was still in the hospital after the recent attack, and someone had to make sure the firespiders were still secure and fed.

She heard the crash of the building's front door and instantly transformed into the superheroine Mykala Phoenix. One of the convenient aspects of the arrangement was that she changed in less than a blink, sometimes even before she knew there was danger. Thus, instead of an attractive scholarly woman in a lab coat, she was a powerful being in a blue tunic, ready to take on whatever was clop-clop-clopping up the hallway, and she recognized that sound.

Mykala grabbed her phone off the lab counter and dialed Paul Phillips.

"It sounds like the alien soldiers just broke into the science building," she said when Paul answered the phone.

The door to the lab slammed open. "And that looks like Deinonychus at the front of the line."

She heard Paul's voice on the phone yell, "Gotta go, hon," and then turned her attention to the tableau before her. The dinosaur stalked into the room followed by several of the tall alien soldiers that had served as sentries for the Astor City City Council when the mayor and the majority of the aldermen were controlled by aliens. (That few people had noticed the difference in the politicians' behavior was a matter of some discussion at the local bars.) Wait, it wasn't just several alien soldiers – they kept coming until there were a dozen, two dozen and more soldiers in the lab, and there seemed to be more in the hallway.

She had never seen Deinonychus in person, and so she almost lost her concentration on the other threats as she stared at the impossibly ancient creature. The reptilian, almost birdlike stare, the long nasty-looking claws, the tail that extended farther behind the rest of the dinosaur's body than logic demanded – she took in the sight as a disinterested scientist might, not in her more immediate role as potential victim of the horrible predator and her army of alien friends.

"Sso," the dinosaur said unblinkingly, pulling up next to a wall beside a bank of windows. "Myke Phoenix sent his little helper to guard the sspidersss. This will be interesting."

Mykala took a deep breath and exhaled a roaring flame that caught Deinonychus full in the face.

"AAAiiiiiieeeeeeee!" squealed the dinosaur. Just at that moment, Myke Phoenix arrived, and rather than coming through a door or window like a civilized superhero, he burst through the wall of the lab and buried Deinonychus under a pile of brick and mortar. Desperate times, desperate measures, you know that drill.

Unfortunately, the attention paid to attacking the dinosaur leader had given the Zembella time to get to the door of the spider room. The tall puppets battered down the door and could be heard ripping screen away from the cages. Sure enough, canine-sized spiders began to appear in the doorway and crawl swiftly to the hole in the wall left by Myke's arrival.

"Be careful! The dinosaur's claws are the only thing that have ever cut me," he called to Mykala as they surrounded the pile of rubble.

"I'll steer clear," she replied, but suddenly found herself seized by three alien creatures. The Zembella grabbed her by the arms and one leg and lifted the warrior princess off the ground. She kicked with the other leg and one alien let go. Given her legs back, she was able to plant her feet, lift the other two aliens and pound them together. Remarkably, none of the three three aliens seemed to lose consciousness. "Why don't they fall?!"

"They're dead already, the blobs are manipulating their actions," Myke said as he pushed and punched the Zembella out of his path. "What we really need is some of that Yucca Daisy shampoo. We have to contact Quincy."

They had learned during their previous encounter that a spray of the ancient shampoo formula cut the connection between alien dead and bloblike being, and a direct hit of Yucca Daisy on the blobs proved fatal. The duck man chemist had reverse-engineered a bottle from the discontinued line and generated a supply against future attacks like this one. The problem with having such an easy solution was when the easy solution was across town and the attack was happening here.

One, then another, and then a small handful of small firespiders, and then a large handful, began to creep and then scurry out of the cage room and through the hole in the wall. Firespiders scattered into the night. The wail of sirens could be heard approaching.

"Someone must have called 911! Help is coming," Mykala called across the room as she shrugged off another four or five Zembella.

"We need to corral all these spiders and the alien soldiers – and is Deinonychus down for the count?" Myke held one Zembella by the hands and used it to swing a cleared area around himself so he could see the bigger picture.

The rubble where the talking dinosaur had disappeared began to move as if something were conscious and digging itself out.

From somewhere nearby came the sound of a truck starting and revving its engine. Headlights blinked on, and there came a screech of tires and the sound of the truck accelerating. The alien soldiers started shuffling out the door and the hole in the wall.

"The blobs must be in a vehicle of some kind," Mykala said, pushing Zembella aside and dashing through the wall. "If we stop them, we'll stop the soldiers at least."

Taillights from a box truck were already somewhat tiny up the street. She started running and pulled up short when a spider the size of an elephant stepped into her path.

The giant arachnid wasted no time. A bright flame washed over her and enveloped the warrior princess for several seconds. Having lost her right hand to those flames once, Terri Travers cried out in anticipation of pain. But Terri was now inhabiting the invulnerable body of Mykala

Phoenix, and the fiery heat made her uncomfortable but failed to disable her.

She drew from her own reserves and shot a countering stream of flame that caught the giant firespider between the eyes.

"SCREEEEEEEE!" said the beast.

"You don't like that either, do you?" Unfortunately, the flaming breath had its limits or she would have kept it up until the monstrous firespider ignited. Once she had argued to preserve the beast for scientific study purposes, but she took the loss of her hand personally, and she was not the only one to have been injured in the monster's attack months earlier.

And having been given custody of a body that had a fully functioning right hand, Terri Travers remembered how much she had lost. Therefore, no longer interested in studying the monster, she followed the flaming burst by charging the firespider and delivering a right hook to the monstrous face. The beast staggered back and climbed a streetlight pole, aiming for higher ground, but the pole bent and crashed to the ground in a shower of sparks. The off-balance spider crashed on top of Mykala.

Back in the lab, Myke Phoenix continued to struggle against a sea of animated alien soldier corpses. Although the blobs could control the bodies from afar, the superhero had figured out that they could not move bodies that were too damaged to work. He had begun using his great strength to its fullest, breaking legs and arms and spines until the remote controllers gave up on trying to move each particular soldiers.

It was grisly work, and as powerful as he was, Myke Phoenix hated to hurt anyone.

"Sorry," he said as he shattered one alien body, then another. "Sorry. Sorry, sorry."

The only mollifying factor was knowing that he was not killing the aliens, for they were already dead, their bodies reanimated by the psychic blobs. The fight was still quite unpleasant.

The aliens stopped trying to attack Myke and started trying to flee. He stepped through the hole to the outside and saw the giant spider by dim streetlight crouched in the middle of a parking lot. He thought the firespider was braced to jump at him, but then it suddenly rolled sideways, a long-haired woman leaped to her feet, and he realized the monster had been on top of Mykala.

"That was not fun," she said with a flourish of her mane. Rather than re-engage, the giant spider turned and scurried into a nearby wooded area, following a cluster of the smaller firespiders. "They didn't come here to fight us; this was all to break out the little ones!"

She turned toward Myke Phoenix just in time to shout, "Behind you! Look out!"

The blond-haired giant turned and instinctively jumped out of the way just as Deinonychus – having dug out from the rubble – leaped toward him. As if anticipating his dodge, as soon as she landed the dinosaur used her powerful feet to change direction and leap again, this time bowling him over with her feet.

She planted her feet on Myke Phoenix's barrel chest and drew her blistered face close to his, reptilian eyes gleaming by streetlight. Without a word she took one clawed finger and cut a deep scratch down the side of his face. Just as years earlier, Myke Phoenix's invulnerable skin yielded and tore under the dinosaur's claws of death.

He pushed her off and leaped to his feet. Immediately a wooziness struck him, and he shook his head as if to clear it. He sank back to his knees.

"Hokey smokes! What's happening?" Myke Phoenix said.

"Well! That worksss more quickly than I dared hope," Deinonychus hissed. "Feel that, hero? That's the poisson that your treacherous friend Quackenbosss created all these yearss ago. You're not going to stop me thiss time, Mychuss my ancient foe. You're dead!"

SWAT!

Mykala Phoenix had picked up the fallen streetlight post, and holding it like a gigantic baseball bat, she swung the pole and struck the talking dinosaur with all of her might. And all of the might of the warrior princess Mychala was very mighty indeed: Deinonychus sailed hundreds of yards through the air and crashed into the trees far across the parking lot.

She dropped the pole and rushed to the side of Myke Phoenix, who was still on his knees and holding his head with both hands.

"Myke! How bad is it?"

"Bad," he said, short breaths coming quickly, and then one big deep breath. "Call Quincy!"

Myke Phoenix pitched forward onto his face and was still.

Epilogue

A phone chirped and its screen lit up a corner of the darkness.

A feathered hand reached groggily toward the light.

"Great godfrey baggins," said a groggy voice. "It's the middle of the night." The little screen gave him Terri Travers' name.

He activated the call. "This better be good."

"Quincy! Myke's been drugged. Poisoned! Deinonychus said it was your formula." The voice of Mykala Phoenix spilled from the phone, breathless, anxious.

"Deinonychus? Formula? I destroyed that formula," said Quincy Quackenbos, his bill agape, suddenly wide awake but not awake enough to remember he had told everyone the formula never existed.

"She must have found it somehow, because he's real bad," Mykala said. "He's real bad, Quincy. We need the antidote. Quickly!"

Quincy Quackenbos swung out of bed, turned on the light and walked to his closet door, phone pressed to his ear.

"Antidote? I never figured I would need an antidote. The whole idea was to kill Myke Phoenix," Quincy said. "Mykala – there is no antidote."

Talons of Justice

Prologue

ON balance, there is more beauty in the world than squalor. From a vantage point miles above the ground, it all looks breathtaking.

Few sights can take breath like the Pacific Ocean, the grandest of all the seas. For thousands of miles in almost every direction is white-capped clear blue water. Above the ocean on this day soared the grandest of all birds.

Here and there, tiny dots of land poked heroically above the waves. The grand bird hovered above one of those dots.

The atoll was barely four-and-a-half miles long and one and a half-mile wide. Its most distinguishing characteristic was a large lagoon on its interior, so large that the actual land mass was a ring barely 500 feet wide around the lagoon. Thick foliage topped by coconut palms covered most of the land, giving lagoon-dwelling birds and other animals some protection from the Pacific winds.

Humans had attempted to settle on the atoll from time to time, but the lagoon was as salty as the surrounding ocean, so potable water was a constant problem for any would-be residents. No one had lived here for decades, and it was just as well. The great bird preferred the solitude.

Very few people have ever seen a phoenix. There's a good reason for that: In all the seven seas and seven continents across this vast plane, there is only one phoenix, and most of the time it preferred to live on this lonely atoll and seven others nearby. The bird had an expected life span of five centuries, and according to the legend it was to burst into flames upon its death, from which blaze would rise a grand new bird to live another 500 years. The pyre more often than not was on the beach of one of these islands. For that reason the little atolls have been named the Phoenix Islands.

The sun was high, and the air was so hot it could have been ablaze this day. The Phoenix rode an air current over the lagoon and watched the horizon.

Years had passed since the Phoenix had become directly involved in human affairs. There had been no need; the great bird had chosen a champion, and then a second. The ancient warrior Mychus and his daughter, Mychala, fought the forces of evil in the world on the Phoenix's behalf, and so the great bird soared and watched, soared and watched.

Suddenly its eyes sharpened and a cry of alarm escaped its throat almost without bidding. Having received a message by means unknown to us mere humans, the great bird turned deliberately and was away from the little island in seconds, flying to the northeast faster than any flying beast can be expected to travel.

A day of accounting had arrived.

Act 1

A hero fallen

"WAK! GIVE THE MAN AIR!!"

Quincy Quackenbos had been awakened from the deepest of deep sleep just 11 minutes earlier, and here he was in a parking lot at the University of Astor City standing over the body of Myke Phoenix. At least he thought it was merely a body, until the superhero groaned and turned himself over onto his back. That movement was Quincy's first clue that his friend was not yet dead.

"OK," the half-man half-duck said, waving a feathered hand in the air as if trying to write on a chalkboard. "OK. OK. What do we have here?"

"The dinosaur – Deinonychus – scratched him, and a few seconds later he just toppled," said a tall, strikingly attractive woman with long, wavy red hair and wearing a light blue tunic.

"OK. That's consistent with what I expected when I developed the formula." The scratch on Myke Phoenix's face was oozing blood. Quincy pulled a cloth handkerchief out of a pocket and pressed it to the wound, soaking it with blood. "Get him somewhere safe." The duck man suddenly looked around frantically. "Where's Deinonychus now?"

"I knocked her into next week with a light pole," said Mykala Phoenix. "She was with the big mama firespider and a boatload of these alien zombies," she said, indicating the strange armored creatures whose carcasses were scattered around the area. "I think they made a strategic retreat. Can you save him?"

"I don't know!" Quincy snapped. "I told you on the phone, the idea was to kill him, not bring him back ever. But I destroyed the formula. That is, I thought I had. How did Deinonychus get the formula?"

The tall woman grabbed the babbling duck man by the arm and squeezed.

"Look, Quincy, we need Myke not to die. Can you save him?"

"Ow?!" The expression of pain made her relax the grip a tad. "Of course I can. If I can make something like this, I can unmake it. I just don't know how much time it will take."

"We don't know how much time we have, do we?"

"No! So if you let go of me so I can get to my lab, I can WHOOOOAAAAAA!"

Mykala Phoenix had a better idea than letting Quincy Quackenbos go and get to his lab. She hauled him up into her powerful arms and took a flying leap.

"I can get you there faster than you can drive," she said as they sailed up, across the sky, and back down again. When they struck ground, she pushed back up with her mighty legs and repeated. Up, across, down, up, across, down, several times, and they landed at the entrance to Quackenbos Laboratories.

"OK, let me down and I'll get to the main lab."

"Which way?" she said, carrying him in her arms and sprinting faster than he could have.

"WAK! All right, fine, that big building over there."

She deposited him in his lab, where he fired up a computer and dropped the bloodied handkerchief into a plastic container to preserve it.

"I'm going to need help. Josiah Petri could be useful – Duckworth, too, but he doesn't know all of the secrets we know about you and Myke; Petri and I would have to be discreet," he muttered.

"What can I do? I'm a biologist, remember," Mykala Phoenix said.

Quincy looked at her.

"You're also all we've got to fight Deinonychus and the spiders and the aliens," said the duck man. "No, you go after them. But your father – yes, I can call him."

"He's still in the hospital!"

"Getting better, though, right?"

"Well –"

"Have an ambulance bring him over here. Myke, too, of course." He lifted the phone to his ear. "Dr. Petri? Quincy Quackenbos. Yes, I know it's the middle of the night, but we need your help."

Medical personnel were hovering over Myke Phoenix when she returned to the parking lot. They had moved him onto a hospital gurney. Several broken hypodermic needles were scattered on the ground from attempts to hook the invulnerable superhero up to an intravenous solution. Finally someone had realized the gash in his face was a way in, and a needle was taped in place at the wound. An attempt to stitch the cut shut had failed, too.

"How is he doing?" Mykala Phoenix asked.

"Are you family?" a paramedic replied, then looked up and saw the phoenix emblem on the superheroine's chest. "Close enough, I guess. He's been poisoned. I don't know what it's doing to him or how fast it's working, because we can't puncture his skin. How did he get this laceration?"

"He was slashed by Deinonychus, the dinosaur."

"So dinosaur claws can cut his skin. That's useful information. You don't happen to be the one who stole the deinonychus claw from the museum last month?"

"No, of course not."

"I'm kidding, don't worry."

From the wooded area that surrounded the university came strange sounds.

"Screeee! Screeee!"

"What in the name of John Wayne is that?" the paramedic said.

"Firespiders," she breathed. "There were dozens of them at large in the area, and zombie alien soldiers called the Zembella – that what these grotesque bodies are. Deinonychus herself took off – unless she's still over there where I dropped her with the streetlight pole."

The medic stared at the tall, red-maned woman in the blue tunic with an expression somewhere between shock and amusement.

"You are having a hell of a night, aren't you?"

"You don't know the half of it. Take him to Quackenbos Laboratories. Quincy Quackenbos is working on an antidote for the poison."

"We were heading for the hospital," he said, "but if that's the case the lab would be a better destination. I don't think he has much time."

"Do that," Mykala Phoenix said, turning toward the woods. "I'm going to round up some firespiders."

"Ms. Phoenix?" She turned. "Are you seeing anyone right now?"

"Right now I'm seeing not enough time to waste answering that question."

The campus was built on a series of rolling hills on the edge of Astor City, surrounded by an arboretum filled with native trees and other flora. Mykala walked urgently through the preserve talking to herself.

"OK, the lab and all of the cages are trashed; where am I going to put these things?" she said, striding purposefully along and looking for little arachnids on the ground – which is why she walked right into a spiderweb stretched across the pathway at eye level.

"Stupid, stupid, stupid," she said, brushing away the sticky stuff and looking up to see a dozen firespiders in the trees.

They all spat fire, bathing Mykala in an incandescent light. Still remembering the searing pain of the giant spider's flame as it ruined Terri Travers' right hand months ago, Mykala Phoenix marveled at her ability to feel the fire with the same searing intensity without damage to her body.

And then she spat fire back at the little firespiders, who made a surprised "screeee" sound and scurried into the dark.

"Girl, if only you were 100 feet tall, there'd be a place for you in the next Japanese monster movie," she said to herself.

The gymnasium locker room! While her mind was distracted by the task of fighting the little firespiders, an appropriate location for locking them up had risen from her subconscious.

"Now, how do we get them there?" She snatched one spider off a tree and another off the ground, lifting them by the scruff of the neck like two enormous, hideous kittens. "They're not that heavy, but I can only carry two at a time." She shrugged. "If that's what it takes –"

A dead Zembella warrior stepped into her path. The firespiders squirmed in her hands. She turned to her right, and another alien soldier was there. She looked to her left, and – long story short, she was surrounded.

Dana Dunsmore Phillips had stopped fearing for her husband's life years ago. After all, he was Myke Phoenix, who always came home from a scrap and turned back into good old Paul Phillips. She had almost forgotten what the fear felt like.

But it had all came rushing back when the phone rang at 3 a.m. and Quincy Quackenbos was on the other line. "Come quickly," he'd said. "I'll do the best I can, but I don't know –"

The stabbing pain in the chest, the tension in her belly – she didn't like this. She didn't like this at all.

Dana grabbed her big purse and rummaged around for her car keys. They had to be in there somewhere. She groaned in frustration and vowed to buy a smaller purse. "What do I need this gigantic bag for?"

"Take me with you," said an androgynous voice from the shelf in the dining room. "There are many forces at play tonight, and you're going to need me to read them all."

"Why not?" she said, her hand finally clutching the keys from the bag full of stuff. She grabbed the Soulkeeper of Kiribati off the shelf and tossed it unceremoniously into the purse.

"How do you fit all this debris in here?" came a voice from the purse as she nearly jumped into the garage and slammed the door behind her.

The golden retriever curled on an easy chair looked up, flickered her eyes and lay her head down again.

Josiah Petri burst into the lab on the run and found Quincy Quackenbos standing in front of a whiteboard scribbling the names of chemicals. Figures and symbols were linked by arrows and circles. It was a formula, and it wasn't. Mostly it looked like the doodles of a desperate duck man worried that the past life he had fled was catching up with him and threatening to kill one of his only friends.

"OK, what do you need?" Josiah said, shrugging off his jacket and getting ready to work.

"I don't know yet," Quincy said, waving a feathered hand at the chaotic writing. "I think this is what worked in the lab; I'm not 100 percent sure of the ratios. Was it two parts of this to one of that, or three parts?"

"That's a deadly compound in any combination. It would literally melt his red blood cells."

"Yes, it would melt your blood or mine, but not Myke Phoenix. That was what was so frustrating for so long, until I finally introduced sodium chloride by accident."

"Table salt?"

"Yes, that was the missing ingredient," Quincy said. "Stupid, isn't it? You whip up a killer cocktail that doesn't have any effect at all until you add a little salt."

"Last month we held off an alien invasion using a shampoo from the 1970s," Josiah said with a grim smile. "Nothing surprises me anymore."

The door burst open again and Dana Dunsmore Phillips exploded into the room.

"Where is he?" she demanded.

"Not here yet, but I think that's him coming," Quincy said, turning his head to the sound of an emergency siren approaching outside.

"Dana Phillips?" Josiah looked confused. "What are you doing here?"

"Why don't you just tell him to change?" Dana said.

"What?"

"Change back into Paul so that Mychus' body can heal," she said frantically. "It worked last time. Myke was dead, for Pete's sake, and he came back good as new."

"Paul is Myke Phoenix?" Josiah said. "Oh my gosh, that explains so many things!"

"Terri told you about turning into Mykala, but she didn't tell you about Paul being Myke?" Quincy said, cracking an actual smile for the first time.

"It never came up!"

"If I may," came a muffled voice from her purse. Dana rummaged and withdrew the Soulkeeper of Kiribati. If it were possible, Josiah's eyes would have grown wider at the voice coming out of the Phillipses' ugly green vase. "Yes, the powers could heal him if he relinquishes Mychus' body, but that would take time that you don't have right now."

"How much time?" Quincy asked.

"That's right," Dana said. "Myke was gone for three months last time. It took that long to repair the damage."

"And if I may be so bold, you need Mychus today," said the ugly green vase. "Now would be good, but sometime around daybreak would be fine. The forces of evil are congregating around town today."

Quincy and Josiah looked at each other. Outside the lab door they heard the ambulance driving up and powering down its siren.

"All righty then," Quincy said. "Let's get to work."

Act 2
Against the alien horde

THE firespider squirming in Mykala Phoenix's left hand grew weary of being held like a bad kitten. It spit a stream of flame that struck the Zembella warrior in their path square in the face. The reptilian-insect-like creature took a step back. That gave her an idea.

Still holding the firespiders, she exhaled a fiery blast at the Zembella to her left and turned her right hand so that firespider was facing the Zembella to her right. As if on cue, the little creature spit fire. Just like that, three dead alien warriors were staggered.

But as she was grabbed from behind, causing her to drop the spiders, Mykala saw that burning the Zembella's faces did not stop them. All three gathered their senses and stepped forward again.

"That's right, the blobs control the Zembella's bodies from afar," she muttered. When the attack on the university lab was breaking up, Mykala had seen a box truck disappearing up the street. Could the alien blob puppet masters be traveling in that truck? "I'll have to track it down."

One of the firespiders wrapped itself around her lower leg and attempted to bite her in the calf. It howled in pain as its jaws encountered irresistible resistance. She kicked, and the spider tumbled away in the dark.

Two Zembella soldiers grabbed her by the arms, and one clamped a hand over her mouth. She spat fire and the hand melted away – she felt a pang of regret as she watched the alien hand disintegrate much like her own hand had months earlier – but the warrior did not lose its grip on her arm.

"That's right, you're already dead. You can't feel that," she said to the silent warrior. The realization unleashed her to be more ruthless than she wanted to be. With the two Zembella still hanging on to her arms, she lifted up and clapped her hands, bringing the two alien heads together with a shattering force that crushed their skulls and cut off the signals from their brains to the rest of their bodies. They clattered to the ground clumsily.

The blobs seized the brains of their puppets, but they were still dependent on an intact nervous system. She reasoned that if she did enough damage to the Zembella bodies – cutting off their heads or crippling their limbs, for example – it would render them useless to manipulation. She had seen Myke Phoenix tearing ferociously through a wave of Zembella earlier that night and was aghast at the injuries he was inflicting on the soldiers. But now she understood: The owners of those bodies were beyond caring or feeling, and their remains were being borrowed.

But there were dozens, perhaps hundreds, of aliens starting to swarm through Astor City.

"Oh, this is going to be gross," Mykala said as she threw a punch that crashed all the way through a helmet and the face behind it.

"We can stay here, powered up and keeping an eye on him, as long as we don't get another call," the ambulance driver said to Brian Duckworth, the CEO of Quackenbos Laboratories Inc. "If someone else needs a ride, we're going to have to take him out of the truck and make him comfortable here."

"But that's Myke Phoenix!" Duckworth said.

"I know who it is, believe me," said the driver. "We've stabilized him as best we can and delivered him to the place where he can get further treatment, and we're just going to have to move on to the next patient when the call comes. But don't worry. Dispatch knows where we are and won't send us anywhere unless there's no one else available."

"Excuse me, ma'am, are you family?" the paramedic asked an auburn-haired woman who approached the back of the ambulance. The fierce look on her face convinced him to back away and let her in to sit next to the blond-haired giant lying flat on a gurney, an IV drip attached to the gaping wound on the side of his face, the only apparent mark on his body.

"Dana," the barrel-chested man breathed. "Sorry I can't get up."

She grabbed his meaty hand and held it to her cheek.

"You just lie there and let people take care of you. Quincy is working on an antidote. Josiah Petri is here and helping out. They're bringing Jacob Travers, too, from his hospital bed."

"Our three mad scientist friends, that should help," he said, attempting a smile. "So what hit me, anyway?"

"It seems Quincy did succeed in developing a poison that could kill Myke Phoenix after all," Dana said, more than a bit of an edge in her voice. "He says he lied because he didn't want to worry us and he thought he'd destroyed all copies of the formula."

"Not all of them, apparently," Myke said, and he tried to lift himself up onto his elbows but couldn't muster the energy and fell back again. "Hokey smokes, what's wrong with me?"

"Don't try to move. The poison is blowing up your blood cells. The less energy you use, the longer you can hang on for the cure."

"Deinonychus is still out there, and the firespiders and the alien blobs and those Zembella things," he said. "Mykala can't fight them by herself."

"And you can't fight them at all," Dana said, sternly and with more of a frightened tone than she wanted. "Take it easy, love. Hang on. Quincy will get you back in the fight."

She hoped she sounded more confident than she felt.

Brian Duckworth flipped on the television in the corner of the lab to see if the alien invasion was making the news. Sure enough, a young man with perfectly quaffed hair was standing in front of the woods with a microphone in his hands.

"– some sort of fight going on behind me now. The alien soldiers that marched on City Hall last month have returned, and so have the small firespiders that made an appearance in town a few weeks before that," the man was saying. "I have unconfirmed reports that Deinonychus, the dinosaur crime lord who disappeared years ago, is somehow involved in all of this as well."

"Look out!" Duckworth yelled at the TV screen, but of course the reporter didn't hear. Nor could he see the alien soldier whose lifeless body was flailing through the air behind him. The strangely reptilian but somehow insectlike soldier struck the reporter square in the back and sent him sprawling, missing the camera by inches, which enabled the camera operator to get a good shot of him spread-eagled on the ground with an alien twitching out the last movements of its non-life on top of him.

"Are you all right, Danny?" the camera operator cried. Danny the reporter waved a hand and crawled out from under. He found the microphone on the ground several feet away.

"I think we're going to fall back to a safer location and pick up this story in a few minutes. Back to you at the studio."

The scene on the screen moved back indoors, where a perky looking woman and a perky looking man stared seriously at the camera with their serious news looks.

"Well, we certainly wish the best to all of the people in that neighborhood, who are now being evacuated," the woman said empathetically.

"If you've just joined us, the scene near the University of Astor City is firespiders and aliens and chaos, oh my," the man said. "Myke and Mykala Phoenix have been engaged for somewhat more than an hour, along with police and sheriff's deputies, with a resurgence of the weird beings that have plagued our city on and off since last winter. We're still trying to confirm reports that Myke Phoenix was taken from the scene by ambulance after some kind of confrontation with the former crime boss and talking dinosaur, Deinonychus. As soon as Danny is set up in a different location, we'll rejoin him. In the meantime, let's see what kind of weather we can expect today. Heather, is it true we all may need an umbrella by this afternoon?"

"Yes, and not just to protect from falling aliens," said another perky woman with a smile.

Duckworth turned from the TV and looked across the lab to see Quincy Quackenbos and Josiah Petri huddled over a computer screen.

"I added that particular component because I anticipated someone would try to develop a way to suck the sodium out of the serum," Quincy was saying as he pointed at the screen. "You have to remember I was working for the

Forces of Evil in the World. I was one of the bad guys. It's an insidious, ingenious concoction if I say so myself."

"OK, so how do we counteract the attack on his blood cells and restore them at the same time?"

They looked at each other in sudden shock. Josiah Petri slapped the side of his head.

"Transfusion!" they said in unison.

"Duckworth, tell those medical folks we need several pints of Type AB positive blood, and we need it fast," Quincy said.

"AB-pos? How do you know –" Josiah said, but caught himself. "Oh yeah, you studied his blood."

"I know everything about his blood."

"But – how do we keep the serum from blowing up all the cells in the new blood?" Josiah cried.

"Duh! How do you think?" snapped the duck man. "We'll stir up the antidote before we give him the transfusion. Wak!"

"Are we that close to solving the riddle? Because a minute ago –"

"No, we're not! So let's get back to work," said the duck man.

Just then a phrase from the television screen caught everyone's attention. Danny the reporter was back on the scene.

"– Mykala Phoenix has left the scene and appears to be hurt."

Quincy Quackenbos, Josiah Petri and Brian Duckworth turned in unison to gape at the television, where Danny was standing in a parking lot somewhere, his hair somewhat askew after being waylaid by a dead alien.

"Again, we saw her fly out of the sky and land just over there, carrying three or four of the insect-reptile things on her back. She shook them off and ran away, chased by a couple of the little firespiders, and it appeared to me as if she was limping. This could be a very serious situation, Myke Phoenix missing and presumably being treated for unknown injuries, and now Mykala Phoenix bidding a hasty retreat. Police are cautioning that people stay in their homes –"

"I have to get out there, I have to help Terri!" Josiah Petri cried. Quincy Quackenbos poked a hand in his chest, and Duckworth grasped an arm gently.

"She'll be all right," Quincy said. "She's as tough as Myke, maybe tougher with that fire-breathing trick she has. Come here, Josiah, I need your help with this. Focus, son. Let's get this done. Brian, do we still have those tankers of Yucca Daisy ready?"

"– new reports that firespiders and aliens are gathering in the area of the Astor City Historical Museum," the perky TV anchor said in a serious tone. "We have a crew heading over there now, and we'll keep you updated. In just a moment, we'll give you the word of the day that you'll need to save and collect to win a new car."

Act 3

The spiders, the fire and the race

ASTOR City was founded in 1877 by the famous industrialist Jefferson Davis Astor. He built a magnificent mansion for his wife overlooking the bluffs of the Shikaakwa River. Emily Wellington Astor lived there until she died in 1943, leaving the grand old structure to the city they loved for use as a museum.

As the sun rose it cast a soft, warm light over the marble stairs leading into what today is the Astor City Historical Museum. The fallen leaves flew around in the grip of a light breeze and crunched underneath as enormous spiders and alien soldiers walked among the trees on the expansive front lawn.

A well-dressed man drove a box truck up to the gated entrance and parked unobtrusively at the curb. He hopped out of the cab and gazed at the morning sun.

"It's going to be a grand day for this time of year," he said out loud. "Are you comfortable in there?"

"This location is sufficient for our needs," said a voice inside his head. "We can manipulate an appropriate number of Zembella and even some firespiders from this distance. We shall not require your services for a time."

"Well, then this would be a perfect time to take a break for a smoke," Smothers said, "if I smoked. Ghastly habit. Mind you, I like a good cigar now and then."

"Why does your species inhale the fumes from burning plant matter? It makes no sense," said another voice he could not hear.

"Surely blobs have activities that give you pleasure but make no sense to the rest of us."

"None that we care to tell you about," a third inside-his-head voice said after a pause.

"All right, then," Smothers said. "I'm going for a little stroll just to get the juices flowing. You three have a lovely morning guiding your puppets and dead alien soldiers as they seize the city."

Inside the box truck, comfortably seated among a lush setting of potted plants, one blob asked his comrades, "Why did Deinonychus tell us not to kill him again?"

Smothers hummed to himself as he took a morning constitutional down the mostly deserted street.

He turned a corner to the sight of blinking police lights about three blocks away. Too late, he noticed a police officer walking up to him.

"Sir, I'm going to have to ask you to come with me," the officer said. "We're clearing the area and setting up a perimeter around the museum neighborhood."

"Goodness gracious me, what's happened?" Smothers said in mock horror.

"You don't have your television on this morning, I guess," said the cop. "The city is crawling with firespiders and aliens. They thought they'd contained them over by the university, but a bunch of them snuck away and your neighbors reported seeing them on the museum grounds. I'd better escort you out of here."

"Oh, no, I can't have that," Smothers said.

"You have no choice, sir, we're evacuating the neighborhood."

"But – but – my medication! I must take my morning pill or my life could be in jeopardy. At least let me go back to my house and fetch that."

The officer sighed. "Where do you live?"

"Just around the corner, over there." Smothers waved vaguely in that direction.

"All right, but let's make it quick." He grabbed Smothers' arm lightly and they started walking together.

As soon as they were around the corner and out of the sight of the roadblock, Smothers broke away and knocked the officer senseless with a roadhouse kick to the jaw.

"Sorry, old chap," he said, straightening his jacket.

"Well done, Smothersss," a hissing voice came from nearby. He looked and spotted a small dinosaur and a giant spider standing in a yard.

"Hello, milady," the well-dressed henchman said. "Why didn't you help?"

"We jusst got here," Deinonychus replied. "And you handled the situation nicely without my assissstance. Let'ss get to the musseum."

They walked back up the hill, past the parked box truck, through a horde of alien dead and firespiders milling about the grounds, and up the marble stairs to the front door of the old mansion. Two Zembella broke the door open and a half-dozen spiders scurried inside. Deinonychus followed. The giant spider stayed on the veranda, being somewhat too large to crawl inside.

Deinonychus stalked down a corridor to a sign that said "OMG! Dinosaurs!" and walked into a large room filled with ancient memorabilia – fossils and models of dinosaur lore. She looked around for, and found, a sign that said, "DEINONYCHUS."

But as she approached the display, she hissed. Instead of what she was looking for, she found an official-looking sign.

"The International Society of Paleontogists has offered a reward of $25,000 USD for information leading to the return of the deinonychus claw that was stolen from this exhibit ..."

"Ssstolen!" Deinonychus cried. "The claw hass been moved?!"

"Doesn't anybody pay attention to the news anymore?" said a firm female voice from the back of the exhibit hall. "That thing's been gone for about two months."

A tall, red-haired woman in a blue tunic stepped through the back doors and placed herself in a stance fit for hand-to-hand combat.

"Mykala Phoenixsss! You were injured. You limped away from the fight."

"I did, didn't I? I limped away right in front of Danny, the TV guy, who noticed and told the whole world about it, and then I followed you here," Mykala said with a shake of her mane. "What can I say? I lied."

Dr. Jacob Travers was a gentle looking man with a big white beard. He always seemed to have an expression of contentment but perhaps a touch of befuddlement, and he would look at home in the front of a lecture hall, studying giant ants, or playing Santa Claus for a group of children.

As he was wheeled into the main lab at Quackenbos Laboratories, he encountered a man who looked like a tall white duck, bill-to-nose with a dark-haired man as if ready to come to blows.

"It's amazing that chemical didn't kill him instantly!" said the dark-haired man.

"I've told you 40 times, that was the whole point in the first place! I'm sorry! Can we get past that and find a counter agent?" quacked the duck man.

"Do you really want to find a counter agent, or has all of this been a ruse to get close to Myke?" Josiah Petri shouted.

"Great godfrey baggins, if that was the plan I would have shot him up myself," said Quincy Quackenbos. "The man's my best friend now, I could have gotten to him any time, why would I let the blasted dinosaur do it?"

"Gentlemen, gentlemen, I don't think this is going to solve our problem," Travers said, reaching up and grabbing each man by the triceps. "What do you say you fill me in on where we are so far?"

Quincy grabbed a piece of paper off the counter and jammed it into Jacob Travers' hands.

"I worked up this formula, using those ingredients, to kill Myke Phoenix," he said.

"Oh my. Oh my!" Travers said as he read the list, reacting to each lethal ingredient in turn. "Oh my, oh my – oh my! And – wait a minute. Sodium chloride? Table salt?!"

"That turns out to be the stuff that makes it all happen," Josiah said. "The poisons didn't work until he added the salt, believe it or not."

"Whether I believe it or not, the salt must be a key," the bearded professor said. "So we counteract the salt."

"It's not that easy," Quincy said. "I added some inhibitors that would increase the effects of the poison if anything is introduced to remove the salt."

"That's downright insidious," Travers said.

"I was an evil genius, if I say so myself," the duck man admitted.

Travers stroked his beard thoughtfully.

"You know, when I put too much salt in the soup, I add potatoes," he said at last.

Josiah stared at him. "What are you talking about?"

"Are you a cook, Mr. Quackenbos? Do you cook?"

"I cook like crazy in the lab," Quincy said. "But I hire people to make my meals."

"Then perhaps it wouldn't occur to you that anyone would use potatoes to remove the saltiness from your soup."

"What are you getting on about? This isn't about soup," Josiah said.

"But don't you see? It could be," Travers said. "Use a potato extract as the base for your antidote."

Quincy Quackenbos appeared to be looking at an object a far distance away. Slowly his eyes came into focus.

"Yes!" He quacked. "Wak! It just might work. Let's give it a shot."

"I hope you two are right about this," said Josiah Petri. "I don't know how much time we have."

Dana Dunsmore Phillips dabbed a cold, wet hand towel on the forehead of Myke Phoenix as the powerful warrior lay feebly on a table. The ambulance crew had apologized, moved him off their gurney, and sped away to another call after all.

"Hang in there, Scoop," she said, using her pet name for her husband, the reporter. The superhero smiled weakly and winced.

"You know, Dana, I could just switch back into Paul," he said. "I'd be just fine, and whatever goes to work when Mychus isn't in this plane would go to work cleaning out this body's systems. This really hurts. I could make the pain go away in a nanosecond."

"But you won't, and you know why," she said softly but firmly. "When Myke died, it took three months to patch him up. You remember those three months when you couldn't switch back into Myke? How do we know how long it would take to fix you back up this time? You want to try battling the forces of evil in the world as plain old Paul Phillips again?"

"Plain old Paul is a pretty tough cookie," Myke breathed, but he didn't change back into his alter ego, either.

"If I may," said the misshapen green vase. "I don't know if Mychus' body could be cleaned up on the other side anyway."

"What does that mean?" Myke said, his voice a little stronger with alarm. "The last time, they patched me up after I bled out and my heart stopped beating."

"That was a fairly straightforward repair job," the vase said. "This poison, it's of *this* world, not that one. I don't know that the resources are there to cleanse the body. I'm not saying they *couldn't* do it, I'm just saying I don't know."

"Great," Dana said. "So Paul would be all right –"

"But we don't know if Myke Phoenix would ever be able to return," Myke said. "After all these centuries, I'd be the guy who lost Mychus forever."

The two humans and the vase let that thought linger in the air for a few moments.

"You hang in there, Scoop," Dana said. "Quincy will work his magic. I know he can."

Mykala Phoenix smashed a Zembella warrior into a marble column with such force that its back snapped. She dropped it to the ground. Under the power of a blob puppetmaster somewhere, it reached out a hand to grab her by the ankle, but its legs no longer operated. She kicked it away.

Several puppy-sized spiders swarmed over her, and she plucked them off. Careful not to ignite any of the displays, she exhaled a stream of fire around herself to dissuade the spiders from coming close again.

It was a bad decision. Encouraged by the example and not having the same care to preserve the museum, four of the big little spiders spit fire at her. Two of them struck her full in the phoenix insignia on her chest, and she shrugged it off. Two of them missed. One of the errant bolts of flame struck the curtains surrounding the tall windows of the exhibit hall. They began to smolder.

"I killed Myke Phoenix, and I can do the same to you," screamed Deinonychus as she raced across the room with her poison-tipped terrible claws fully extended.

"You have to get near me first," Mykala said, leaping high into the air and over the charging dinosaur, twisting her body in the air to avoid colliding with a skeletal Tyrannosaurus rex model.

Four Zembella warriors surrounded her and grabbed her. She whirled as hard as she could with her arms extended and her palms sideways, striking them each with such force that they crumpled to the ground, necks snapped.

"Sorry, sorry, sorry, sorry," Mykala said to each in turn as the blows landed. "I hate this."

The talking dinosaur charged again, and Mykala leaped again, this time managing to punch the little creature in the back of the head while avoiding the claws as she flew over. For good measure, after Deinonychus skittered across the floor, stood up and turned back, Mykala spit a wall of flame that caught the already burned dinosaur in the face again. The clawed menace shrieked in pain.

WHOOMP!

Mykala Phoenix looked in horror as the curtains on either side of one tall window erupted completely in flames that licked against the wall and ceiling. Deinonychus looked at the fire, as well, and scampered out of the room. The little firespiders ran after her, sensing an escape route, but eight Zembella strode toward the superheroine as a second set of drapes ignited.

"This does not look good," she said, bracing for the alien soldiers' approach.

"OK, OK, OK," Quincy Quackenbos said. "Let's see what we got."

The duckman cut off a swath of his blood-soaked handkerchief and laid it on the laboratory counter. In his feathered hand he held a test tube filled with a gray, pasty substance. He poured several drops of the serum on the handkerchief. The blood fizzed and bubbled.

"Check it out," Quincy said.

Josiah Petri seized the handkerchief, thrust it under a microscope and peered into the eyepiece. A few seconds passed.

"I'm not sure," he said. "I think maybe, but maybe not. What's it look like to you?"

Jacob Travers took his turn at the microscope.

"I see what you mean," he said, looking first to Josiah Petri and then to the duck man. "It could be working, but it's hard to say for certain."

Quincy Quackenbos looked intently into the eyepiece and, after a few seconds, grunted.

"Close enough," he said. "I think we've got it."

"'Close enough'?" Josiah scoffed. "Quincy, we have to be sure about this. We may only get the one chance."

The duck man gripped the test tube a little more firmly and opened a drawer, withdrawing a syringe.

"There's only one way to be sure," he said. "We've got to try it."

In 18 years, Myke Phoenix had been punched, battered, tossed through the air and generally abused in every way that a bad guy can abuse a good guy. He had said "ouch" countless times, because it turns out that being in possession of a bulletproof body does not exempt a person from feeling pain from the impact of death-dealing implements against his impenetrable (except via velociraptor claws) skin.

But Myke Phoenix had never screamed in agony. That was why a grim chill coursed through Dana's body when she heard the sound and felt the ancient warrior's body shudder convulsively.

"Hokey smokes," he said, sweat streaming off his forehead. "It hurts like the dickens when your blood cells explode."

"Come on, Paul, you can do this. It can't be long now," Dana said.

"I'm pretty sure you're right," Myke said. "It can't be long. I think I'm going to slip away and you'll be stuck with Paul Phillips, maybe for good."

"If Myke dies, yep, he'll turn back into Paul," said the Soulkeeper of Kiribati. "The good news is Paul will be just fine."

"The bad news is we don't know how long it will be before Mychus comes back," Dana said.

"Or if he can come back at all," Myke whispered. He sighed, leaned back and closed his eyes.

"Hey!" Dana said, shaking the warrior. "I need Paul back, but the world needs Myke right now. You hang on, mister. Hang on, Myke!"

Myke Phoenix seemed to be staring at something on the ceiling. He took a deep, raspy breath, exhaled loudly and shuddered, and his body relaxed completely.

"Myke?" Dana said, a tear escaping her eye. She braced herself for the instant when her husband reappeared, safe and sound, dooming the world to whatever Deinonychus and her minions had in store.

The door burst open and Quincy Quackenbos raced into the room, followed by Josiah Petri and Jacob Travers in his wheelchair, all of them breathing heavily.

"Stand aside!" Quincy barked, and Dana jumped aside.

Quincy brandished the syringe and looked at the superhero in despair.

"Oh my – are we too late?" asked the duckman.

"Not yet, he would have changed," she said.

"OK, here goes," he said, inserting the hypodermic needle into the gash in Myke Phoenix's cheek, the only place where the superhero's body could be penetrated. "This better work. And get that blood transfusion ready in case it does."

Act 4

Rise of the Phoenix

SMOTHERS climbed back behind the wheel of the box truck in time to watch three tankers rumble through the gates to the Astor City Historical Museum. The big trucks were emblazoned with the logo and name "QUACKENBOS."

"The Yucca Daisy is here," Smothers said out loud. "I wonder what took them so long."

"They have brought the lethal substance?" a voice spoke inside his head from the compartment behind him. "Take us to safety."

"Your wish is my command," the well-dressed henchman said, reaching to turn the truck's emission.

"FREEZE!"

He turned to see the barrel of a loaded gun pointed at his face. The officer he had knocked senseless held the weapon on him while flicking on his radio. "Command, I'm at the box truck parked outside the museum with the party who assaulted me before. I need immediate backup."

"10-4," replied the radio.

"What's in the back of the truck, bloke?" the officer said. Suddenly he howled in pain, dropped the gun and held his hands to his head. A moment later he relaxed and looked up at Smothers without emotion.

"This isn't the truck I was looking for. Move along," he said, waving the truck down the street. "Move along."

Smothers started the engine and pulled away.

"I wondered how long you chaps would wait to borrow his mind and get me out of there," he said out loud.

"It was enjoyable witnessing your fear," a blob's voice spoke into his mind. "It was something that makes no sense but gave us pleasure."

Smothers laughed in spite of himself.

"Well, we're going to lose almost all of your Zembella, the firespiders are scattered all over town, and the deinonychus claw was stolen before we had a chance to steal it ourselves," he said. "And oh yes, the museum is burning down. All told, a less than successful affair."

Smoke was pouring out of the windows and flames licked out from inside the Astor City Historical Museum when fire crews arrived on the scene. And they stayed in their trucks when they saw the scene. Alien beings marched back and forth among a cluster of firespiders on the front lawn.

And if that weren't enough, a giant spider jumped off the museum's roof – the very elephant-sized firespider that had menaced the city months ago and recently reappeared.

And if *that* weren't enough, a large window broke and out tumbled a four-foot-tall dinosaur with nasty-looking claws.

"Mother of Mayo, that's Deinonychus!" the fire commander yelped. "All hands, stay in your trucks until someone can secure the scene! We can't save the structure if we're all dead."

"Secure the scene!" someone yelled. "How is anybody going to secure *this* scene?" Truth to tell, between the fire and the walking dead aliens and the firespiders and the talking dinosaur, the scene looked very insecure indeed.

But then another figure tumbled out the window from the smoke – a red-maned woman wearing a blue tunic and looking very formidable in her own right.

"That's that Mykala Phoenix!" someone pointed out the obvious. Or perhaps not so obvious; this was still very early in Mykala's career.

She plowed into two Zembella and contorted them into grotesque shapes.

"Sorry, sorry," she said.

Her appearance emboldened the operator of one of the Quackenbos tankers, who jumped out of the cab and charged the long hose attached to the truck. As five Zembella stormed toward him, the man opened the hose and sprayed them with a substance that had the consistency of shampoo – largely because it *was* shampoo, the reformulated Yucca Daisy, which had proven toxic to the blobs.

The Zembella dropped like stones as the shampoo struck, cutting the connection between the dead aliens and their equally alien puppet masters.

"That is a much tidier way to knock them off than I was trying," Mykala said to herself.

The other two tanker operators jumped out and deployed their own devices, and the Zembella began to scatter. But they were taking more of a risk than they realized.

Mykala Phoenix was the first to see that Deinonychus was charging toward the Yucca Daisy tankers. The dinosaur ran fast, but Mykala was faster. She tackled Deinonychus and sent them both sprawling on the lawn. Seeing how close the little dinosaur had come, the tanker operator dropped his hose and hopped back into his truck.

Both combatants scrambled to their feet and faced each other. Deinonychus held out her claws and stepped forward slowly; Mykala stepped backward. Her back was to the burning building.

Two little firespiders ran up and sprayed Mykala with fire. She spit back at them and spit fire at the dinosaur for good measure. This time Deinonychus dodged the stream of flame and feinted with her deadly, poison-tipped claws. Mykala backed up again, and backed, until her back was to the wall. She could feel the furious heat from the burning building and stared at the little dinosaur barely 10 feet in front of her, holding her clawed hands and beckoning.

The red-maned hero shook her head. For a moment she could swear she saw a man with the face of a duck running across the lawn behind the dinosaur, and a large figure striding through the smoke in front of him.

"Come, little Mykala Phoenix, come meet your fate," Deinonychus said, giddy with triumph. "Come to die. Come to –"

A powerful booming voice interrupted.

"Not today, you little vermin," the voice said. "She's not going to die today."

Deinonychus whirled and stared, incredulous, at the man standing tall before her, surrounded by the swirling smoke, his blond hair tousled by the wind caused by the billowing flames, the image of a phoenix emblazoned proudly across his barrel chest. His massive hands were balled into fists, and he looked as angry as he looked mighty.

"It ends today, here, Deinonychus," Myke Phoenix said. "This ends now."

"Impossssible," Deinonychus said. "Impossible!"

As villains as villainous as this villain often manage, Deinonychus recovered quickly from the shock of seeing Myke Phoenix recovered from the fatal wound. She whirled back and struck viciously at Mykala Phoenix with her poison-tainted claws, gauging a deep slash across her collarbone.

That was the only blow she was able to land before Myke Phoenix grabbed Deinonychus by the scruff of the neck, tossed her into the air like a softball and punched, sending the dinosaur sailing 200 feet across the lawn and smack into a tree trunk.

"Quincy!" Myke barked. The duckman scurried up to Mykala, who was already unsteady on her feet. She sank to the ground as Quincy reached her side.

"Easy, young lady, easy," the duck man cooed, withdrawing a syringe and injecting a gray substance into the gash in her chest. "Good thing I insisted Myke bring me along in case something like this happened."

"SCREEEEEEEE!" Quincy looked up and saw the gigantic face of the elephant-sized firespider, which hauled back and spit a wall of flame in their direction.

Mykala threw her arms around the duck man and put her back to the spidery fire, absorbing the full impact with her invulnerable body.

Then she turned and landed a punch that staggered the giant arachnid, which dropped back.

"Holy cow," Quincy muttered, smelling the odor of singed feathers.

"Run, Quincy! Get out of here," Mykala shouted, pushing him away and standing to face the giant spider. Underneath, smaller firespiders darted here and there, apparently released from any alien control and running around at random.

Empowered by the arrival of a second superhero, the Quackenbos tanker drivers and firefighters leaped out their trucks and got down to business. The Zembella started walking toward the shampoo trucks until their first wave was stopped, err, dead in its tracks by the Yucca Daisy spray. The alien soldiers then began to flee the scene in droves.

Myke Phoenix ran over to the tree where the evil little dinosaur had landed. Deinonychus was on her feet and snarling.

"You've been a thorn in my side for 20 years, hero," the dinosaur spat. "Why won't you die?"

Lster, the big blond man thought of many ways he could have responded to that question. He could have explained that antidotes can be crafted to counteract poisons. He could have made a crack about how even a dark rose has its thorn. He could simply have proclaimed that he was just too stubborn to die as long as evil stalked the earth.

In the heat of the moment, he just hauled off and caught Deinonychus under her reptilian chin with a powerful uppercut that launched the little dinosaur another 200 feet toward the cliff.

She landed in a heap and rolled several feet before catching herself, sinking her terrible claws into the ground and snarling up at the man in the white uniform stalking toward her.

This time, instead of making a speech, she launched herself at him, turning herself in the air so she struck him full in the chest with her ugly three-toed feet, sinking six deadly claws into his sinews. Blood quickly stained the phoenix insignia and he roared in pain.

"Maybe you didn't get enough poison before, hero," Deinonychus snarled. "Or maybe Quackenbos failed after all. But I can still slash you. Die, you dimwitted fool, die!!!"

Quincy's antidote was working perfectly – the new dose of poison had no effect on Myke Phoenix. He grabbed the dinosaur by the throat with all of his might, pried her off his chest and hurled her at another tree overlooking the river. She struck with a sickening thud and bounced onto the ground, scattering several firespiders, which spit streams of fire in surprise and alarm.

But still Deinonychus rose.

Around the corner of the burning building crawled the giant firespider. Mykala Phoenix was on its back attempting to control it like a bronco buster. The monster shrugged her off and stared at the tableau before them.

Myke Phoenix, bleeding from a half-dozen wounds to his chest, walked cautiously toward the little dinosaur, who stalked step by step toward him.

"Die, damn you," Deinonychus said, reaching down, grabbing a little firespider with her deadly claws and squeezing. The little beast burst into flames, and the dinosaur hurled the flaming corpse at Myke Phoenix.

Myke dodged. Deinonychus reached down again, killed another firespider and threw it in a flaming ball at the superhero, who kept coming.

The dinosaur grabbed a third firespider.

"Why – won't – you – DIE?!" she shrieked, closing her claws around the little beast and creating a third flaming ball to throw at Myke Phoenix.

"SCREEEEEEEEEEEE!"

The giant firespider had watched as the dinosaur sliced three of her little cousins and used them as flaming weapons. Now she scrambled toward Deinonychus with purposeful fury.

"Get back, Mykala!" Myke grabbed her and stepped out of the path of the stampeding spider.

The huge monster locked her jaws around the waist of the little dinosaur, who snarled and raked her terrible claws across the firespider's multiple eyes.

"SCREEEEEEEE!" the firespider cried and spit a stream of flame that enveloped Deinonychus. Flailing from the fire and still locked in the spider's jaws, the dinosaur slashed and slashed until, like the smaller arachnids, the giant creature also erupted in fire.

Refusing to let go of her flaming captive, the great firespider staggered to the edge of the bluff and toppled over. The blazing monsters bounced once, twice, thrice before crashing onto the rocks on the banks of the mighty Shikaakwa River, where – now motionless – they burned together for hours.

The gracious mansion that Jefferson Davis Astor built for his beloved Emily would smolder for days. Myke and Mykala had cleared the way for firefighters faster than anyone believe possible, so the crews were able to save some of the back rooms, and of course the stone walls and foundation held, but any attempt to restore and rebuild the museum would take millions, and the priceless collections were lost forever.

Myke and Mykala Phoenix stood on the banks of the Shikaakwa River with Dana Dunsmore Phillips, Josiah Petri and Quincy Quackenbos, next to the charred bodies of a giant spider and a small dinosaur. Police tape surrounded the area around the bodies.

"You're sure this was her?" Dana said. "It's burned beyond recognition except for those horrible claws."

"Dana, we watched them go over the side in flames. I never took my eyes off them," Myke said. "And you can't substitute those claws. She was the last of her kind, the *only* one of her kind that anyone has seen for millions of years. This is the body of Deinonychus, hon. No doubt."

"What about the claw that was stolen from the museum?" she said, refusing to believe that the evil one had not somehow escaped.

"Did you read a lot of comic books when you were a kid, Dana?" Quincy said. "This body has two feet. The museum display was only one foot. Whoever stole the deinonychus fossil, it's not attached to this body. Believe it, kid. The witch is dead."

"I'll do an autopsy if you'd like," said Josiah – for he was the Astor County medical examiner, after all, "but I can pretty much guarantee the story is over for one criminal mastermind."

"And for this poor creature," said Mykala, touching the carcass of the giant firespider. "I can't help but feel sorry for her. She was the product of my father's misguided genetic engineering. She was just an animal; she meant no one any harm."

"'Misguided' isn't quite the word I'd used to describe it," Quincy said. "He was an idiot to tinker with nature that way."

"I don't disagree," Mykala said. "At least when he refused to stop tinkering, he didn't produce another monster of this size."

"That'll be some consolation while we spend the next month rounding up all of the puppy-sized firespiders that are still wandering around town," Myke Phoenix said as they began to walk away. "And anyway – Hokey smokes!"

"Oh my stars," Dana Dunsmore Phillips said when she saw why Myke had stopped in his tracks.

"Great godfrey baggins," said Quincy Quackenbos.

Josiah Petri and Mykala Phoenix gaped silently.

Perched on a large piece of driftwood on the riverbank was the largest – and most beautiful – bird any of them had ever seen. Its feathers seemed to glow in the setting sun, especially the tail feathers that flashed reds and golds and blues and greens. Its beak was as red as a rose, and the rainbow hues streamed from head to tail.

As the five companions stared in awe, the bird sang a melody as precious as life itself that melted their hearts. And then it flapped its wings and nodded.

"The Phoenix," Myke whispered, as if any of them had any doubt what they were witnessing.

"Good to see you again, old friend," said the Soulkeeper of Kiribati from the depths of Dana's purse, "as if anyone could see anything from in here."

Dana pulled the vase out and cradled it in the crook of her arm. The Phoenix nodded again and chirped musically.

"It came to help," the Soulkeeper said, "only to find you didn't need its help. Well done, it says. Well done."

They stood on the river bank in the sun without another word. Then the great bird nodded a third time, raised its wings and took to the sky.

Epilogue

FIVE wine glasses were raised over Paul and Dana Phillips' dining table that evening. Paul had proposed making his special lasagna, but Josiah suggested he had worked hard enough today, and so they ordered pizza.

"You know, we make a good team, the bunch of us," Dana said as they drank their wine and tackled the pizza. "All those years it was just Paul and me – and the Soulkeeper. It's nice to have help."

"You needed the help," said the vase, back in place on the top shelf next to the table. "And you'll need it again. The forces of evil in the world are just getting started."

"Oh, let's not go there tonight," said Terri Travers, accepting a slice from Josiah Petri. "Has anyone slept since yesterday? In the last 24 hours I've had enough evil for one lifetime."

As if to mock that sentiment, the house began to shake and a roaring sound seemed to surround them. Goombah started barking. Paul Phillips and Terri Travers transformed into Myke Phoenix and Mykala Phoenix, and they dashed out onto the back deck.

"Please, oh please," Mykala Phoenix said fretfully. "We're all so tired."

They saw, rising into the sky from the wooded area a few miles away, a round aircraft of some kind, lights dancing in the dark, flaming exhaust hurling toward the ground as the craft lifted straight into the sky. The body borrowers' ship rose and rose and rose until it was a dot against the night slightly larger than the stars.

"Do you think they'll be back?" Quincy said as they gathered back inside – chasing the golden retriever away from the pizza boxes. "You beat them a couple of times now."

"I don't know," Paul Phillips said – for Myke had transformed back into their middle-aged host sometime during the spacecraft's departure. "The first time around, they tried the old 'we come in peace' routine. This time they lined up with Deinonychus. I'm surprised they just turned tail and left."

"Well, we did beat their pants off," Terri Travers said, "or we would have if they wore pants."

"I don't think we've seen the last of them," Josiah said. "They'll be back."

"I think you're right," Paul said.

"But we'll be ready for them, with our warriors," Quincy said, raising his glass.

The phone rang just then, the phone that Paul carried for the business of the Astor City Beacon.

"Oh, great, a hot news tip," Paul said. "Just what we need right now, huh?"

"Let it go to voicemail, Paul," Dana said pleadingly.

"The news never stops, love, you've always known that," he said, pushing the button to answer the phone. "Astor City Beacon."

"Mr. Phillips?"

"Yes, ma'am, how can I help you?"

"My name is Avis Malone. I'm a paleontologist with the Museum of London. Perhaps you've heard of me."

"Hmmm, the name does ring a bell."

"It ought to. I am, after all, the leading paleontologist in the world."

"I'll take your word for it."

"Don't just take my word for it, a modicum of research will show you that it's acknowledged fact throughout my profession that I am the best at what I do. I know more about dinosaurs than any living soul. It's important that you understand that fact."

"OK, OK. How may I help you today?" he said, a little testily.

"Yes. Well. I was just reading your news story about Deinonychus' attack on Astor City, and I wanted to correct something you wrote."

"Well, I do want to get the facts straight. What needs to be fixed?"

"This reference to Deinonychus being the last of her kind."

"That's an acknowledged fact. The last deinonychus supposedly died millions of years ago."

"No, Mr. Phillips, they didn't. You see, there are more deinonychus animals still alive on this Earth," Avis Malone said. "And I have seen them."

A Myke Phoenix
Christmas

A Myke Phoenix Christmas

DEINONYCHUS was dead, to begin with. There is no doubt whatever about that. She had plunged over a cliff in flames – and in the clutches of a giant spider – and they landed on the rocks below with an emphatic thump that chased the life out of both of them.

Deinonychus was as dead as a doornail. Now, I haven't a clue what makes a doornail any more dead than any other inanimate object, but that has been a familiar saying for at least two centuries, and so, to be familiar, I drag it out of the box and say it again, to emphasize and make clear: Deinonychus was as dead as a doornail.

For 20 years, give or take, the impossible little dinosaur had been a thorn in the side of law enforcement and especially Myke Phoenix, the superpowered warrior who watched over Astor City, a medium-sized urban community like most other American cities except for its superpowered watchman.

Some medium-sized cities are unique because of their location by a great lake or tucked in the mountains. Some medium-sized cities sport a professional sports team or mighty college. Astor City, founded at the conjunction of two grand rivers, one wide enough to support a small chain of islands, was once best known for its water-dependent manufacturing facilities, but these days its claim to fame was Myke Phoenix.

The unfortunate side of having your own superhero is that your town attracts supervillains. And Deinonychus was the most villainous of these. She was so evil that it took the combined efforts of Myke, Mykala Phoenix, and a genius who happened to be half man and half duck to finally send her to her just rewards.

And so Astor City, its residents, and its superpowered protectors looked forward to Christmas with expectations of peace and good will among all, because that is what the season is about, of course, and because there was no chance that an evil talking dinosaur could disrupt the festivities.

Evil being what it is, however, the absence of an evil talking dinosaur does not preclude the absence of evil.

Which brings us to Christmas Eve.

Once upon a time, in a medium-sized city called Astor City, Sam Benson gazed out his living room window waiting for snow.

It wasn't snowing. In fact, it hadn't snowed since Thanksgiving. There wasn't a flake of snow to be seen, in the air, on the ground, nowhere.

"I want it to snow," Sam said. "It's Christmas Eve. Why won't it snow?"

"Oh, honey, it's still Christmas if there's no snow," Lily called from the kitchen. "Is the pizza guy here yet?"

"Pizzaaa!!!" two children screamed and went running from their rooms to the front window and around the living room and back to their rooms.

Sam sighed and walked into the kitchen, where Lily was mixing something in a bowl.

"Pizza on Christmas Eve. I don't know," he said.

"Oh, stop, you," she said. "I'm making all this stuff for the big meal tomorrow with your parents and my brother and their kids. There's no time to make a special meal tonight."

Sam shrugged.

"When I was a kid my mom would make magic bars for Christmas Eve, and my dad would read out of the Bible and we'd have milk and magic bars, and then we'd sit up and wait for Santa Claus until we fell asleep," he said. "We'd magically wake up in our beds with a Christmas stocking stuffed with goodies, and then it would be Christmas morning."

"That's sweet," Lily said.

"It *was* sweet," he said. "I feel like our kids should have something like that on Christmas Eve."

"Maybe next year."

"Yeah, maybe. But they're losing this year."

"Oh, you grump. Tomorrow will be all the Christmas magic they need. Go look for the pizza guy."

He snorted. "OK, I'll go look for the pizza guy."

Looking out the front window, Sam could taste his mom's magic bars in his imagination – chocolate, coconut, graham cracker sweetness. The crust would crumble in their hands, the chocolate would be all gooey and they'd lick their fingers. That was what a merry Christmas was all about.

A car pulled up to the front of the house with a light on top that said "Pete's Pizza." Sam grabbed his wallet and headed outside.

The moon on the asphalt so lacking in snow gave the luster of midday to objects below.

"How much do I owe you?" Sam called as he walked down the sidewalk toward the street. He was looking in his wallet to fish out a $20 bill and didn't notice the delivery guy until he heard the growl.

"What the bejeebers?"

The young man in front of him was wearing a baseball cap and frothing at the mouth. No, really, there was white froth around his lips and dripping on his scraggly beard. He looked like an old movie about a wolf man. And he was growling like a mad dog. One thing he was not doing was carrying a box of pizza.

"Holy moley!" Sam Benson cried.

The crazed wolf man guy came running at Sam and literally jumped into the air at him. Sam closed his eyes, cringed and braced for an impact that never came.

Instead, he heard a "whoomp" sound and the growling stopped momentarily.

He opened his eyes and instead of a young man in a baseball cap, he saw a tall, red-haired woman wearing a blue tunic with a short skirt. The image of a bird rising from ashes was emblazoned fetchingly across her chest. He looked, saw the wolf man kid sitting on the ground, and looked back at her.

"Wha – you're Mykala Phoenix!" Sam said.

"That's right," the woman said just before the bearded pizza driver barreled into her, growling again. "I'd stay and chat, but this guy has me preoccupied." She picked him up and threw him across the street.

The wolf man ran off into the night, and Mykala Phoenix sprinted after him.

Sam looked into the car. There was no pizza in the pizza delivery car.

"Oh, man."

Sam's car was parked in the driveway. He fished out his keys and jumped in the car. The pizza place was in a strip mall a few blocks away. If delivery wasn't going to work tonight, maybe he could get some takeout.

As he sped away, Lily opened the door and stepped into the night. Looking at the pizza car, its engine still running but no one in sight, and seeing that Sam's car was no longer in the driveway, she looked up and down the street.

"Sam?" she called. "Sam, where are you?"

"That was weird," Sam muttered as he drove the few blocks to the mall. He turned on the radio and a country singer was crooning.

Silent night, holy night,

All is calm, all is bright.

Round yon virgin, mother and child,

Holy infant so tender and mild,

Sleep in heavenly peace,

Sleep in heavenly peace.

His eyes welled with tears. No snow, no magic bars, and a bloodthirsty pizza driver, but still, after all, it was Christmas. The music brought him back. His eyes were so blurry it looked liked two cars had been turned over in the pizza joint's parking lot.

He rubbed his eyes and looked again.

Two cars *were* turned over in the pizza joint's parking lot. He could see at least two people jumping up and down near the cars and waving their arms at each other.

In years to come telling this story, Sam would tell people he still didn't know why he pulled into the parking lot and got out of his car.

"It was like I was in a bad horror movie and was just compelled to do the stupid thing that would get me in the greatest danger," he would say. "I guess I was really hungry and just wanted to bring some pizza home."

He pulled into the parking lot, staring at the overturned cars and the wild men jumping around them. The cars had been tipped in the lot right in front of the pizza joint's front door, but there was still room to get in.

"Hey guys," he said, walking up to the restaurant doors.

"No! No! No!" They ran up to him and stood in the entrance. "Woo! Woo! Woo!"

"Come on, are you kidding me?" Sam said. "Let me in, guys, I just want to buy some pizza."

"PIZZA! You want PIZZA?" said the young man nearest to him, who was wearing glasses and a blue shirt embroidered with the pizza joint's logo and the name NATE. "I'll show you some PIZZA, man. Come here! Come here!"

"I don't think so," Sam said, backing off. But the kid in the blue shirt walked toward him calling, "Come here! Come here! I got PIZZA."

Suddenly there was a white wall in front of Sam blocking his view of the crazy kid.

It was a huge man in a white uniform, and he seemed to be cradling someone in his arms. He set the person down, and Sam saw that it was a man wearing a duck mask with a tank of some kind strapped to his back.

"I think you boys want to leave this gentleman along," the man said in a commanding voice. The man in the duck mask was fiddling with the nozzle of a hose attached to the tank.

"NOOOO!" shouted the kid with the glasses and the blue shirt. "Want to give him PIZZA!" And he hopped up and down impatiently.

"Cool your jets a minute, Nate," the white-suited man said. "You getting it there, Quincy?"

"Yeah, I got it. Step aside."

Sam realized with a jolt that he was standing behind Myke Phoenix, the superhero, and the man in the duck mask wasn't wearing a mask, he was Quincy Quackenbos, the duck man who used to be a criminal genius.

"Hokey smokes!" Sam said.

"That's my line, buddy," Myke said.

Quincy sprayed the contents of the tank into the faces of the rampaging pizza drivers.

"PIZZA! Woo! Woo!" they cried, and then their shoulders sagged a bit and intelligence returned to their faces. "What the bejeebers just happened?"

"Ee-yup," Quincy said, looking at Myke Phoenix. "That went well."

"Incoming!" shouted a female voice behind them. They turned to see Mykala Phoenix walking up with a firm grip on the wolf man, who was squirming and howling at the moon. "Got another one for ya, Quince."

A blast of Quincy's goo in the face, and the bearded pizza guy calmed right down.

"It was the tomato sauce," Quincy said. "Whoever – or whatever – spiked the sauce really wanted these boys to go nutso."

"I think Pete's Pizza is closed for the night now, friend," Myke Phoenix told Sam. "Are you OK?"

"I'm fine," Sam said. "Just a little shook up, I guess."

"Can't blame you," Myke replied. "It's not every Christmas Eve that pizza drivers go berserk all over town."

"No, it isn't. Thank you, sir. I think you may have just saved my life."

"Hey, it's what I do," Myke Phoenix said with a smile, then turned to go. "Merry Christmas!"

And Sam heard him exclaim as he ran out of sight, "And to all a good night!"

When Sam walked into the front door of his home with a bag of frozen pizzas, Lily came running out of the kitchen and threw her arms around him.

"Where have you been?" she cried. "I was worried sick. You went out to pay the pizza guy, I heard a commotion and when I came out nobody was there except the pizza delivery car. What happened?"

"Well, the pizza joint didn't work out, so I went down to The Food House and bought a couple of frozen pizzas," he said. "I hope that's OK."

"Oh, honey! We can't bake frozen pizzas. I have all sorts of stuff in the oven for tomorrow," she said. "Cookies, and your mom's magic bars. You're going to have to throw some leftovers in the microwave."

"That'll do," Sam said, and suddenly he took Lily in his arms and gave her a smoochabulous kiss, perhaps the most smoochabulous kiss he had given her since they were first married and the pastor said, "You may kiss the bride."

"Wow! What was that for?" she said, blinking in surprise.

"Pizza! Where's the pizza?!" The kids had suddenly appeared at their side.

"No pizza tonight, but you know what?" Sam put his hands on his knees and opened his eyes wide as innocence. "It's Christmas!!!!" And then he chased them around the living room as they squealed with delight.

"Don't knock over the tree!" Lily giggled. "Sam, what happened? You were so mopey before."

"I bumped into a couple of superheroes and a talking duck who saved me from some crazy people and set me straight," Sam said. "Remind me never to complain at Christmastime ever again. It's the most wonderful time of the year."

"You got that right," Lily said. "Now help me get those cookies out of the oven. I guess maybe we can sneak those pizzas in between the bakery. Oh, look!"

Outside the window big, fluffy white flakes of snow were falling and swirling in the night breeze. Yep, it was Christmas, all right.

FINIS

About the author

WARREN Bluhm is a wordsmith, journalist and podcaster who lives not far from the shores of Green Bay with his beloved, two golden retrievers (Willow The Best Dog There Is™ and Dejah Thoris, Princess of Mars) and their cat Blackberry.

To see what he's up to, visit warrenbluhm.com.